SARAH

SARAH takes up the story of one of the most intriguing characters in Joyce Marlow's highly praised first novel, KESSIE.

At the beginning of the First World War, Sarah Whitworth is a pacifist, determined to have no direct involvement with a conflict in which she can see no sense. But when her brother Tom volunteers for the army, she decides to serve as an auxiliary nurse at the Eastern Front – a decision that will change her life.

In the middle of war-torn Russia, Sarah meets the charismatic revolutionary Mikhail Muranov, and begins a relationship that will force her to choose between her love of homeland and family or her love for Mikhail Muranov.

**Also by the same author,
and available from Coronet:**

KESSIE

About the author

Joyce Marlow was born in Manchester. She
became an actress, before turning to writing
such highly acclaimed works as THE
PETERLOO MASSACRE, THE
TOLPUDDLE MARTYRS, CAPTAIN
BOYCOTT AND THE IRISH, THE
UNCROWNED QUEEN OF IRELAND and
MR AND MRS GLADSTONE: AN
INTIMATE BIOGRAPHY. Her first novel
KESSIE won great praise and also won her the
Elizabeth Goudge prize for the best Historical
Novel of 1985. She has just completed the final
part of the KESSIE trilogy, ANNE.

Sarah

Joyce Marlow

CORONET BOOKS
Hodder and Stoughton

For Patrick with love

Copyright © 1987 by Joyce Marlow

First published in Great Britain in 1987 by Hodder and Stoughton Limited

Coronet edition 1988

Printed and bound in Great Britain for Hodder and Stoughton Paperbacks, a division of Hodder and Stoughton Limited, Mill Road, Dunton Green, Sevenoaks, Kent TN13 2YA (Editorial Office: 47 Bedford Square, London WC1B 3DP) by Richard Clay Limited, Bungay, Suffolk. Photoset by Rowland Phototypesetting Limited, Bury St Edmunds, Suffolk.

British Library C.I.P.

Marlow, Joyce
  Sarah.
  I. Title
  823'.914[F]   PR6063.A65/

  ISBN 0-340-42364-1

PART ONE

1

Sarah wedged the piece of wood between the upper and lower halves of the window frames. One of the sash-cords had snapped but it should hold now, she reckoned, giving the wood an extra shove. In the old days, not so long ago, Billy Cartwright would have come round to mend it, but Billy had been killed in the battle for Hill 60.

The murky December light was fading fast, wreaths of fog were drifting over the damp rooftops of Moss Side, spiralling from the alleyways, hovering over the cobble-stones. Within a couple of hours the noxious vapours would have formed into a still, silent, browny-grey mass and you wouldn't be able to see the houses on the other side of the street. Sarah was about to draw the curtains, to shut out the descending gloom, when she heard the muffled sound of the cheering.

The cheers had to be for Tom.

A few minutes later his tall lean figure rounded the corner, emerging from a swirl of fog. Behind him trailed a good-sized crowd, shadowy figures in their caps and shawls, but Tom's vitality, his confident strides, the assured set of his head, pierced the gloom. He saw Sarah silhouetted in the window and raised his hand in greeting. His spectral escorts gazed up at their hero's sister, but even with the window shut and the swathes of fog between them she could feel the hostility. Returning Tom's greeting with a wave, Sarah drew the curtains and went into her little scullery where, in anticipation of her brother's arrival, the kettle was simmering on the gas-ring.

By the time another loud cheer had died away and Tom

had climbed the stairs and let himself into her flat she had warmed the pot and the tea was nicely mashed. He carried the tray into the sitting room and perched it somewhat precariously on the rounded end of the ornate brass fender she had found in a local junk-shop, pushed home on a borrowed hand-cart, and polished to its present gleaming splendour. Sarah removed the tray to a safer position on the table and poured out two cups of tea, leaving the pot and the water jug to keep warm in the hearth. When he had drunk his tea and scoffed most of the ginger biscuits, lounging in the armchair with his long legs stretched across the hearthrug, he extracted his tobacco tin from his jacket pocket and expertly rolled a cigarette between his fingers, licking the paper to make it hold, before he lit the end.

Tom Whitworth, Member of Parliament for The Dales, must surely be the only Junior Minister of the Crown to roll his own cigarettes, and Sarah reckoned he continued to do so partly from habit, but partly to prove success hadn't gone to his head and he remained one of 'us'. She went on watching as her brother inhaled deeply on the tobacco and blew out several smoke rings, waiting for him to say why he had come. They usually met when Tom was in Manchester but he had not trailed out to Moss Side on a dreary afternoon, interrupting his hectic workload, to chit-chat. Maybe Tom wanted her to loosen her ties with the Manchester Peace Committee, to tone down her demands that honourable peace negotiations be entered into forthwith, because they were embarrassing for him as a Junior Minister? If he did, Sarah had no intention of complying.

Then casually, as if it were a further piece of chit-chat, he said, 'I wanted to tell you personally, Sal. I've accepted a commission as a Second-Lieutenant. In one of the new Pals Battalions of the Manchester Regiment.'

The clock on the mantelpiece ticked loudly, a tiny pocket of gas in one of the coals burning in the fire hissed as it escaped, and as if responding to the sound the gas in one of the lights on the wall plopped and spluttered. Staring at Tom, watching the thick black hair flopping on to his

8

forehead, Sarah's stunned brain had only one coherent thought: if you're joining the army, you'll have to have your hair cut. After a moment, when she had recovered from the shock, furiously she said, 'You've gone on at me some and often about your being more likely to end the war by having power, by being in Government. So what's changed? Why are you suddenly more likely to end it by leading men to their deaths in the trenches?'

They had a good old set-to, rehashing the arguments they'd thrown at each other since the outbreak of the war, since Tom had, so shamefully in Sarah's opinion, denied his Socialist principles by supporting the war effort and then, earlier this year, by accepting Lloyd George's offer to be his second-in-command at the newly created Ministry of Munitions. In fact Sarah had been torn in two by the appointment, her pride in her brother's achievement, in Government at his age and coming from their poverty-stricken background, battling with her revulsion that he should be a Junior Minister of *Munitions*. Now she demanded to know what Kessie felt about him enlisting. Had he thought about his wife and children? Tom told her not to be ridiculous. Of course he'd thought about Kessie and the kids – didn't any man of sense and sensibility in wartime? – and of course he'd discussed his decision with his wife, endlessly over the last few months. Kessie understood why they had been forced into this war and why he could no longer sit and watch, even from the Ministry of Munitions, but had to be there, by the side of the men he was supposed to represent.

'Then why've you accepted a commission, even as a lowly Second-Lieutenant, if you want to be by their side?'

A slight frown clouded Tom's face before he said, 'I wanted to enlist in the ranks. But Kessie pointed out the men who regard me as their spokesman in peacetime will expect me in the same role in wartime.'

'I see.'

Sarah sank back into her chair. Actually, she did see Kessie's point, given the rotten arguments for fighting the war, a subject on which she and her favourite sister-in-law had agreed to differ. Was it so surprising that Tom had enlisted? Or was it more surprising that he had kept out of the fray for sixteen months? As he himself said, he'd never been a great one for sitting on the sidelines, and embedded in her brother's tough, sometimes ruthless character, there was a romantic streak. It was evident in his passionate love for England, for the moors, for the people who lived in the smoky cotton towns of Upperdale, their own birthplace Mellordale, and Lowtondale, which were collectively known as The Dales. With the men of The Dales, Tom's own constituents, responding in their thousands to the call for a Citizens' Army to knock the hell out of the Huns and send them reeling all the way to Berlin, was he likely to have held back? Obviously Kessie had decided the answer was no.

Breaking the uneasy silence, Tom said, 'I shan't be killed, Sal. I'm a born survivor. We create our own fate. It's fateful I'm joining a Pals Battalion. "Pal" comes from the Romany for brother, you know. My gipsy blood will see me through.'

His voice had a certainty that transcended the belief of all men who marched off to war, but it sent a shiver down Sarah's spine. And Tom was now grinning at her, the dimple in his chin stretching. When he started to talk about their gipsy blood, a subject which he knew irritated her because it was pretty diluted by now – it had been their beloved, long dead Mam's brother who had been the full-blooded gipsy – and grinned like that, Sarah knew she could abandon hopes of further serious discussion.

'Do you want another cup of tea?' she asked.

'I wouldn't say no.'

When they had drained the teapot and Tom had polished off the last of the ginger biscuits, he said he'd better be on his way, his eye on the trails of fog that were now slipping through the window joints and floating forlornly around the room. There was no need to look outside to know the miasma had thickened and he wanted to catch the six o'clock train to London, Kessie and the children. At the door Sarah and her brother did not embrace. They had never gone in for sloppy behaviour; they had no need to; the bond between them went back to infancy as the last two of Mam's large brood, born after a gap that had separated them from the rest of their siblings.

'I shan't stop preaching pacifism,' Sarah said.

'I don't expect you to. You know I respect your views, though I don't share them.'

He had shown some courage, Sarah acknowledged, some remnants of his Socialist principles when hecklers had interrupted his support-the-war-effort speeches. In answer to their shouts, 'What about that sister of yours?' he had shouted back that the freedon of the individual conscience and the right to propagate deeply held convictions were among the reasons they were fighting this war.

'Are you coming down to us for Christmas?'

'No. Tell Kessie thanks, but no.'

'Come down and see us before I get my posting.'

'When will that be?'

'I report to the training camp in the New Year. There's twelve weeks basic training for subalterns. So any time in April.'

Sarah said she would consider the suggestion.

For a long time after her brother had gone she sat in front of the fire, watching the coal burn to an orange mass, its glow and warmth slowly falling to ash. Rowing against the tide of this war was a hard, unpopular task. The People's Centre she and Tom had jointly, proudly, opened before the war had collapsed about Sarah's reviled pacifist ears. Folks she'd known for years crossed the street to avoid talking to her, shop assistants pointedly ignored her, kids danced behind her, chanting, 'Hun lover, go and live in Berlin', 'Cowardy, cowardy custard', 'German bum-licker' and similar uplifting slogans. Sarah gazed at the mantelpiece on which an array of the white feathers she'd received in the post was stuck in a clay pot. Probably it was only because Tom was her brother that she hadn't had a brick chucked through her window.

If she was being honest she couldn't say she was smitten by all the members of the Manchester Peace Committee.

11

In fact, in the old suffragette days she would have labelled half of them as cranks with obsessive bees in their bonnets, but war was an obscenity, this particular war was particularly obscene, and you had to find your allies where you could. There were moments, like now, when she felt weary and discouraged, endlessly playing a tune few wanted to hear; though that was no reason for not playing it. At such moments she reckoned it would be a comfort to have a marriage like Kessie and Tom's, to have one person in the world to whom you were infinitely precious, to whom you could always turn. Her sole liaison with a man had been a disaster, and after the Edward Dawson business Sarah had decided she could live without men and the physical side of things, even though the sexual desire sometimes troubled her in the stillness of the night.

Poor Edward, who had obviously abandoned his Marxian principles for the greater glory – or mass hysteria – of fighting for King, Country and Empire. She had seen his name among the long columns of those who died in the shambles of the Dardanelles campaign earlier this year. Dawson, Private Edward James, East Lancashire Regiment, killed at Gallipoli. She had shed a few silent tears for him.

The embers of the fire had almost died. Sarah shivered. Then, resolutely, she stood up. At the advanced age of thirty-two, the likelihood of her finding true love, or even a decent working relationship with a man, was not high, but old maids unencumbered by personal ties, untroubled by emotional disturbances, were very useful persons to have around. Her tasks were to continue to do her utmost to bring about an honourable peace and to ensure that the next generation of Edward Dawsons were not killed thousands of miles from their homelands.

In the middle of April one of Kessie's long chatty letters arrived, with the vital news reserved for the final paragraph: 'Tom's now completed his twelve weeks basic training and he's just learned he's under orders for France. But he's been given a week's leave first and he said you

12

promised to visit before he sails. Please, please, do come, Sarah. The children are dying to see you. And so am I. Fondest love, as always, Kessie.'

There was a postscript which read: 'I enclose £5 as an advance birthday present. It will leave you with no excuse to say you can't afford to travel to London.'

Five pounds indeed! Even if she travelled first-class that sum would cover her return fare from Manchester to London four times over, but it was typical of her ever generous, ever tactful sister-in-law. Mind you, Kessie had never been short of the odd bob or two and, since her beloved Papa's death last year, by Sarah's standards she was a rich woman.

Hastily, Sarah rearranged her teaching timetables. She had originally trained as a teacher, so once her People's Centre had collapsed, friends had rallied round to find enough private pupils to keep her head above the financial waves. Not all her pacifist friends, however, appreciated the irony of her dashing down to London to wave her favourite brother off to the war. Undeterred, Sarah went. She travelled on a train packed with soldiers, more lambs for the slaughter, and when she reached Euston station she found that Kessie had sent the Rolls-Royce, which had been a contentious wedding present from her Papa, to meet her.

Excitedly, as they drove through the streets of wartime London, the young chauffeur informed Sarah that he'd enlisted in the Middlesex Regiment and hoped he too would soon be off to France. She wanted to say he shouldn't be excited by the idea of fighting Germans like himself, he should be working with them for a better world, but she didn't. It wasn't this young lad's fault if he'd swallowed the propaganda he'd been fed, and how did she explain to him why her Socialist brother had decided he should go? Murmuring non-committal responses to his exuberant chatter, Sarah gazed out of the Silver Ghost.

The atmosphere in London was just the same as in Manchester, pedestrians cheering the khaki-clad platoons as they marched along the roads, the cards stuck in front windows proudly announcing that the man of this house was already serving his King, Country and Empire, and the Silver Ghost was having to purr slowly up Highgate Hill behind a convoy of chugging military ambulances. At the top of the hill the motor car turned past the green where two horses were quenching their thirst at the water trough after their long haul from the Archway. As they crossed South Hill to the row of Georgian houses that lay in tree-lined seclusion back from the road, Sarah recalled how swanky the one in the middle of the row had seemed to her when Kessie had first bought it, though for real swank she now appreciated it was left at the starting post.

Having wished the young chauffeur the best of British luck – what else could she do? – Sarah thumped on the big brass door knocker of her sister-in-law's house in The Grove. Her knock was answered with customary dourness by Kessie's devoted housekeeper, Maggie, who regarded emotions as things to be kept battened down and Sarah herself as a bit of an upstart. There was, however, nothing dour about the greetings from Kessie or the children.

It was lovely to see them all again.

Tall, slim, elegant in a fine wool, green and white check-ered suit and a white silk blouse, her glossy chestnut hair parted in the middle and swept back on both sides, Kessie was looking well, Sarah was glad to see. Her sister-in-law's heart had been badly affected by her imprisonments as a young suffragette and the difficult birth of the twins Kate and Mark, but she appeared to be achieving the right balance between not overdoing things, not precipitating the heart attack male specialists predicted, and leading a reasonably active life.

After the greetings, one little hand in each of hers, Anne and Con conducted Sarah up the stairs to the first floor. Anne said, 'You're sleeping in our bedroom, Aunty Sarah. We've gone up to the attic.'

'That's noble of you.'

'Acksherly, we don't mind,' Anne confided. 'We like being in the attic, don't we, Con?'

Her younger sister nodded.

Her nieces' bedroom was a light, airy room at the rear of the house, overlooking Kessie's flower-filled conservatory, the velvety lawn, and the borders in which the spring flowers were unfolding. Beyond the fruit cages and the apple tree at the bottom of the garden were the woods and the open expanse of Parliament Hill Fields. The view was a distinct improvement on the one from Sarah's flat in Moss Side, and at The Grove there was also the luxury of a bathroom with its constant supply of boiling hot water gushing from the geyser, and a separate *indoor* toilet.

For the next few days she enjoyed Kessie and Tom's company. By unspoken agreement they avoided contentious subjects, nobody mentioned her brother's imminent departure, and being with the children was a real pleasure for Sarah. She inspected Anne and Con's bedroom in the attic, which was stuffed with pictures, books, toys and bric-à-brac, and she wondered if Tom ever contrasted his daughters' possessions with the one-eared furless rabbit, the wooden hoop and the few tenth-hand books that had been their childhood hoard? Still, as Kessie had once observed rather crossly, 'I thought Socialism aimed to level up, not down', to which she had replied, 'It does, Kessie, it does.'

Proudly Anne showed Aunty Sarah the full-scale map of the Western Front which was pinned above her bed, with the little Union Jack flags marking the British positions from the Ypres Salient, the only piece of Belgian soil left in the Allies' hands, down to the Somme region of northern France. In the afternoons she collected Anne and Con from the kindergarten down the hill, though Anne said in September, when she was seven, she would be moving into the *big* part of the school. She played games with them, she read them stories, and she did her best to satisfy Anne's insatiable curiosity which was not to be fobbed off with simplistic answers – 'Yes, but *why*, Aunty Sarah?' the child insisted.

It was a joy to watch Kate and Mark's toddler steps daily becoming firmer, helping them to shape words, bouncing them on her knee, kissing the thick black hair that was growing just like hers and Tom's. In the evening she gave the twins their baths, for Kessie's servants, Vi and Ruby, had left The Grove: Ruby at the start of the war, rushing forward her marriage before her young husband marched off to Flanders, now herself the proud mother of a baby girl; Vi more recently, to work in a munitions factory.

Then, slightly to Sarah's surprise, Kessie informed her that she had invited her old suffragette friends, Didi and Stephen, to dinner on Thursday evening. The surprise was because Tom and 'Didi', thus known from her initials D.D. for Dorothy Devonald, had never been the best of friends. However, it transpired that she and Stephen had only just returned home after having served with one of the Scottish Women's Hospital Units in Serbia. Tom had agreed he would be interested to hear about their experiences in that remote Balkan kingdom whose contretemps with the Austro-Hungarian empire had precipitated the war.

On the Thursday evening they heard the front door knocker bang and voices in the hall and almost before Maggie could open the sitting room door to announce the arrival of the guests Dorothy bounced in like a ping-pong ball, throwing her arms round Kessie's neck, saying how lovely it was to see her.

'Hello Tom.' In the same crisply offhand voice she said to Sarah, 'Oh hello, I didn't expect to see you.'

Sarah shared her brother's opinion that Miss Devonald was a ferocious little madam with reactionary views about everything except women's rights, but just as she had made a resolution not to argue further with Tom about his decision to enlist, she had decided to keep her mouth as tight shut as possible should Didi sound off about the war. After all, she too was a guest in Kessie's house and in two days' time her beloved husband, and Sarah's favourite brother, would be away to the fighting.

Behind Dorothy strode Stephen, actually Doctor Serena Abbott, but as she herself said, 'I ask you, do I look like a Serena?' to which the answer had to be, no. For allied to a broad face and Eton-cropped hair, she had a jolly, booming, slap-the-thighs manner which at times, in Sarah's opinion, was almost a caricature of the manly woman. She didn't know Stephen Abbot particularly well, though they had met in their suffragette days, but what she knew Sarah quite liked.

Stephen enveloped Kessie in a bear-hug and briskly shook hands with Sarah and Tom before enquiring how Tom was finding life in the jolly old army. That was a query he was only too willing to answer.

'Do you know what the adjutant said to a poor young bugger who arrived at the training camp with me? He said "Jesus wept! Who's your tailor?" How's that for a greeting when at the age of nineteen you've volunteered to fight for your King and Country?'

Tom continued by observing that three months in the army subject to lunatic rules and regulations, idiotic discipline and hierarchic snobberies had reinforced his conviction that England's social structures had to be torn to pieces before there could be any hope of building a just, equitable society. One of the few good things to be said about the war was that it had activated the process of social demolition. Far too many people were on the move, including women, for them ever to settle back into their prewar grooves.

With considerable pleasure Sarah listened to her brother holding forth. Initially, she reckoned, his comments were intended to rile Didi, but they finished as a statement of Tom's beliefs. Rile Dorothy they did. Throughout the recital, her deceptively innocent face, with the round, gold-rimmed glasses perched on the little nose, grew increasingly tight with anger. (Her eyesight had been ruined by her prolonged imprisonments as one of the youngest of militant suffragettes.) Dorothy had, however, been brought up not to interrupt her elders and she managed to contain herself until Tom had had his say. Then, as he turned to Stephen, obviously about to ask about her experiences in Serbia, she burst out, 'You need discipline in life, Tom. You most certainly need it in armies. Whether you like it or not, most people need to be led, by those whose education, background . . .' Dorothy paused for a second and looked at Tom who was now comfortably relaxed in the armchair, smoking as usual, '. . . or natural abilities have fitted them for leadership. What you regard as a load of tommy-rot . . .' From the way she spoke the phrase she conveyed her disapproval of Tom's language, '. . . is part of the essential discipline of any good army. It's what makes it strong in dark days and ultimately enables it to snatch victory from the jaws of defeat. As one day soon the Serbian army will.'

During this tirade Dorothy jumped up and stood facing Tom, who was regarding her with his most sardonic expression. As she continued her tiny body was almost shaking and her tones acquired a tremulous note.

'If you'd retreated with the Serbian army in midwinter, as we did, struggling through snowstorms and blizzards, up those precipitous mountains in Montenegro, through those twisting valleys, dragging oxen and guns and pack ponies, accompanied by a horde of women and children, you'd know the value of discipline. It was discipline and devotion to duty that kept the Serbians, and us, going. Wasn't it, Stephen?'

Dorothy swung round towards the older woman, but without waiting for a reply she pushed her spectacles furiously up on her nose, took a deep breath and said abruptly, 'Please excuse me. I'm going to wash my hands.'

After she had run from the room it was Stephen who broke the startled silence. Although her language was her usual slangy style, her tone was sombre.

'Sorry about that, chaps, but it was a rough old do. Hundreds of thousands of us set off through those mountains. In the end we had to abandon those who couldn't keep up, which meant most of the women and children and old folk and some of the walking wounded, to the mercy of the elements, brigands and the advancing Bulgars. As 'twas, only a quarter of the Serbian army made it to the Albanian coast and half of them had to be lifted on to our evacuation ships. By golly, you should have seen Didi encouraging people to keep going. She's only knee-high to a grasshopper, but for the last two days

18

and nights she carried a baby whose mother had died. The little mite survived.'

Stephen twitched her nostrils, a peculiar habit of hers, and Sarah saw the tears welling in Kessie's eyes. Then Stephen said, ''Tisn't only that's upset Didi, though. She's just heard her brother Georgie's gone west. Copped a packet during some "stunt" at Givenchy and died of his wounds. Gather he's been awarded a posthumous Military Cross, though personally I've never considered that much help.'

'Oh God,' said Tom.

'Why didn't she tell us? Georgie was her favourite brother. Why didn't she cancel this evening?' Kessie cried out to Stephen, who shrugged her large shoulders in a 'You know what Dorothy's like' gesture.

While a distressed Kessie went to comfort her young friend, Tom excused himself and, left alone with Stephen, Sarah said, 'How did you come to be in Serbia? In case you don't know, I'm a pacifist. So I haven't followed the doings of our gallant allies with the usual patriotic enthusiasm.'

'You don't have to be on the defence with me, old girl.' Had she sounded defensive? Sarah wondered. 'My sentiments are pacifist, too. But I'm a doctor, and if men will insist on blowing themselves to smithereens and involving women and children in their war games, then it's my job to patch 'em up as best I can. How did we come to be there? Thereby hangs a tale.'

Stephen informed her that immediately upon the outbreak of the war her old friend and colleague, Doctor Elsie Inglis, had raised the huge sum of £50,000 for several fully equipped Scottish Women's Hospital Units. Having raised her Units – ambulances, X-ray cars, trained women doctors and nurses, volunteer orderlies – she had wanted to place them at the service of the British Army.

'You'll never believe what some base-wallah at the War Office said to Doctor Inglis. "My good lady, go home and sit still. Our commanding officers have no wish to be saddled with hysterical women."'

'I believe it!' said Sarah.

'The French and Belgian Governments showed more sense. We've Units working for them on the Western Front. Then the Serbians said they'd like us to join them. By golly, they needed us, Sarah, virtually no medical facilities and typhus rampant when we arrived. Darned shame, though, isn't it, we're not allowed to help our own British lads? Still a good way to go on the equality front.'

Sarah certainly agreed with the last sentiment.

Maggie came in to announce that dinner was ready and they went into the dining room to join Tom, Kessie and Dorothy. As they sat down, Dorothy said, 'My brother died as he would have wished. Doing his duty for England and for freedom. We shall mourn the passing of his life, but we shall not weep for the glory of his death.'

Defying anyone to offer sympathy, she stared at the tureen as Maggie ladled out the Mulligatawny soup. Sarah glanced at her brother, soon to depart to do his duty for England and freedom, but his face had its particularly attentive expression which meant his mind was miles away and he was not going to waste his breath arguing with Miss Devonald. She looked at Kessie, who shook her head imperceptibly. Maybe she was right, Dorothy had had a basinful, whatever you thought of her, and Sarah had vowed to keep quiet this evening.

After breakfast on the Saturday morning of Tom's departure for France, the family assembled in the sitting room. Why did the sight of her brother in his uniform – well cut khaki jacket and breeches, fine cotton shirt and tie, glinting buttons, polished leather of boots, gun holster and Sam Browne belt – stir even her pacifist blood? Because she too fell victim to the sartorial romanticising of the glory of war? Once they were all present and correct, Kessie signalled to the excited children to give Daddy their presents before he set off for the Western Front. Despite the huddlings in corners and the whispered conversations with Mummy and Aunty Sarah that had been going on all week, Tom did a beautiful act of being supremely surprised that any such thought should have entered any of their heads.

Kate and Mark's offering consisted of coloured crayoning scrawled on a piece of white cardboard. Con had made a cat from papier mâché which she had painted bright orange and which she told her father he could call either Amber or Jasper after their cats, 'cos she wasn't sure whether it was a boy or girl cat. Anne, who like her mother hated sewing, had laboriously embroidered a sampler which had the word 'Daddy' in red silk in the centre, surrounded by blue and white flowers to complete the patriotic colour scheme. Kessie gave Tom one of those new cigarette lighter things. Sarah just stopped herself from saying 'And don't smoke yourself to death', because you didn't make remarks like that these days, before she handed over her gift, a leather-bound, gold-edged copy of the *Complete Works of William Shakespeare* which had cost a small fortune.

'Your old copy was falling to bits, so I reckoned you could do with a new one.'

Tom smiled at the emotion wrapped in the brusque tones, 'Thanks, Sal.'

Then it was Maggie's turn and she presented him with a five-year diary which had a padlock and key. All Tom's charm was in his thanks, the charm he'd inherited from their Mam, as he said he hoped Maggie didn't believe the war was going to last another five years! But he was obviously, genuinely, touched by her gift and the aptness of her choice, for Tom had always enjoyed writing which he did with considerable facility, though his spelling left a lot to be desired. While he was expressing his thanks, Kessie signalled to Anne and Con, who trotted towards the occasional table on which sat a mysterious humped object, covered by a chenille tablecloth.

Sweeping into the deepest of curtseys, Kessie said, 'And now for your very last present, sir, a gift from your devoted, dutiful wife and your loving, obedient offspring. Unveil it, children dear.'

Anne and Con pulled off the tablecloth and Sarah was as astonished as her brother by the sight of one of the very

21

latest, most compact types of portable gramophone which reproduced excellent sound without the aid of a horn. Kessie opened the lid, which was as gleaming brown as the leather of Tom's boots, and explained that you took out the handle to wind it up, thus, fitted it in there, and put it back when you'd finished playing your records, of which six could be carried in this pocket in the lid. She'd chosen six of Tom's favourite records, including Elgar's 'Nimrod' variation, though obviously he could make his own selection, and she'd consulted everybody she knew who'd been in the trenches and they all said a gramophone was an absolute must, and if you had one you were the pride of your company . . .

Having presented her splendid gift with aplomb and humour, Kessie was now babbling somewhat emotionally. As Tom slipped his arm around her waist and kissed her gently to express his thanks, the door knocker banged. Anne rushed to the window.

'Your taxi's here, Daddy,' she shouted. 'Oo, and there's lots of people outside.'

There was pandemonium as Maggie answered the door and the driver carried Tom's baggage and the gramophone outside. Tom's officer's stick could not be found and everybody searched frantically until eventually Anne discovered it underneath the chenille tablecloth on the floor. In the hall Tom hugged the children, telling them to be good and to help Mummy while he was away. He touched Sarah's nose with his long forefinger.

'Don't do anything daft, Sal. Keep an eye on her for me. See she doesn't overdo things.'

Sarah shooed the even more excited children across the small paved front garden to give Kessie and Tom a last few seconds together. She saw her sister-in-law bury her head on her brother's chest and how she envied their loving closeness. Oh God, or fate, or something, keep him safe, see he is among the survivors.

Then Tom was climbing into the taxi and slowly the vehicle moved away from the kerb. The crowd of neighbours and well-wishers that had gathered to see off one of

22

Highgate's once reviled but now highly esteemed inhabitants, cheered and waved their Union Jacks. Eluding her mother's grasp Anne ran alongside the taxi, blowing kisses with one hand, clutching their elegant female cat, Amber, with the other. Little Con copied her older sister, holding up inelegant male Jasper and waving his paw, and their father leant from the window, waving and blowing kisses back. The children stood on the pavement until the tail of the taxi disappeared down the hill, and with it the last glimpse of their Daddy's smiling face.

Close to tears, Kessie said, 'He will be all right, won't he?'

''Course he will,' Sarah echoed her brother's words. 'He's a born survivor, is our Tom.'

2

'Isn't it a lovely evening? Now sit, Horatio, sit!'

It had been a dreary summer's day but the sun had suddenly emerged about five o'clock and it was now a beautiful, turquoise-coloured evening, so Sarah and Kessie had decided to have a gentle stroll. They had wandered down through the woods beyond The Grove and were approaching the ponds on Parliament Hill Fields when Dorothy came bounding towards them. By her side strode Stephen and in front of them, straining on its leash, was a puppy.

'Sit, I said, sir, sit.'

The puppy took no notice of Dorothy's peremptory tone but ran round and round her legs so that the hem of her orderly's skirt was pinioned by the leash. While she unpinioned herself she greeted Kessie enthusiastically, but she ignored Sarah who presumed the rebuff was due to Didi learning of her pacifism. Then Dorothy said, 'Isn't it wonderful news about Tom? You must be proud of him.'

The news that Tom Whitworth, the Labour MP for The Dales, had been awarded the Military Cross for his bravery in the battle for Mametz Wood had made the headlines.

Kessie said, 'Oh yes, we are.'

The sad lack of enthusiasm in her voice was lost on Dorothy who asked, 'Have you heard from him recently?'

'We had a few pencilled, scrawled lines the day before yesterday, saying he was bearing up. And he's now an acting captain.'

'Jolly good show!'

Kessie glanced down at the puppy, 'Is it yours?'

'Not exactly. A friend of mine's been posted to a hospital in Malta, so she's asked me to look after Horatio until she gets back. He's blind in one eye, aren't you, poor old thing? That's why he's called "Horatio". After Lord Nelson.'

'Doesn't seem to affect him much.' Stephen gazed rather sourly at the puppy which was now barking furiously and staring up at his new mistress with moist eyes, pleading to be allowed to rush around.

A couple of young soldiers walked slowly past them, wearing the distinctive lobelia-blue suits, white shirts and red ties which were the hospital uniforms of other ranks. They gave hesitant, grateful smiles towards Dorothy and Stephen who were themselves both in uniform.

'Do you think they're from Endell Street?' Dorothy asked Stephen as the soldiers walked on. 'I forget what they look like once they've left us.'

They were both working at the Endell Street Hospital where Flora Murray, a staunch pre-war suffragette, was the doctor-in-charge, and Louisa Garrett Anderson was the chief surgeon. On the outbreak of the war, unlike Doctor Elsie Inglis, they had not bothered to offer their services to the War Office but had taken off for France, where the powers-that-be were more desperate for trained medical staff. With the mounting stream of casualties from the Western Front the War Office had approached them, and Endell Street had become the first military hospital in Britain to be run by women surgeons, physicians and nurses.

'I can't tell you what it's like at the moment,' Dorothy turned to Kessie. 'They're littering the corridors, we're so overcrowded, and we're operating round the clock, aren't we, Stephen? And some of the wounds are gruesome. I fell over a basket outside the operating theatre yesterday, stacked high with amputated limbs . . .'

Horatio managed to pull free from her grasp and raced up the slope, his leash trailing behind him. Dorothy chased after him, but as she caught up with the puppy, he barked joyously and set off again with her in hot pursuit.

'That'll keep her occupied for a while,' said Stephen. 'He's a right little terror, I can tell you. Personally, I have the gravest suspicion about him being blind at all. Why don't we sit down?' She took Kessie's arm and led her to a vacant bench. 'Sorry about that, but tact isn't Didi's middle name.'

By heck it isn't, Sarah thought. Describing baskets of amputated limbs to the wife and sister of a man fighting in the battle of the Somme! Not that Miss Devonald would care about her feelings, but Kessie she was supposed to adore. As she sat her down on the bench, Stephen patted Kessie's arm but she made no reply and the strain, the desperate worry for Tom, were only too evident in her face.

It was nearly three weeks since the news had broken that five British army corps had 'gone over the top' on a twenty mile front in the Somme region, that this time the breakthrough had been made, the Germans were being pushed back, and victory was in sight. Victory had not yet appeared but the casualty lists had, column after column of them, day after day. Each time the door knocker banged at The Grove, Kessie and Sarah held their breaths in case it was a telegraph boy with the buff envelope whose contents would regret to inform them that Captain E. T. F. Whitworth had been killed or seriously wounded.

In silence the three of them watched Dorothy's efforts

to catch Horatio. At one point she almost succeeded when he stopped to cock his leg against a tree, but at the last moment the puppy eluded her outstretched hands and set off at a fresh gallop. Stephen broke the silence by saying, 'What's the Consultative Committee up to? Any fresh developments?'

Recently, Parliament had woken up to the fact that half the men fighting for their country would, on the old franchise and electoral registers, be ineligible to vote in the victory General Election. Therefore something must be done, but the buggers had proposed that the extension of the vote be based on war service, which would not include women's sterling efforts. That information had aroused women's suffrage bodies of every ilk, all of which had been in a comatose state since the outbreak of the war. A Consultative Committee had been set up, and Sarah had travelled to London as a representative of the north-western area. Almost immediately on her arrival the battle of the Somme had started. Kessie hadn't asked her to stay on at The Grove, Sarah hadn't volunteered, she'd just stayed. As it was holiday time there was little problem about her pupils and, to be honest, for the first time in her life she was not panting to return to Manchester, though she was doing her best to push the possible reasons why to the back of her mind.

In answer to Stephen's question about the Consultative Committee, she said, 'The latest buzz is they're considering giving the vote to all men over the age of twenty-one. We're all agreed about one thing. If that's the way the wind's blowing, then they're giving us the vote, too. Another rumour says even our dear Prime Minister believes women can no longer be denied the elementary right to put their crosses on a ballot paper, in view of their splendid war work.'

'Not old Asquith,' said Stephen, 'I don't believe it!'

'I'll believe it when we actually get the vote,' said Kessie.

After a pause Sarah said, 'Are you and Dorothy working permanently at Endell Street now?'

'Not sure. Doctor Inglis has been asked to take another

26

hospital Unit abroad. So we're holding our horses to see what happens.'

'Where will it be, if you do go, this time?'

'Bit hush-hush at the moment. Better keep the old lips buttoned.'

A breathless Dorothy returned with Horatio firmly on his leash. 'Now sit, sir, sit.'

Exhausted by his gallop across Parliament Hill Fields the puppy flopped down at her feet, and Dorothy beamed triumphantly. But Stephen stood up and yanked on his lead. 'Come on, matey, your temporary mistress and I are on duty soon. Walkies back home.' As they departed, she put her arm round Kessie's shoulder, 'Keep your pecker up, old girl.'

Sarah and Kessie decided it was time to go home too, and as they were strolling up through the woods Kessie said suddenly, 'I'm always going to remember where I was, and what I'd just listened to, when I heard the battle of the Somme had started.'

'Yes,' said Sarah.

The raucous cries of the newspaper vendors – 'Tremendous battle on the Somme. Read all about it' – had greeted them as they had emerged from Southwark Cathedral on that beautiful late afternoon of 1 July, 1916. They had just listened to an inspiring performance of Brahms' *Requiem*. The hideous irony of that particular music at that particular moment – requiem: music for the repose of the souls of the dead – was haunting Sarah too.

'What is happening, Sarah? Half the Pals Battalion have been wiped from the face of the earth. There's hardly a soul in The Dales hasn't lost somebody. Think how many men we know personally who've already been killed, gassed, or hideously wounded. And how many of them went on 1 July? How many casualties were there on that first day?'

'I don't know,' Sarah said, 'and I don't reckon we shall until the war's over.'

'Have you looked at Anne's map recently? I have. Because she's not sure where to move her flags. I'm not surprised. As far as I can make out, the furthest advance is less than a mile. In some places they hardly appear to have advanced at all. They gave up at Loos after three weeks. How much longer is the carnage on the Somme to continue?'

Kessie's husky voice trembled with passion, an accusingly interrogative passion. Sarah could only repeat, 'I don't know, Kessie. I simply do not know.'

There was a great deal she was beginning to feel she did not know. The emotions were raging round her head, at war with her reason, which was a disconcerting position for someone like herself whose beliefs and objectives had always been certain and clear-cut. More vehemently than ever she was opposed to the slaughter, now on a more mind-numbing, soul-sickening scale than ever before, but which as before appeared to be achieving nothing except waste, pain, heartbreak, suffering. Her reasons said she should therefore be fighting harder than ever for an end to the conflict. Yet she was not a coward, she was not a German bum-licker, and she wanted to avenge the blurred faces of the dead that stared up at her from the pages of 'Today's Casualties' in the local newspapers Kessie regularly had sent down from Lancashire; the faces of lads she had gone to school with in Mellordale, boys she'd taught in her early days in Manchester. Reason said vengeance was a terrible thing, yet emotion said Tom had been right. The dogs of war had been unleashed and she had as little hope of quietening them as Dorothy had with that puppy. The best option now, the one in which both Kessie and Tom believed, was to be a participant, to help alleviate the misery, to save what lives you could, to be able to bear witness once it was all over.

Why didn't she?

Because of the likes of Mrs Pankhurst and Dorothy Devonald screaming that all real women were at a white heat of belligerent rage, one hundred per cent behind their menfolk in the Great War for Civilisation. Because the vote had yet to be won, to establish women's rights as citizens, to consolidate the gains the war had ironically, but undeniably, brought them. Because Kessie was at the end of her tether and needed her, and loyal support for your nearest and dearest in their hour of trial – Kessie she loved more than any of her own sisters – was a creed in which Sarah believed.

A week later Sarah sat in a stationary train, listening to the anti-aircraft guns barking away like berserk hounds of the Baskervilles. Last year when she had visited London the air-raid precautions had been pathetic, on the premise, she suspected, despite the evidence to the contrary, that the Huns had not, could not, and would not get their Zeppelins through. The regulations introduced this year, ordering everything to be 'blacked out' after lighting-up time, had turned night-time London into a funereal city and caused innumerable street accidents, but they had obviously been sensible. This business of stopping all trains and damping down the fires in their engines during a raid in case a Zeppelin pilot glimpsed a glowing coal, seemed to Sarah to be overdoing things.

The rest of the passengers in the compartment had exhausted their conversational powers some while back. They seemed convinced that the continuing battle of the Somme was a great victory, any road, and Sarah had not made herself popular by disagreeing. Fortunately, it was a long-distance train and she could therefore stretch her legs in its corridor. She managed to push her way through to the emptier space near one of the doors where an argument was in process about the use of the toilets while the train was stationary.

'My little Freda can't hold herself no longer.'

'Your little Freda should be at home in bed at this time of night, my good woman.'

Not all men had changed their attitude towards women, Sarah thought. Then she heard the female voice booming, 'For heaven's sake, the regulations say the toilets should not be used while a train is standing in a station. We are not standing in a station. We are stuck somewhere outside Clapham Junction. Let the poor child have her piddle.'

29

It had to be Stephen. It was. She espied Sarah and shouted, 'What are you doing on this benighted chuff-chuff, old girl?'

'What are you?'

Stephen had been stretching her legs too, but she was travelling first class and she insisted that Sarah accompany her to her virtually empty compartment. When they reached it the compartment was deserted and Stephen said perhaps the two old buffers who had been there had decided to leg it to Waterloo station. After a brief argument as to who should explain first how they came to be ill-met by moonlight, Sarah kicked off. She said she'd been to a meeting of the Consultative Committee which, for complicated reasons she would not bother to explain, had been held in the wilds of Surrey.

'So what's happening on the jolly old suffrage front?'

'Mrs Pankhurst has just let it be known that votes for women should be cast aside. All that matters at the moment are votes for men who are fighting for their country.'

'Well, I'll be jiggered! How jolly helpful of her!'

'Isn't it? Fortunately, she no longer has much clout in suffrage circles. Too busy flying around on her patriotic broomstick. So it's only a temporary gumming up of the works, the most militant, vehement, prewar advocate of votes for women doing a complete about-turn. Apart from that, yet another of those parliamentary committees is going into session, to try and work out the electoral reforms. Give or take arguments about tactics, we're trying to make sure they don't forget to include women.'

'You sound disenchanted.'

'I am a bit,' Sarah admitted. 'No matter. What are you doing? Are you on your way to Endell Street?'

'Lordy, no. Didn't Kessie tell you? No, she can't have. Only told her myself this afternoon when I dropped by to ask after old Tom. Gather there's no recent news. No, I've finished at Endell Street. Just been trying to persuade a gin-sodden wreck of a nurse to pop over with us to Russia. Can't say I was sorry when she declined the offer.'

'Why are you popping over to Russia?'

As she asked the question Sarah started to laugh. The phraseology was so ridiculous she couldn't stop herself. Leaning her broad shoulders against the plush upholstery of the first-class compartment, spreading her legs wide so that her skirt dipped between them in unladylike fashion, Stephen laughed with her.

'First began talking like this after I'd floated the idea of training to be a doctor. Come from South Devon, you know, very conservative area and all my family are huntin', shootin', fishin' types. Young Serena as a doctor, hah, hah, ho! So I turned myself into a bit of a buffoon. Laughed it all off. Showed I wasn't a bit hurt by their cruel jokes. Found it useful when I started working in a general hospital, too, with those *buggers* of male doctors, to use one of your brother's favourite words. Been at it so long, it's become part of me.'

Understandingly, Sarah nodded. She now knew why Kessie was so very fond of Doctor Abbot. She again asked, 'What about Russia?'

'Ah yes. Remember I told you Doctor Inglis might be taking another Unit abroad? Well, she is. Since the collapse of Serbia, the boys who made it through the mountains on that epic retreat have regrouped. Two Serbian divisions are now attached to the Russian army. During last year's capers we took to them and the Serbians took to us and they've virtually no medical facilities, so Doctor Inglis has agreed to take a Unit out to Russia. We've no problem getting volunteers for our Motor Transport Section, driving the ambulances, that sort of lark. Didi's volunteered as a driver this time. Dashed good driver she is too, so she'll be accepted, specs or no specs. But we're scratching around to fill the medical sections. Most of the good professional nurses and volunteer orderlies are already serving somewhere.'

After only a few seconds' pause Sarah said, 'Would you take me?'

'We'll take anybody, old girl, providing they're literate and numerate and don't knock back the gin.'

Would they indeed? Sarah thought. Stephen noticed her

31

raised eyebrows. With a hearty smack she smote her head, saying she hadn't meant it like *that*, they'd leap at Sarah, and was she serious?

Was she? Sarah asked herself.

The question had shot to the surface like one of those newly tapped oil wells. Whoosh. It had been a gut reaction, an instinctive response to the turmoil inside her, the battle between reason and emotion. Like her brother Sarah believed you made your own fate and that there were fateful meetings, moments, incidents, occasionally portents. It was by seizing them that you shaped your life. Encountering Stephen on an air-raid stranded train at the moment when she was looking for volunteers to go to Russia and Sarah herself was racked by the urge to do something positive had to be fateful.

It was gone six o'clock and the summer dawn had long since cleared the night-sky before a weary Sarah finally reached The Grove. Once Kessie was up and she could find a quiet minute – with Anne and Con now on school holiday, there weren't too many of those – she would discuss the subject of Russia with her, to see what Kessie's reactions were and how badly she still wanted or needed Sarah by her side. To an extent, it depended on what happened to Tom.

Sarah let herself into The Grove with her own key and to her surprise she heard the murmur of voices from the sitting room. Maggie was always up with the lark, but Kessie wasn't, and they were too low-pitched to be the children's voices. Any road, they wouldn't be downstairs at this hour. Wearily she took off her hat and coat and hung them on the hall-stand, then bracing herself for . . . for anything, she went into the sitting room.

Wrapped in her dressing gown Kessie was sitting at one end of the sofa. At the other end, in her orderly's uniform, was Dorothy Devonald – what the heck was she doing here at this hour? As Sarah came into the room Kessie's head swung round and her eyes were sparkling with tears, but *sparkling* was the right adjective. She jumped up and ran across the room – with her suspect heart Kessie wasn't supposed to move at those speeds – and threw her arms round Sarah's neck. Excitedly, breathily, she said, 'He's in England, Sarah! Wounded, but not too badly. He was brought to Endell Street, just after the air-raid and . . .'

Almost as excited as Kessie, Dorothy forgot her manners and interrupted. 'I was just about to go off-duty, almost my last actually. I'm leaving for Russia soon and I'm having a holiday first. Well, sister called me over and said, "A Captain Whitworth has just been brought into St Ursula's Ward – everywhere's so crowded we're taking officers as well as men – and I think it's Kessie Whitworth's husband. Isn't she a friend of yours?" Well, I fell into the ward and there was Tom! I tried telephoning but nobody was awake. So I came on up and I thundered on the door knocker like that messenger in *Macbeth*, didn't I?'

Laughing breathlessly, Kessie nodded. Dorothy's voice acquired a briskly professional edge, as she went on: 'Tom's wounds are nothing to worry about. A shell burst near him and a fragment shattered his right arm. But he's left-handed, so that was lucky, and it'll heal soon anyway. And a chip of marble embedded itself in his head. It came from a headstone in a cemetery, apparently. Goodness knows what they were doing there. Head wounds bleed like stuck pigs and that was Tom's main problem. He lost a lot of blood before they got him to the advanced dressing station. But rest and good food will soon build him up. They'll start the process at Endell Street. They have a first-class record of getting men fighting fit again.'

Hurrah for them, Sarah thought, as Dorothy beamed at them.

'Once Tom's out of hospital, which shouldn't be too long, he'll be sent away to convalesce. Then you'll be able to complete the building-up process, Kessie. Oh,' Dorothy put her finger thoughtfully to her lip, 'seeing I'm off to Russia, you wouldn't like to look after Horatio for me, would you?'

There were limits even to Kessie's helpfulness. As she shook her head, saying the puppy would not get on with her cats, the front door knocker banged. A few seconds later Maggie entered the room with the no longer dreaded buff envelope of the telegram. Kessie slit open the envelope, glanced through the contents and threw the telegram into the air. As they watched the piece of paper fluttering to the floor, she giggled.

'They regret to inform me that Lieutenant, Acting Captain, E. T. F. Whitworth – how pompously precise – has been wounded. For which three hearty cheers!'

Somewhat to Dorothy's disapproval Kessie went on giggling. It was a sound which had in the past occasionally irritated Sarah, but she hadn't heard it in a long, long time, and at the moment it was pealing out like a carillon of bells.

3

'Let me introduce you to Captain Kendle who, like me, has the dubious honour of promotion to that rank. Guy, meet my sister Sarah who's a holy terror. She's also off to Russia on Thursday.'

Captain Kendle took her hand, smiled, and asked if he should call her Sarah. Immediately liking his straight-forward manner, even though he had one of those posh, slurred accents, she nodded vigorously.

'Then you must call me Guy. Why are you off to Russia?'

After Sarah had told him she was going as an orderly with the Scottish Women's Hospital Unit, to nurse the Serbian wounded, he said, 'Good heavens! Have you travelled much before?'

'The furthest I've been is to Kessie's house on the Isle of Wight!'

'It should be an exciting experience then!'

His laughter was infectious, his attention focused – none

of that blank-faced gazing some upper class buggers had when they spoke to her, their eyes darting to see if more important folk were around. He had an air of what Sarah could, reluctantly, only describe as 'breeding' and she saw why he was nicknamed 'the Prince'. They all had nicknames on the Western Front, the unreal reality of life in the trenches demanding something less formal than the customary surnames, but not extending to the intimacy of christian names. Tom was known as 'Piper' from 'Tom, Tom the piper's son'. Undoubtedly Guy Kendle's nickname was well-chosen. The pieces of his personality added up to a fairy-tale Prince Charming who was making Sarah feel like a fairy princess. She could stop behaving like a romantic schoolgirl, she told herself severely, because Kessie had informed her that Captain Kendle was a married man with a twelve year old son.

Sarah glanced towards her sister-in-law and her brother – how good it was to see Tom on his feet again. His right arm was still in a sling, slower to heal than Miss Clever-Clogs Devonald had suggested, his black hair cropped from his head wound, and he was leaner and tenser than when he'd sailed for France four month's ago but he was here, alive, and almost well.

They were on the terrace at Chenneys, a beautiful early Tudor mansion of mullioned windows and elegant chimney stacks, situated not far from the coast in rural Kent. In the morning sunlight the stonework was a mellow ochre colour, and the terrace looked out over herbaceous borders, rose bowers, billiard table lawns and an ornamental lake. To reach the house they had driven through acres of rolling parkland, with deer munching at the verdant grass, and passed a summer house à la Marie Antoinette which was twice as big as the house in which Sarah and Tom had grown up in Mellordale.

Chenneys was the home of the Marchal family, pronounced 'Marshall'. The peculiar spelling, according to Kessie, derived from their Maréchal ancestors who had landed with William the Conqueror in 1066. A wing of the mansion had been made over as a convalescent hospital for officers, but this section remained the family's preserve. Apart from being born with a very large silver spoon in his mouth, their host, Philip Marchal, was a highly successful playwright whom Kessie and Tom had met at the first night of his latest comedy, *Love me for Ever*. Following that encounter Kessie had organised a war-distress, charity matinée of one of his earlier plays and they had become good friends so when Tom reached the convalescent stage, Chenneys was the obvious place for him and he'd suggested his friend Guy Kendle come here too.

Sarah looked at Philip Marchal as he stood talking to Tom and Guy. All three men were in their early thirties, much the same height, hovering round the six feet mark, and there wasn't any superfluous fat on any of their bodies, but Philip had neither Guy Kendle's easy, careless charm, nor Tom's more conscious, challenging variety. If, however, you liked immaculate grooming, sleek hair, teak brown and neatly parted in the middle, elongated features and a haughty expression, Sarah supposed Philip Marchal wasn't bad looking. And he was *Sir* Philip now. His elder unmarried brother had been killed on the Somme and the title had passed to him.

After everybody had greeted everybody Philip led them across the terrace and into the house. He had a bad limp in his right leg and within a short while of Sarah's only previous meeting with him he had answered her unasked question: 'I am not a war hero, Miss Whitworth. When I was six years old I was thrown from a pony, which then trampled on me. My leg never recovered from the animal's and my mutual dislike.' As Philip's honoured guests they were staying the weekend and two maids conducted them up the ornately carved stairway to their bedroom. When they reassembled on the terrace for mid-morning refreshments, a wide-eyed Anne whispered, 'Did you see the peacock in the bathroom, Aunty Sarah?'

Sarah nodded. The bathroom in question was tiled in pale green, with a peacock flaunting its mosaic eau-de-nil and turquoise tail over the sunken bath. In the swanky stakes, Chenneys was definitely a front runner.

After they had consumed the refreshments, the butler appeared with a camera which he set up on a tripod in the middle of the terrace, for among his other talents Philip was a gifted photographer. It was he who had taken *that* picture of Tom in his uniform, a waist-length shot in which her brother's lean body was turned three-quarters towards the camera, his gloved hands resting on his officer's stick, his empty gun holster just visible, the dark eyes quizzical beneath the peaked cap, the devilish smile hovering on his lips. In the euphoria of knowing that Tom was safe, Kessie had let several interested newspapers have copies of the photograph, a gesture which had turned Captain Tom Whitworth MC, MP, into a national hero, for elderly ladies, middle-aged matrons, romantic lasses and hero-worshipping lads had taken his dark good looks and his Military Cross to their hearts.

Immediately the camera appeared bossy-boots Anne tried to organise her siblings into a nice group round Mummy and Daddy, Aunty Sarah and Uncle Guy. Little Con who wanted everybody to be happy, bless her, complied with her older sister's commands, but Mark who had more than a touch of his father's devilry, exhibited it by sticking out his tongue at Anne and pinching his twin sister, whereupon Kate, who was a born show-off, howled histrionically. Within seconds there was uproar on the terrace.

Above the hubbub came the blare of a tooting horn and at considerable speed an open touring car, dark green in colour, swung round the curve of the drive and in a crunch of flying gravel bucketed to a halt. The noise on the terrace stopped and everybody froze, as if they were playing a game of 'statues', staring at the motor car. The driver was a woman who flung open the door, waved her hand at them, and called out, 'Hello everybody.'

Ye gods and little fishes, Sarah knew that voice with its anglicised transatlantic twang, but it couldn't be . . . Anne broke the frieze on the terrace by running to the balustrade and shouting, 'It's Aunty Alice. It's Aunty Alice. Hello, Aunty Alice.'

By heck it was, Alice Conway in person, looking not a day older than when Sarah had last seen her, just before the outbreak of the war. Kessie had told her that Alice had gone back to the United States when her father was taken seriously ill, but apparently he'd died soon after she reached New York. No wonder even Kessie hadn't recognised her old friend because nobody knew she was back in England. Personally, Sarah had reckoned Alice would stay in the safety of her native land until the war was over which showed how wrong you could be because here she was, sweeping up the steps from the drive.

Untying the scarf round her motoring hat, taking it off, patting her golden hair, Alice called out, 'Philip, you must forgive me, arriving like this, but I only reached London last night. When I telephoned The Grove this morning, Maggie told me everybody had come here for the weekend. I was just dying to see you all, so I thought why not? I jumped into the Napier and she drove down like a dream. I can't tell you how wonderful it is to see you.'

With arms outstretched, symbolically embracing them all, Alice reached the terrace. Kessie said how lovely it was to see her, quarrels forgotten the children jumped up and down, Philip said she was very welcome and of course she must stay the weekend. Tom introduced the one person she did not know, Guy Kendle, and he was favoured with Alice's golden smile.

'It's bliss to be back, though the crossing from New York was fearful. We "zig-zagged" most of the way because there were enemy submarines around. It's a very spooky feeling, I can tell you, wondering whether the ship is going to be blown from under you and you're about to be deposited in the icy Atlantic.'

Imperiously Alice directed the footman to carry her luggage from the Napier. That took some time because he was decrepit, the young able-bodied men on the estate having followed their late master, Sir Aubrey Marchal, to the war. When the cases and hat-boxes were on the terrace – Alice never travelled lightly – she handed round presents from New York to Kessie and Tom and the children, and to Philip. She apologised to Guy.

'I didn't know you'd be here, Captain Kendle.' Briefly she smiled at Sarah, 'Or you, Sarah.'

Sarah responded to the reflection upon the unlikelihood of her being at Chenneys by saying, 'How's Johnny?'

She felt the need to mention Alice's actor husband, Jonathon Conway: one, because she had always liked his uncomplicated, theatrical personality; two because it was through Johnny's playing the lead in *Love me for Ever* that any of them were here, and three because Guy Kendle was now gazing at Alice with a mesmerised look on his face.

She said her husband was fine but of course he couldn't accompany her today, because he was earning royalties for Philip with a matinée and evening performance of his play. Her tone suggested that Johnny would be better employed fighting on the Western Front like Guy and Tom. A maid conducted her inside, presumably to a ready and waiting spare bedroom. Sarah's presumption was correct because when Madam returned she had changed into the palest pink taffeta skirt, in the very latest calf-length style, naturally, which showed off her slim legs and trim ankles. Mind you, Kessie had adopted the style too, and she said it was immensely practical, not having skirts trailing round your ankles. Alice's rig-out had a matching pink jacket over a white silk blouse, on her feet were pink court shoes, and her pink and white hat was anchored at an angle on her upswept golden hair. She looked striking, to say the least.

'Shall I cause an uproar if I suggest taking photographs?' Philip enquired.

Not understanding the remark Alice blinked, but Kessie smiled at him, 'I think I can guarantee calm this time.'

This time the children were on their best behaviour and they had a jolly session, with Philip telling them to relax, to take no notice until he called out, because he wanted the groupings to be informal. The butler stood behind him, moving the camera at his master's bidding, and Alice talked throughout, elaborating on the spookiness of the Atlantic crossing. When Kessie said Sarah would soon be embarking on the wartime seas, incuriously she said 'Really?' She proceeded to tell them how peculiar peace-time New York seemed after wartime London and Paris, though she had no doubt her native land would soon be in the war on the Allies' side. Alice also told them she had returned via Cherbourg, so naturally she'd gone to see Christabel in Paris.

'She sends you her love, Kessie.'

Precisely how from Paris Christabel Pankhurst expected to do anything about votes for women, or for the British war effort about which she ranted with as fearful a jingoism as her mother, Sarah could not begin to imagine. But then she personally had lost her faith in Christabel and Mrs Pankhurst several years ago.

'I had this made in Paris.' Alice indicated the pink and white outfit. 'And a simply lovely evening gown I must show you, Kessie.'

'Are the fashion houses still functioning?' Kessie asked in surprise.

'I'll say they are. The French are fighting to uphold their culture against the Teuton. And what could be more French than *haute couture*?'

What indeed? Sarah thought. Personally she'd always considered Alice a spoiled selfish Madam, certain life was a bowl of cherries especially laid out for her, and with the average rich person's awareness of how the lower half lived – none at all. She had to admit, however, that what she'd originally regarded as a fashionable fad on Alice's part had turned into a genuine dedication to women's emancipation and until the day she died she would bear that ugly scar across the back of her left hand, her souvenir of the demonstration that had gone into suffragette history as 'Black Friday'.

When the photographic session was finished, the butler disappeared with the camera and tripod, only to reappear with a maid bearing drinks for the adults and cordial for the children. Sarah thought perhaps Alice's unexpected, uninvited presence wasn't a bad thing. Nobody would ever accuse her of being dull and her attention-grabbing personality – part conscious, part natural? – took their minds off the war. On this most heavenly of late August days, in these fairy-tale surroundings, that was not in fact too difficult a feat, apart from the glimpses of the other convalescent officers, sitting or strolling round their wing of the house, or the noise they heard just before they went inside for luncheon which sounded like distant thunder and made them all gaze at the cloudless, pearly heavens.

'What's that, Daddy?' Anne frowned.

Philip replied, 'It's the guns firing on the Somme, Anne.' He glanced from Guy to Tom. 'We heard them clearly during the preliminary bombardment in the last week of June. And on 1 July itself.' He looked back at Anne. 'We hear them from time to time now.'

Anne stared up at her father. 'They must be awfully noisy close to, Daddy.'

'They are, me luv.'

They've driven some men mad, Sarah thought. Shell-shock, that's what they call it now, finally admitting that minds can be wounded too. It was not until the rumbling ceased that either her brother's or Guy Kendle's bodies relaxed. They were so dissimilar in background and out-look that only a very special experience could have forged what was obviously a very special bond between them. Tom hadn't said much to her about the fighting, but he had observed that if you wanted to know what Gehenna was, you could pick anywhere on the Somme, though the choicest spots had been, and were, those once bosky woods: Trônes, Bernafay, Mametz, Bazentin-le-Petit, Delville, High, or Thiepval.

After luncheon the nursemaid Philip had hired for the weekend took the twins inside for their naps. Through the languorous, shimmering heat of the afternoon the rest of them sat on the lawn in the shade of immemorial elms and oaks, supplied with cool drinks by Philip's servants. Kessie fell asleep on the *chaise longue*. Tom smoked while he played word games with Anne and Con but his eyes were

41

on Kessie's recumbent body and the gentle rise and fall of her breasts. Just occasionally they caught Sarah's in the recognition that all this was one hell of a long way from the back streets of Mellordale or Moss Side.

'I expect you miss your brother?' Sarah enquired conversationally of Philip.

'Not particularly. We had nothing in common. He was hearty and sportive and liked young men.' He eased his gammy leg before saying, 'For his sake I regret his death. I had no desire to inherit the title, which my brother enjoyed as a prefix to his name. But I had no objection to inheriting Chenneys.'

Ask an idle question and sometimes you got a sharp answer. Johnny Conway had said Philip Marchal had a reputation for being a caustic so-and-so which presumably he had earned by openly saying things most folk left unsaid. Mind you, he could afford to, with his wealth and position allied to an actual talent as a playwright.

What about him and Kessie?

Normally Sarah reckoned she was slow on the uptake about people's emotions, who was lusting after or coupling with whom, perhaps because she tried not to think about that sort of thing, but after seeing the two of them together in the last few hours even she realised Philip was besotted by Kessie. Not a barbed word was flung in her direction, in her presence those cold grey eyes almost assumed a warmth, the haughty expression softened, and for her nothing was too much trouble. Who else would have hired a nursemaid to ease Kessie's weekend? Sarah returned her attention to Philip who was saying to Alice, 'Lady Maltravers? I met her the other week sailing off to her arduous war work, towed by her maid and two Pekinese.'

'Has Lord Maltravers recovered from his unfortunate accident?' Alice enquired sweetly.

'I doubt it. Which is among her ladyship's problems. But if I'd have been his dog, I'd have bitten him in the bollocks.'

Alice's bell-like laughter pealed out. It was the politeness with which he used words like 'bollocks' that was part of

Philip's verbal ammunition. Sarah was uninterested in society chit-chat so she asked Guy, who was apparently well travelled, if he had been to Russia. Regrettably no, he said, which brought that conversation to a standstill.

There had been no problem about her signing on for a year as an orderly in the Russia-bound Scottish Women's Hospital Unit. Kessie said Tom's wound would keep him on home-leave for at least three months, and personally she considered he had now done his bit and could with a clear conscience remain in England and rejoin the Government. Although she would miss Sarah, she must follow the dictates of *her* conscience. So Sarah had been up to Manchester and put her furniture into storage.

After tea the twins were taken to bed by the nursemaid, then Kessie and Tom played several games of 'Happy Families' with the older girls before Kessie said it was their bedtime. Loudly Anne protested it wasn't fair, this was a special day, and she should be allowed to stay up late.

'I keep telling you, life isn't fair,' Kessie said. 'The sooner you learn that lesson the better. You've already stayed up an hour later than usual. If you go now, Daddy'll read you a bedtime story.'

Anne's expression said she hadn't the slightest doubt her adored and adoring Daddy would read her a story whatever the hour, but reluctantly she followed obedient little Con to kiss Aunty Sarah and Uncle Pip, which was what the children called Sir Philip Marchal.

'Where's Aunty Alice and Uncle Guy?' Anne then said.

Glancing across the terrace to the herbaceous borders and the rose garden, Sarah suddenly realised she hadn't seen either of them since tea. It was a very good question.

Where were Alice and Guy?

Guy had just pushed open the door of the summer house and was holding it ajar for Alice to enter. It had been he who had casually suggested they take a stroll in the golden evening light of the perfect English summer's day, one of the loveliest lights in the world, he considered, and the one he most missed abroad. Alice had needed no cajoling to accept the invitation and to agree about the beauty of the golden light. Apart from anything else, she was glad to escape from the clamour of the four Whitworth children. There were times, she felt, when the Victorian precept that children should be seen and not heard, or neither seen nor heard, was to be recommended.

As she entered the single room of the summer house, her pink skirt brushing against the fine wool of Guy's khaki slacks, she felt the heat of his body and she turned to smile at him. Avoiding her gaze, he stretched out his arm towards the sofa which stood on the far side of the room, but he *had* closed the door and he *had* indicated the cushion-strewn sofa on which they could both sit, rather than the individual wickerwork chairs that flanked a low table. Having seated herself in the middle of the sofa, Alice watched as Guy walked towards her, bending down to place his officer's cap on the table. He had been wounded in the thigh during the murderous battle for High Wood and his movements were stiff.

Kessie had once accused her of totally ignoring other people's emotions and reactions, which had never been true. It was merely that Alice hated moaners and whiners and believed people should stand up for themselves. During the walk through the parkland she had noticed the minute Guy's step had faltered, immediately suggesting they rest because *her* feet were aching, though it had been he who had indicated the summer house half-hidden among the trees.

Guy eased himself on to the sofa. He left only a few inches between them but he was still avoiding her eyes. Instead he gazed at the rich golden light shining through the trees beyond the latticed windows, dappling the wooden floor, glinting on the coat of arms of the City of Manchester that was his regimental cap badge. Breaking into the chorus of birdsong, the only sound in the stillness of the early evening, eventually he drawled, 'What a charming place. It reminds me of my favourite spot at home. That's an arbour below the gardens which are

44

my wife's pride and joy. Do you know Lancashire, Mrs Conway?'

'I know The Dales. That's where I first met Kessie and Tom. We all campaigned for Tom when he first stood for Parliament. Us suffragettes, I mean.'

'Ah yes, of course. *My* Lancashire, the detached part of north Lancashire, is entirely different from the industrial cotton belt. You must visit us, Mrs Conway, and allow me to show you the beauty of fell and hill and lake.'

'I should like that.'

It was deliberate, Alice felt sure, the constant reiteration of her married name and the repeated mention of his wife. She didn't care if he had ten wives because something quite extraordinary had happened since her arrival at Chenneys. Neither of her husbands had proved to be the ideal mate. Franklin had turned out to be a beast and as for Johnny, well, Alice was rather bored with him, though he wasn't bad in bed. Once upon a time she had imagined Tom to be her destined mate, but in the last few hours any lingering desire for him had vanished. From the fact that they were sitting here at all, from the tenseness of Guy's body and the way he was refusing to look at her, he was obviously as aware as she that they had been born for each other.

What was he going to do about it? What was she? Her nipples had hardened against the silk of her chemise, her limbs were trembling for the weight of his, her crotch was damp, the muscles contracting fiercely, aching to close upon his shaft deep inside her. If he didn't stop talking about the beauties of his home, Ryby Hall, and north Lancashire, she was going to burst into flames. Then Alice saw the twinge of pain mar his elegant features, as he adjusted his thigh into a more comfortable position. That was quite extraordinary too, the tender concern she felt for Guy. While Alice had always been convinced that the majority of men were idiots, and it was only when she realised they were powerful idiots whose strength had to be countered that she became a suffragette, certain men as individuals she had as surely always liked. Sexual passion

45

was something she understood and relished. A feeling of tenderness towards a man was a new emotion for Alice.

She put her hand on his thigh. 'Shall I rub it better?' Then she laughed. 'That's what Poppa used to say to me when I was a little girl and I'd bruised myself or something.'

Guy caught her hand in his, raising it to his lips and kissing her fingers. His head turned towards her, and over the edge of the white flesh of her hand into which his white teeth were now biting, his eyes were burning. He had the most beautiful eyes, nut-brown in colour, sensitive, vulnerable eyes fringed with thick lashes like a girl's. His lips were on hers, their mouths were open, tongues licking and coiling, she was stretched backwards across the sofa, his weight was upon her and she could feel his heavenly hardness. His hands were supporting her neck so that their lips could continue to meet, their teeth to bite, their tongues to probe. After a while, breathing heavily, they broke apart. He tore at the buttons of his jacket, wrenching it from his shoulders, dropping it to the floor, his fingers pulled at his collar and stud, furiously unknotting his tie, while Alice threw off her pink bolero and her fingers fumbled frantically with the pearl buttons of her blouse.

Abruptly, with his vest hanging down his trousers, his fly buttons half undone, he stood up, turning his back towards her. His voice hoarse with passion he said, 'This is lunacy, Alice. We can't. We mustn't. You're a married woman. I'm a married man.'

Suffering rattlesnakes! He wasn't going to become the perfect English gentleman at this juncture. While he stood with his shoulders shaking, taking long deep breaths, Alice continued to discard her clothes. Then she too stood up and padded towards him. Slipping her arms round his waist, first she nuzzled the nape of his neck into which the fine brown hair grew so neatly, before slowly, sensuously, sliding her protruding nipples across the smooth skin of his bare back. In as light a voice as she could manage, she said, 'We all make mistakes, Guy.'

'I'm a Roman Catholic.'

'I don't mind.'

With a slight laugh he swung round. The laughter trailed away as his brown eyes surveyed her naked body.

They sat on the terrace, Tom by Kessie's side, Philip *faute de mieux* by Sarah's. Her brother appeared at last to have become aware that their host was, to say the least, enchanted by his wife. Tom was being amorous and possessive, stroking Kessie's hair, kissing her hand, whispering in her ear, making her blush and giggle, a performance to which she apparently had no objections and which announced: should you be entertaining any ideas, *Sir* Philip, she's mine.

The cloudless daytime sky was a suffusion of exquisite turquoise, flecked by wispy pink clouds, and the sun was a fiery spreading mass. Reflected in its light, the lake beyond the rose bowers was a pool of iridescent bronze, the mullioned windows of the house seemed as if they were on fire and the early Tudor stone was the chestnut colour of Kessie's hair. In the distance the gently rising meadows, the stubble cornfields and the copses that surrounded Chenneys were tinged with scarlet.

'Cooee.'

Coming up the steps was Alice, with Guy by her side. Her hat was in her hand and in the glorious light her hair was a burnished gold and she was a tall, slim goddess from the land of nectar and ambrosia.

'We had a heavenly walk. Isn't it a fabulous evening?'

Ever the good host Philip enquired if they would like a drink. Alice and Guy both said they would, the butler appeared as if by magic – was he permanently in a hovering position? Sarah wondered – and in two shakes of a lamb's tail they all had fresh drinks. Alice was in what Sarah could only describe as a 'cooee' mood, gazing at Guy with rapture, and he couldn't take his beautiful brown eyes off her. One of the buttons of his jacket was missing, Sarah noticed. They've been making love, she thought, but they can't have been, they only met this morning, things like that don't happen in our world. Only too apparently, they did. What were Alice and he thinking about? They were both married and he had a young son. Not that trifles like that would perturb Alice, who was a taker of anything she wanted. But what about Guy? His manner was carefree, his charm insouciant, but he had those sensitive eyes. Still, if he was smitten and wanted to suffer, and make Alice's husband and those close to him suffer, there was nothing she could do about it.

The twilight was gathering and Philip asked if they wished to go indoors, but they all said no, it was such a beautiful evening. Philip murmured to the butler that they'd have a late dinner, and Sarah thought of the cook keeping the food warm.

'During our stroll,' Guy drawled, 'Mrs Conway told me about the suffragettes. And about your present struggles for the vote. I gather you're the expert, Sarah.'

'My expertise is in the past tense. I am off to Russia on Thursday. I'm leaving the continuing struggle in other capable hands. Including Kessie's and Mrs Conway's.'

The asperity of her tone made Guy blink, but it wouldn't occur to him that he'd made her heart flutter, would it? *Mrs Conway* indeed! Sarah now appreciated why he'd immediately called her by her Christian name. She was his pal Piper's holy terror of a sister, to be regarded in the same pally light.

By her side Philip stretched his leg. Her asperity hadn't been lost on him now, had it. One day, she reckoned, he would write a sophisticated three act comedy about a group of disparate people drawn together by women's suffrage and men's suffering. One act would be set on the terrace of a beautiful country house, where the seemingly beautiful people – the outer layers were subtly peeled away in Philip's plays – sat looking at the rising moon glittering across the lake . . . and by heck, champagne was served!

Sarah's eyeline took in the butler, whose fingers were expertly prising the cork from the bottle. The cork shot across the terrace, landing at Sarah's feet. As she bent to pick it up, the bubbly liquid spewed into the air and the butler moved swiftly to pour it into the glasses. Weren't

48

they supposed to be lucky, champagne corks? Not that she believed in such nonsense, but it would be a memento of a heavenly, and interesting, day. When Sarah looked up everybody was on their feet, silhouetted against the velvety sky, filled champagne glasses in their hands. Kessie smiled at Philip who raised his glass.

'Pray lift your glasses, ladies and gentlemen, to drink a toast to Sarah who has volunteered to serve our distant allies. May God, or if she prefers it, good fortune, smile upon her endeavours and bring her safely back to England. May we all soon stand here with her again, in a world at peace.'

PART TWO

4

The icy rain was lashing across the River Danube, stinging Sarah's face, soaking through her grey cloak and uniform, dripping from the brim of her orderly's hat. In the make-shift shelter on the quayside, half-open to the elements, she examined the hundreds of wounded Serbian soldiers who had been ferried down by the Unit's ambulances to await evacuation by river. Her now expert eye picked out the most seriously wounded men. She pointed to the stretchers the Serbian orderlies were to lift on to the barge.

On the gangplank of the large Danube barge Jenny Macdonald was assisting the walking wounded, which in this neck of the woods included those who could crawl on all-fours. Sarah called out to her, 'How many more stretchers can you fit in?'

'About a dozen, I guess.'

It seemed to Sarah that she had known Jenny Macdonald for a lifetime. Yet it was less than four months since they had first met in the lounge of the North Western Hotel in Liverpool. She had been sitting having a cup of tea when the young woman in civilian clothes, with a mop of curly red hair and a fresh-scrubbed face liberally sprinkled with freckles, had flopped into the leather armchair next to hers. Her smile had been warm and when she'd spoken the accent was transatlantic. Sarah had presumed she was with the posse of Canadian nurses who had lately disembarked in Liverpool en route for the Western Front.

'Gosh no, I'm with you. I've joined the Scottish Women's Hospital Unit. It's just that I haven't gotten my uniform yet. And I'm not Canadian. I'm from Newfound-land. We're a different breed entirely. We're the oldest British colony in North America, you know. Shall I order some more tea? Then we can get properly acquainted.'

Over tea Jenny had handed out information at a cracking pace and Sarah had wondered whom she reminded her of, before realising it was her own young self, though maybe she hadn't been so cheerfully, unselfconsciously outgoing.

'And my grandfather emigrated from Scotland during "the Hungry Forties". I guess he settled in Newfoundland because it's like the Highlands. He started a pulp-mill and it prospered and my father runs it now. We have a nice clapboard house just outside St John's. I'm very fond of my island home but it is a bit *parochial*. You know what I mean? So I persuaded my mother into letting me visit Edinburgh. Half my relations still live in Scotland, you see. I'd only just arrived when the war broke out. Do you smoke?'

Sarah had shaken her head. With unpractised non-chalance Jenny had lit a cigarette and blown out a cloud of smoke.

'My mother cabled to say Callum and Hamish were both volunteering. They're my brothers and I have a younger sister called Fiona. I thought I'd stay over a while to greet Hamish and Callum when they arrived in England. Well, I did, and gosh am I glad I did, because we had fun together in London and we shan't ever have such fun again. Callum was attached to the Canadian Division near Ypres. April 22nd, 1915. I guess you won't remember the date, but I do. The first-ever gas attack. They had no gas-masks, nothing, and Callum was in the thick of it. I went to see him regularly when he was brought to a hospital in Oxfordshire. I almost thought it might have been better if he'd died. You know what I mean?'

With a slight frown Jenny had regarded the glowing end of her cigarette.

'Well, eventually they shipped Callum back home be-cause they couldn't do anything for him. I guess he'll cough his lungs out one day soon. He'll be twenty-one at the end of the year. Then Hamish was wounded on the Somme. He was at Beaumont Hamel on 1st July. Gosh, he said that was terrible, but the Newfoundlanders put up a terrific fight. I think Hamish will be okay but I was filled with rage. I just knew I had to do something. My aunt – I call her Aunty – in Edinburgh is a friend of Doctor Inglis and she told me they were looking for people to go to Russia with one of the Scottish Women's Hospital Units and they weren't being too difficult about ages. I'm not twenty-three, you see, and they won't take you in the other outfits until you are. Why did you join?'

Briefly, Sarah had filled in the background to her road to Russia. Jenny had looked at her in astonishment. She'd never met a pacifist face to face before, she'd said. All her family were four-square behind the war effort. Then she had sat up excitedly.

'I've just realised. You're Captain Tom Whitworth's sister, aren't you? Gosh, you must be proud of him. I'd just love to meet him.'

You and several thousand other lasses, Sarah had thought wryly, and *gosh* was she fed up with being identified as Tom's sister.

From that moment Jenny had attached herself to Sarah, treating her like an infinitely wise older sister, constantly saying, gosh, didn't she know a lot about everything and what a splendid, liberated life she'd led. How immature these lively, intelligent, middle-class girls were in so many ways. Kessie had been just the same, though she'd learned about life the hard way during her suffragette years. Sarah had reckoned Miss Macdonald might have a similar experience in the months that lay ahead.

The long sea voyage from Liverpool to Archangel Sarah had found fascinating, if at times 'spooky' to use Alice's word, particularly when the alarm had sounded and they'd had to race on deck to stand by the lifeboats. Fortunately, it had turned out to be a whale blowing its way through the water, not a German submarine, and the young sailor who had raised the alarm had looked a right Charlie. The best that could be said of the even longer journey from

Archangel to Odessa was that they had crossed Russia from the White Sea to the Black Sea. And how many folk could say they had done that?

In Odessa the Unit had been treated like royalty, bands playing, civic dignitaries in full swarm, gala performances and banquets laid on. After three days enjoying a luxurious life that had no connection with the misery and destitution they had witnessed in Archangel and other places along the route, Doctor Inglis had addressed their assembled ranks.

In her brisk voice she had said, 'You will all be aware that the Roumanians have entered the war on our side. Fierce fighting is now taking place in the Dobrudja region of their country. Our services are urgently required to nurse the Serbian wounded who are fighting with their Russian and Roumanian allies. You will start packing immediately. We leave after luncheon. At all times remember that you are British women and you have a duty to uphold the honour of our country. And whatever happens – stick to your equipment!'

After an agonisingly slow train journey southward from Odessa they had arrived in Megidia to find the town shell-shattered and deserted. For several days, with Doctor Inglis unable to obtain any clear orders as to where they should proceed next, they had watched the hideously beautiful sight of the Black Sea port of Constanza burning, a hazy red glow during the day, a brilliant orange against the sky at night. Finally the orders had arrived for them to move on which, Sarah quickly appreciated, was a euphemism for retreat. The last nine weeks had been a nightmare of unpacking the equipment, setting up advanced dressing stations, cleaning out filthy temporary hospitals, nursing the wounded, dismantling the equipment and retreating through the increasing chaos of the Dobrudja. Westwards the ambulances and the supply wagons, Doctor Inglis, her nurses and orderlies, including Jenny and Sarah, had trundled through the cold, the mud and the crowds of refugees towards the River Danube, along the river back towards Russia as one shattered

Danube town after another fell before the advancing Germans, Austrians and Bulgars.

Doctor Inglis' constant exhortation to Stick to the Equipment had become the Unit joke, but she had quickly recognised Sarah's organisational ability and placed her in general charge of the stores, so Sarah had the additional burden of ensuring that everything from blankets to tins of golden syrup, to theatre equipment and Ludgate boilers, were safely en route to their next destination. To begin with, class consciousness had reared its ugly, tiresome head and several of her middle-class fellow-orderlies and most of the working class nursing sisters had objected to Sarah giving them orders. By briskly pretending she had not heard the objections and by being efficient, Sarah had won the Unit's respect. To date, she had lost only twelve tins of golden syrup – which she felt sure the Roumanians had appropriated. As far as Sarah could see at the moment, there was no end in sight. The Danube town of Braila, their present base, was already under shellfire with much of the opposite bank of the river in enemy hands. She had no doubt they would soon be 'moving on' again.

From the top of the gangplank Sarah surveyed the barge, now packed as tightly as a tin of sardines with wounded Serbians, and Russians and Roumanians. She therefore instructed the captain to cast anchor, or whatever they did with barges, and to sail down river. While they had been finishing the loading, the Unit's ambulances had brought down further casualties. From lack of sufficient shelter many of them were lying in the pouring rain so, pausing only to stretch her aching shoulders, Sarah said to Jenny, 'Right. We'd better start loading the next barge.'

Suddenly she saw them standing on the quayside, staring at the confusion of casualties, the two men from the British armoured cars. What a surprise that had been, encountering the armoured car squadrons of the Royal Naval Air Service in some godforsaken hole! Nobody had told them there were British troops of any kind operating in southern Russia or Roumania, let alone with powerful Rolls-Royce and Lanchester armoured cars.

'Don't just stand there,' Sarah shouted at the RNAS men. 'Lift some of those stretchers and get them on to that barge over there.'

What a relief it was to be able to bawl in English!

As she walked down the gangplank, the smaller of the two men cheekily saluted her, 'Aye, aye ma'am.'

With Sarah, Jenny and the few Serbian orderlies he and his mate worked tirelessly in the incessant rain in the back-breaking task of bending down, lifting the stretchers, carrying them on to the barge and packing them in as tightly as possible, while the walking wounded milled around getting in their way. All the while the smaller of the two men chatted to the wounded, saying things like, 'Come on sunshine, let's get you on HMS *Royal Oak*', or as his foot slipped on the wet cobbles and the stretcher lurched, 'Oops-a-daisy, sorry about that, mate.'

None of the wounded understood what he was saying, indeed many were too far gone to care, but the cheerful tones brought smiles to a few lips and the determined Cockney chirpiness – he had quite a strong Cockney accent – lightened the arduous, depressing task. Then Sarah heard the shriek of an approaching shell and instinctively she ducked her head.

'Helps if you close your eyes, too. Dunno why, but it does.'

As she lifted up her head, her eyes open, he winked at her. He was a cheeky bugger! Noting that the shells were for the moment falling short, landing in the Danube, in her briskest voice Sarah suggested he help the girls who were unloading the wounded from the back of the latest ambulance to have arrived.

Darkness had fallen before they had cleared the quayside of casualties and seen the barge on its way down river. Sarah suddenly realised that he and his mate had disappeared. She asked Jenny where they were. Jenny said they had been ordered back to the armoured cars and had presumably driven off to the fighting zone, wherever that might now be. Sarah did not even know his name. She thought he might have said goodbye.

Desperately tired, she and Jenny struggled through the panic-stricken streets of Braila to the hospital to find Doctor Inglis in the entrance hall addressing her remaining staff, the Unit having by now split into three groups to try to cope with the flood of wounded from this disastrous campaign. Doctor Inglis had been in the operating theatre all day. She looked as exhausted as Sarah felt, her face like a crumpled monkey's, her red hair wispier than ever. As she nodded for Jenny and Sarah to fall in, it did not in the least surprise Sarah that she should be giving her 'troops' a stern lecture.

'I have already spoken to the Transport Section, who are among the worst offenders in this respect, and I am now telling you. I will not tolerate swearing. Not only is bad language unbecoming in a woman, unbefitting our sex but, I repeat, we are here in this country as the representatives of Britain. Is that clearly understood?'

'Yes, ma'am,' they chorused.

Listening to the scream of a shell overhead – the enemy gunners had found their range – Sarah did not know whether to laugh or to cry. Having got her reprimand off her chest, Doctor Inglis proceeded to give them the not unsurprising news that the situation in Braila was desperate and they were therefore to fall back on Galatz which was some twenty miles further along the Danube, actually on the border of Roumania and Russia. The Transport Section which had so offended her sensibilities and patriotic pride had, she told them, already left by road. She herself would travel with a few of the gels in her own car as usual (her private vehicle, an enormous Studebaker, had come with her from Scotland) and the rest of them would travel by train.

'Whitworth.'

'Ma'am.'

'Two of the cars are *hors de combat*. They're already in a truck attached to the train for Galatz. You will be in charge of the truck and you will see the cars reach Galatz safely.'

'Yes, ma'am,' Sarah said.

Jamming on her trilby hat, Doctor Inglis strode off to prepare for her drive to Galatz.

5

By the time they reached the railway station in Braila the rain had turned to sleet. Not that it made much difference, Sarah thought, as she pulled her sodden cape around her. Telling the other lasses to stick to each other as much as to the equipment, she pushed her way through the frightened mob of civilians – a sight she'd become only too familiar with – towards a Russian officer. It was the Russians who were supposed to be in charge of this campaign, God help them all, for Sarah's opinion of the efficiency and competence of the Russian army hierarchy was now infinitely lower than Tom's of the British.

Not without difficulty, because the officer spoke no English and her Russian remained limited, she managed to make herself understood. He pointed to a train standing on the far platform which he assured her was the one bound for Galatz and said he personally would escort her on board. Sarah was thanking him, trying to explain that she had other nurses with her, when she heard Jenny's voice shrieking above the general tumult.

'That train's going out. Those are our cars on board. Gosh Sarah, they're leaving without us.'

Steaming from the nearby platform was a train, with their loaded truck. Shouting to Jenny, 'Come on, come on', Sarah started to run, frantically shoving people out of her way. She had to get on that train, she was in charge of that truck, and Doctor Inglis would have her guts for garters if she lost the cars. On the edge of the platform was a line of Russian soldiers, their guns cocked to stop people storming the departing train. Behind her she could hear Jenny panting breathlessly.

'What do we do now, Sarah? It's going without us. It's going. Oh . . .'

In front of them was a young soldier, his fur hat framing a broad, peasant face. He was very nervous, his fingers were twitching on the trigger, and he could fire any minute, Sarah knew. There was only one hope. Above Jenny's long drawn-out wail of anguish, she stabbed her finger repeatedly towards the train and her uniform, while she yelled, '*Shotlandskaya bol'nitsa. Shotlandskaya zhenskaya bol'nitsa.*'

Slowly the light dawned in his eyes and he nodded. '*Shotlandskaya.*'

Thank the Lord, the fame of the Scottish Women's Unit, driving their ambulances, nursing the wounded, always turning up where they were most wanted *with* their equipment, had reached him. The last carriages of the train were clinking slowly past but fortunately one of them was a goods wagon, its sliding door open. While hands stretched down to help pull Sarah and Jenny into the wagon, the young soldier pushed from behind. Packed with Russian troops the wagon stank, but the men were stolidly polite and made a space for a breathless Sarah and Jenny to sit down on the straw.

'I think I shall die of asphyxia,' Jenny said.

'Not until we get our hands on that truck.'

In any group there was always a spokesman and in the light of the single oil lamp swaying with the motion of the train, Sarah's eyes sought the least bemused and subservient among this bovine lot. Just because they were treated like cattle didn't mean they had to behave as if they were, she thought, irritatedly. Then she found the right face. He turned out to be a bright lad and they held a halting conversation. After she'd gained as much information as possible, she said to Jenny, 'You will be unsurprised to learn they have no idea where they're going. But they doubt it's Galatz because that's where they've just come from. I knew it! Those gilded Russian officers are after

61

our cars so they can do a bunk all the way back to nice civilised Odessa.'

Jenny laughed at Sarah's ferocity. 'Could have been the usual muddle. They won't get far in our two. They're clapped out. What do we do? Get off at the first place we stop at and grab the truck back?'

'Yes.'

It was not an easy task to accomplish but when they reached a station, Sarah managed it. By throwing in the name of every Grand Duke and Russial general she could think of, by miming and dredging up every Russian phrase she knew, she managed to convince another officer and the station master that if they did not unhitch the truck and reattach it to a train bound for Galatz immediately, execution by the tsar, followed by the eternal flames of hell, would be their fate.

Then two totally unexpected things happened. First of all a British officer and a petty officer from one of the armoured car squadrons marched down the platform, kitted out with their knee-boots and sheepskin overcoats. All the Women's Unit had strong indiarubber boots, brought with them from England, thank heaven, but Sarah looked enviously at the sheepskins. The Russians had promised them warm coats, but what they'd been presented with had been a pile of untreated skins which presumably they were expected to treat and sew together themselves. Maybe one day they would, because she hadn't lost them and they were among the stores en route for Galatz. While the British officer was explaining that his lorry had broken down and needed to go by rail, who should come bounding along the platform but Dorothy Devonald.

During the voyage from Liverpool to Archangel she had ignored Sarah, spending her time with the members of the Transport Section who considered themselves infinitely superior to the nurses or orderlies, talking in lordly tones about double-declutching and the merits of the Ford cars. On the journey from Archangel to Odessa she had addressed only a few words to Sarah but here she came bounding along the platform, almost throwing her arms round Sarah's neck and calling her by her christian name.

'Sarah! Am I glad to see you! Where is this? How far are we from Galatz? We received an urgent message to pick up some Serbian wounded and we've been driving through the mud ever since. I thought we'd better find out where we are. And if there's a train leaving for Galatz, Vera's leaving with it. She's gone down with 'flu or something.'

The discussion as to who should travel in what became almost acrimonious. The RNAS officer said he and his petty officer would drive Dorothy's ambulance and the ladies could go by train with their precious truck and his broken down lorry. Adamantly Dorothy said she was *not* abandoning her ambulance, and the idea of not letting Doctor Inglis down and not losing any of the equipment was paramount in all their minds. By comparison, danger appeared a trivial item. Obviously Vera Johnson was ill, shivering violently with a fever, so she must travel on the train.

Jenny settled the argument by saying, 'The train's going out any minute now. It's got a head of steam. I propose that you and I go with Dorothy, Sarah, and take it in turns to navigate and nurse. And the lieutenant will look after our truck, won't you?' She held out her hand to him, 'Bye. See you in Galatz which is beginning to sound to me like the golden city of Samarkand, or Camelot, or something.'

Everybody laughed. Vera was helped into a carriage and the armoured car men climbed into the truck. As the train steamed out the lieutenant shouted, 'Take care. They're retreating through the Dobrudja like bats out of hell.'

As if we didn't know, Sarah thought.

'Don't worry,' Dorothy said, 'I've a pistol in the cab and I'm a first-class shot. It was my brother's personal property and it came home with his effects from Givenchy. I snaffled it. I thought it might come in handy.'

Apart from the fact that she had no business to be

carrying a pistol, did Dorothy imagine that information was likely to cheer Sarah up?

Progress from the start was inchingly slow. 'Tracks' had been fitted to the four rear wheels of the ambulance, which enabled Dorothy to drive in bad conditions but reduced speed. The main problem however was the clogged roads. People were not so much fleeing through the Dobrudja like bats out of hell as plodding along with the dogged hopelessness of folk tramping from somewhere that had been home to anywhere they could find refuge. There were streams of them: men, women, children, ancients with long white beards, grandmothers swathed in black; some with push-carts, others with horse-drawn carts and bullock carts piled high with pots and pans, crying babies, squealing pigs and squawking hens. Trailing behind them were dogs and cows and goats. Mixed up with the civilian refugees were the ragged columns of dishevelled Roumanian soldiers.

'Huh,' Dorothy snorted, as they passed another group of retreating soldiers. 'Doctor Inglis was right. What they need is some good Scotch porridge in their bellies.'

She leaned out of the cab to pump several derisive blasts on the horn.

As darkness started to fall on the third evening, Sarah decided that tough as her upbringing and her suffragette years had been, wretched as the journey from Archangel had appeared, chaotic as their earlier retreats had undoubtedly been, she had only just begun to realise how bitterly cold and desperately weary you could be, yet remain *compos mentis*. The flaps of the hood of the cab were down as far as they would reach but the sleet was turning to snow which was swirling through the gaps and over the top of the windscreen. She did not know how Dorothy was managing to keep going in the nightmare conditions, her feet endlessly on and off the clutch and brake pedals, her left hand constantly pushing the gear lever in and out of neutral, up and down, her right hand wiping her spectacles, both hands manoeuvring the heavy steering wheel.

'Are we still travelling north?'

They had now lost the stream of refugees and had not the faintest idea where they were. The only thing they knew was that Galatz was twenty miles to the north of Braila. Among the equipment in the ambulance was a compass which, in the dim light of their side-lamps, Sarah again leaned out to consult.

'Yes.' After a pause she said, 'How much petrol do we have?'

'Enough to get to the North Pole. What the blazes is that?'

Through the whirling snow, in the swathe of the head-lights, Sarah saw a horse-drawn cart plodding along with humped figures in its back. Something fell from one of the figures, directly in their path, but the cart plodded on and the figures made no move. The fallen bundle lay in front of them. Swearing furiously, Dorothy jammed her foot on the brake, sending the ambulance into a terrifying skid. Sarah shut her eyes, bracing her body for the crash, as Dorothy shouted repeatedly, 'Damn and blast this country, damn and blast it, damn and blast it.' After a seemingly interminable slide Sarah realised they had stopped. Slowly she opened her eyes to find that the ambulance had come to a halt on the edge of a steeply dropping embankment. Turning her head she looked at Dorothy who was slumped over the wheel, her shoulders heaving, now swearing softly to herself.

'Are you all right?'

'Yes.'

'Well done.'

'Light me a cigarette, will you?'

Inexpertly, with difficulty, Sarah lit one and handed it to Dorothy. Then above the thump of her heart and the howl of the wind, she heard a different howl.

'Listen.'

But Dorothy was puffing furiously on her cigarette. Sarah listened hard and she was sure she could hear the sound. She climbed from the cab and battled her way through the driving snow towards the bundle, directed by the noise, and in the darkness she almost stepped on it. Bending down she picked it up. It was a baby, she could feel it, she could hear it, bawling its head off. Cradling it to her body, she struggled towards the ambulance where Jenny had emerged from the back and was standing anxiously by the cab.

'What is it? What happened?' She peered at Sarah. 'Gosh, I don't believe it.'

They crowded inside the cab where Dorothy stared at Sarah and the screaming baby in absolute astonishment. Clutched against Sarah's bosom, soothed by her and Jenny, slowly it stopped crying and looked up at Sarah with watery grey eyes, its mouth puckering into a sucking moue.

'No, me little luv, I can't feed you,' Sarah smiled faintly. 'But you're all right, aren't you? You have malleable little bones and you fell into the snow, didn't you? And babies are tough little things and you're all right. You'll live to tell the tale.'

'I've seen some things in this goddammed country,' said Dorothy, 'but how could they? How could they drive on, the unutterably callous swine?'

Perhaps it was because they were feeling shattered by their escape from a serious accident, but Jenny suddenly started to lecture them about swearing, giving an extremely good imitation of Doctor Inglis in her ladylike patriotic British mood. They laughed uproariously which made the baby smile and them laugh even more. When their somewhat hysterical merriment had subsided, Sarah cranked the stalled engine and, directed by Jenny, slowly Dorothy reversed the ambulance. Then with Jenny once more in the back with the wounded, Sarah cradling the baby in her arms, off they drove again.

When they caught up with the cart which was still plodding through the worsening conditions, they saw why nobody had stopped. The horse was on its last legs but the humped figures in the back were already dead. Kept alive by the dying warmth of its mother's body, the baby must finally have slipped from her grasp.

Further along the otherwise deserted road they came upon a farmhouse which proved to be deserted, too. They found a pile of wood in a shed, and with the help of the less seriously wounded Serbians, as on the previous nights, they lifted the stretcher cases from the ambulance and managed to get a blazing fire going. Jenny produced a bottle, Dorothy cut the finger from a rubber glove for a teat, while Sarah made a feed from condensed milk and hot water. After the baby had gulped the food down and Sarah had winded it, she changed it and found it was the sex she had expected – female.

'Of course,' said Dorothy.

'What shall we call her? said Jenny. 'You found her, Sarah, you christen her.'

Sarah thought and said, 'Tania. It's a pretty name and it sounds Eastern European.'

Solemnly Jenny said, 'Tania, in the name of the Father, the Son, and the Holy Ghost.'

After they had settled the wounded for the night they huddled round the fire. Sarah rocked baby Tania in her arms and soon she was asleep. Then Dorothy said, 'I could do with a couple of hours' kip but I think we should keep moving. It's stopped snowing at the moment but I'm sure it's going to start again soon. If we get stuck here in the middle of nowhere in a blizzard . . .'

There was no need for her to complete the sentence. Glancing at the men lying on the floor, Jenny said, 'Unless we get them to Galatz and Doctor Inglis soon, I doubt some of them will survive. They're wonderful men the Serbians, so heroic and stoic. They have such faith and trust in the Scottish Women's Hospital Unit and us in particular. I find it touching.'

'We'd better justify their touching faith,' Dorothy said in her crystal-clear tones. 'We go on then?'

Sarah and Jenny nodded their agreement.

When they were ready to leave, in an ominously heavy

dawn light they had a row about who should look after Tania for the rest of the journey. Jenny took it for granted that the baby would travel in the rear of the ambulance where it was warmer, and also because the Serbians had adopted Tania as a mascot and would help to keep her amused. The quarrel made Sarah realise how utterly exhausted they all were, tense with the fear that the ambulance might break down or, for any number of reasons, they might never reach Galatz. And how could she expect Jenny to know that holding the baby in her arms, feeding her, changing her, had given her an intense pleasure and satisfaction? Because the one thing Sarah wanted in the world was a babe of her own, and the one action she now regretted above all others was not keeping the child that the dead Edward Dawson had given her.

With Dorothy, but without Tania, Sarah climbed into the front cab to resume her navigator's job. They set off once more through the silent already snow-covered world; silent, that was, apart from the thud of the guns in the distance. And Dorothy had been right about the weather. Within a couple of hours it started to snow again, softly at first, but with increasing windswept intensity, and the driving conditions were appalling. Then the ambulance began to weave from side to side and Sarah realised that Dorothy had fallen asleep. Shouting loudly at her, she grabbed the steering wheel. With a jerk of her head, Dorothy woke up, blinked at Sarah and the road before taking the wheel back in her own hands.

'You can't go on much longer, Didi.'

It was the first time Sarah had ever actually called her by her pet name. After listening to the story of the retreat through Serbia she remembered saying to Kessie that should she, heaven forbid, find herself in a similar desperate situation, she probably would not mind having Miss Devonald by her side. She could now confirm that she did not.

'I'll go on as long as I can. We must reach Galatz soon. Keep me awake, Sarah.'

Sarah kept her awake by loudly reciting poetry, drawing

on the stock they had been forced to learn by rote at school in Mellordale and on the poems with which she'd later tried to interest her classes in Manchester. She had always memorised easily and she started off with chunks of *The Rime of the Ancient Mariner*, followed by the *Ode to Autumn* and the *Ode to the West Wind*.

After Sarah had recited *Porphyria's Lover*, which was one of her favourite poems, her memory started to play tricks and she found herself shouting the first lines of every poem she could remember.

'I wandered lonely as a cloud, That floats on high o'er vales and hills,

'Childe Roland to the dark tower came,

'The barque that held the prince went down, The rolling waves swept on,

'And what was England's glory then, To him who mourned a son?

'Tiger, tiger, burning bright, In the forests of the night,

'Abou Ben Adhem (may his tribe increase!), Awoke one night from a deep dream of peace.'

Her mind was drifting into a dazed numbness, her eyes blinking into the swathe of the headlights and the long tunnel of greyness beyond. That was what the world consisted of, endless greyness and a small patch of white. You had to keep the white patch clearly in your sights until it turned into a glorious dawn. Desperately, she carried on reciting.

'Haste thee nymph and bring with thee, Jest and youthful jollity,

'She stood breast high amidst the corn,

'The curfew tolls the knell of parting day . . .'

Sarah's voice trailed away, her lashes began to flutter, her eyelids were dead weights. She didn't care about anything any more, she just wanted to go to sleep . . . no, she didn't . . . she had to stay awake for some reason she couldn't recall . . .

'Sarah, Sarah, look.'

The excited croaking sound brought her back to consciousness. Ahead of them, the lights of a town were winking. It had to be Galatz. Her voice cracked with fatigue and emotion, Dorothy started to sing.

'As I went down to Strawberry Fair, Ri-fol, Ri-fol, tol-de-riddle-ido . . . we made it, Sarah, we made it!'

About a quarter of a mile further along the road, spectral in the snow, Sarah saw a monstrous shape coming towards them, with a hump on its back and two gleaming yellow-white eyes.

'What the heck's that?' The fear that Galatz had already fallen and a dreadful German, Austrian, or Bulgarian contraption was about to capture them trembled in her voice.

Reassuringly Dorothy rasped, 'Don't worry, it's one of ours. It's one of the Rolls-Royce armoured cars.' With unusual irony she added, 'The Royal Navy has arrived.'

Pressing her foot on the brake pedal, hauling on the handbrake, she brought the ambulance to a slithering halt not far from the armoured car. Both of them sat there, blinking owlishly, watching four men climb from the turret and plod towards them through the drifting snow. The RNAS officer approached Dorothy and saluted them both, which was a compliment.

'We're very glad to have found you, ladies. We'll escort you into Galatz. All well?'

Dorothy nodded. Croakily, she said they had a nurse and thirteen Serbian wounded packed in the back. Oh, and a baby. In the wavering, ghostly light of the two vehicles' headlamps, Sarah saw the officer's eyebrows go up and she thought he muttered, 'Jesus'. Then, as Jenny's head appeared by the officer's side and he saluted her, the passenger door opened, a shadowy face peered in and the cheerful Cockney voice said, 'Come on, Miss, put this round you.'

He was taking off his sheepskin coat and wrapping it gently round Sarah's shoulders. She didn't know why, because it was no more perishingly cold than it had been for hours, for days, but she was shivering violently.

'It really is nice to see you again, Miss. We were almost giving you up for goners. Our lieutenant was dead worried when he arrived in Galatz and you still didn't turn up. The commander tore him off a strip for leaving you. By the by, your truck's quite safe, and an orderly friend of yours, a young lady named Miss Agnes Turnbull, has your cases. She picked them up on Braila station. I think we ought to get acquainted, don't you, if we're going to keep on meeting like this. Petty Officer Sewell at your service. Harry to me mates. May I know your name, Miss?'

'Whitworth.' Hoarsely Sarah managed to say through chattering teeth, 'Sarah to my friends.'

'Sarah Whitworth! I knew I knew the face! Was your driver a suffragette, too?'

'Y-es,' her teeth chattered.

'That explains things, don't it?'

Did it? Sarah went on shivering.

6

Galatz was not the golden city of Samarkand, nor Camelot. On the contrary the situation was about as cheering as in the other Danube towns they had visited, with the civilian population streaming out towards Reni, the next town down the river. After Sarah had enjoyed a good sleep in a warm bed and eaten a hot meal in the hospital dining room she was summoned to Doctor Inglis' office. Briskly informing her that she, Dorothy and Jenny had done a good job in getting the ambulance through, Doctor Inglis carried on, 'Want to put you in the picture, and it's not a bright one. The Russian Red Cross are pulling out of Galatz. *They say* all further casualties can go straight through to Odessa on trains which *they say* will be forthcoming. Personally, Sarah, I have my doubts.' The use of her Christian name gave Sarah a fair idea of what was to come. 'Now, there are Serbians fighting outside this town and after what happened before, I swore on the Bible that I would rather be captured again than forsake my wounded Serbians.'

Doctor Inglis had been taken prisoner during the 1915 campaign in Serbia itself. Earlier in their retreat they had left badly wounded Serbians behind as they had 'moved on', not appreciating how bloody Balkan feuds remained. The advancing Bulgars, they had subsequently learned, had massacred them all.

'A few of us have decided to stay. Be glad if you'd stay with us. I must emphasise that if you do you face the possibility of capture. The Russians have refused to answer for our safety. But Commander Gregory from the armoured cars has assured me he will see us out, if the worst comes to the worst. The decision is yours, Sarah. Your response has to be voluntary.'

You're a clever old monkey, Sarah thought, as she volunteered to stay in Galatz, either until there were no more wounded Serbians to nurse or to the bitter end. In the afternoon she saw Dorothy and Jenny off on the train to Reni. Dorothy was going because she'd caught a filthy cold on the journey to Galatz, Jenny because somewhere along the route she'd cut her hand and it had become infected. They were taking baby Tania with them. Sarah felt quite tearful as she kissed her goodbye and the child held out her skinny arms to be lifted into Sarah's. She was sniffing hard to stop herself crying when suddenly, to Sarah's astonishment, Dorothy kissed her.

'It was good to have you by my side on the last lap. I don't think I'd have made it without you. Incidentally, I think that petty officer's sweet on you. He has that look in his eyes.'

'Don't be daft,' Sarah replied.

On her way back to the hospital an RNAS lorry stopped in front of her and Harry Sewell leaned out. 'Can I give you a ride anywhere?'

According to the strict rules and regulations of the Scottish Women's Hospital Unit they were forbidden to consort with members of the opposite sex, other than in an official capacity. But then officially, Sarah didn't suppose Harry Sewell was authorised to give rides to females, even if they were his compatriots in uniform and they had worked together in nightmare conditions. Gratefully she nodded her head. He opened the passenger door and she climbed into the cab.

As they drove towards the hospital he said, 'We've just been told we're leaving Galatz. If the Russians have anything to do with it, I expect we'll end up in Timbuctu.' Then in a solicitous tone he asked, 'How are you feeling now? Are you fully recovered from your ordeal?'

'I'm fine, thanks. It wasn't so much of an ordeal. Not for these parts, any road.'

She saw Harry smile at her bravado, but he made no comment. When they reached the hospital he jumped from the cab to help her down. Rather awkwardly he held out his hand. 'Well, look after yourself. Hope to see you again very soon. And happy Christmas!'

Sarah had completely forgotten. It was Christmas Eve. As she shook his hand she thought maybe the sudden awkwardness indicated that he was a bit stuck on her but she had neither the time, nor the energy, to bother about that sort of thing at the moment.

Apart from an air-raid which caused a few casualties, it was quiet in Galatz over Christmas, and on Christmas morn itself Doctor Inglis held a simple service in the hospital which Sarah attended. She found it comforting, though she was also finding it more difficult than ever to believe that God existed especially when the guns started with a thunderous clamour, the sky was once more filled with the green showers of rocket flares and the tidal wave of casualties surged in.

The next five days were the nightmare to end all nightmares.

Sarah could only be grateful her body was so tired that her mind stopped thinking, other than enabling her to perform the immediate tasks she was presented with. During those five days, over a thousand wounded men a day struggled into the hospital, either on their own, carried by their comrades, or ferried by the Unit's few remaining ambulances. To begin with, there were just the twelve British women who comprised the rearguard, including Sarah, to deal with those thousands of casualties. Doctor Inglis was the only surgeon left in the whole of Galatz and she disappeared into the operating theatre, instructing Sarah to take charge of the wards.

It was rather like telling her to take charge of a raging bush fire, Sarah felt, but they found bales of straw in a deserted stable which they spread everywhere – in the corridors, in the dining room, between the beds in the wards, anywhere to give the exhausted, wounded Russians, Roumanians and Serbians something to lie upon.

At some point during the second day Sarah was standing by the window, having a few seconds' breather before she sorted the latest influx of casualties into some order of priority. One of the lads lying in the corridor was crying for his 'Mamocka' – that sounded the same in any language – when Sarah heard the rumble. Looking out of the window, she saw several of the British armoured cars and lorries draw up in the hospital's forecourt and the RNAS men start to lift more wounded from the backs of the lorries.

'Another batch coming in. Fetch some more straw,' she called out.

When she went down to the entrance hall to meet the latest batch, she noticed Harry Sewell. She was pleased to see his cheerful face, though she hadn't time to let him know. Briefly, he told her they'd been ordered back to defend Galatz and, horrified by the sight of the Russian wounded lying by the sides of the roads in the freezing conditions, they'd scooped up as many as they could. The most important thing as far as Sarah and her friends were concerned was that the RNAS men had a naval surgeon and several orderlies with them. The orderlies set to work immediately and the surgeon went straight into the operating theatre. Sarah was later given a message that she was to drop whatever she was doing and go down to the quayside where she was to organise a mass evacuation of the wounded by river. The promised trains to transport them to Odessa had not arrived and did not look like doing so.

Among the depressing huddle of wooden shacks on the quayside Sarah took stock of the situation, then briefly returned to the hospital where she issued her orders. Their interpreter Louie was to accompany her to the quayside, their ambulances and the RNAS lorries were to be loaded with wounded and driven down, and the walking wounded were to start walking. Back at the waterfront Louie transmitted Sarah's orders to the remaining barge owners, namely that they were to sail down river to Reni with the wounded, departing as soon as they had their full complement.

'They've not the least objection to leaving Galatz,' Louie said, 'but they say they won't go until they know how much they're to be paid for their services and who'll pay them.'

'Tell them the Russian army,' Sarah said, thinking, they'll be lucky. 'And you can also tell them from me, if they don't do as they're told, they'll be shot. By those British troops over there.'

Sarah waved her hand towards Harry Sewell who had just arrived with a convoy of the RNAS lorries. At the back of her tired brain, she thought: good old pacifist Whitworth!

They worked all day and by the light of the flickering lamps rigged up by the RNAS men, they worked all night, to the steady growl of the ambulances and lorries driving backwards and forwards to the hospital. As Harry Sewell helped her to lift a stretcher on to a barge, Sarah said, 'It's darned cold, but at least it's not raining.'

Acknowledging their previous efforts in Braila, Harry grinned at her. At one point in the small hours, when Sarah's energy was at its lowest ebb, she revived herself by having a sharp up-and-downer with some Russian officers who were standing around doing nothing in particular, and kicking two Roumanians who had fallen asleep.

'You're a right little Napoleon, aren't you?' Harry said.

'You can't expect *them* to work all day and all night. They're not members of the Scottish Women's Hospital Unit!'

By eight o'clock in the morning they had despatched thousands of casualties down the Danube. When Harry was driving her back to the hospital, he said, 'I take my hat off to you, Napoleon, to all of you.'

'Thank you.'

At the hospital Sarah saw Doctor Inglis coming out of the operating theatre. Her grey-blue eyes were glazed with fatigue, her hair was stuck to her head like corkscrews, and she walked past without noticing Sarah.

'Has she had a break at all?' she asked one of the old dug-outs of a nursing sister.

'Only briefly. Been operating fifty-eight hours nonstop. Cook kept her going, kept us all going, with supplies of hot soup.'

There was considerable pride in the old dug-out's voice and Sarah thought: you've earned it, you've turned up trumps and risen to this grisly occasion. By her side Harry said, 'And a special hat off to your lady doctor. By the by, when did you last have any sleep, Napoleon?'

'Keep still. Stop making such a fuss.' Sarah finished her examination. 'You're a big baby. All you have is a broken nose.'

'Oh thank you, Miss Whitworth,' Harry Sewell said. 'I liked my nose the way it was.'

After she had cleaned the abrasions, she stuck a piece of lint and a plaster over his nose. 'That's the best I can do. Try not to hit it again and . . .'

'I didn't hit it. I fell off me motor bike into a great big shell hole.'

'Try not to fall into any more shell holes and you should be all right. Do you want a cup of char? I was thinking of making some.'

'I wouldn't say no.'

They went into the adjoining cubicle which contained one of the Unit's primus stoves, a kettle and the diminishing hoard of tea and tins of condensed milk. To Sarah's surprise Harry Sewell propelled her towards the battered chair and sat her down, and while he brewed up he informed her his Ma had trained him to make the best cup of rosie lee in the whole of Bethnal (which he pronounced Beffn'l) Green. After he had handed her a mug of tea he perched on the end of the work-bench.

'Here's to 1917,' Harry held up his mug, 'and here's hoping it'll be brighter than 1916.'

'Yes,' said Sarah.

While she had been sleeping the sleep of the dead, Harry had gone out on a reconnaissance on his motor bike and fallen into the shell hole. Now here she was sitting in the cubicle with him and not feeling guilty because most of the wounded had been evacuated and the floodtide of casualties had become a trickle, if for the ominous reason that the resistance was, they gathered, collapsing.

Harry was making her laugh with tales of his family's last prewar working holiday hop-picking in Kent, but half of Sarah's brain was listening for the monstrous, thudding noise of the guns that had been part of her daily life for nearly four months.

'In a strange way, you do miss the sound of 'em once they stop, don't you?'

He was surprisingly perceptive and underneath that chirpy, jocular exterior, Sarah reckoned there was quite a serious, sensitive soul. She recalled his awkwardness as he'd wished her a happy Christmas and what Dorothy had said. Was he sweet on her? Had he 'that look' in his eyes? At the moment she couldn't see them because they were squinting down his bandaged nose. When they were visible they were a cheerful grey.

Abruptly she asked, 'How old are you?'

He looked surprised at the question but answered promptly, 'Twenty-seven.'

'I shall be thirty-four this year.'

'Which means you're thirty-three now. You don't look it, if I may say so.'

No, well, maybe she didn't, it came from her being so

77

small. She had inherited Mam's smallness of stature and Dad's lack of charm, while Tom had been blessed with Dad's height and Mam's charm. Sarah thought they'd better get the age difference straight, just in case Harry Sewell had taken a fancy to her. Briskly she went on, 'How do you come to be in the armoured car squadrons? And what on earth are they doing in the Royal Naval Air Service?'

'She's inquisitive, too, is Napoleon.'

'If you call me Napoleon again, I shall hit your nose.'

With a grin, followed by a grimace as the widening of his mouth hurt his nose, Harry explained. He was a motor mechanic by trade and when the war broke out he'd been working at a toffs' garage in Knightsbridge. Among his customers was Mr Locker-Lampson MP, who was also in the Royal Naval Reserve, and he'd had this bright idea of forming the armoured car squadrons as a sort of mobile task force. The only problem was the navy didn't want them, so they'd been shunted into the new Royal Naval Air Service, which brought them to the second problem. Armoured cars were no more useful in the air than on the ocean waves. In Harry's opinion they'd been sent to Russia because nobody could think what else to do with them.

The armoured cars had sailed from Liverpool at the end of 1915, in good time to get stuck in the ice in the White Sea. Months late they'd finally steamed into Archangel, then they'd gone right down to the Caucasian mountains, via Odessa. They'd seen Mount Ararat – no Noah's Ark on top – and were on their way to Baghdad when suddenly they were ordered to the Dobrudja, via Odessa.

'I see,' said Sarah.

Harry was grinning at her and grimacing again, when from outside in the corridor Doctor Inglis' voice boomed. 'Whitworth.'

Sarah adjusted her cap and bade Harry farewell.

The next morning she was in the kitchen, eating a bowl of porridge before she went on duty, when Harry put his head round the door. 'Good morning.'

'Good morning. How's your nose? There's some porridge in the steamer.'

'Painful. Thanks, I've had me breakfast. All right if I come in for half a mo'?'

'Yes. One thing about being the last of the Mohicans is that rules and regulations go by the board. What was that racket in the wee small hours?'

'That was us blowing the last pontoon bridge across the Danube. Have you heard the other news?'

'We've won the war? Sarah sprinkled more sugar on her porridge. 'Go on. Surprise me.'

'A couple of hours ago the Russians pulled out on the last train to Reni, every mobile man jack of 'em. The railway line is now *nichevo*.'

Sarah stirred the porridge and smiled at Harry's use of the Russian word *nichevo* which the British troops had adopted to mean: no more, gone, finished. 'How long before the Germans or the Austrians or the Bulgars get here, do you reckon?'

'Dunno. We'll do our best to stop 'em.'

Sarah did not see him again until later in the afternoon. She was in the ward, changing a dressing, when she heard a hissing noise. Looking up she saw it was Harry standing in the doorway, going 'Pst, pst', and beckoning to her. She shook her head at him. Doctor Inglis was further down the ward, examining a patient who needed an operation, and the relaxation of rules and regulations did not include RNAS petty officers clomping in to speak to her orderlies when they were on duty. When Sarah had finished changing the dressing he was still lurking in the doorway, beckoning urgently, so with a quick glance at Doctor Inglis who appeared to be absorbed in her examination Sarah moved swiftly to the door.

'What is it?' she whispered. He pulled her into the nurses' cubicle and shut the door. 'What on earth . . . ?'

'Just listen, please.' There was no trace of cheekiness in his face, nor jocularity in his manner, so she listened. 'We're all being taken off, with the cars. The barges have come for us. Our lieutenant's going barmy. First we was ordered here to defend Galatz. Now we're ordered out, without defending it.'

'Does Doctor Inglis know?'

'Our lieutenant's just seen her to explain the situation.'

Yes, Sarah thought, that was typical of her, to come from such a conversation straight into the ward, to examine a probably dying man in preparation for a tricky operation. They had volunteered to stay to the bitter end, if necessary, so now that Galatz was being abandoned she had no need to consult them.

'Sarah. Can I call you Sarah?' She nodded. She'd been thinking of him as Harry for several days. 'I shouldn't be here. I should be loading the cars. I just wanted to say . . . well . . . take care of yourself, won't you? Commander Gregory won't let you down. He knows these waters like the back of his hand. Qualified Danube pilot he is. He'll find a barge for you from somewhere. And he'll get it into Galatz. He's a good bloke.'

From the anxiety in his voice, Sarah presumed there weren't too many barges left in the vicinity and getting them in and out of Galatz was becoming difficult. With a smile she said, 'Doctor Inglis has absolute faith in Commander Gregory. He's a Scot, you see, like her.'

Harry laughed and then he said, 'I love you, Sarah.'

Or at least that was what she thought he said, but the words were gabbled.

'Thanks for the nose-bag.' He said that clearly and with a touch of the old flippancy. Patting his bandage he gave a yelp of pain, and was gone.

After she had completed the operation, in a matter-of-fact tone Doctor Inglis put them into the picture Sarah already knew. She told her to start checking and packing the equipment into the ambulances which were to leave forthwith for Reni by road, taking with them as many of the remaining wounded as they could carry. A skeleton rearguard, which Sarah presumed would include herself, would stay to nurse those who were left behind and the casualties still trickling in. Suddenly, she felt quite calm. Maybe Commander Gregory would produce a barge from somewhere to evacuate the rearguard and their wounded, but if capture was to be their fate, so be it.

Inside, the sitting room was glowingly warm, the flames leaping in the grate, their red and yellow tongues twisting and licking round each other. Outside, the snowflakes were drifting past the window, muffling sound, though the backfire of a motor engine echoed loudly.

'That's Humpty Dumpty falling off the wall,' Kessie said. Both her guests regarded her in astonishment, then laughed as she explained. 'Tom's taken Anne and Con to the theatre. I promised them I'd listen for the crash as Humpty Dumpty fell.'

Solemnly, Kessie had made the promise because the girls had been disappointed that Mummy was not going with them; she was supposed to be resting, storing up her energy for the party they were having tonight. But first Alice had turned up unannounced, then Philip had telephoned to ask if he might call as regretfully he could not now join them this evening. Having thawed himself out he was moving away from the fire, lowering himself into an armchair, easing his gammy leg into a more comfortable position. In bad weather Kessie knew the leg troubled him, in the same way as the scar on the back of Alice's hand played her up.

'I don't think I've known it so cold in all the years I've been in England.' Alice made that sound like a century. She had in fact first come to London twelve years ago, though admittedly at times it had seemed like a hundred years. 'It was just as bad in Paris. Guy says it's simply unbelievable in the trenches. Can you imagine living in a hole in the ground in these conditions? And being shelled and shot at into the bargain?'

Kessie could. She had a vivid imagination and she'd been doing little else but think about the frozen stalemate on the Somme.

'Isn't it pretty?' Alice had taken a cigarette case from her handbag and was holding it up for them to admire. It was very pretty, a slim gold case, with tiny birds enamelled on one side, and in the firelight the colours gleamed exotically. 'Guy gave it to me for Christmas.'

Despite the increasing difficulty of obtaining civilian travel permits for France, or indeed anywhere outside the United Kingdom, Alice had managed to wangle one and had spent Guy Kendle's leave with him in Paris. Insofar as her friends were concerned she made no effort to cover her tracks but when her attention was captured by man, dog, or worthy cause, to use an Americanism Alice went the whole hog. She also had a tendency to flaunt her male conquests. It had been just the same when she'd first met Jonathon Conway. Johnny says this, Johnny says that, and what, Kessie wondered, was Alice's husband saying now?

'I'm sorry you can't be with us this evening after all, Philip.'

'I'm sorry, too, but I've just learned I'm sailing for New York tomorrow morning.'

'What?' Alice stubbed out the cigarette she had just lit and jumped up from the chair, smoothing down the folds of her flared tartan skirt. 'Why didn't you tell us? If I dash back home, write some letters and wrap up some parcels and get them round to your apartment, will you deliver them for me in New York? Momma would love to see you. She's lonesome now Poppa's gone and she worries dreadfully about me over here in the air-raids, so you can reassure her. She'd love to meet you. She adores titled people. You won't mention Guy, though, will you? Momma doesn't know about him. Yet.'

'I wouldn't dream of mentioning Guy,' Philip said. 'It might be wiser if you mentioned him less.'

Alice wasn't listening. She was out into the hall, with Philip limping behind to assist her into her coat. Returning with him to the sitting room, affectionately she kissed Kessie.

'See you tonight. Guy's so pleased "old Piper" will soon be back with him in those ghastly trenches. Why do they call each other by those silly names?'

In a flurry of glossy fur coat and hat, escorted by Philip, Alice was gone. Within a few seconds Kessie heard the purr of her Silver-Ghost's engine starting up and its soft thrum-thrumming as Alice gave it full throttle. Due to her weak heart Kessie had been forbidden to drive, an edict she had reluctantly accepted, and as Tom showed no interest in learning and her faithful driver/mechanic had been killed on the Somme, she had loaned the Rolls-Royce to Alice for the duration of the war. When Philip came back into the sitting room for several seconds they looked silently at each other in the subdued light of the flames. He broke the silence.

'Why didn't you tell me Tom was returning to active service?'

'Why didn't you tell me you were likely to be going to New York?'

'I thought he was being invalided out of the army and joining Lloyd George's administration.'

'Didn't most people? Including our new Prime Minister. Are you going to New York because you thought Tom had accepted Lloyd George's offer and would therefore be staying in England for the rest of the war? Why are you going, anyway? Is it to do with your work in the War Propaganda Bureau? To bang the patriotic drum for Britain? To convince the Americans they should enter the war? Or because *Love me for Ever* is opening on Broadway? Or is it a bit of all those reasons?'

'You frequently accuse me of not answering your questions, Kessie.' Philip smiled slightly. 'My not doing so could be because I hardly need to bother. You answer them for me. Your assumptions are in essence correct. The situation has grown . . . fraught, shall we say?'

Leaning her head back on the sofa, Kessie thought, yes, fraught was the word. Tom had become increasingly scratchy, occasionally as downright rude as only he could be, about Philip's role in his family's life. At one point he had accused Kessie of having an affair with the lah-di-dah bugger. Charitably she had attributed this to his still being in pain with his injured arm, though she had told him he was the last person who had any right to complain if she did have an affair. At this Tom had become virtue outraged. Since her closeness to death, he'd proclaimed passionately, he had known she was the only woman for him and he had not so much as laid a finger on another woman. From the widening of his dark eyes as he said this Kessie doubted it was the truth, the whole truth and nothing but the truth, but after the frontline trenches on the Somme she didn't think a casual, animal 'shag' in one of the brothels that apparently littered the rear areas counted.

How right was Tom to be worried? How attracted was she to Sir Philip Marchal?

In the low glow of the fire his elongated features were a golden brown which made him look like an El Greco figure. She *did* like him, his mordant, barbed wit made her laugh, and with Tom away it had been extremely useful to have somebody who was so astonishingly devoted and would do anything she asked of him. She was always conscious of his masculinity and his desire for her; not that he'd made any overt sexual approaches. Just occasionally she wondered what it would be like to make love with another man and thought if she ever took the plunge it would be with Philip, but mostly she regarded him as she had her cousins in childhood days, an interesting male friend and ally. Although Philip was only two years older than Tom somehow he seemed much older. Indeed, it was difficult to imagine him ever having been young and she gathered he'd had a miserable childhood. What she really objected to was Tom's dictating whom she should see, or not see, in his absence. Anyway, Philip himself had decided to cut loose by going to America, though whether he would have gone had he known Tom was returning to active service was an interesting question.

'You didn't answer my question,' he said, almost as if he were a mind-reader, 'why didn't you tell me Tom was returning to the front?'

'We were going to tell everybody tonight. That's the reason for the party. Farewell to Tom. Obviously he's already written to Guy, who told Alice who's not noted for keeping her mouth shut. Do you want the light on?'

'Do you?' He had this irritating habit of batting questions back to her which perhaps explained why, Kessie thought, she answered so many of them herself.

'No, I like sitting in the firelight. We could do with some more coal on the fire, though.'

While Philip obliged, carefully using the tongs to manipulate the coal from the scuttle to the grate, he did not enquire why Tom was returning to the front when he had been asked by the Prime Minister to stay at home and join his Government. Perhaps he guessed that Tom was going back because he felt he owed a duty to those who had no choice in the matter.

They were sitting in the light cast by the freshly leaping flames when the muffled clop of horses' hooves and the children's excited voices were heard outside. The front door opened and banged shut and Anne and Con rushed into the room, eager to tell their mother about the pantomime.

'Why are you sitting in the dark, Mummy?' Anne asked.

'Why are you?' Tom clicked the main switch by the door and Kessie blinked in the harshness of the electric light. 'Hello, Philip.' He looked at Kessie. 'I thought you were having a rest.'

Tom was in his uniform which he now hated wearing unless he had to but his daughters, Anne in particular, were so proud of him in it that Kessie had told him to put it on and not be a spoil-sport. His anger at Philip's presence was making him glower darkly, but glowering had always suited Tom's personality and in his uniform he looked stunningly handsome, pulsatingly alive. Kessie knew she was his, and he was hers, warts and all.

When he discovered why Philip had called Tom's temper subsided and he was at his most charming, wishing him a safe passage across the submarine-infested Atlantic. They were in the hall, saying goodbye to him, when there was a bang on the front door knocker which Anne and Con hurried to answer. Anne's legs were longer so she got there first to greet the post-woman with the early evening delivery. Swiftly, Anne shuffled through the envelopes –

she was always on the look-out for postcards for her collection – before she handed them over to Kessie.

'There's a letter from Aunty Sarah, Mummy. I know her writing.'

'How is Sarah?' Philip paused in the act of buttoning his coat.

'All right,' said Kessie, 'as far as we know.'

The full bombardment of Galatz started at five o'clock in the morning and it was a stunner, the shells screaming and shrieking, the explosions thudding and thumping, the floors and walls of the hospital shaking, plaster falling from the ceilings. The fresh onslaught of the guns shattered Sarah's recently acquired calm. She didn't want to be captured by the Bulgars, or by anyone, she wanted to be safely in Reni, she wanted to see Harry Sewell's cheeky grin.

Laboriously, they carried the remaining wounded into the main downstairs ward where they wrapped them in blankets, ready to be evacuated. They were all feeling pretty dazed by the bombardment when the doors were flung open and in strode an officer. In the dim light Sarah decided it must be a Bulgarian officer, as did the patient she was tending because he crossed himself repeatedly with the right-to-left Russian Orthodox blessing. Then the upper-class British voice rang out clearly.

''Morning, ladies and gentlemen. Ready to leave? Quick as you can, please.' It was Commander Gregory.

7

When they finally reached the safety of Reni an exhausted, anxious Sarah searched for Harry Sewell's figure among the crowd on the quayside waiting to greet the Scottish heroines. Where was he? The answer, which she learned from Jenny, would have been unbelievable except that nothing was beyond belief here. Harry's armoured car squadron had been ordered back to Galatz, which was to be defended after all. At this news Sarah almost burst into tears but she took a deep breath to control her emotion and sent out one of her prayers: please keep him safe.

The Unit had been allotted an extraordinary folly of a house, with a pagoda on top of a tower, as their quarters in Reni. Sarah found that Jenny had 'bagged' a pleasant room beneath the tower for the two of them to share. After she had semi-collapsed on to the truckle-bed, she asked where baby Tania was.

'Don't worry,' Jenny replied soothingly. 'I've found a splendid woman in the town to look after her.'

Sarah sat bolt upright. 'What do you mean you've found a splendid woman in the town to look after her? I'm looking after Tania. But for me she'd have died of exposure. Where is she? Take her to me this instant.'

As Sarah struggled to stand up the tears poured down her face. She was sobbing and shouting at Jenny who, after listening to the tirade in astonishment for a minute, abruptly turned on her heel and marched from the room. She continued to shout and sob until Jenny returned with a glass of whitish liquid which she ordered Sarah to drink. Realising that she was as close to hysteria as she had ever been in her life, Sarah swallowed the sleeping draught and when she awoke it was to discover that she had slept for forty-eight hours. As soon as Jenny came off duty from the hospital, brushing aside Sarah's apologies, she said she would take her to see Tania.

Reni appeared to be something of a dump, with unpaved streets and ramshackle wooden houses, but the minarets of a mosque and the dome of an Orthodox church brightened the skyline and it had a decent market place. Down by the River Danube Jenny turned into one of the houses in a dark, narrow street, knocking on the door to the left of the entrance hall. The knock was answered by a round-faced woman in her early twenties. In her terrible

Russian, using an extremely formal mode of address, Jenny introduced *Gospozha* Nekrasova.

The room they entered was as dark as the street outside and cluttered with heavy furniture, but within half-an-hour Sarah had established a good relationship with Mariya Fyodorovna – the use of first name and patronymic was the polite formula. She also accepted that Jenny had done the right thing. In fact it had been clever of her in refugee-packed Reni to find a woman who obviously loved children – she had two happy looking toddlers of her own – and, with a husband away fighting with the Russian army, only too glad of the money for looking after Tania. As Jenny said, what on earth would they do with the baby when they were ordered to move on again.

The likelihood of their moving on again in the immediate future became increasingly remote. Reni stood on the confluence of two rivers, the Danube and the Pruth, so there was always a wind blowing across both stretches of water. When it started to snow once more, two wind-whipped blizzards collided in a screaming frenzy over the rooftops of the town. After the snowstorms had abated the temperature dropped and it went on dropping steadily, ten, twenty, thirty degrees of frost. Sarah had neither seen, nor felt, anything like it. The whole town was ice-bound, the unpaved streets were turned into skating rinks, icicles hung thick as bunches of bananas from the eaves of the wooden houses, and it was so cold your breath emerged in gasping vapour that almost froze on your lips. First the River Pruth, then the Danube itself, froze absolutely solid from bank to bank.

With 'General Winter' in command the fighting came to an abrupt halt. Consequently, mercifully, there were fewer casualties to nurse, mostly frostbite or pneumonia cases from the frozen trenches. The last months, however, had taken a heavier toll than Sarah appreciated, or, believing herself to be a tough, liberated woman, had wanted to appreciate. For the first time in her life she was sleeping badly, lying for hours staring into the darkness, listening to Jenny's steady breathing, her mind as restless as the sea, endlessly swishing backwards and forwards, then surging with emotion.

Kessie had once accused her of viewing life in terms of black and white. Maybe she'd been right and things were a deal more complicated than Sarah had allowed. Having witnessed the horrors of war she was more than ever a pacifist, yet she did not regret coming to Russia and nursing her way through the Dobrudja retreat. In practice, she now greatly admired Doctor Inglis and Dorothy Devonald, whose attitudes in theory she disliked, in Dorothy's case detested. And what was she to make of herself, sensible Sarah, becoming so emotional about baby Tania, screaming at Jenny, and worrying herself sick over a man she hardly knew?

The British armoured cars were frequently in Reni and though Harry Sewell was not among their crews, Sarah learned from his mates that he was in the trenches outside Galatz which had been successfully defended. From time to time she received a chirpy message from him which told her to keep smiling, though nothing else. Had Harry ever actually said 'I love you, Sarah'? Or had she imagined the words in those desperate hours in Galatz?

Slowly, Sarah started to unwind, and for the first time since they had left Liverpool she unpacked her cases properly. Neatly, she arranged the champagne cork from Chenneys, the children's farewell gifts, and the few books she had with her, on the bedside table. In a prominent position she placed the photograph of Tom (which Jenny thought was stunning) and several of the pictures Philip Marchal had taken on that heavenly August day and which Kessie had forwarded.

'You're a romantic at heart,' Jenny said.

'Not really. They cheer the place up.'

Sarah was determined to get her emotions under control again.

As often as her duties allowed she visited Tania, always taking with her a parcel of food and toiletries. The gratitude with which Mariya Fyodorovna received them made her cross, but she was never cross with Tania who always held out her arms to be lifted in *Tyotya* Sarah's the minute her 'Aunty' entered the room. How she longed to keep the baby as her own. The idea of adopting Tania and taking her back to England niggled at the back of her mind. Was it a feasible notion?

Through Mariya Fyodorovna she met Mr Lohvitzky who lived in a room on the floor above. He was a retired school-teacher, a real gentleman, Sarah was assured, who spoke English and would be only too happy to give her Russian lessons. Mr Lohvitzky, whom she addressed as such in English fashion, was tall and thin. He wore a suit that had gone green with age and made him look like a desiccated grasshopper. His delight in his English pupil was unbounded, though being a gentleman he had to pretend he didn't really need the money.

Russian was a fiendish language and by comparison English grammar was a doddle, but Sarah persevered. If she didn't start to learn Russian properly while things were comparatively quiet and she had time on her hands, she never would. One evening she sat hunched on her truckle-bed, her Russian-English dictionary, notebook and pencil to hand, while Jenny lay propped on her bed reading *The Thirty-Nine Steps*, a new novel that had recently arrived in a parcel from her 'aunt' in Edinburgh, and smoking. In Sarah's opinion, like most members of the Unit she now smoked far too much.

'I have just spent a quarter of an hour,' Sarah said, leaning against the bedroom wall, 'translating the following ever so useful, everyday sayings: "Scythe-mow the grass while there is a dew", and "The gathering of the storks heralds the spring".'

'Well, if you will learn Russian . . .'

Jenny ducked her head on to the pillow as Sarah threw the dictionary at her.

Mr Lohvitzky was quite hurt when Sarah said she'd like to learn colloquial Russian but she did move on to translating sentences such as: 'Last week he was in Petrograd, this week he is in Moscow, next week he will be in Odessa, and where will he be next year?'

One of the benefits of being stationed in Reni, bitterly cold and windswept as it remained, was that letters and parcels started to arrive with reasonable regularity. Everybody agreed that news and goodies from home were boons and blessings beyond compare. Faithful Kessie who wrote every single week had already informed her that Tom had returned to active service. Sarah's heart had turned over at the news, though she couldn't say it surprised her. She could only hope her brother's gipsy luck, or something, would keep him safe. Then the letter from Tom himself arrived, stamped with the heavy Cyrillic characters that Sarah was now easily able to translate as 'Passed by the War Censor', though this was obviously untrue. No war censor would have passed his comments.

Tom's idiosyncratic spelling – 'rhumors', 'schrapnell', 'terrable', 'inishitive' – somehow gave an added impetus to his savage account of life on the Western Front, winter 1917. The weather there was obviously as fearful as here on the Eastern Front because Tom wrote that his priority was trying to ensure that none of his lads actually froze to death. He said he was having some success with the prevention of 'trench feet' too, which might stop them dying from pneumonia. His other priority was turning the deafest possible ear to the 'stunts' imbecile staff officers, safe in their châteaux miles behind the front lines, enjoyed arranging 'to keep the men on their toes'. Unfortunately, Guy had been forced to lead one such idiot raid against the Boche trenches last week and had caught a piece of 'schrapnell'. It was a Blighty wound, he was back in England and Tom missed him like nobody's business, but he reckoned 'the Prince' should be all right within a couple of months.

Amen to that, Sarah breathed, remembering Guy Kendle's insouciant charm and the sensitive brown eyes that had made her heart flutter on that beautiful day at Chenneys. Kessie had informed her that Alice's and his affair was as passionate as ever and had said she couldn't imagine how it would be resolved without causing pain to several people, not least to Johnny Conway who, with compulsory conscription, had received his call-up papers and was now in the army. Poor Johnny, Sarah thought. Still Alice's husband always appeared to take life as it came.

Early in March there were further terrible blizzards in Reni but fortunately by now they all had warm jackets. Through Mariya Fyodorovna, Sarah had found a tanner and a cobbler willing to treat and to stitch those sheepskins into coats. When the latest blizzards subsided Dorothy drove into the town from Odessa, where she had gone with the Transport Section to organise much needed repairs to the Unit's vehicles. As she jumped from her Ford she looked like a miniature armoured car man, not because she too had acquired a sheepskin jacket, but because she was wearing trousers tucked into her long indiarubber boots.

'Gosh!' Jenny said, surveying the trousers. 'They look practical. Where did you get them?'

'I had them made in Odessa. They're *immensely* practical. Personally, I'd recommend them for all women on active service.'

From the passenger seat Stephen emerged, though she was still wearing her officer's uniform of calf-length skirt, long belted jacket and turned-up trilby hat with a tartan band. Enveloping Sarah in a bear-hug she said, 'Good to see you, old thing.'

'And it's good to see you. How long is it since we parted in wherever-it-was?'

'Must be getting on for five months.'

While they were climbing the stairs to their room Sarah noticed how Stephen had aged. What would she be, pushing forty? She looked every day of it, lines etched on her broad forehead, streaks of grey in her Eton-cropped hair, none of which had been there when they had landed in Archangel. Neither her hearty manner, nor her slangy speech, had altered and Sarah was glad they had not, though on occasions in the past, like Kessie's giggling both had irritated her.

After she had slumped into their best chair, Stephen

said, 'Didn't know what I was letting you in for, that night stuck in the train outside Clapham Junction. What! Gather it was a fair old nightmare in Galatz. Not that we went to the vicarage tea-party. Roumanians running like hares in all directions and every darned bridge they sent us to blown to smithereens. Finally trundled over the river with our ambulances at Tulcea, just as the Russians were laying the charges to blow the last pontoon bridge there. And a tricky old journey that was. Very wide the Danube at Tulcea.'

Having allowed herself the luxury of indicating something of what her retreat through the Dobrudja had entailed, boomingly Stephen said, 'Where's our Elsie? Haven't heard a dicky-bird from her in weeks. Has she taken off into space?'

'Doctor Inglis has gone to Odessa,' Sarah said.

'Dammit!' Stephen leant back in the chair, her legs wide apart. 'We'd be better off communicating by carrier pigeon.' Then even more boomingly she changed the subject because it ill-became her to criticise their leader and the Unit's operational problems in front of a junior member such as Jenny who wasn't even an 'old chum'. 'What's the situation like in Reni? Very dodgy in Odessa. The natives are growing restless. Can't say I blame 'em, but it's all very tense.'

They discussed the rumours that were flying around about trouble in the capital city, Petrograd, on account of the dreadful food shortages, the appalling casualties, the crassly incompetent way the war was being conducted, and the astonishing unpopularity of the tsar.

'Something's definitely up,' Stephen twitched her nostril furiously. 'They've started censoring my *Times*. Thick black lines through whole columns. Presume it's through the Russian news.'

The *lèse-majesté* of anybody daring to censor *The Times*, which Stephen had sent regularly from London, made them all laugh.

Dorothy and she decided to stay in Reni for a few days, to see if 'our Elsie' returned from Odessa so that Stephen could have a much desired 'confab' with Doctor Inglis.

Although the snow had stopped falling the weather remained perishingly cold and fuel was in as short supply as food. In typical fashion, within two days of her arrival Dorothy had discovered that not only was there a plentiful supply of logs in the woods on the far side of the Danube and the area was not in enemy hands but there were twenty of their cars and RNAS lorries currently in Reni and the ice was thick enough to bear their weight across the river.

'We're going over in a convoy tomorrow. Operation fuel-forage. Should be fun. Are you coming, Sarah?'

She declined the invitation. The journey to Galatz had diminished Sarah's appetite for motoring, particularly on ice, but Jenny went on the expedition, as did Stephen. In the early afternoon Sarah was in her room, off-duty, when her friend Vera put her head round the door, saying there was somebody to see her downstairs in the lobby. It could be one of her several friends in the town, Sarah thought as she came down the main staircase, and even when she saw the flat cap, the sheepskin overcoat and the knee-boots she reckoned it was one of Harry Sewell's mates bearing another of his cheery messages.

Whipping off his cap, he turned round and said, 'It *is* nice to see you again, Miss!'

'Harry!' Sarah wanted to fling herself into his arms but instead she gazed at his nose with a professional air. 'It's set beautifully. You'd hardly know it'd been broken.'

'You might not. I assure you I did!'

His eyes said he wanted to talk to her, and she wanted to talk to him, but if she took him up to her room Sarah knew she would be shot at dawn. So they sat in the common room drinking tea with five of her orderly friends, all of whom appeared to be greatly interested in her relationship with Petty Officer Sewell. Harry regaled them with funny stories of life in the trenches outside Galatz, which had obviously been as unfunny as Tom's in the trenches on the Somme, the only difference being the absence of staff officers dead keen on 'stunts'. Eventually Harry said he must be on his way. Sarah accompanied him to the front door of the folly where she whispered, 'Did you see that pagoda thing when you came in?'

'How could I miss it?'

'There's a separate staircase. I'll get the key. It'll be a bit parky but we can have a talk, if you'd like.'

He nodded and left. Sarah waited a few minutes, then casually she said she thought she'd stretch her legs and climb up to the tower to see if the others were on their way back.

'Aren't you energetic?' Vera commented.

Despite the sunshine it was cold up in the tower, shiveringly so, and naturally Harry wanted to put his sheepskin round Sarah's shoulders.

'Why don't you keep your coat on *and* keep me warm?'

Smiling at him, she started to undo the big buttons down the front of his jacket. She didn't know what had come over her because she'd never behaved like this with a man before. At the thought of actually facing Harry, however, her nerve failed and turning her back towards him she snuggled into the coat.

Slowly, Harry's arms enfolded her.

For a long time, silently, they looked out across the Danube. The view from the top of the pagoda tower was spectacular, at least on a day like today. The sun was glinting on the snow-packed rooftops of Reni, turning the icicles into shimmering chandeliers, making the frozen river gleam like highly polished metal, while a pinkish-blue haze hovered over the dark outlines of the islands and the woods on the far side of the river, and the cars and lorries returning from their fuel-foraging expedition appeared to be gliding along like ice-gondolas.

Eventually Harry spoke. 'I took to you, you know, Napoleon, the moment I saw you on that quayside in the pouring rain, loading those barges. I volunteered to go with the party to find you outside Galatz, you know.'

Sarah snuggled closer against him, it was lovely and warm in his arms. After another pause he said, 'Did you catch what I said when I was leaving Galatz?'

'I might have. I'd like to hear it again. To make sure I heard aright.'

There was an even longer pause, during which he tightened his grip round her and she was sure she could feel his heart beating.

'I'm not much good with fancy words, but you're special, Napoleon. I'd be honoured if you'd consider being my wife, one day, when this is . . .'

Sarah had little practice in letting her personal emotions flow freely. All she could say was, 'Oh Harry.'

Then, disentangling herself from his grasp, she swung round, put her arms round his neck, tilted her head back and looked up into his face. His expression was ever so tender, yet longing, and slowly his mouth came down upon hers and they kissed. When their lips separated Sarah put her head on to the serge of his tunic, thinking it had been much nicer than being kissed by Edward Dawson.

Abruptly she lifted her head. 'I reckon you'd better know. I am not a virgin. I had a liaison with a man once. He's dead now. He was killed in the Dardanelles. I didn't love him and it wasn't very successful.'

For several seconds he stared down at her, his face set. Dropping her arms from round his neck Sarah thought, oh heck, that's torn it. But she'd had to be honest with him. Then solemnly Harry said, 'I'm not a virgin neither. I've been with one or two women. I think they're still alive. None of them were up to much.'

They were both laughing helplessly and he took her in his arms again. 'You really are something special. I want my head testing but I love you, Napoleon.'

She didn't mind being called Napoleon, not the way Harry said it. There was something else she had to tell him but he was lifting up her chin and they were kissing again and it was even nicer. She would have to tell him about Edward's child and what she'd done, wouldn't she? But not today. Their gasping breath was hanging like puffs of smoke in the coldness of the air, Sarah could feel the excitement in her own body and more than sense it in his.

Gently, slightly to her chagrin, he held her ar arm's length, his hands resting on her shoulders.

'Shall we be officially engaged? Or shall we leave it until the war's over and . . .'

The door burst open, a colder blast of air hit the room, and Dorothy's clarinet tones said, 'Vera said you'd climbed up to . . . oh.'

Harry walked to the window where he stood with his back to them, looking fixedly down, his neck very red. Sarah stared straight at Dorothy but beating a retreat, hasty or otherwise, was not her style.

'I say, I am sorry. Hello, Petty Officer Sewell. I am glad you and Sarah . . . shall I shut up? Or shall I tell you the news?'

'Why not? Seeing you're here?'

'Well, this letter was waiting for me.' Dorothy waved the sheets of paper in her hand. 'Just now when we returned. We had a jolly good forage. Gathered masses of wood. It's from an old chum. She says that the parliamentary committee has finally reported on the terms for a new electoral Bill. They're unanimously agreed all men over the age of twenty-one should have the vote. That'll include you, Petty Officer Sewell . . .'

Harry emitted a strangled sound, though whether it was of frustration, fury, or amusement, Sarah was not sure.

'But the committee has only recommended by a majority that some women be given the vote. My chum says if any of us actually get it, it'll be women *over the age of thirty-five*. Vera says you had a letter from Kessie by the same post. What did she have to say?'

'The same as your chum. Those are the main proposals. Kessie's up in arms and . . .'

'I should jolly well hope so!' Furiously Dorothy pushed her spectacles up on her nose. 'After what we went through in the Dobrudja, how dare anybody deny me the vote?'

'Hear, hear! How dare they!' Harry turned round and Sarahy was uncertain whether or not he was being ironic.

Dorothy took the words at their face value and beamed at him. Sarah could have strangled her.

97

8

When Kessie arrived at the hospital she found Tom sitting wrapped in his dressing gown in the basketwork chair. As soon as he asked if she'd bring a packet of fags with her tomorrow she knew he was feeling better.

'Fags! If you think I'm bringing in packets of cigarettes, or your tobacco tin, you can think again. If you have any sense, you'll stop smoking altogether.'

His dark skin was losing its greyish tinge but he still had a racking cough from the bronchial pneumonia he'd gone down with in the trenches in this bitter, bitter winter of 1917. This time he'd been brought to the Queen Alexandra Hospital in Highgate to convalesce, which made visiting easy. It was a beautiful house, one of Sir Alfred Mond's palatial mansions before the war.

'There's some grapes in there.' Kessie plonked the basket she was carrying on to the bedside cabinet. 'They've been 'specially sent up from the hothouses at Chenneys. I wrote to Philip to tell him about your pneumonia and he must immediately have cabled from New York.'

'How jolly decent of him.' Tom stretched out his left hand, plucked a plump purple grape from the bunch and popped it into his mouth. 'Not bad. Well? What's the latest news from the suffragette rialto?'

'Oh, I'm so angry I could scream.' Furiously Kessie kicked out her leg, caught her ankle on the foot of the bed and let out a yell of pain. While she held up her ankle for Tom to massage, which he obviously enjoyed doing, and the touch of his fingers across her silk stockings was to say the least pleasant, she said, 'It looks as if we're going to compromise on votes for women over the age of thirty.'

'That'll mean you'll be eligible, me luv.'

'That is not funny.' Tom agreed it was not. 'They're trotting out all the old arguments. Women outnumber men in the country, now more than ever before, therefore we have to take note of the backwoodsmen's fears of petticoat government. If we push for full adult suffrage on the same terms as men, in one fell swoop, we might get nothing at all. Half a loaf is better than none. All the nonsense we've heard a hundred times before which has nothing, absolutely nothing, to do with the equity and justice of our case. But we're organising a demonstration to show the strength of our feelings. If they try to backslide this time, to wriggle out of giving *any* of us the vote, well, I wouldn't like to answer for the consequences, war or no war.'

Tom was still in the Queen Alexandra Hospital, though ambulant and coughing less, when the first women's suffrage demonstration since the outbreak of the war took place. Kessie came straight from the rally to report to her husband. It was just like the old days – I wish you'd been there to see it – thousands of us marching through the streets of London with the banners flying. Well no, actually it wasn't quite like the old days. We had representatives from scores of our new trades walking in the procession. There were . . .' Kessie ticked them off on her fingers, 'dentists, tanners, typesetters, stokers, spot-welders, bakers, brewers, butchers. Oh and there were two girls driving steam rollers decorated with suffrage bunting and a couple of women chimney sweeps in their top hats! And there were several women grave-diggers, waving cheerfully! I took Anne and Con with me and Anne said, "We shall have the vote, shan't we, Mummy?" I said, "Yes! If it's the last thing your mother does!"' Tom held out his hand and with a slight frown said, 'Don't overdo things, Kess.'

She took his hand but ignored the comment. 'The next thing we're organising is a deputation of women war workers to 10 Downing Street. We're arranging it to coincide with the motion they're introducing into the House of Commons, that the electoral proposals be incorporated forthwith into a Bill. It's to make sure they don't forget the women's proposals, measly as they are, while they're at it. I wish you could be there to speak for us, Tom.'

'So do I, me luv.' Tightening his hold on her hand, he pulled her towards him and Kessie sat on his lap. '*Don't* overdo things. You're looking very tired.' Then he grinned wickedly. 'I want you on your feet, well active, any road, when I get out of here.'

Continuing to ignore the plea not to overdo things, Kessie went with the deputation to 10 Downing Street. When the serious business was finished, Lloyd George drew her into a corner where, apart from flirting outrageously (did he ever let up?) he enquired about Tom's health.

'I trust he will not again be returning to the trenches. They talk about minefields and enfilading fire over there. Believe me, Kessie, metaphorically speaking, we have them over here. I need Tom in my Government.'

'We haven't discussed the subject,' she said. 'He isn't fit enough yet.'

'When he is, not only discuss it, but stamp your feet, the way you stamped them at me in the old days.'

'Speaking of which . . .'

'As many women as cold political reality will allow shall have the vote. I promise you.'

The same day, the motion that the electoral proposals be incorporated into a Bill passed through the House of Commons, including votes for women, over the age of thirty anyway. But the cold political reality decided that the Bill would be a House of Commons measure which meant that every clause would be debated as a separate issue, passed or thrown out as such, with MPs voting according to conscience, whim, or how much pressure was exerted upon them. So there was still a long, long way to go, Kessie knew, before any of them would be able to put their crosses on a ballot paper and call themselves full citizens of their own country.

A few days after the deputation and the news about the Bill, she was in the study at The Grove, dealing with a pile of letters from Tom's constituents in The Dales, when the region of her heart started to ache dully. For an hour it continued to ache and she was almost as breathless as Tom had been. The experience scared Kessie so much that, though she didn't say a word to her husband, she telephoned Mr Seagrave, the heart specialist who had attended her after the birth of the twins. He was now working at a military hospital but he agreed to see her in Harley Street.

After Mr Seagrave had examined her, he said, 'You are without doubt, Mrs Whitworth, the most extraordinary of my patients. When you were told to stay in bed, you started to walk around. You should have had a fatal heart attack, but you did not. Since then, for somebody with your heart condition, you have led an extremely active life. However, if you continue at the pace you have obviously been pursuing, in my considered opinion you will unquestionably have a major heart attack, which may or may not be fatal. Is there anything else you wish to know?'

Kessie said no thank you, and Mr Seagrave too enquired after her gallant husband. Prewar, she recalled, he'd been awfully snooty with Tom – a Socialist with a Lancashire accent – but for her gallant husband's and their children's sake, she decided she really should take his advice this time.

It was nearly Easter before Tom was discharged from the hospital. They decided to cross to Willow Bank, Kessie's house on the Isle of Wight, so that he could continue his recuperation in the island's comparatively mild, unsooty, unsmoky air. Tom agreed Alice could accompany them, not that he had much option because Kessie and Alice had already decided she should. On the boat going over from Southampton, Kessie heard Anne lecturing Kate and Mark about behaving themselves, because Daddy still wasn't terribly well, and the twins were being angelic, if for them that was a relative term.

The afternoon after their arrival, the three adults sat peacefully in the sitting room at Willow Bank, the four children having been invited to a birthday party. The sun was streaming through the large bay windows and it seemed as if the most ferocious winter Europe had endured in decades might, at last, be drawing to an end. At the bottom of the long sloping garden the winter jasmine was still in bloom, but the leaves were budding on the trees, the grass was sprouting again, and along the borders the unfolding cream, yellow and white of the jonquils, daffodils and narcissi were nodding behind the emerging deep blue of the grape hyacinths.

The conversation was desultory, although one piece of interesting news came from Alice, who had bumped into Christabel Pankhurst looking well and glad to be back in London.

'Isn't it strnge how things work out?' Kessie said. 'Mrs Fawcett, the non-militant, has proved to have the steely tenacity of purpose as far as votes for women are concerned, while militant Mrs Pankhurst and Christabel have been careering all over the place, even if they have finally come back to the quaint idea that some women at least should have the vote. Personally I never got on particularly with Sylvia Pankhurst, but we were staunch allies in the battle for the young working women's vote, even if we lost it. Personally, you know how I once adored Christabel and you remember her stomping through the Dales, really in touch with the mill-girls, but I doubt she's perturbed by the fact that they're being denied the vote.'

'She isn't,' said Alice.

The grandfather clock in the hall chimed three o'clock. Although the boat from Southampton was not due until four-thirty and it took no more than half an hour to drive the trap from here in St Lawrence to Ventnor – less the way Alice drove it – Kessie was not surprised when she said she'd go in early to do a bit of shopping. She was like a cat on hot bricks, waiting for Guy's arrival on the island.

'I'll come with you. The fresh air'll do me good.' Alice did not look enchanted by the offer of his company, but Tom continued, 'I'd like to greet Guy, too. He is my friend, tha knows. Might look peculiar if Mrs Jonathon

Conway met him on her lonesome, any road. You'll have ten days of him, more or less to yourself.'

With mock coquettishness Alice fluttered her lashes. Kessie told Tom to wrap up well, to put on his 'British warm' and his hat because the sun would have gone down before they returned from Ventnor. Muttering that he wasn't in the damned trenches and he wasn't going in his damned uniform, he went into the hall. When Alice moved to follow him, Kessie mimed for her to shut the door.

'Be discreet, please, Alice. People are mightily interested in us at the moment, Tom in particular, our war hero, MC *and* bar.'

Before he collapsed with pneumonia Tom had been involved in a 'stunt' which had earned him another Military Cross, for the ludicrous reason, he said, that he'd completely lost his bearings in the filthy, freezing darkness of no man's land and stumbled on a surprisingly empty Boche trench, which had been hailed as an example of dashing initiative by Division.

'The Isle of Wight is a small place and small places breed gossip and . . .'

Sweeping towards her, Alice interrupted. 'Don't worry. Guy's an English gentleman, so his middle name is Discretion. I shall be as inconspicuous as a church mouse.' Kessie suppressed a giggle at the impossibility of that comparison, and Alice bent down to hug her. 'Nobody but you would have let us come like this.'

Occasionally, particularly bearing in mind what Alice had once done and the devastating effect it had had upon her, Kessie thought her present connivance and support were pretty noble. But Alice's outrageousness had always attracted her and she had more life in her little finger than staid respectable folk had in their whole bodies.

Tom opened the door. 'Come on, Alice, if you're coming.'

He had put his 'British warm' officer's overcoat over his civilian suit and he was wearing a scarf, Kessie was pleased to note, though his thick black hair was hatless. Crossing towards her, he kissed her gently.

'You're to rest this afternoon. That's an order.'

'Sir.' Smartly Kessie saluted.

In the glow of the bedside lamp the perspiration shone on their entwined, beautifully sated bodies. Languorously Alice ran her hands over Guy's damp skin, kissing the livid scar beneath his breastbone. It would always be there, but his latest battle wound would fade as the suffragette battle honour on the back of her hand had faded. She was proud of both scars.

The embers of the fire in the grate were almost dead and the clamminess of their now still bodies made Alice shiver slightly. Guy responded by tucking the bedclothes tightly around her, before he lit two cigarettes. Silently they lay smoking, his arm around her, her head on his shoulder. Suffering rattlesnakes, Alice thought, if he wasn't going to bring up the subject of his wife, then she must – before she gave him her other news.

'What did she say when you told her about me?'

The mournful hoot of the foghorn on St Catherine's headland sounded, for on the drive back from Ventnor a sea-fret had crept over the cliffs and up through the trees, later thickening to a heavy mist. Despite the warmth of the blankets and his body, Alice shivered again at the sound. Guy tightened his grip round her, drawing her closer to him, but it was several more seconds before he spoke, during which time the plaintive, plangent notes of the foghorn echoed through the dense night air.

'Nothing much, really.'

'You did tell her, didn't you?'

'Sort of, yes.'

'You're a moral coward, Guy Kendle.'

He laughed in his charming, deprecatory, English fashion. 'It's not that *entirely*, my darling. She and I both come from recusant Catholic families. I've tried to explain what that means.'

The explanation meant nothing to Alice. She failed to

see why the refusal of Guy's and his wife's ancestors to take the Oath of Supremacy to Henry VIII, in 1534 for heaven's sake, should affect her and Guy's future relationship. To use a vulgar Americanism, his wife sounded a pain in the arse. Guy was the eldest son and heir to the Ryby estate. At the age of twenty-one, just down from Cambridge University, he had dutifully married the girl his family had chosen. Whether they had ever been happy together Alice was unclear, but his wife had duly borne a son. In giving birth she had nearly died and thereafter the marriage had died in all but name. For Guy had been warned that another child could kill his wife and a good Catholic woman could not possibly use any form of contraceptive. She had proceeded to monopolise the child, leaving Guy to his own devices which had included travelling round the world. Did she expect him to spend the rest of his life satisfying his sexual desires with hole-in-the-corner *affaires*?

Apparently yes, because Guy was saying, 'She is my wife. I am her husband. Until death us do part. For her there is nothing to discuss. Unless I bring shame upon the honoured name of Kendle, she is uninterested in what I do, or what I feel.'

'She's going to have to be interested and start discussing things.' Alice took the cigarette from between his fingers, stubbing it and her own into the ashtray on the bedside table. In her clearest, anglicised New York accent she announced, 'I'm enceinte, Guy. You know when it happened.'

It had happened the day before Guy went north to Ryby Hall to see his family, when they'd had luncheon at one of those charming hotels overlooking the Thames in rural Richmond. In the clear cold sunshine they'd gone for a walk, their desire had overwhelmed them and Guy had not practised *coitus interruptus*. Not that she'd wanted him to, though normally Alice took rigorous contraceptive measures because the thought of having a baby frightened her.

'Are you sure?' he murmured. 'Can you be sure?'

'Yes.' She had only missed one period but Alice just knew she was enceinte and, astonishingly, she was glad. Having a child, she had now decided, was something a woman should experience and to bear his would not be, could not be, frightening. 'I don't know what Johnny will say, and frankly I don't care. I shall just tell my "dear husband" I want a divorce. Are you pleased?'

'My cup of happiness runneth over, my precious, my dearest, my beloved . . .' He went on murmuring endearments and kissing her and saying he'd adore a little girl, just like her. Not that Alice had expected any other reaction, but in regard to what they were going to do and how he was now going to persuade his wife to divorce him his answer was similar to Mr Asquith's notorious wartime words, 'Wait and see.'

A couple of days later they were in Ventnor to buy last-minute Easter presents, strolling through the steep narrow streets in a family party that consisted of Tom, Guy, Anne, Con, and Alice herself. They were just about to enter the Crab and Lobster Hotel, to treat the girls to tea, when from the raucous cries of the newspaper vendors Alice learned the momentous news she had been waiting to hear for months. She took it as a good omen for her baby girl's future.

When they returned to Willow Bank, Anne raced into the sitting room where Kessie was ensconced on the sofa. Alice had noticed how tired she looked and that her lovely skin had acquired a worrying, slightly waxen pallor, so it was a good idea for Kessie to rest as much as possible. It was also good training for her personally to be with the children.

'Mummy, Mummy,' Anne said breathlessly. 'America's come into the war! Hurrah, hurrah! Aunty Alice is pleased.'

'I'll say she is.' Holding Con's hand, Alice swept in. She hoped her little girl would be a combination of Anne's intelligence and spirit and Con's sweetness and obedience. 'Now we're finally in, the war'll soon be over.'

Even Guy joined in the chayaking that greeted this remark but Alice smiled and said with the good old US of A on the Allies' side that had to be the truth.

Anne perched on the sofa by her mother's side. 'Will you write and tell Aunty Sarah, Mummy? About America.'

'I expect she'll hear the news,' Kessie smiled.

After she'd written her weekly letter to Sarah, Kessie decided she could no longer postpone writing to Dorothy, to explain why they had compromised on votes for women over the age of thirty. It was not, Kessie felt, a situation that it would be easy for Didi to accept or to understand, far away in the turmoil of revolutionary Russia.

9

'Who are these Bolsheviki?' Dorothy asked, as she unpacked the picnic basket. 'A Russian soldier lectured me for half an hour this morning before he allowed me to move my own ambulance. His English was quite dreadful and I hardly understood a word he was saying. He said he was a Bolshevik.'

'They claim to be the majority – that's what the name derives from – among the left-wing groupings,' Sarah said.

'That doesn't mean much. Everybody's left-wing in Russia at the moment.' Dorothy peered at a parcel of the local skinless sausages. 'What's a *soviet*?'

'A council,' said Sarah. 'It's Russian for council.'

'Oh, I see. From what I understood my soldier to be saying, they're setting up *soviets* in factories, on farms, *and* in the army. Did you ever hear anything so ridiculous? Imagine having a council meeting just before you go into battle.'

'They're already having them, Didi. They're . . .' Harry stopped speaking as little Tania shot past him as fast as her hands and knees would carry her. As he caught her she yelled loudly, still protesting as he handed her back to *Tyotya* Sarah who pacified the child by feeding her titbits which she ate greedily.

Having returned from another stint in the trenches outside Galatz, Harry had formally requested permission of Doctor Inglis to escort three members of her staff, Nursing Orderlies Whitworth and Macdonald and Driver Devonald, on a picnic. Permission had been granted, for since Harry had been the only RNAS man available to attend the Unit's Easter Sunday service, metaphorically speaking Doctor Inglis had taken him to her not over-ample bosom. Sarah had brought little Tania with them because, fond as she was of Mariya Fyodorovna, she was no believer in the virtue of fresh air and the baby spent far too much time cooped up in that dark room. In one of the Lanchester lorries they had driven to this slight incline behind Reni. Spring had definitely come, for as Mr Lohvitzky's phrase-book had it, the storks had not only arrived, they were nesting. Every clump of bushes, every tree in sight, was festooned with their untidy nests.

As she handed round the plates, hard-boiled eggs and hunks of rye bread, Jenny said, 'I think the *soviets* are the most democratic things I've ever heard of.'

From the minute they had learned about the riots in Petrograd, followed by the astonishing news that the tsar had abdicated, and then by the demonstrations in Reni itself, Jenny had been in a state of euphoria. Everything that was happening was absolutely, unquestionably wonderful, and every spare minute she was down in the town, snap-shotting history-in-the-making with the posh new camera she had bought from an impoverished Russian. She had photographed the crowds in the market square, and the orators who had shot up like early morning mushrooms, standing on the street corners, waving their arms, shouting about the new era of freedom and justice for all.

'They're a fascinating lot, the Bolsheviks,' Harry said. 'At least the ones I've met are.'

'Really?' Dorothy looked at him with surprise and

interest. Seeing that normally she was such a snob, the two of them got on amazingly well and Sarah reckoned it came from a mutual absorption in the insides of motor vehicles. 'Where did you meet yours?'

Harry was only too eager to tell them. During his recent stint in the trenches, he said, they'd been watching a Taube aeroplane dropping leaflets over the Russian lines when suddenly the Russian soldiers had leapt out of their trenches and poured into the British ones. Apparently, the German leaflets said their beloved tsar had been deposed by the brutal English.

'Well, that made us the heroes of the hour. The Russians hugged and kissed us, very emotional they were. After that they kept on leaping into our trenches, chattering away like a pack of . . .' From the slight hesitation Sarah guessed Harry had been about to say 'schoolgirls' or some such comparison, but he amended it to, '. . . seagulls. Very matey and excitable they were and they had this bloke with them, as their political commissar. His name's Mikhail Muranov and he's a character and a half. He speaks astonishing English. You'd like him, Sarah, he can quote passages of John Milton's poems off by heart.'

That did surprise Sarah. Milton was one of her personal favourites, but not the easiest of English poets to comprehend, let alone quote passages from.

'And Mikhail's a Bolshevik. They're sort of Marxians, aren't they?'

Sarah nodded at which Dorothy exclaimed, 'What? You mean followers of that dreadful man, Karl Marx?'

Sarah suppressed a smile. She doubted Dorothy had the faintest idea what the dreadful Karl Marx had advocated.

'They're in favour of votes for women, Didi,' Harry said, 'all women. You're to be equal in their new regime. Mikhail has a lot to say about women's souls being as fine as men's.'

'Really?' Dorothy's fury at the news from home that the suffrage societies had compromised on votes for women over the age of thirty had not abated, not even after reading a ten-page letter of explanation from Kessie. 'Women's emancipation will certainly make a change in this country. Personally, I'll believe it when it happens.'

'It's going to happen,' Jenny said emphatically. 'It's all going to happen here. You don't seem to realise you're living through the greatest, most momentous, stupendous upheaval in European history, maybe in the world's history.'

Unimpressed Dorothy said, 'Who wants a drink?'

Sarah gave Tania a cup of the delicious local fruit cordial which she lapped up greedily. Either she was a naturally greedy baby or, more likely, she was not getting enough to eat at Mariya Fyodorovna's – nobody in the household was. Sarah made a note to scrounge more food for them. Having had her fill Tania's little eyelids started to flutter and her head to nod. Sarah settled her on her lap thinking what a beautiful feeling it was to have a bairn enfolded against you. They were all fairly somnolent now, Dorothy and Jenny stretched full-length on the grass, Harry by Sarah's side.

Behind them the barren winter steppe was a multi-coloured carpet of spring flowers, below them the Danube was almost blue, the woods on the far bank where Dorothy had led the fuel-foraging expedition a mass of green. What a sight the Danube had been when it finally started to thaw, huge slabs of ice cracking like the craziest of crazy paving, then the dark rivulets between the melting slabs widening and spreading until suddenly, one day, the last blobs of ice had gone and the Danube was once again a great sheet of water flowing freely towards its delta.

This natural phenomenon had seemed to Sarah to reflect the extraordinary events that were shaking Russia to her old, apparently immovable foundations. She herself considered the revolution a magnificent expression of the human spirit, the final eruption of a people goaded beyond endurance, but with Russia being such a vast country and the rumours flying as freely as the wild geese in the skies above, her excitement was tempered by the need to discover exactly what was happening.

Harry was watching her with a fond, almost sloppy,

smile. Was he entertaining visions of one day picnicking with her and Tania in the hop-fields of Kent? Sarah had mentioned her dream of taking the little girl back to England. Or was he imagining her with *their* child on her lap? Everybody in the Unit accepted that they were sweet on one another and would in the fullness of time marry, including Doctor Inglis. Sarah looked at Harry's curly brown hair and the cheerful face with its leathery skin and she was sure they would marry but she did wish he would . . . What? Be less willing to defer to her as 'Napoleon', more openly loving and demonstrative? Why didn't she take the initiative? Because she had been brought up to believe that in sexual matters it was men who led? She'd taken the lead with Edward Dawson when it had suited her, so why not with Harry whom she liked a lot more than she'd ever liked poor old Edward? Because this time she was frightened of her emotions?

With a deliberate spontaneity which made Sarah certain he had been chewing over the proposal for some time, Harry said, 'That Mikhail Muranov I told you about, he's addressing a meeting in Reni this evening. He's invited me. He's a splendid turn, even if you don't understand what he's saying. He'd like to meet you, I know. He likes us English, though him and his mates think we should all return home pronto. Why don't we go to hear him? I have your officer's permission to escort you young ladies for the day!'

'Why on earth should they want us to go home?' Dorothy demanded, 'after all we've done for them?'

'Never mind about that,' said Jenny. 'Do let's go.'

The sun was sinking westward in a scarlet disc, the Danube was aflame with its light, the wooden buildings round the market square were a fiery bronze and the faces of the crowd glowed. The whole scene might have been stage-managed by the gods with a small 'g' (for the Bolsheviki did not believe in the Almighty with a capital 'G') to match the colour of their revolutionary red flags.

'That's him,' said Harry, 'he's a striking fellow, isn't he?'

111

'Gosh,' said Jenny, 'he certainly is.'

Several men were standing on the makeshift platform but it required no effort to decide which was Mikhail Muranov. He was not the tallest, about five feet nine inches, but his figure overwhelmed the others. His body was thick-set, his shoulders and chest broad, he had a wide forehead, wide-set eyes, wide mouth, but it was his hair that riveted the attention: long blond hair – though the sunset was turning it to auburn – astonishingly cut into a medieval pageboy style. He was wearing a Russian shirt with a high neckline and buttons down one shoulder, and baggy trousers tucked into knee-length boots. Having become an expert on boots during the freezing winter months, Sarah noticed they were a good, strong, real leather pair.

Then he started to speak. His voice was deep and resonant, his gestures were as expansive as his personality, arms flung outwards to embrace the crowd, upwards to chastise the heavens, and he was as spellbinding as Mrs Pankhurst or Tom or Lloyd George at their very best. At his peroration he threw up his arms to the darkening sky and declaimed Milton's lines, first in English – obviously he'd noticed their presence – then in Russian:

Long is the way
And hard, that out of hell leads up to light;
Our prison strong; this huge convex of fire;
Outrageous to devour, immures us round.

No prison, Mikhail Muranov's voice thundered in his own language, however strong, however fiery, could now contain the outraged spirit of the Russian people, and however long and hard the road from the tsarist hell, they were marching towards the Bolshevik heaven.

For a few seconds the echoes of his voice trembled in the gathering darkness, then the applause broke, people surged forward and the red flags formed a fluttering barricade around him. Sarah felt as if she had been released from a hypnotic trance, Jenny looked as if she'd been

112

dunked in a vat of sweet wine, Harry had a pleased expression on his face, as if Mikhail Muranov were his personal property, and even Dorothy was shaking herself like a little dog emerging from the water.

'I say, he can speak, can't he? I should think he's a dangerous man.'

'Double gosh!' Jenny turned the seraphic smile on to Sarah who had teased her about the constant use of 'gosh'. 'Can we meet him, Harry?'

'They're having a bun-fight and a discussion afterwards. I've got the address. We're all invited.'

Looking more than ever like an ancient grasshopper Mr Lohvitzky came towards them, and having examined the address he offered to escort them. It did not surprise Sarah that Mr Lohvitzky should have attended the public meeting because he was always regaling her with long sad stories about his father's land being stolen by a rapacious landlord. The dear old man was not, however, a believer in the Pankhursts' old suffragette cry, 'Deeds Not Words', of which Sarah had thoroughly approved and still did. He much preferred talking about his woes to doing anything about them.

At the door of the given address, Mr Lohvitzky bowed and wished them goodnight. When Sarah suggested he come in with them he looked shocked, and she wasn't sure whether this was because he hadn't been invited and no Russian gentleman of the old school would dream of going anywhere uninvited, or because instinctively he behaved deferentially towards his leaders, whoever they might be.

Inside the small crowded room, there was nothing deferential about anybody's behaviour. Everybody seemed to be shouting at the tops of their voices and although there was a preponderance of men Sarah was glad to note several women were present. The air was already thick with smoke and without exception the women had cigarettes in their mouths or fingers. It was clear that here as much as at home smoking was one of the badges of the emancipated woman. For a short while they stood by the door, their ears assailed by the noise, watching the animated faces and the gesticulating hands, before Harry bellowed in a surprisingly loud, commanding voice, 'Mikhail'.

The wide smile cut Mikhail Muranov's face, he stretched out his arms and the gesture created a path for them. Harry introduced them to Mikhail who took each of their hands in a hearty grip, before persuading them they should have a tumbler of vodka, rather than tea from the samovar.

'You are welcome, welcome,' he said in English. 'My good friend Harry and the fair damsels from distant England's shores.' He gulped a mouthful of vodka. 'The heiresses to Oliver Cromwell, the first great revolutionary, truly the chiefest of Europe's men, and to the sublimest of revolutionary poets, John Milton.'

Behind her spectacles Dorothy's brown eyes blinked rapidly. For her, Oliver Cromwell was the double-dyed villain who had martyred King Charles I and John Milton was a sublime Christian poet. Mikhail gulped another mouthful of vodka and said, 'And which of you is the mountain nymph, sweet liberty?'

'I am,' Jenny said promptly.

'Then you shall sail home, sweet nymph, and proclaim to your fellow countrymen and women that in Russia the bourgeoisie have dug their own graves and the rise of the proletariat is a reality.'

Within minutes they were sitting on the floor listening intently. His command of their language was, as Harry had said, astonishing, laced with Milton's words and spoken in a good middle-class accent – not too posh, more like Kessie's than Dorothy's. Sitting at his feet, Jenny agreed with everything he said and violently disagreed with Dorothy's pronouncements. Sarah knew she wouldn't get anywhere with him like that. Russians loved arguing, and she could see he was thoroughly enjoying his set-to with Didi. Sarah had no intention of letting Mikhail Muranov get away with some of his more outrageous statements, particularly his asides in Russian to his comrades, but she wanted to fire her first real salvo in his language. Carefully she rehearsed what she had to say in her head, remembering everything Mr Lohvitzky had taught her.

'I am what Karl Marx called a "true" Socialist with such contempt. I believe in . . . a constant fight . . . but without violence . . . against our masters.'

The words did not emerge as fluently as she had hoped but Mikhail swung round to her, congratulating her upon her excellent Russian and, realising that she knew something about Marxianism which was more than Dorothy, or Jenny did, giving her his full attention. Mikhail had flattered her by saying she spoke excellent Russian but it was good enough to enable Sarah to argue with his comrades too. The women truly seemed to be equal, as confident and articulate as any of the men, full of splendid plans for the emancipated future, sharp at pouncing upon 'old tsarist taints', the casual assumptions that men would do this and women would do that because that was the way things had always been in the past.

To start with Sarah had not much liked the vodka, but in best Russian fashion she took another gulp of the second, or was it third, tumbler, and found the fiery taste had definitely improved. She was feeling ever so happy and clever, telling the comrades that if they did succeed with their Marxian revolution, old Karl Marx would turn in his grave. In his time he'd said some very rude things about Russia and he'd been adamant the revolution would happen in an advanced industrialised country like England. Mikhail had moved closer to her and was now propped against the wall, his booted legs stretched in front of him. Leaning forward, running her fingers along their dusty, leathery length, in English Sarah said, 'Where did you get those boots? And where did you learn to speak such splendid English?'

Gulping a mouthful of vodka – he didn't half knock it back, Sarah thought, though it appeared to have no effect on the fluency of his speech – with a grin he said, 'I bought the boots in Odessa, and I had an English governess called Miss Thompson who considered John Milton the greatest poet who ever lived. In that, if nothing else, she was right.'

'Are you rich? Go on,' Sarah smiled up at him, 'tell me all about yourself. Where do you come from? What did you do before the war? Why aren't you in the army? How did you . . .'

'"Sabrina fair, listen when thou art sitting!"' Mikhail declaimed, '"Listen for dear honour's sake!"'

With another smile Sarah said, 'I'm listening.'

He said he came from Odessa and yes, his family was rich, though they had long been among the liberal intelligentsia, conscious of their inherited wealth, of the immense gulf between rich and poor in Russia and the clamorous need for sweeping reform. His parents were Mensheviks but at university he and his brother Piotr had become convinced that only a Marxian tourniquet, as applied by the Bolsheviks, could stanch their country's grievous wounds. Piotr was currently stationed in Reni, which was why Mikhail had temporarily left revolutionary Odessa to descend upon this boring town as a political commissar. He was not in the army because he was unfit for military service.

'Unfit?' Sarah's eyes travelled up and down his body which was as sturdy as an oak tree.

'I am deaf in one ear.'

Perhaps it was the majestic tone in which Mikhail made the statement, suggesting that all the best Bolsheviks were, that made Sarah laugh. For the moment he looked distinctly unamused but she couldn't stop laughing, then she was choking and he was calling for a glass of tea, making her drink it, patting her back.

'Are you all right?' Harry called out anxiously.

'Stop hitting her.' Jenny's nursing instincts overcame her adoration of the superb Mikhail Muranov. 'It doesn't do any good.'

Spluttering, Sarah managed to regain her breath and wipe the tears from her eyes, assuring everybody that she was fine again. Mikhail had stopped patting her back but he had slipped his arm round her shoulders. The touch of his fingers through the cotton of her blouse, the closeness of his broad chest, the scent of his masculinity, sent delicious shivers through Sarah's body. The other effect was to make the muscles of her groin contract in a way no man's proximity had done before, including Harry's, though she'd experienced the sensations by herself in bed. The smooth, silky blond hair was swinging against her cheek and her fingers itched to stroke its pageboy length.

Steady on Whitworth, she told herself in best Doctor Inglis fashion. He's just being friendly, he isn't likely to be interested in you, though he is about your age, so calm down, dear. Any road, you've more or less promised to marry Harry Sewell once the war is over and it'll be a happy union because he's a nice lad. Moreover that woman with the sharp intelligent face and mane of tawny hair looks as if she regards Mikhail as her private property, notwithstanding its proposed abolition and the severing of bourgeois family chains.

Yet Mikhail was the most exciting creature she'd ever met and she'd known some in her time, starting with Tom, but they all had a certain English restraint, even Tom, bounds beyond which they would not tread. Sarah could not imagine any limits which Mikhail Muranov would consider inviolate and if she didn't altogether approve of that, it *was* exciting.

So was the way he was stroking the back of her neck.

Jenny was looking sleepy and Sarah thought she wouldn't mind having a kip herself, particularly with Mikhail's arm around her. Good old Harry was frowning. He said loudly, 'Well, our commander's been up to Petrograd. Your Mr Kerensky has told him your army's planning a summer offensive.'

'He is not our Mr Kerensky, and the offensive will fail,' Mikhail said majestically. 'The Russian people will not fight for tsarist generals in Kerensky's clothes. They will not again go into battle without rifles, without ammunition, without boots, without food in their bellies, without good reason, to be slaughtered in their millions like ants in an antheap.'

There was a silence. Then Dorothy stood up and from her unimposing height managed to look down through her spectacles with considerable dignity, throwing accusing looks at Mikhail. 'While you are mutinying, we shall be

117

caring for the casualties. And if we don't gallop back to our quarters, chaps, we shall be on the carpet. Personally I have to be up at the crack of dawn to drive my ambulance to Tuchook where there's an outbreak of typhus.' Stephen was with a small section of the Unit in Tecuci and had sent an urgent message requesting further ambulances and nurses.

Leaping to his feet, towering above her, Mikhail bent down to kiss her on the forehead. 'For myself, I thank you and all the members of the *Shotlandskaya Zhenskaya Bol'nitsa!*' The way in which he rolled out the Unit's name in Russian, the 'sh' and 'zh' sounds deep and rich, made it sound the noblest of institutions. '"Servants of God, well done. Well hast thou fought thy fight."' Then he roared, 'But it is the wrong battle you are engaged in.'

The farewells were noisy and emotional and they were exhorted to go forth to spread the Bolshevik message. Jenny said she certainly would. Outside it was a beautifully clear, starlit night but the air was quite chilly and its impact made Sarah realise she had drunk more vodka that she had imagined. What had she said to those dedicated, determined, intelligent Russians? Apart from Dorothy who was marching in front, they were all somewhat squiffy, proceeding in less than straight lines. Jenny was chattering away like a starling about what a wonderful man Mikhail Muranov was and how it had been the most fascinating, educative – except she couldn't pronounce the word properly – evening of her entire life.

'He's not as bad as I expected,' Dorothy said over her shoulder. 'I just don't understand how any sensible, intelligent person can be a Bolshevik. The only thing they have the right idea about is us women and our equality.'

'What did you think to him, Napoleon?' Harry murmured in Sarah's ear which he then tried to kiss.

Pulling her head away she said, 'He's a character and a half, like you said.'

Harry did not attempt to embrace her again.

When they reached the gates to the folly, with the moon shining on the pagoda tower, Dorothy said, ''Night, Harry.

118

See you sometime, somewhere, and the best of British luck in the meantime.'

'And to you, Didi. 'Night ladies. Sleep well.'

Sarah watched his compact shape disappear into the shadows and a twinge of an emotion from which she rarely suffered assailed her. It was guilt. For as they had been leaving the noisy, stuffy, smoke-filled room, Mikhail had again slipped his arm round her shoulder and nodded his head towards Harry.

'Is he your man?'

After only a second's hesitation, without looking at Harry, she'd said, 'No.' And she must have been drunk because she'd then nodded towards the girl with the tawny mane and said, 'Is she your woman?'

Without any hesitation Mikhail had replied, 'No. We are holding a party next week, an al fresco Russian party. "Come thou goddess fair and free, Come and trip it as you go, on the light fantastic toe."'

10

Round the campfire the Russian soldiers were dancing, swinging wildly backwards and forwards, one arm holding the partner's waist, the other up in the air. Breaking apart they leapt as high as the flames, arms wide, legs opening like scissors to touch their outstretched hands. Now four of them were squatting on the ground, folding their arms, and with backs straight, heads erect, they began to shoot their legs in front of them. The tempo of accordions and fiddles increased, everybody was clapping their hands, faster and faster, as the booted legs flashed in and out.

'Gosh,' said Jenny, 'did you ever see anything so exciting?'

When Mikhail had issued the invitation to trip the light

fantastic toe at an al fresco party, apart from not realising he meant Milton's words literally, Sarah had assumed that by 'we' he meant his Bolshevik comrades would be hosting the party. The day after their session with the comrades, however, an official invitation had arrived for the Unit to attend a celebration with their Russian allies. While Doctor Inglis disapproved as strongly as ever of her 'gels' flirting, notably with Russians, she was always keen to cement good relations, so the invitation had been accepted.

The Russian soldiers had finished their amazing dancing. Now the accordions were wheezing into action again, the fiddles scraping, and one of the higher ranking officers came towards Doctor Inglis, clicking his heels, bowing, proffering his hand.

Laughingly she shook her head. *'Pas moi. Je suis trop âgée. Mais les autres, les jeunes filles, oui, oui.'*

Most of the higher ranking Russian officers spoke French, though whether they understood our Elsie's was, according to Stephen, a moot point for her grammar was minimal and her accent atrocious.

'Come on, gels, on your feet. Enjoy yourselves.'

The junior officers came towards them, clicking their heels, bowing politely. Mikhail strode straight for the spot where Jenny and Sarah were sitting, but although Jenny made to rise to her feet he ignored her and hauled Sarah upright.

'"And if I give thee honour due",' gravely he inclined his head, '"Mirth admit me of thy crew, To dance with her, and dance with thee",' he smiled as he led Sarah into the open space round the fire, '"In unreproved pleasures free".'

'You really do know your Milton, don't you? Well enough to paraphrase.'

'Yes.' He flung her the full length of his arm and brought her swiftly back towards him. Momentarily their bodies touched and Sarah felt as if she had been plugged into a live electric socket. 'So do you, *moya* Sabrina. Well enough to know that I paraphrase. Now follow my movements. Let the pleasures freely flow.'

120

To begin with Sarah was uncertain of herself, so were her stumbling, laughing fellow-orderlies. Although she hadn't danced in years, back home in Mellordale it had been an activity she had once enjoyed, if more decorously than this, and she did have a natural sense of rhythm. Soon her feet were tripping and stamping, her body was bending and weaving in harmony with Mikhail's, and her gipsy skirt was swirling around her. Sarah didn't know why she'd put it on, except Doctor Inglis had told them to don their glad rags and this multi-coloured skirt and white satin blouse she'd bought in Reni were the gladdest rags she possessed.

Fresh logs were being thrown on to the fire, showers of orange sparks were shooting upwards to the blue-black sky, suddenly Sarah realised that everybody else had stopped dancing and she and Mikhail had the ground to themselves. For a few seconds she hesitated, glancing at Doctor Inglis, but she was smiling and nodding her head in approval.

'Ayee-yay!' Mikhail shouted.

All Sarah's senses were then concentrated on the insistent thrum of the music, the rhythm of the clapping, on his body in front of her, leaping against the backcloth of the flames, stamping his feet, sashaying backwards and forwards with his arm around her waist, breaking away from her, again seizing her hands and galloping her round the fire, his hair sweeping over his shoulders, brushing against her face; and on her own body, her legs, her arms, lithe, supple, sinuous, the skirt swishing round her thighs, the breeze ruffling her short hair, the warmth of the fire fanning her cheeks. Sarah had never in her life felt so exhilarated, so superbly free, so much of a . . . gipsy. A little of her grandmother's blood ran in her veins and she threw back her head with the sheer joy of being alive and of dancing with Mikhail Muranov.

The bows of the fiddles were scraping frantically, the pleats of the accordions were being squeezed furiously, the clapping was rising to a crescendo. Mikhail took her in his arms, he was holding her up in the air, up towards the heavens, he was swinging her round and Sarah felt as if she were on a flying trapeze. Then the music stopped, she had her feet back on the ground, and she was laughing breathlessly. With her head tilted back she looked up at Mikhail who bent his down and whispered, '*Obezhayu tebya, moya dikaya angliiskaya roza.*'

I adore you, my wild English rose. Oh she adored him, with the long suppressed wildness of her gipsy ancestors.

Mikhail took her hand in his and led her towards Doctor Inglis and the top Russian brass. Together they bowed and his long hair swept the ground.

'Didn't know you had that in you, Whitworth,' Doctor Inglis said, smiling broadly. Her reactions were unpredictable, though Sarah then realised why she was pleased because she said, 'Shows what we British can do in every respect, eh?' The doctor-in-charge reasserted itself, 'You'd better put something round your shoulders, otherwise you'll catch a chill.'

An officer produced a coat for Sarah. Still the Russians went on shouting and applauding, and fleetingly she wondered how many of them supported Mikhail's Bolshevism, though it didn't matter. Nothing mattered, except being with him.

Sarah expected Mikhail to arrive at the folly, or the hospital, or to contact her in some way, but two interminable days and nights went by without sight or sound of him. The rest of the Unit shared Doctor Inglis' view that she had put up a jolly good show – where had she learned to dance like that? – but Jenny's behaviour was tiresome. On-duty she spoke to Sarah only when it was essential to do so; off-duty she lay on her bed in their shared room, her nose in a book, smoking more heavily than ever. Her lone comments, uttered in her most twangy, laconic Newfoundland voice, were concerned with Harry whom she'd bumped into while shopping in the town, and with the stupid way the characters in the novel she was reading, who imagined themselves to be head-over-heels in love, behaved.

Then Agnes Turnbull said, 'Will you do my shift for me,

Sarah? I'm feeling mouldy. I've got the foulest of . . .' She dropped her voice, for though she was an advanced young woman she had been brought up not to mention such things, '. . . monthlies. I'll do the weekend shift for you.'

Sarah said of course she would. A free weekend would give her time to find out what had happened to Mikhail. How she wished Kessie were here in Reni, so she could talk through the wild tangle of her emotions.

Immediately after an early breakfast on the Saturday morning Sarah went down into the town. First she visited the Nekrasovs, handing over a food parcel which Mariya Fyodorovna received with her usual tearful gratitude – which today irritated Sarah more than usual. She didn't stay long because even Tania had lost her all-absorbing charm, though maybe that was because she was in a crotchety teething mood. Through the narrow unpaved streets which Sarah now knew almost as well as the streets of Mellordale or Moss Side, across the market place, along the flyblown quayside, she searched for Mikhail or his comrades. The atmosphere in the town was like a seething cauldron, ready to boil over at any moment, if nobody seemed sure in which direction, and though several groups with red flags passed by Sarah she didn't know any of the faces.

How could Mikhail have danced with her like that, how could he have said he adored his wild English rose, and then dropped her as if she were a faded petal? Disconsolate, yet angry, Sarah retraced her steps. As she rounded a corner she marched straight into Harry.

Oh heck! she thought. Brightly she said, 'Hello, how's tricks?'

'Fine.'

His cheerful grin was not in evidence, but he turned round and accompanied her along the street. They were crossing the market place when he said, 'I hear you treated the Russians to a display of gipsy dancing the other night.'

Which little bird had told him that? What had Miss Macdonald said? For some reason Sarah gave him the information she normally kept secret. 'My grandmother, my Mam's mam, was a full-blooded gipsy.'

'Truly?' Sarah nodded. 'Didn't know it was Gipsy Napoleon.'

Then Harry said he must be on his way, as he was under orders to drive one of the lorries to take food supplies to Queen Marie in Jassy. Supplies. Jassy. The two words buzzed in Sarah's head. The Unit's urgently needed medical supplies from Britain were stuck in the old Moldavian capital which, since the fall of Bucharest, had become the seat of the Roumanian government. Doctor Inglis was going spare over the delays, Sarah was disgusted with Mikhail Muranov and her own idiotic behaviour – she could do with a break.

'Will you take me with you?'

Harry stared at her in amazement as Sarah explained why she wanted to go to Jassy. He repeated that he was under orders, on an official mission with another member of the squadron.

'Who?'

'Bert Cox.'

'He wouldn't bat an eyelid if the Maharajah of Jodhpur or a gorilla came with you.'

With stout loyalty Harry defended Bert Cox – he was a good bloke to have in a tight corner – but Sarah saw him weighing the attraction of her company, the Unit's need for its medical supplies and the phlegmatic stolidity of Cox, against the fact that he had no business to take a passenger, in particular a woman, on a RNAS mission without permission. Seeing him wavering, she said everybody improvised in the chaos of wartime Russia and once they'd got the Unit's supplies on the move, even if they were found out they'd be forgiven. Exigencies of the hour and all that. Then a thought struck Sarah.

'You are coming straight back, aren't you? You're not staying in Jassy?' Harry said they were staying overnight, driving back tomorrow. 'That's all right then. I'm not on duty until Monday morning.'

Her eyes wide – Sarah had only recently appreciated

how fetching that looked – she gazed up at him. Harry sighed and smiled ruefully. 'All right, you little gipsy witch. We're leaving in . . .' He pushed back the sleeve of his jacket and consulted the large, new-fangled wrist watch. '. . . In three-quarters of an hour, and I'd better get my skating boots on. Look, to be on the safe side, I'll pick you up outside the town, near where we had our picnic. Can you make it in time?'

'Never fear. Sarah will be there.'

They had driven about half a mile from the rendezvous when Sarah saw the unmistakable figure striding towards them, the long blond hair shining like an angel's in the bright sunshine. Mikhail leapt in front of the lorry and Harry swore softly as he applied the brakes.

'Whence are you bound?' Mikhail's excellent English occasionally had an archaic ring.

'To Jassy,' Harry replied.

'I shall accompany you.'

Through gritted teeth Harry said, 'This is not a public omnibus. It's a British lorry on an official mission.'

Mikhail smiled broadly at Sarah who thought: well, I could be part of the mission. There was no stopping him in any case. He was like an elemental force, a human tornado, or hurricane, or earthquake. Swinging his body into the back of the lorry, he settled himself alongside Bert Cox and the food supplies for Queen Marie. In a cloud of dust they resumed their journey. After a few minutes Mikhail leaned his head round the side of the partition that held the rolled-back hood, the silky hair brushed against Sarah's cheek, and half in English, half in Russian, he said, 'What a wondrous sight to behold, *moya samaya dikaya vsekh angliiskikh roz.*'

Sarah did not enquire how he had managed to survive without the wondrous sight of his wildest of English roses for the last week, she just knew she felt twice as alive now he was sitting behind her. Replying in Russian she said, 'Why do you want to go to Jassy?'

'I don't, though it will indubitably be a useful occasion.

All such occasions are. I want to be with you, my beauty, the cynosure of neighbouring eyes.'

She suppressed a smile. Mikhail was impossible with his endless supply of apposite Miltonic lines. Testily Harry said, 'Do you think you could ask him to speak English? Where I come from it's considered ill-mannered to jabber away in a language people don't understand.'

'My profoundest apologies,' Mikhail said in English. 'I forget that you are not as fluent in our tongue as little Sarah.'

You do nothing of the kind, Sarah thought, you know perfectly well he speaks no Russian. But Harry had lost the advantage by asking *her* to ask Mikhail, rather than making the request himself, and Mikhail's calling her 'little Sarah' had added insult to injury. For several miles they drove in silence towards Galatz. Sarah was relieved when they crossed the border into Roumania without going into the town which held so many memories. She presumed Mikhail had fallen asleep in the back, if only for the reason that he was rarely quiet when he was awake. Eventually, she broke the silence.

'Would you like me to navigate?'

'The map's by your side.'

After she had consulted it, with some surprise she said, 'It's quite a long way to Jassy, isn't it?'

'Yes.'

Obviously Harry was still angry. Unaccustomed to being at the centre of a triangle with two men apparently interested in her, Sarah was unsure how to deal with the situation. Her unease was heightened by the knowledge that she had no business to be in the lorry and if anything went wrong not only she, but Harry, would be in severe trouble. Despite her uncertainty and misgivings, the sheer joy of Mikhail's wanting to be with her buoyed her spirits, so cheerfully she surveyed the countryside.

The flat steppe lands shimmered in the heat, carpeted with the fading colours of the spring flowers. In the villages whitewashed houses gleamed in the sunlight, the shed blossom of cherry and almond trees lay heaped on the ground like confetti, acacias were a brilliant yellow against the pale blue of the sky, and willows wept into ponds. Slowly, the Lanchester lorry started to climb into lusher countryside and time seemed to have stood still in these parts. Women wrapped in voluminous skirts and headscarves were tending the vines on the terraced slopes, men were working the soil with ancient wooden implements, and on the higher ground shepherd boys were guarding the sheep.

But time had not stood still. Even here the present intruded.

The terrain had levelled out and they were driving through flat, scrubby uplands when in the distance Sarah saw the column of soldiers coming towards them. A few seconds later the volley of shots sounded in the calm air. Sarah sat up, her body tensing. In Reni they had heard the rumours that, as Mikhail had predicted, the Russian army was disintegrating, soldiers refusing to fight or deserting. For all they knew the Austrians could suddenly have taken advantage of the unstable situation and broken through the Russian lines. These could be enemy troops advancing towards them. She looked at Harry and she could see his brain working fast, deciding whether to drive on or to retreat. As the echo of the rifle shots faded, he chose the former course. He kept one hand steady on the steering wheel but the other dropped to his right side. Quickly, he extracted his bayonet from its scabbard and laid the blade across his knees. The steel flashed wickedly in the bright sunlight.

'There's a rifle and a shotgun behind you, Sarah.'

Her heart thumping, Sarah turned to find the guns and to see Mikhail and Bert Cox leaning round either side of the partition. Harry asked if Cox had fixed bayonet, Bert said he had, and in the same calm, commanding tones Harry went on, 'Give the guns to Muranov, Sarah. You can shoot, I presume?'

Mikhail let out a string of expletives and Sarah was glad Harry did not understand Russian. After she had handed the guns to Mikhail he shaded his eyes to peer at the advancing column, but the glare of the sun and the dust raised by their feet still made it difficult to identify them.

'They could be Russian,' Mikhail said.

'They could be anything,' Harry retorted.

Sarah's armpits were damp, the palms of her hands sweating, her stomach muscles quivering, but Harry was driving the lorry steadily onwards and she was not going to show fear. She would do whatever had to be done, short of actually killing anybody. Then Harry yelled, 'Hell's bells!'

The steering wheel was slipping through his hands like a serpent, frantically he was trying to control the lorry as it veered across the road bumpity-bump, lurching and swaying across the scrubby ground. Sarah felt sure they were about to turn over, she was clinging to the top of the windscreen which was stupid because the glass would smash as they crashed, but with one last bucketing leap Harry managed to stop the lorry.

'Gordon bloody Bennett. That's all we needed. An effing puncture. Pardon my French.'

'Don't mention it,' Sarah gasped.

There were guns and faces all around them. For several seconds Sarah stared at them, temporarily so stunned by her second experience of the malign unpredictability of motorised vehicles that she felt neither fear nor surprise. Then the babble of voices penetrated her mind, she realised they were speaking Russian, they were pointing at her in amazement, excitedly saying it was a woman. One of them said it was a *Shotlandskaya* woman and Sarah smiled with relief. She turned to Harry. 'It's all right. You can re-sheath your bayonet. They're friendly.'

Mikhail had jumped from the back and was saying, 'What happened? What is the matter?'

'The matter is our tyres are made of rubberine for the cold of the Russian winter. In the heat of the summer they tend to burst,' Harry replied drily.

'May I be of assistance?'

'Unless you know how to change a wheel, no.'

128

Harry and Bert Cox set to work to remove the damaged wheel and to replace it with a spare one. While they worked, sweating profusely in the hot sun, half the column milled around offering helpful suggestions in Russian. They were a motley collection of deserters, or true patriots in Mikhail's eyes. He had seized the opportunity to spread the Bolshevik message and was standing in front of the lorry addressing the other half of the men. Every so often several of them excitedly fired their rifles, producing the sound that had so alarmed the occupants of the lorry only a short while ago.

Eventually Harry shouted, 'For Pete's sake, Sarah, tell them to sling their hooks. And get him to hold his meeting and them to do their rifle practice somewhere else.'

Tactfully Sarah translated Harry's requests and the would-be helpful Russians moved back a few feet, while the loquaciously spouting Mikhail retired with his audience to the shade of a scrubby tree.

When the spare wheel was finally fixed and they were back in the lorry, the Russians cheered them on their way. The heat of the day was dying and as they drove through the foothills of the Carpathians the air grew clearer and the distant bulk of the mountains loomed against the late afternoon sky. They dropped down into Jassy surrounded by its bowl of hills, but by the time they reached the outskirts of the city the dusk was falling. Stopping the lorry, Harry shouted to Mikhail to find out where the royal palace was. Mikhail leapt from the back and strode away but he had to accost several people, none of whom seemed lively, before he discovered the required information. Striding back to the lorry, he opened the passenger door and said he would come in the front now, to give directions.

'Little Sarah may sit in my lap.'

Little Sarah had no need to look at Harry's face to know how this proposal had been received. Quickly she climbed down to the road and Bert Cox helped her to clamber over the damaged wheel and into the back of the lorry. Slowly, in the fading light, they drove into Jassy.

Dorothy had passed through the town earlier in the year

and she had said it was a terrible place. Sarah saw what Didi had meant.

Bundles of human rags lay in the gutters, bone-skinny children with heads grown too big for their bodies huddled on the pavements, lacking the energy even to beg. There was none of the normal clatter and clang of a city, though once upon a time, before starvation engulfed it, Jassy must have been a proudly beautiful place, with medieval houses, baroque buildings and intricately carved churches. The few carts and vehicles appeared to be moving on deadened wheels, and the few better-dressed, fatter-looking inhabitants were hurrying silently along, with a detached manner and unseeing eyes.

With the Union Jack fluttering from its bonnet the Lanchester growled slowly through the silent streets and people stood to attention, or tried to, saluting as the lorry passed them. Sarah wanted to sink to the floorboards with anger and embarrassment. Near the centre of the town, in the fast descending darkness, they located the royal palace which was an extraordinary, new, mock-Gothic structure. Apart from being five times as large and lavish, it reminded Sarah of the Town Hall in Manchester.

11

Sarah's arrival at the palace with the food supplies for Queen Marie created only mild surprise. The doings of the Scottish Women's Hospital Unit had passed into local legend and legendary figures could not be expected to behave like normal women. A maid conducted her up a vast staircase into a sumptuous bedroom, dominated by a four-poster bed hung with damask drapes. Carefully, the young girl unpacked Sarah's flannel nightdress and dressing gown, laying them out at the foot of the bed, before extracting her toothbrush, hairbrush, face-cloth, small towel and bar of soap, which she placed on the huge dressing table where they looked absolutely ridiculous. The maid then pantomimed having a wash which Sarah reckoned she could do with, so she nodded.

She was standing by the window, gazing at the moon shining on the gardens below, the impotent anger at the contrast between the luxury of the palace and the sights beyond the railings rushing through her blood, when the maid returned. With her were two large women carrying a porcelain bath, above which clouds of steam were floating. The maid laid the mats she was carrying on the carpet, the two Amazons placed the bath in the middle of them then, holding up Sarah's moth-eaten old dressing gown, the maid indicated the embroidered screen near the bed. When Sarah emerged, wrapped in the dressing gown, the slightly smaller of the two women darted behind the screen to pick up her clothes. Curtseying, both Amazons left the room.

Being helped into the bath, having her hair washed, her body lathered by other hands, being helped out and enveloped in a fleecy towel, then being dusted with a sweetly smelling powder, were among the more extraordinary sensations of Sarah's life. As a once-in-a-lifetime experience she had to admit it was sensuously pleasant and at the moment she was feeling unusually sensuous, abnormally conscious of her body, a condition she refused to admit was solely or wholly the result of Mikhail Muranov's proximity.

There was a knock on the door and the smaller woman re-entered, bearing Sarah's underclothes and her grey orderly's uniform, all immaculately ironed. Deciding she had best let the maid continue to perform the incredibly useless functions for which she had been trained, she allowed the girl to brush her hair and to dress her. When the last button of her uniform was done up, the maid swivelled the full-length mirror on its polished oak stand into a position from which Sarah could inspect herself.

Having battled with the problem of long hair and lice

on the journey through Russia and the retreat through the Dobrudja, once in Reni she and Jenny had found a good hairdresser among the refugees and had their locks shorn. Sarah's thick, straight black hair was now cut sleekly into her neck, with a three-quarter fringe across her forehead. The style suited her, emphasising the colour and size of her dark eyes, somehow softening the sharpness of her features. The image reflected in the mirror showed her hair mahogany tinted by the overhead light, her dark skin had a healthy glow, and in the well-pressed uniform her figure was trim. She would never be a Gaiety Girl – not that she wanted to be one – but Sarah reckoned she would more than pass muster. She smiled at the girl to express her appreciation and the reflection told her she had nice teeth too.

Downstairs they were conducted into a splendid panelled room hung with oil paintings, and were seated round a satin-smooth table, gleaming with silver-gilt cutlery and crystal glasses. Harry sat bolt upright, staring at the array of knives and forks and spoons as if they might bite him, while Bert Cox looked as if he'd been struck by lightning, silently accepting whatever was offered, watching which eating implements other folk picked up before slowly fumbling with his selection. Mikhail hardly ate anything, waving his hand at the servants, pushing his plate away with hugely disgusted gestures. Sarah felt much the same, except she was hungry. What had they been doing bringing food supplies to the palace? Ensuring, presumably, that large meals could continue to be served. Although he ate little, Mikhail drank a fair amount but the alcohol did not loosen his tongue. Instead he sank into a thunderous gloom.

A Roumanian officer, who spoke surprisingly good English, dined with them, though unsurprisingly he refused to speak Russian to Mikhail, there being little love lost between the Russian and Roumanian allies. The officer informed them that King Ferdinand was not at the palace but Prince Carol was and before they departed he wished personally to thank the gallant Englishmen for their ser-

132

vices to Roumania and, the voice dropped to a hushed tone, on being acquainted with the news that one of the Scottish nurses had come with the supplies, tonight Queen Marie wished to meet Miss . . . ?

'Whitworth.'

Sarah saw the officer's agonised expression, but nobody in Russia or Roumania could pronounce her surname properly, apart from Mikhail, and she didn't feel like being helpful.

When they had finished the meal Mikhail stood up and bowed ironically to the Roumanian. 'I shall go into the town.'

'I'll come with you,' Harry said.

'As you wish,' Mikhail replied with melancholy grandeur.

The Roumanian officer leered at them but Sarah doubted they were going in search of a brothel, which was what the lecherous smile assumed. It was more likely Bolsheviks and spare wheels. As the men left the room, Bert Cox walking phlegmatically behind, Harry grinned for the first time since they had left Reni.

'Pussy cat, pussy cat, where have you been? I've been to Jassy to see the Queen. Enjoy your audience, Napoleon.'

The palaver that went on before she was finally escorted into Queen Marie's presence would, Sarah reckoned, have reduced anybody of a nervous, deferential disposition to a quivering wreck, though she was assured there would be no language problem. As Miss Votvurt was aware *their* beloved Queen Marie was a grand-daughter of *her* great Queen Victoria. It was a fact of which Sarah was unaware, though it did not surprise her, because old Victoria's grandchildren littered the thrones of Europe.

Her Majesty was seated in an embroidered armchair in a room overburdened with heavy furniture and *objets d'art*. The chamberlain advanced towards Queen Marie with Sarah, as instructed, following a few paces behind. He bowed so low his nose almost hit the ground and after he had straightened himself up Her Majesty held out an elegantly manicured hand which, as also instructed, Sarah touched briefly and lightly. Despite her anti-royalist sentiments, bearing in mind the reason she was in Jassy, she had managed to make her knees perform the expected obeisance. As she rose from curtseying, contrary to instructions she gazed at Queen Marie who was an astonishingly beautiful woman, with wide eyes and perfectly proportioned features including a jewel of a nose, though she was too heavily made-up and wearing the weirdest get-up of flowing white robes.

'We are pleased to see you, my child. We hold the Scottish Women's Hospital Unit in the highest esteem. What is your name? It is unlikely, we suspect, to be "Votvurt".'

'It's "Whitworth", ma'am.'

'Ah,' Queen Marie smiled slightly. 'And which part of Scotland do you come from?'

Sarah tossed up between Edinburgh and Glasgow and settled for the latter. The Queen said 'Ah' again, Glasgow was not a city she knew well, which was a good thing because Sarah didn't know it at all. Her Majesty then said she wished to satisfy her curiosity. Was it true that the nurses had themselves manned the armoured cars during the regrettable retreat through the Dobrudja? Sarah said, no ma'am, though a vision of Dorothy rat-tat-tatting away on the guns, given half the chance, flashed into her mind. Had Miss Whitworth been among the gallant nurses to whom the Queen had presented medals at Tecuci?

'No, ma'am.'

'That is an omission we shall rectify.'

In a flutter of white drapes Queen Marie waved her hand towards the courtier who walked to an ornate table, to return with a small open box, in the velvet lining of which a medal was nestling. With a further white flutter, the Queen wafted a hand towards Sarah.

Oh heck, Sarah thought, to have that pinned to her uniform she was going to have to kneel down. Still, the whole situation was straight from the Arabian Nights, it had been ever since Mikhail had jumped into the lorry, so without feeling too much of a hypocrite she knelt in front of Queen Marie. As the medal was pinned to her grey dress, she wondered if it carried a pension. In Reni they had all been presented with St George's Crosses by a pomaded, gilded Russian prince and the high-bred idiot had solemnly informed them the decoration carried a pension of one rouble a month for life, barely enough to buy a small cake of soap.

'Thank you, ma'am. It is a great honour to receive this medal from Your Majesty's own hands.'

The Queen smiled graciously.

Having been firmly told that under no circumstances was she to initiate any conversation or to ask questions, but merely to reply briefly to any asked of her, Sarah looked up at Queen Marie.

'May I beg a favour of Your Majesty, on behalf of Doctor Inglis and all the members of the Scottish Women's Hospital Unit? Our supplies, urgent medical supplies, have unfortunately been held up here in Jassy. Would it be possible for Your Gracious Majesty to intervene to . . . um . . .' Sarah's command of flowery language deserted her and in a rush she said, '. . . get our supplies to Reni where they're needed?'

For a few seconds there was a silence, during which the gentle tick-tock of the ormolu clock on the mantelpiece sounded to Sarah like thunder. From the aghast expression on the chamberlain's face she felt that he would, if he could, order her head to be chopped off. Then Queen Marie said, 'We shall make enquiries, my child.'

Sarah's boldness, however, brought the audience to a close and she was escorted to her bedroom where the maid was waiting to undress her. Suddenly feeling absolutely exhausted Sarah allowed her to do so, to pull back the damask counterpane, to assist her into bed, to show her the night-light, to turn off the main lamp, to curtsey and to leave the room.

The softness of the feather mattress and the silkiness of the sheets soothed her weary body but her mind refused to relax, churning over the day's events and the utter, amazing ludicrousness of her, Sarah Amelia Whitworth from Inkerman Street, Mellordale, being in a royal palace. The anger at being here, rather than out in Jassy doing something useful – though what? – again sent the blood rushing through her body. And how had she, who not so long ago had decided she was one of life's useful spinsters, managed to get herself into a situation in which one man was green with jealousy and as for the other . . . thinking about Mikhail Muranov did nothing to calm her blood or restless mind.

There was a tapping on the door. Sarah sat up in bed, her hand felt for and lit the night-light. Her body tense, her mind half-expectant, she called out, 'Who is it?'

The door opened. It *was* Mikhail.

Breathing deeply, Sarah stared at him. He was wearing his day clothes but he had loosened the high-necked blouse so that the folding flap hung down and in the glow of the night-light she could see his throat and the top of his chest. Throwing his arms out wide, in an upward, part supplicating, part demanding gesture, he said, 'May I fully enter?'

The archaic English underlined the implication of his words: the room, and you. As Sarah nodded he advanced towards her, softly quoting:

What hath night to do with sleep?
Night hath better sweets to prove,
Venus now wakes, and wakens Love,
Come, let us our rites begin.

As he walked towards the bed, all the while reciting from *Comus*, he shed his clothes. Sarah had never before seen anybody undress with such bold casual ease, and she watched, mesmerised. Then he was standing by the looped-back drapes of the four-poster, smiling down at her, and he was stark naked. She had never before seen the naked body of an adult male. His was as strong and as sturdy as a tree trunk, his skin was as smooth as polished

136

oak, apart from the line of blond hair running from his navel to the cluster round his private parts. Slowly, her bewitched eyes travelled up towards his face. Still smiling he bent down and with two swift movements he threw the bedclothes to the foot of the bed and pulled the flannel nightdress over her head. Instinctively, Sarah clasped her arms across her small breasts and closed her eyes, for she had never before revealed her naked body to a man.

He was lifting her up, dropping her down in front of him, holding her tightly, flesh against flesh, running his hands up and down her back, pressing her into his crotch. Sarah still had her eyes closed but she could feel him stiffening and thickening, his erection sliding between her legs.

'Relax, my beautiful English rose, relax. Shed your protective thorns. Let your senses bloom.'

With a long shuddering sigh, Sarah opened her eyes and looked up at him. The passion she had subdued for so many years erupted like a volcano. They fell back on to the bed. She was doing things and wanting him to do things to her that she had barely imagined even in the eroticism of her solitary nights. When he thrust himself inside her she felt as if she were a virgin, except her channel was widely, wetly open, but the ecstatic sensation his entry produced was unknown to her. Sarah was roused to a previously unbelievable pitch of pulsating, wriggling, gasping desire as their bodies threshed from side to side of the huge four-poster bed. She responded to his endearments and sexual cries with words she had not known were in her vocabulary, obeying his ravishingly exotic commands. She rode him like a pony, arching her back, thrusting out her breasts, dangling them for him to lick and bite. Then he was rolling her over again and his full weight was upon her, pressing her down into the softness of the feather mattress. They were travelling in unison, faster and faster, upwards and upwards to the heights of Parnassus, the peak of Olympus. She was a hotly running stream and his flood was joining with hers in a confluence of love, a supreme climactic moment that Sarah had never before experienced.

She cried out, 'Give me a baby, Misha, give me a baby.'

Across the breakfast table Sarah gazed at Mikhail, talking animatedly to Harry, his head flung back, the sun burnishing the sleek length of his hair, his hands gesticulating. She wanted to take them in hers, to dance with him in the bands of sunlight streaming through the windows, and to shout, 'I've found out what love is, irony of ironies, in a royal palace, in the arms of a Bolshevik who recites John Milton's poetry like Comus himself! And I am *only* thirty-four years old. The best years of my life are ahead of me.'

'Wake up, Napoleon,' Harry was flicking his fingers under her nose. 'I said, how did it go with Queen Marie last night?'

Emerging from her rapturous reverie of how it had gone with Mikhail, Sarah described her audience with the Queen, which made even Bert Cox laugh and Harry regard her fondly. Realising that in her intoxicated happiness she had flashed him a dazzling smile, the guilt flooded through her. She would just have to tell Harry the truth. It was one of those things that had happened. She could do nothing about her great liking for him in the face of her overwhelming love for Mikhail. At least she hadn't given herself away, as Alice Conway and Guy Kendle had that day at Chenneys – not that she cared if anyone knew except the decent thing would be to tell Harry personally. Maybe his unawareness of her glorious love stemmed from the fact that apart from wishing her 'Good morning' and winking at her as he entered the breakfast room Mikhail had taken little notice of her.

After they had finished the meal, Harry and Bert were led off for their audience with Prince Carol which left Sarah with Mikhail, and a horde of servants. In English she whispered to him, 'I love you, Misha.'

'I love you, *moya lyubimaya, moya* Sabrina.'

The response was somewhat distracted. Then he jumped up and said he was going into the town. Sarah said she would come with him but Mikhail said it was Bolshevik business and her presence, as an Englishwoman, would not be helpful. With a smile and a wave of his hand, he was gone. A maid conducted Sarah into a morning room where disconsolately she flicked through an illustrated book about Roumania, with English captions. What a lot of interesting Roman and Byzantine sites they'd failed to notice in the Dobrudja, she thought sardonically, though she had one memory of the Emperor Trajan's wall emerging in red-gold splendour as the sun broke through an early morning mist.

'That was a wash-out,' Harry said when he and Bert returned from their audience with Prince Carol. 'No cosy chats for us. Half asleep and dead bored he looked. What's happening about your supplies?'

Their supplies – the reason why she had come to Jassy. Purposefully, Sarah went in search of their Roumanian officer whom she didn't locate, though she found Queen Marie's chamberlain who frostily informed her that Her Majesty had issued instructions in regard to the hospital supplies, which could not be implemented today because today was Sunday. Back in the morning room, when she gave Harry this information he said they were staying another night anyway. He hadn't got the damaged wheel repaired and he wasn't driving back to Reni without two good spare wheels unless it was absolutely essential. In the middle of the afternoon Mikhail appeared and, on learning they were staying another night in Jassy, disappeared. He was not present at dinner and after their Roumanian officer had retired they started to talk about England, Harry regaling them with stories of his Cockney relations, even Bert Cox joining in with tales of life on the squire's estate in Suffolk. Sarah realised they were homesick. She had the feeling that Russia and Roumania were on a different planet from England and this was an extraordinary interlude in all their lives.

It was quite late when they went up to their rooms, but Sarah did not feel in the least bit sleepy. Wanting, wanting, she lay in the four-poster bed, waiting, waiting for Mikhail to enter. Eventually she must have fallen asleep because she was awakened by the maid drawing back the curtains and a cup of real English tea being placed by the bedside. When she saw Mikhail at breakfast she intended to be coolly off-hand, but he was not at the breakfast table and Sarah did not know whether to be pleased or angered that he had not returned to the palace. Immediately the meal was finished she went into action to track down their supplies. Their Roumanian officer assured her they would shortly be en route for Reni, but Sarah had heard similar assurances hundreds of times in the Dobrudja so she said she personally wanted to check them. It took several hours of politely nagging persistence before she was finally driven to a large shed in a siding of the railway station. Inside the shed were the wooden crates stamped in English and Russian: 'Medical Supplies. Scottish Women's Hospital Unit. Reni. Urgent.'

On past evidence they would continue to sit there for another month, or two, or six, so she had herself driven back to the palace where Harry said he'd given up on the spare wheel. He agreed to drive the Lanchester to the station, but by the time he and Bert Cox and Sarah had loaded the Unit's medical supplies into the back of the lorry, it was already dusk. Harry said he was definitely not returning to Reni in the dark unless he had to, which he hadn't, so they stayed another night in the royal palace.

About midnight, as Sarah was slipping into sleep, there was a knock on the door. It was Misha, with a bottle of wine and two glasses under his arm. Extraordinary interlude in her life or not, absent for the best part of two days or not, she jumped from the bed and ran towards him. Ensconced in the embroidered armchair, with their arms entwined, they drank from the other's glass. The bottle of sparkling wine drained, Misha pulled her to her feet, shouting:

Meanwhile, welcome joy and feast,
Midnight shout and revelry,
Tipsy dance and jollity . . .

Throwing off their garments, they danced around the room clapping their hands and singing, their naked bodies touching, parting, swaying, undulating as they had on that night round the campfire, until eventually they collapsed in each other's arms on to the feather mattress of the four-poster bed.

The next morning, after a large breakfast, they finally left Jassy. Their Roumanian officer wished them 'Drum bun!' which meant 'good journey' in Roumanian. As on the inward lap Sarah sat in the front with Harry, while in the back with Bert Cox and the Unit's crates Mikhail promptly went to sleep. Sarah herself was feeling pretty tired but she had to tell Harry the truth. She owed him that.

'Harry,' she began, 'there's something I have to tell you. I . . .'

He interrupted. 'You don't have to explain. I'm not that blind. Or deaf, Napoleon.' He gave a short, bitter laugh as her pet name slipped out and for the first time in her life Sarah felt herself blushing. Had she and Misha been so noisy in their lovemaking last night? 'Don't worry. I shan't call you "Napoleon" again. I hope you know what you're doing, Sarah, and you don't get hurt. If you ever need me, you've only to ask.'

The tears prickled Sarah's eyes and she put her hand on his wrist, a gesture she would not have made a few short weeks ago. He had stirred her emotions, but it was Mikhail who had unleashed them. 'I'm sorry, so very, very sorry, if I've hurt you.'

At least she had been saved one unpleasant task. She did not now need to tell him that not only had she had a liaison with a man who'd been killed in the Dardanelles, she had conceived his child, and because she had not wanted his child she had procured a messy back-street abortion which had brought her close to death.

She wanted a child by Misha.

While they were on the road to heaven that first night in the royal palace in Jassy, Misha had assumed it would not be the first time for her – how unlike an Englishman!

– and with a certain arrogance, asked if she had already taken precautions. Sarah had replied in the affirmative, which had been untrue, she had taken no precautions whatsoever. Whether, as a result of her botched abortion, she could have the baby she so desperately wanted, Misha's baby, was a moot point.

12

From the shade of the willows weeping round the pond Sarah watched Jenny and Dorothy's bravura arrival, the dust kicking high behind them as they cantered down the narrow roadway and into the village square on two of the superb Cossack horses the Russians had loaned to the Unit. Barely knowing one end of a horse from the other, Sarah had travelled here with Mariya Fyodorovna and Mr Lohvitzky in the convoy of bullock carts and the local market carts with their basketwork hoods that had left Reni in the mid-morning. The bullocks had bells round their necks, ribbons flew from the carts, and the jollity of the passengers, the presence of so many families with their children, showed that most of them regarded the trip as an outing, a few hours away from the town and the fast deteriorating situation; not necessarily as an endorsement of the best known Bolshevik in the area, Mikhail Muranov, whom they had come to hear speak.

Sarah had returned from Jassy with Harry to find Doctor Inglis spitting fire and brimstone and Commander Gregory in none too happy a mood either, but both had calmed down, as Sarah had predicted they would, when they'd seen the Unit's supplies stacked in the back of the lorry. Almost immediately Harry and the armoured cars had left Reni to take part in the great summer offensive in Galicia which, as Mikhail had anticipated, was a shambles, with whole Russian divisions refusing to fight. Nonetheless the casualties had been appalling; and the supplies vitally needed. At the moment there was a lull in the fighting, so when Sarah had casually suggested they might spend their day off in the country listening to the always interesting Mikhail Maranov, Dorothy as well as Jenny had fallen in with the suggestion.

Tania tottered towards her *Tyotya* Sarah, who caught her by the waist and held her up to the trailing willows. Kicking her legs which still weren't as chubby as they should be, she gurgled happily. In comparison with Kessie's children as babies, Sarah had to admit Tania was slow on the uptake, but she was nonetheless a little love. In England – though Sarah had not yet worked out how to transport her back home – where she would be given lots of love, stability, good food and a good education, Tania would grow into a fine young woman.

Lowering the little girl to the ground, Sarah smiled at Mariya Fyodorovna and her toddlers and at Mr Lohvitzky. Mariya Fyodorovna was in traditional costume, a full-length pale lemon dress with a wide skirt and puffy sleeves caught in tightly at the wrists, on top a dark green apron, its high bib elaborately ruched and embroidered, a small fringed shawl draped round her shoulders. The inevitable headscarf, worn by all but the 'ladies' of the region, was a silky, Sunday-best affair. Fastidiously, Mr Lohvitzky brushed the drifting pollen from his ancient suit. A slight breeze was now stirring the willows, rustling their silvery undersides, cooling the ferocious heat of the afternoon.

There was a murmur among the crowd already thick in the square, followed by cheering, and Sarah saw Mikhail's instantly identifiable figure moving among them, the page-boy hair bleached platinum by the weeks of unrelenting sunshine.

'Mikhail,' she waved as she called out, 'Mikhail.'

Not immediately, which was typical, but after a while he came towards them. His advent caused Mr Lohvitzky to brush his suit furiously and Mariya Fyodorovna to blush with nervous excitement. Sarah reckoned it would be the next generation at least before the likes of them faced the likes of Mikhail four-square. Bending low under the drooping willows he squatted on his haunches by their side, giving Sarah a wink but otherwise greeting her as if she were no more than an acquaintance.

That he loved her still faintly astonished Sarah, but that uninhibited, extrovert Misha wished to keep their liaison quiet, did not. For though he held John Milton, Oliver Cromwell and the English Civil War in glorious esteem, and as a consequence was not without admiration for England, the majority of his Bolshevik comrades were vociferously unadmiring of her native land. Misha's involvement with an Englishwoman was not therefore something he wanted to shout about, and as Sarah was unaccustomed to flaunting her personal emotions the secrecy did not bother her.

'Hello, you've found a nice cubby-hole.' Dorothy crawled under the willows. Seeing Mikhail she said, 'Oh hello. I thought we'd come to hear you speak.'

'You have,' Mikhail stood up, nodding to Jenny who was behind Dorothy.

Jenny gushed about wanting to talk to him after the meeting, whereupon he bestowed his widest smile upon her, though Sarah doubted she came high on his list of priorities. As he pushed apart the curtain of the leaves, lifting the children in front of him, he whispered to Sarah, 'You I will see after the meeting, *moya* Sabrina, yes?'

With a brief smile, she nodded. Then Jenny insisted they stay just where they were for a few seconds, because the sun was absolutely in the right place, the willows and the pond made a lovely backcloth, and she wanted to take a picture. She extracted her camera from the satchel round her shoulder, squinted through the viewfinder, and waved them into a tighter group. Naturally – it seemed natural, anyway – Mikhail assumed the central position, Sarah stood on one side with Tania in her arms, Dorothy on the other, Mr Lohvitzky and Mariya Fyodorovna self-consciously forming the wings, her children in the foreground.

The photograph taken, Mikhail strode through the crowd, which parted before him as the Red Sea before Moses, towards the red flags fluttering in the gentle breeze round the makeshift platform. Following in his wake, Sarah and her friends found a good position near the front.

From the minute he started to speak Mikhail had the crowd in his thrall, with the demagogic orator's ability to wipe the mind clean of doubts, to make the audience believe that what he was uttering was the truth, the whole truth and there could be no other truth. Must all power be with the *soviets*? Yes. Must there be an immediate truce on all fronts and a just peace between peoples? Yes. Must the land be given to the peasants and workers control industry? Yes and yes. Must there be an honestly elected constituent assembly in Russia? Absolutely yes. Who cared for the people and would bring these urgently required measures to pass? None but the Bolsheviks. The shadows were lengthening round the platform as he neared the peroration, he was holding his arms wide to the heavens, his voice was soaring, and Sarah was expecting him to quote Milton.

Then it happened.

The sound came first, the steadily increasing thud which made the ground tremble. Momentarily Sarah wondered if it was the prelude to an earthquake before she realised that the thudding noise was coming from one direction only, from the roadway that led into the square to the far left of the platform. On the platform Mikhail stopped in mid-sentence, his head swivelled round and with simultaneous movements hundreds of necks turned towards the thunder of oncoming sound.

Emerging from a cloud of dust, cantering two abreast, they swept into the square, riding straight through the crowd towards the platform. Sarah saw the black Cossack hats, she saw the sun glinting on the guns, she saw them spitting orange flames, before she heard the terrible rat-tat-tatting.

'Dear God,' she heard Dorothy shout, 'they've got machine-guns.'

For what seemed to Sarah an eternity she stood trans-fixed, clutching Tania to her bosom. In that eternity, amidst the screaming pandemonium, the clang of the horses' hooves on the hard-baked earth, the snort of their nostrils, she saw the Cossack soldiers reining, swerving, sharply turning their steeds round and round, up and down, in and out of the domino shapes of white sunlight and lengthening shadow. All the while the Cossacks fired the heavy machine-guns from the backs of their horses, suddenly lifting them in the air in a *feu de joie*, so that the bullets dropped like hailstones on to the kingdom below, the kingdom of the primordial god Chaos.

'Get under the platform,' Dorothy's voice shrieked. 'Under the platform.'

There was blood running from the platform and Mikhail had disappeared.

Clutching the howling Tania in her arms, Sarah lunged towards the wooden planks but as she moved she was hurled to the ground. Fleetingly, as she fell, she noticed that Dorothy was in a crouched position, her left hand on her right knee, to steady her upraised right hand.

In her right hand she held a pistol.

Lying with her face pressed into the shaking, reverberat-ing earth, above the murderous cacophany, Sarah thought she heard the sharper, evenly spaced sounds of Dorothy firing the pistol. There was a heavy weight on top of her. She had to get up because Tania had fallen from her arms as she fell. She had to find the little girl, as she had to find Mikhail, but she could not shift the weight which was shutting out the light, muffling sound, so that Sarah could feel, rather than hear, the continuing chaos. The weight, she realised, was of dead bodies, pushing her down into the bowels of the earth, into those nether regions from which all the demons of hell had emerged, slowly suffocat-ing her . . . The next thing she knew her head was on somebody's shoulder and a cup was being held to her lips.

'Come on Sarah, drink this.'

The voice was Dorothy's. How terribly English it sounded, crisply, commandingly redolent of governesses

146

and nursery teas. Sarah sipped the water and muzzily shook her head. Propped against Dorothy's shoulder she was sitting not far from the platform which had collapsed, its blood-spattered planks leaning drunkenly in the air. Slowly her eyes travelled round the square.

Round the platform and piled by the two narrow exits were bodies, human and animal, lying in grotesque attitudes that Sarah had seen before, positions which in life their limbs could not attain. Overturned carts, fragments of the basketwork hoods, red flags, shoes, a gaudy headscarf, a bunch of twisted ribbons, were strewn across the square. The full realisation that the gunfire had stopped, the snorting horses and their Cossack riders had departed, and that the sounds she could hear were screams of agony, children's sobs, and shrieks of lamentation, came after Sarah's eyes had absorbed the images.

Then, by her side, she noticed the long thin body stretched out and the stain seeping from it was darkening the shadows. From the suit, the old, well-pressed, green-with-age suit, Sarah knew it was Mr Lohvitzky's dead body. Dorothy's gaze followed hers.

'He was machine-gunned,' she said brusquely. 'He must have died instantly. He can't have suffered.'

The words jarred Sarah's dazed, numbed mind. Loudly she said, 'Where's Tania?'

'I think she's with Mariya Fyodorovna. She's over there.'

Struggling to stand upright, Sarah said, 'Where's Mikhail Muranov? What happened to him?'

'He was alive last time I saw him.'

Dorothy tried to persuade her to stay put, but Sarah reacted so fiercely that Didi helped her to walk the few yards towards Mariya Fydorovna who was propped against the wall of a house. Her legs were stuck out in front of her, her beautiful lemon dress and the ruched, embroidered apron were blotched with blood, and her toddlers were clutched one under each arm. Tania was not with them but although Sarah shook her hard, asking where the little girl was, she realised it was no use. Maryia Fyodorovna and her children were not badly wounded, but she was in a state of total shock, her eyes staring blankly, her sole movements a convulsive jerking of her arms round the cowering bodies of her two little boys.

'I must find Tania.'

Desperately, Sarah's eye searched through the mayhem. The far side of the square by the pond was still sunlit, a mockingly bright light which shone on the willows weeping into the blood red water. Suddenly she saw him, or rather she first saw the sun gleaming on his platinum hair. In his arms he was carrying a child, not Tania, the shape was too large, but Misha had survived.

Suddenly Dorothy rushed away, shouting, 'What on earth do you think you're doing? You're supposed to be a nurse. Have you seen Tania? She's missing.'

Dully Sarah's gaze followed Dorothy, who was furiously hitting Jenny's arm. Jenny herself was standing calmly snap-shotting. What an extraordinary thing to do, Sarah thought, and she herself was a nurse, she should be helping with the wounded. But she had to find Tania. Where was she?

It was the dress she recognised, the blue-check gingham, ankle-length dress that Mariya Fyodorovna had made for her with the material Sarah had bought in Reni. She was lying face downwards, squashed between two obviously dead bodies, quite close to the platform. Why hadn't she noticed her before, Sarah thought, as she ran towards the child, but the sudden movement made her feel dizzy and she had to rest for the moment. Closing her eyes she put her fingers to her forehead, massaging it vigorously to clear the fuzziness. When she opened her eyes Dorothy was on the ground, lifting Tania into her arms. Stumbling towards them Sarah sank to her knees and commanded, 'Give her to me.'

Gently, with her index fingers, Dorothy closed the wide-open, staring grey eyes, the way little Con closed the eyes of her dolly. Tania was not a doll, she was a little girl, *Tyotya* Sarah's little girl.

'She's dead, Sarah.'

'Of course she's not dead. Give her to me.'

Silently Dorothy placed the limp body into Sarah's arms,

before furiously she pushed her spectacles up on her nose. There was congealing blood round a livid bruise on Tania's right temple, matting the browny-gold hair, but her body was quite warm. Rocking the little girl in her arms, kissing her hair, softly Sarah started to sing the lullaby Mam had sung to her when she was a bairn.

'Don't, Sarah, don't.' Dorothy's voice was croaking with emotion the way it had during the drive to Galatz.

'Oh no,' Jenny was kneeling beside them, saying no, over and over again. The child could not be dead. They could not have found her in the snow outside Galatz and christened her Tania in the name of the Father, the Son and the Holy Ghost, for her to die a few months later in the sunshine outside Reni. It was stupid, too pointless, too futile a gesture even for God, the Father, or His Son, or the Holy Ghost.

'Somebody's got to ride back to Reni to get help.' Dorothy jumped up. From the satchel over her shoulder she pulled out a handkerchief to blow her nose, and the pistol fell to the ground. Sarah saw a hand pick it up and she knew it was Misha's before she heard him speak.

'I think I owe you my life.'

As if she were watching a scene in a strange play, Sarah saw Mikhail bow slightly as he handed the pistol to Dorothy, who stared at it for several seconds. Then in a flat voice she said, 'It was my brother Georgie's. He died at Givenchy. They send all their personal belongings home, you know.'

'You are a good shot and you have a cool head. You came prepared. So should we have done.'

Suddenly, the fury erupted in Dorothy. She almost spat at Mikhail, 'Why can't you fight the real enemy, the Huns, instead of fighting each other and slaughtering the innocents, you and the damned Cossacks.'

'The Cossacks slaughtered my people with Lewis guns given to them by the English, your people, who trained them to use your English guns.'

'Not to murder helpless men, women and children, they didn't, that's not what they trained them for.'

149

Frowning, Sarah looked at Mikhail and Dorothy. What were they shouting about? Who cared whose guns they were? The only thing that mattered was that a few hours ago Tania and the rest of them had left Reni for an afternoon's outing and now they were . . . Sarah's mind accepted the fact. Tania was dead, murdered, her little skull shattered.

Misha dropped to his knees by her side. The wrathful expression banished, gently he touched her shoulder. 'Come, Sarah, there is work to be done. You are needed.' Then, his voice at its most tender and compassionate, softly he recited, '"O fairest flower, no sooner blown than blasted, Soft silken primrose fading timelessly, Summer's chief honour . . ."'

His deep voice flowing over her, kneeling as if they were in church, with Milton's lines of lamentation they performed the last personal rites for the dead child.

13

The Daimler took the steep hill out of Ryby-in-Furness village with majestic ease in top gear, Kessie noted, and as it turned a sharp bend the chauffeur pointed out Ryby Hall. Built in the local grey stone, beautifully proportioned, probably late eighteenth century, she thought, it stood amidst trees on the hillside, overlooking the sweep of Lake Coniston. In the bright July sunshine the water was reflecting the blue of the sky, the white of the swiftly moving clouds, and the green and purple of the heather-strewn hills. Brooding over the lake at the far end, the Old Man of Coniston sheered up to the sky.

When they drew up in front of the entrance to Ryby Hall, Kessie adjusted Anne and Con's bonnets and repeated what she had said a dozen times on the train.

'You're to be on your very best behaviour. Don't speak unless you're spoken to.'

'Not at all?' Anne asked. 'Not even to Uncle Guy's little boy?'

'Yes, well, you may talk to him. And he's not little. He's five years older than you are.'

A middle-aged footman ushered them into a cool, elegant room, where Mr and Mrs Kendle senior, Mrs Guy Kendle and her son Julian, were waiting to greet them. The boy was like his father in looks, already quite tall, if gangling with thirteen year old awkwardness, and he had the same soft brown eyes as Guy, the same thick lashes, the same long neck that tilted to one side as he spoke. Not that Julian, or Anne and Con, were allowed to say anything much because the minute the introductions were effected, the children were led away to have luncheon by themselves.

'You have two pretty daughters,' Mr Kendle murmured.

'Thank you,' said Kessie.

In fact, Anne was not a pretty child, striking perhaps with her dark eyes and unusual copper-coloured hair. Con was more conventionally pretty, with neat features, softly waving auburn hair and the dimple in her chin like Tom's. As they disappeared her daughters did look nice, their fine cotton dresses beautifully pleated, white gloves and knee-socks immaculately clean, patent leather, ankle-strapped shoes shining, straw bonnets demure.

'God has, I believe, blessed you with two other children, Mrs Whitworth,' Mrs Guy Kendle said softly.

'Er yes.' Kessie seldom thought of her children as blessings, though she supposed they were. The remark had doubly startled her because Mrs Kendle – Guy had never mentioned her Christian name – had spoken as if God were a personal friend.

'Such a pity your husband was unable to accompany you,' said the older Mrs Kendle.

Tom had not the slightest idea she was visiting Ryby Hall. *En famille* they were staying in The Dales and they had been invited to a Thorpe family wedding in north

Lancashire but Tom had never been overfond of Kessie's relations and at the last minute he had cried off, pleading political duties. Leaving the twins in Tom's hands, she had travelled to the wedding with her other daughters. Kessie had also hatched her plan, designed to stop Alice putting into practice her recent threats to have things out with *that woman* person to person, by promising to make a detour to Ryby Hall and speak to Mrs Guy Kendle herself. What she was going to say on the subject of her husband and his mistress, his pregnant mistress, Kessie had not the faintest notion.

Luncheon was a deadly affair, the servants obsequiously dishing out the food, of which there appeared to be no shortage at Ryby Hall, and everyone speaking in hushed tones. Mr Kendle Kessie did not dislike but, though she hated to admit it because she thought women should stick together, she had no rapport with the two Mrs Kendles. Physically they were not alike – the older woman was a brown-haired Junoesque figure, while Guy's wife was a pale, very pale, version of Alice – but mentally mother and daughter-in-law came from the same peapod.

'Do you not find short skirts *draughty*?' Mrs Kendle senior enquired, though what she meant was 'immodest'. Both women's skirts swept the ground.

'No. They're very practical in this day and age.'

'It depends what sort of life one leads,' Mrs Guy Kendle said softly. 'You are, I believe, politically active?'

'Yes. Wasn't it exciting, the debate about votes for women?' The two Mrs Kendles looked as if it were the least exciting news they had ever heard, so Kessie continued with extra vivaciousness. 'I must say it was gratifying, after all our years of struggle, to see the Commons chamber absolutely packed. I've never heard such a buzz of anticipation before a debate and, though I say it myself, Tom made a brilliant speech . . .' The two Mrs Kendles blinked simultaneously and Kessie realised why Guy never mentioned his wife's christian name. In this house such usage was taboo. She amended her error. ' . . . my husband, I mean. When the debate was over, I just crossed my fingers and held my breath. When the count was announced and it was 385 in favour of our inclusion in the Bill and only 55 against, I wanted to stand up and sing dear old Ethel Smythe's *March of the Women* at the top of my voice! I really do believe we are on our way to making the breakthrough at last, and obtaining the vote for a few million women at least!'

The older Mrs Kendle said personally she had never been able to understand the fuss about women's suffrage. She enlarged upon the themes of the laws of God and nature and the separate spheres the Almighty had wisely ordained for men and women. Mrs Guy Kendle entirely agreed with her mother-in-law. Both ladies were glad the vote, if it were to be given to women, should be restricted to older, responsible females of the better type. Remembering the reason for her visit and what Tom always said about wasting your energy hitting your head against brick walls, with difficulty Kessie restrained her temper.

After the Nesselrode pudding had been served, young Mrs Kendle said her husband had informed her that Mrs Whitworth's sister-in-law was serving in Russia. They did communicate then, Kessie thought, although the tone indicated that Mrs Kendle had her doubts about going quite so far, geographically and otherwise.

'You must be concerned for your sister-in-law's safety, Mrs Whitworth,' said the older woman. 'The news from Russia is quite awful, is it not? One can only pray, as we do, that the latest offensive will be successful, though with those dreadful Jewish agitators creating havoc for their own purposes and . . .'

'Which dreadful Jewish agitators?' Kessie's anger got the better of her manners.

'Do you not read *The Times*?' The extra softness of Mrs Guy Kendle's voice rebuked the rude interruption. 'These Anarchists, or Leninites, or Bolsheviks, or whatever they call themselves, they are all Jewish terrorists. There's that Trotsky man and that Lenin person's real name is Zederblum.'

'Really? It's not what my sister-in-law tells me in her letters and she's on the spot.'

'So are *The Times*' correspondents.' The young Mrs Kendle's voice was so quiet that Kessie had to strain to hear her words. 'One may perhaps believe they have a wider perspective and a greater political understanding than your sister-in-law, if you will forgive my saying so.'

This time with the greatest difficulty Kessie controlled her temper and her tongue, and eventually the meal came to an end. She could only hope that Anne and Con had enjoyed the company of Julian Kendle more than she had his mother's or grandmother's. When they were back in the cool elegance of the drawing room and the children were ushered into the adults' presence, Anne's expressive face said they had not.

Leaning over the back of the armchair in which Kessie was seated, she whispered, 'He's horrible, Mummy. He doesn't like girls and he's terribly stuffy.'

Gently, Julian's mother coughed. Well-mannered little girls did not whisper in company. In her soft, contained voice she suggested that after they had allowed their food to digest, her son might take Mrs Whitworth's daughters for a walk round the estate.

'Not too far. And keep to the paths.' She turned to Kessie. 'I'm sure you will wish to have a rest, Mrs Whitworth. Your health, I believe, is not, alas, of the best.'

When she was upstairs having her rest, Kessie wondered how on earth Guy and that woman had come to marry. They could never have had anything in common; except of course their Roman Catholicism and their landed heritage. After about half an hour, Anne's voice floated through the shaded but open window.

'I don't want to see your chapel.'

'Neither do I.' Little Con's voice supported her sister.

'In fact, I don't want to go for a walk with you at all.'

'Neither do I,' said Con.

'That makes three of us.' Julian's voice was about to

154

break and it swooped between a boy's treble and a man's growl.

After a pause Anne said, 'Is there anything interesting to see?'

'Of course there is,' Julian said indignantly.

'Well, show us that then.'

The crunch of their feet on the gravel receded. A further half hour elapsed, while Kessie lay staring at the stuccoed ceiling and the floral designs on the anaglypta cornices, her mind as restful as the guns thundering on the Western Front. Then there was a knock on the door and the maid entered to enquire if Mrs Whitworth would care to join Mrs Guy Kendle in the arbour. Holding a parasol over her head to protect her from the sun, a footman escorted Kessie to the arbour. It was a journey of delight.

In front of the house ran a grey stone wall, against which stood the tallest flowers, hollyhocks, delphiniums, monk's hoods, arum lilies, lupins, gladioli, then came the tiger lilies, huge white-faced marguerites, ranks of iris, candytuft, phlox and fragile gypsophila. A spread of orange eschscholtzia held their petals wide to the sun, strawberry coloured geums extended their delicate circles, and in the rockery yellow roses of sharon massed behind the blue of the lobelia and the white of the alyssum. The herbaceous borders led into the rose garden where the trellises were thick with ramblers, magnificent blooms covered the bush roses in every colour from palest white to darkest crimson and rare purple, and the perfume was intoxicating. The rose garden dropped down into the arbour which was the shady bower of poets' dreams, formed partly by man in an intricate lattice-work of climbing plants, partly by nature in overhanging trees.

Kessie knew both why Guy loved the place, and why he had fled.

His wife was sitting on a rustic bench in the shadiest part of the arbour. Graciously, she motioned for Kessie to join her, asking if she had enjoyed her rest. Politely, untruthfully, Kessie said she had, before genuinely enthusing about the loveliness of the gardens. Mrs Kendle admitted she oversaw their perfection and there was a trace of enthusiasm in her voice. Then enough was obviously enough; one must not exaggerate.

'I wonder where the children are?' She pushed her hand at a cloud of midges which rose like fermenting beer, to hover above her head.

'Anne and Constance love exploring.' Kessie felt she should employ Con's full, proper name.

'Do they?' It was not, Kessie felt, a feminine trait of which Mrs Kendle approved. After a pause, during which she again hit out at the midges, she said, 'Do you know what I miss more than anything since the outbreak of hostilities?' At this sign of a confidence, Kessie leaned forward interestedly. 'Our chaplain volunteered in 1914 and we have no resident priest on the estate.'

'Tom says the RC padres are among the very best. Everybody respects them, whatever their religion, because they go into the front-line trenches and make themselves useful.'

Kessie had aimed to be friendly but her remarks were received like a dollop of cold porridge. Perhaps she should have said 'my husband' and she should not have said 'RC', or suggested that padres weren't always useful. Surprisingly, Mrs Kendle continued the conversation.

'In wartime one needs spiritual comfort more than ever, does one not? One needs to hold firm to one's moral values. The breakdown of morality in some areas is most distressing, do you not agree? One reads of the fearful rise in the rates of illegitimacy, of women who, in the urge to gratify their animal lusts, are heedless of the sanctity of marriage. I am sure that is not what you envisaged, Mrs Whitworth, when you fought for what you see as women's rights.'

Her words had not exactly emerged in a rush, but the tempo of Mrs Kendle's softly measured speech had increased. She wants me to know, Kessie felt sure, that she's aware of her husband's liaison with another woman, with whom I'm more than acquainted, and it sounds as if she knows about Alice's baby too. If she does, what a bitter pill that must be for her to swallow, for Alice had told Kessie the marriage had disintegrated years ago, shortly after Julian's birth, when doctors had warned that another child could kill Mrs Kendle.

Looking at her swatting away at the midges – if she left them alone, they might swarm off – Kessie felt a pang of pity for her. What could she say to a woman who had built a defensive moat round her emotions and pulled up the drawbridge? Which was of paramount importance to Guy? His love for Ryby Hall, or his love for Alice and their unborn child? Kessie was considering these fearfully difficult questions, when echoing up through the woods came the sound of the children's voices.

'Julian dear,' Mrs Kendle called out. At least she used her son's christian name. 'We're in the arbour.'

Abruptly the voices stopped. There was quite a long silence, followed by some whispering. Mrs Kendle called out peremptorily, 'Julian, what are you doing? Come and escort Mrs Whitworth and me back to the house.'

The crackle of dry twigs underfoot preceded the children's slow appearance, in single file, under the archway into the arbour, Con first, Anne next, with Julian bringing up the rear. In the appalled silence Kessie put her hands to her mouth to stop herself from laughing out loud. Comparatively speaking Con looked respectable, apart from her squashed bonnet, but Anne was gloveless, the pleats of her dress were filthy, her flattened bonnet and sodden socks were in her hand, and she was hopping on one ankle-strapped foot because the other was shoeless. As for Julian – Kessie clamped her hand over her mouth – his young country gentleman's outfit of fine tweed jacket and knickerbockers was not only soaking wet, it was covered in green slime, and his boy's bowler had had a dent in it.

Mrs Kendle rose slowly to her feet, stretching herself to her full height, and she was as tall as Kessie. 'What on earth have you been doing?'

'I'm s-sorry, M-mama, b-but . . .' Julian stuttered.

Anne hopped forward. 'It was my fault. I wanted to

paddle in the stream, 'cos it was hot, and I took my shoes and socks off and my shoe shot over the waterfall and Julian tried to rescue it but the stones are all covered in moss and they're very slippy and he fell into the water. Con and I went to rescue him and I trod on Julian's hat and Con's too and she trod on mine. And it wasn't Julian's fault, honestly it wasn't, he was trying to rescue my shoe.'

Anne's explanation tumbled out like the waterfall over the mossy stones. The picture of the three of them rushing around trying to rescue each other and stamping on each other's hats, made Kessie feel quite hysterical and she knew her shoulders were shaking. Mrs Kendle, however, was looking straight at Julian who was standing awkwardly, his head to one side, gangling over the two girls.

'I k-know I was in ch-charge, M-mama. I-I accept f-full responsibility.' He managed to get 'responsibility' out without stammering.

His mother transferred her icy gaze to the girls and said in icier tones, 'You had better return to the house, wash yourselves, and retire to your rooms.'

'But we haven't had our tea,' Anne protested.

'Your tea!' Mrs Kendle came as near to expressing real emotion as Kessie now considered her capable. 'Little girls who behave as you have just behaved go to bed without their tea.'

Kessie could have hit her. Any pang of sympathy for the woman disappeared and in as icy a voice as Mrs Kendle's she said, 'Please don't bother about tea. We shan't be staying the night. We'll leave immediately.'

Anne sneezed loudly. Mrs Kendle surveyed her bedraggled form and said, 'Please do not be stupid, Mrs Whitworth.'

Seizing Anne by one hand, Con by the other, Kessie marched them under the archway and up towards the house. The action was to prevent her really losing her temper and to stop Anne from saying anything more because her scowling face said she did not like her mother being called 'stupid'.

'We're sorry, Mummy,' Con said as Kessie marched

them through the rose garden. 'And Julian's quite nice, acksherly, when you get to know him.'

'Good. And so you should be sorry.'

'I hate this place,' Anne said, 'I want to go back to Daddy.'

You're not the only one, Kessie thought, though she could hear Tom's voice saying: what the hell did you think you were doing, traipsing up to Ryby Hall, knocking yourself out, poking your nose into other folks' affairs?

14

They buried Tania and Mr Lohvitzky side by side in the Russian Orthodox cemetery in Reni. He had been a practising member of that branch of the Christian faith, Sarah knew, and so long as it was decently done it did not matter to her how or where Tania was laid to rest. Misha and she had paid their last respects in the carnage of the square.

Since that shattering afternoon she had seen him once, briefly. A note had been delivered to the hospital, asking her to meet him at their usual rendezvous in a couple of hours' time. Asking Vera to cover for her, Sarah had slipped away to the boathouse on one of the lakes outside the town. The tall reeds, the floating mats of water plants, the yellow and white of the water-lilies were as peacefully beautiful as ever, but Sarah had stared blankly at them as she listened to Mikhail talking. He was a marked man, he was therefore returning to Odessa, but he would almost certainly be going to Petrograd where the struggle was entering its final phase, he would keep in touch, and if she could come to Petrograd . . .

'Why don't you have your hair cut?' she remembered

saying. 'You might as well go around with the imperial crown on your head.'

Then she had wept and he had kissed away the tears, murming endearments, *Sarochka moya, moya lyubimaya*. They had clung to each other and as they parted he had said, '*Vstretimsya snova.*'

Would they ever meet again?

The days following the funeral passed in a blur. They were not particularly busy at the hospital, at least not by Dobrudja or recent standards. Largely unoccupied, Sarah's mind went over and over that afternoon like the needle across a gramophone, always sticking in the groove that if only she hadn't called out to Mikhail and they hadn't followed him, Tania might be alive because the worst of the casualties had occurred around the platform. Sarah kept telling herself that 'if only' were the two most futile words in the English language, but it didn't help.

Jenny developed the photographs she had taken that afternoon. They were among the best she had shot, the ones taken during and after the massacre vivid and terrible, the one before happily informal. In the centre of the group Mikhail looked magnificent, the sun gleaming on his long blond hair; on the outside, standing like a long thin pole, Mr Lohvitzky had the hint of a smile on his thin lips; with her short hair and trousers Dorothy looked like a lad; and in Sarah's arms little Tania beamed up at her *Tyoten'ka*. The scalding tears ran down Sarah's cheeks. She could hardly bear to put the picture by her bedside but it was the last tangible memory of the child and the old man. Sometimes in the middle of the night, when Sarah woke panting and sweating from the nightmare in which she was buried beneath a pile of dead bodies, helplessly watching the shining black Cossack horse cantering towards Tania and crushing her skull, she switched on her torch and lay on her bed, gazing at the happy images Jenny's camera had captured.

'Are you going to be a photographer, when this lot's over?' she asked Jenny. 'Seriously, professionally, I mean?'

A look of astonishment at Sarah's amazing perspicacity flickered across Jenny's face before she said, 'I admit I have thought about it. I'll need to learn more about the job. But it is an increasingly important form of history, isn't it? The pictorial record. We women should be involved.'

'It's your gut reaction, to photograph a scene. When I first noticed you, you were calmly snap-shotting among the carnage.'

Stung by this comment which she obviously took as a criticism of her behaviour, Jenny said, 'You're cool and calm when you're nursing, when your personal emotions aren't involved. We have to be, otherwise we couldn't function.'

'True,' said Sarah.

Within a few days they were again nursing round the clock, as the wounded flooded in from another catastrophic offensive. In a terrible way Sarah was grateful, because it took her mind off her grief and sense of guilt, and she was so tired when she fell on to her truckle-bed that the nightmares stopped.

Stephen and Dorothy returned from somewhere called Varnitza which was in the foothills of the Carpathians, where Stephen had been in charge of a field dressing station and Dorothy had joined her. They had welcome news of Harry and the armoured car squadrons which when last heard of had been at a place called Kozova.

'Though I expect they'll have retreated by now,' Stephen said. 'It's chaos, Sarah, absolute *bloody* chaos.'

'Still it was jolly exciting at Varnitza, wasn't it?' Dorothy said, while the three of them snatched a hasty cup of tea before going on duty. 'We were really in the front lines there. Before the shooting match started I persuaded one of the Russians, quite a decent chap actually, to take me into a forward trench. It was about ten feet high which meant I couldn't see anything, so I climbed up the fire-step. The Russian chappy assured me nobody took snipers seriously in that neck of the woods. It was a narrow valley and I could see the Germans across the river. In fact, one

161

of them waved at me, so I waved back. Got a bit noisy in the end though, didn't it, Stephen?'

Stephen nodded and her nostrils twitched rapidly as she said, 'We were shelled for two days and nights at that range. Had to pack up eventually and scarper in the dark. Had the distinct feeling I'd been there before.'

Literal-minded Dorothy frowned, before the light dawned. 'Oh, you mean it was like the retreat through Montenegro and the Dobrudja. Oh yes!'

At times, listening to Dorothy, you could be forgiven for thinking she was an entirely emotionless, nerveless creature, though Sarah knew that was not true. From her infancy, she decided, Didi had viewed life as open warfare, to be waged against selected opponents, her governesses, her brothers, idiot men who wouldn't let women have the vote. Now there was this Great War in which her particular temperament was given full rein and official blessing. For Dorothy was of the rare breed that thrived on danger, rising like a cork from a champagne bottle to occasions such as driving to Galatz, waving at German soldiers, or coolly firing her pistol at a Cossack horseman with a machine gun.

They were into the sweltering month of August before the flood of casualties became a trickle, and the year's contracts Sarah and Jenny had signed with the Scottish Women's Hospital Unit were nearly up. Half the Unit, on shorter-term contracts, had already gone home. With the chaotic conditions in Russia few replacements had arrived, and Doctor Inglis was trying to persuade the members of her diminishing band to sign on for a further unspecified period.

'Have you heard?' said Jenny, 'Didi's volunteered to stay. I can't think why. She's always going on about how much she hates Russia and the Russians and their beastly revolution. I thought she'd be off home like a shot the minute her contract was up.'

If you don't understand why she's staying – because Stephen is – I shan't bother explaining, Sarah thought.

They were sitting on their truckle-beds, the sticky heat

was like a mass of tiny ants crawling over their skins, so in unladylike manner they had both stripped to their under-garments. Jenny had taken to wearing those new-fangled bust-bodices which she said were ever so practical and stopped you flopping all over the place, but as Sarah hadn't much to flop she still wore her camisole.

'I think I shall volunteer to stay, too,' Jenny said. 'I know the fighting's worse than futile now, but those poor misguided boys need somebody to tend their wounds, don't they?' You'd also like to stay in the thick of the revolution, Sarah thought. 'What are you going to do?'

'I think I'm going home.'

'Really?' Jenny's face dropped. 'Gosh, Sarah, why? Oh, I shall miss you.'

Sarah did not explain why, but the other day in the market place somebody had slipped a note into her hand. It was from Misha, giving her an address in Petrograd where he could be contacted. Those members of the Unit who had already gone home had travelled via Petrograd. There was nothing to keep her in Reni now, except perhaps a sense of duty and Sarah felt she had given her fair whack of that. She loathed the heat as much as she had hated the freezing winter, day after day of unrelenting sunshine, and although they all got on well together considering their diverse backgrounds and beliefs, after twelve months of close proximity she reckoned she could do with a change of companions. Sarah had therefore decided not to sign on again but to go home via Petrograd where she would find Misha and . . . well, they'd see when they met.

Then the delayed cable from Newfoundland arrived and after Jenny had perused it she said, 'I shan't be staying after all.'

What was it now? Sarah wondered. Had her brother Callum finally coughed his lungs out? Or was it her brother Hamish who had again been wounded during the battle for Vimy Ridge? Full of concern she crossed to Jenny who with a frown, explained, 'My parents ask me to return to England to be with Hamish. They say I should see my aunt before I see him. What do you think that means?'

Sarah had no idea, but like the worried Jenny she could not believe it boded anything good.

A few hours later she was summoned to Doctor Inglis' office. The Venetian blinds were drawn, to shade the fierce sunlight, and she was sitting behind her desk. Sarah approached smartly and saluted, but Doctor Inglis merely nodded her head.

'Sit down, Sarah.' As she sat down, she thought: the last time she used my christian name was to ask me to stay in Galatz. What's coming this time? It was nothing dramatic, though it underlined the fact 'our Elsie' did not miss much. 'You have decided to go home, have you not?'

'Yes, ma'am.' There was no need for elaboration with Doctor Inglis. The statement was sufficient.

'In that case, I think it would be a good idea for you to leave with Jenny. I have extracted two sets of travel documents from the Russians. I do not like the idea of Jenny travelling by herself. You speak Russian, which she does not, and I have the highest regard for your initiative and courage, if not for your respect for rules and regulations.'

As she made this last statement Doctor Inglis' lips twitched slightly. Sarah recalled standing in this self-same spot after her return from Jassy, listening to the old martinet tearing her off a strip about her flagrant disobedience and the utter irresponsibility of leaving without letting anybody know where she was going, conveniently overlooking the fact that if Sarah had told anybody, she wouldn't have been allowed to go.

Now she was saying, 'Right. Off you go. You will, of course, check the supplies before you leave, and produce an inventory. You and Jenny are booked on the train for Odessa the day after tomorrow.'

As Sarah stood up to leave, Doctor Inglis also rose and a band of sunlight seeping through the Venetian blinds caught her face. Everybody in the Unit knew she was not well, she was obviously tired and had lost a good deal of weight, but with the pressures she was under and in this heat that was unsurprising. Suddenly seeing her in the harsh sunlight, Sarah realised she was ill as opposed to being somewhat unwell, and needed a damned good rest. Watching Doctor Inglis' step as she accompanied her to the door, Sarah noticed that had lost its spring too. Only the voice remained as incisive as ever.

'Take care of yourself, Whitworth,' she said, holding out her hand.

The renewed use of her surname was, Sarah reckoned, to modify any idea that the old martinet had grown quite fond of her and held her in some esteem. She pressed Doctor Inglis' hand which was like a child's, so thin and light. 'Please take care of *yourself*. Look after *yourself*.'

'Don't worry about me. The Inglises are a fighting breed.'

They certainly are, Sarah thought. Withdrawing her hand, she saluted smartly. 'It's been a privilege to serve with you, ma'am.'

'Thank you, Whitworth.'

Doctor Inglis looked genuinely touched by the tribute.

They parked the Silver Ghost in the lane and hand-in-hand they walked between the hedgerows entwined with dog roses and honeysuckle. It was as heavenly a day as the one at Chenneys when they'd first met, the sun enveloping a cloudless sky, the air sweet with the scent of summer flowers, only the song of the birds and the hum of the bees disturbing the drowsy silence. They came to a gap in the hedge and with his arm round her shoulder, Guy wheeled Alice through it and slowly they climbed the path towards the brow of the hill. When they reached the top Alice cried out with delight. 'Oh Guy, it's beautiful.'

Below them lay the gently rolling Kent countryside, the archetypal English checkerboard landscape that Alice had grown to love, green fields, gold of ripened corn, orchards and copses and winding lanes, divided by their dear little hedges. In the distance, shimmering in the sunlight, was the crowning glory of the view, the Gothic pile of Canterbury Cathedral, its towers rising with serene majesty from the rooftops of the city.

165

'Was this really the pilgrims' first sight of the cathedral?'

'On the old Pilgrims' Way from London, yes.'

Alice turned her face towards Guy. Seeing the expression in his eyes, hastily she unpinned her hat and let it fall to the ground. When they emerged from the lingering embrace, partly to allow his tumescence to subside Alice guessed, Guy made a great fuss about picking up her hat.

Then he said, 'Would you like to sit down and have a rest for a while, my darling?'

Alice nodded. He took off his Sam Browne belt and unbuttoned his jacket. Momentarily she wondered how much else he proposed to discard, but he was spreading his jacket across the grass. She protested, 'You'll get it dirty.'

'It'll brush clean. Rather that than soiling your beautiful dress.'

It was a lovely dress of softest white tulle embroidered with tiny red flowers, which she had bought in Paris in July 1914 when she was on her delayed honeymoon with Johnny. Originally it had a wide crêpe-de-Chine belt and an underskirt that dropped to the ankles, but worn without the belt and long underskirt it made the prettiest, up-to-date maternity gown.

Guy lowered her gently on to his spread jacket before he sat down beside her. She leaned her head against his shoulder and tenderly he ran his fingers over the swell of her stomach. Placing her hands over his fingers, pressing them against the increasing firmness of the child within her womb, she said, 'What shall we call her?'

'I've always liked Jane,' he said.

'Jane? It's a bit "plain Jane". I like Margaret. Margaret Kendle. Yes, it has a flow.'

'How about Margaret Jane?'

'Margaret Jane Kendle. That's nice.'

Guy made no comment about Kendle as their daughter's surname but he was a bit of a moral coward. That or he disliked hurting people, even that wretched wife of his. From what Kessie had said after her abortive visit to Ryby Hall, she sounded simply frightful. It was wicked of her to

166

shut Guy off from his own son who clearly, desperately needed the affection of a loving father. Perhaps when the war was over and they were settled in their own house they could have Julian to live with them and his half-sister, Margaret Jane. Until the war was over Alice had now accepted that Guy was not going to do anything about divorcing his wife, so when Margaret Jane arrived in the world, temporarily she would be illegitimate.

'When am I going to read your poems? Kessie says Tom thinks some of them are really good and Tom does know about poetry. It was one of the things about him that surprised me when I first met him. Coming from his background, I mean. And if you've let *him* read them, it's about time I did.'

'I'm still revising them, my darling.' Guy nuzzled the back of her neck. 'But old Piper's approval has swayed me in the direction of seeking publication. The minute I consider them satisfactory, you shall read them. You're not expecting pretty couplets about sunset over the trenches and our gallant boys cheerfully knocking the hell out of the Hun, despite the less than cheering conditions?'

'From you?' Alice turned her head towards him. 'Certainly not.'

For a few seconds the brown eyes were sombre, seeing sights Alice didn't want to know about. Then he smiled at her, the honey charm dripped from him, and he was nice enough to eat. Stretching out his hand towards her hat, he lifted it up and placed it on her head.

'I am thinking about penning some couplets about you, my love. In that hat. You looking ravishing in it.'

While she had been turning out a hatbox the other day, Alice had found the old hat. It was a huge cartwheel of white folded straw and she remembered wearing it soon after she'd first arrived in England, down at her sister Verena's house in Sussex. For fun, to amuse Guy, knowing she still looked fetching in it old-fashioned though the style was, Alice had brought it with her for their few days in Canterbury.

In his most languid, drawling voice Guy said, 'Talking

of ravishing, when you've had your fill of the pilgrims'
view of Canterbury Cathedral, may I suggest we return to
our tavern, have an early supper, and retire to the bedroom
occupied by Captain and Mrs Hartley?' They had registered in Alice's maiden name. 'There to indulge in a little
gentle exercise?'

'I think that's a lovely suggestion.'

It would be the last time they made love for some time.
For early tomorrow morning Guy was catching the train
to Folkestone, to board the troopship back to the Western
Front.

Before she finally left Reni, Sarah climbed the stairs to the
top of the pagoda tower to have her last look at the town.
Through the open window the Danube was the same colour
grey as the first time she had set eyes on the great river,
only now it was the greyness of a serpent somnolent in the
heat. Fleetingly, Sarah remembered standing in this room
on that bright, chill, winter's day with Harry, but sadly she
had no emotion left for him, only the wish that he was safe
and that the future would be kind to him. Down in the
market square, where she had first seen Mikhail in the
gaudy sunset, the carts with their basketwork hoods were
trading and the memory of that festive convoy trundling
out of the town sent a shiver down Sarah's spine.

She would not be sorry to say goodbye to Reni.

For several minutes she stood with her head against
the window jamb. She was being punished for having
terminated the embryonic life of Edward Dawson's child.
The one and only time in their liaison they had not been
'careful' she had conceived, but willingly, wantonly, wildly
'careless' as she had been each time with Misha, she had
not conceived his child. With a deep sad sigh, Sarah went
down the stairs and walked into the town.

At Mariya Fyodorovna's room the heavily bolted door
was opened only after she had called out loudly, repeatedly, that it was she, Sara Amosovna. How long ago it
seemed that Mariya Fyodorovna had asked her what her
father's christian name was and when Sarah had replied

'Amos', had proceeded to address her as Sarah-daughter-of-Amos. Sobbing loudly, Mariya Fyodorovna thanked Sara Amosovna for her many kindnesses, she kissed the toddlers, wished them all good luck, and left.

From a market cart she bought a bunch of flowers, before walking to the cemetery where she placed the flowers on Tania and Mr Lohvitzky's grave. Silently, for several minutes, she knelt in front of the simple headstone which she, Jenny and Dorothy had paid to have erected. Inscribed in Cyrillic lettering were the facts they knew and the words they had deemed appropriate.

Tania. Born 1916. Killed 1917.
Sergei Pavlovitch Lohvitzky. Born 1849. Killed 1917.
    Requiescat in pace.
In memoriam. Scottish Women's Hospital Unit.

15

The journey northward was a nightmare, if not of such epic proportions as those days in Galatz. It was a little over a hundred miles from Reni to Odessa but it took the train three days to cover the distance and when they finally reached Odessa it was a frighteningly different city from the one they had arrived in just under a year ago, with armed troops patrolling the streets and the sound of gunfire echoing from the docks. Fortunately, a station official recognised their grey uniforms. Babbling about the *Schotlandskaya Zhenskaya Bol'nitsa* saving his son's life in the Dobrudja, he found them seats on the train bound for Petrograd. Or at least the grateful official hoped it was Petrograd-bound.

The train was packed beyond capacity. It started and then halted at isolated Russian stations with their long platforms stretching from nowhere to nowhere, and as they sat and sat in the suffocating heat they could hear the thud of heavy artillery in the distance. Children howled, bodies sweated, tempers grew short, fierce arguments flared. Food was difficult to obtain, though at least Sarah and Jenny had the money and goods to haggle and barter with the peasant women on the station platforms.

In some towns they passed through, where on the south-ward journey bands had played, blood was running across the platforms, and at places along the track where flowers had been thrown, decomposing bodies lay. Yet in other towns the crowds were cheering the Bolshevik orators, the red flags were waving, and pinned to the wooden palisades of one shattered village Sarah saw the crudely printed banner, 'Education for the People'. Armed personnel, military and civilian, were constantly boarding the train, demanding documents, and when they saw the grey uniforms they shoved their way towards Sarah and Jenny.

'Gosh,' said Jenny after Sarah had kept calm during their third interrogation, 'we're not popular round here, are we? Why don't they like us?'

Unquestionably, Jenny had grown up during the twelve months since they had sailed out of the River Mersey, but in some ways she remained amazingly immature and naïve. Sarah reckoned she should by now have appreciated that most Russians regarded most foreigners with suspicion and the Bolsheviks in particular regarded all English people, which for them included a lass from Newfoundland, as lackeys of their capitalist masters who were pursuing the war for their own nefarious purposes.

The fourth inspection of their travel documents and the demands to know what they were doing in Russia were conducted by two women wrapped in bandoliers, the car-tridge loops stuffed with bullets. Having satisfied the com-rades that she and Jenny were not *provokatori*, not spying tools of their capitalist taskmasters, Sarah was subjected to a long harangue about the slanderous lies being spread by the Junkers and the bourgeoisie as to the true nature, the genuine proletarian fraternity, of the All Russian

170

Congress of Soviets. As the comrades moved on to interrogate other suspect passengers, they raised their hands in a clenched salute and chanted, '*Za Revolyutsiyu! Za Sotsializm!*'

After a pause Jenny said, 'It is encouraging to see women in command, equal partners in the revolution, isn't it?'

'Personally,' said Sarah, 'I've never been impressed by women hell-bent on proving they can be as aggressive, rude and humourless as any man. Nor by those who enjoy kicking, when they should have learned the lesson of being kicked. Nor by those who use sixteen words when one will do.'

'Oh.' Jenny frowned. After a further pause she said, 'What do you want to do when the war's over, Sarah?'

Without hesitation Sarah replied, 'Stand for Parliament. Once we have the vote and we can.'

'Gosh yes,' Jenny's normal enthusiasm returned and she clapped her hands. 'Sarah and Tom Whitworth, brother and sister Socialist Members of Parliament. Oh yes, I like that idea!'

So did Sarah, though might it be circumvented by what happened when she saw Misha in Petrograd?

On the afternoon of the thirteenth day of their journey the train finally drew into the Moscow Station in Petrograd, which was as chaotic as any they had passed through. As they struggled with their luggage, several people spat at their uniforms. A cab-rank was still functioning but none of the cab-drivers was eager to take the *Angliichanki* to the British Embassy. Eventually, one of them agreed to drive them there for twenty-five roubles. Sarah's Lancashire soul, bred in penury, was outraged at the thought of paying such a vast sum for a cab, but her cases now felt like lead weights. Jenny said, 'For goodness sake, Sarah, it's only money. I'll pay.'

Only money! There spoke the well-heeled young supporter of the Bolshevik revolution!

When they reached the British Embassy, a large solid building overlooking the River Neva, surprisingly the cabby helped them with their cases. Then, tipping his whip to his cap in a somewhat old-fashioned gesture, Sarah felt, he wished them God speed back to England, which was an unrevolutionary benediction. As Jenny thundered on the door knocker of the Embassy she said, 'People are nice really, aren't they?'

'Sometimes, little Miss Sunshine.'

After a considerable amount of argy-bargy and explanation they were allowed inside the building. While a Russian servant dressed in most unrevolutionary knee-breeches and a jacket covered with gilt buttons carried their luggage upstairs, one of those languid, drooping upper-class English twits said, 'We expected you days ago.'

'There is a revolution going on,' Sarah snapped tiredly, 'or has it escaped your attention?'

Jenny and Sarah were advised not to set foot outside the Embassy. Having consulted the large-scale map of the centre of Petrograd pinned to an office wall, Sarah wrote a brief note saying she had gone out on a personal errand but she would be quite safe. Deliberately, she left the note in a prominent position on the twit's desk. Dressed in a plain navy skirt and jacket, with a scarf tied low on her forehead in peasant fashion, Sarah then slipped quietly out of the building by an unattended side door. Quickly she walked round to the front, turned right and walked along the embankment of the River Neva towards the Alexandrovsky Bridge.

On the far side of the river the sun was golden on the stonework and domes of the Fortress of St Peter and St Paul, and undoubtedly Petrograd was a beautiful city. As in Reni there was the same curious mixture of normality and abnormality, of life going on while the revolution seethed towards boiling-point, though perhaps here the air of hopeful excitement was stronger than the fearful uncertainty. The columns of men with rifles slung over their shoulders were singing lustily as they marched over the bridge towards the Finland Station. Between the posters announcing art exhibitions, performances at the Alexandrinsky Theatre and the latest ballet at the Mariyin-

sky, Sarah noticed the armed men lurking in shop door-
ways. When she reached the high walls of the
Preobrajensky Barracks she had to flatten herself against
them, as the horses pulling the limbers and full gun-
carriages clattered furiously past.

Yet all was tranquil as she cut through the Tavricheski
Gardens. By the lake, beneath the trees, little boys in
sailor suits played with their boats, little girls in flounced
dresses and frilly hats pushed their dollies in miniature
prams, women in silken gowns, parasols raised, strolled
with men in smart suits and Homburg hats. On an ornate,
circular stand a band was playing.

Without difficulty or retracing her steps, Sarah found it;
the Cyrillic lettering on the placard told her she was in the
right street. At the far end, almost on the corner of the
Suvorovsky Prospekt, she stopped, not because her heart
was beating rapidly and her skin was ridiculously clammy,
but because there were two armed guards outside the
house. She hadn't thought of having to present her creden-
tials, to persuade unfriendly-looking comrades to let her
in. Taking a deep breath Sarah walked towards them.

The guns in both hands were trained on her. Who was
she? What did she want?

'I'm Sara Amosovna. I'm looking for Mikhail Muranov.
I'm a friend of his from . . . from Odessa. Is he here,
comrades?' she said in Russian.

Dear old Mr Lohvitzky had taught her well. From him
and from Misha she had learned a good accent and her
Russian obviously passed muster. One of the comrades
shouted to somebody inside and while Sarah waited, trying
to seem unconcerned, people flowed in and out of the
building, showing their passes to the guards.

A small, thin young woman appeared on the doorstep.
She had a fierce intensity of manner, as if every second
was too precious to waste. 'Sara Amosovna?' As Sarah
nodded, the young woman's glittering eyes flashed her
up and down. Presumably she fulfilled the requirements
because she was ordered to follow.

Inside the house typewriting machines clattered, a

telephone was ringing, voices shouted, folk pounded up and down the stairs, rushing in and out of rooms. Sarah's young guide took the stairs at the double, but her heart beating fast, she walked more slowly. The staircase was circular and as she rounded the curve she saw him on the first floor landing. Framed in the doorway, the afternoon light was streaming through the window behind him, making a halo of the blond hair, which he had *not* had cut.

'*Sarochka moya*! *Kak ya tebya zhdal!*'

He held out his arms and her nervous tension evaporated.

Crying, 'Misha, Misha!' she hurled herself into them.

Pulling the scarf from her head, he ruffled her hair and held her tightly. She felt like a little bird enveloped in his embrace, her heart fluttering wildly. It was wonderful to see him and he wasn't just a breath of fresh air, he was a gust of the strongest, purest wind. She loved him and she wanted to stay with him for ever.

'Misha,' another voice sounded peremptorily.

Releasing Sarah from his grasp, he propelled her into the room and sat her down on a chair laden with papers, again saying how much he had missed her. Asking Irina Beriasovna to find some tea, he strode out, promising to be back in a minute. Comrade Irina obliged with a glass of lemon tea and disappeared. A man came in and started to search frantically through a pile of papers on the desk – the whole room was covered in pieces of paper – before he lifted Sarah to her feet and found what he was looking for among the letters on the chair. Everywhere she sat, somebody came in and wanted to look through the documents underneath her. One man asked her to take this message immediately. When Sarah said she wasn't a courier, he swore with obscene Russian gusto and stormed out.

It was a good hour before Mikhail returned. He went straight to the desk where he pulled out a drawer, extracted a bottle of vodka and a cup, poured himself a generous measure, and held the bottle up to Sarah who shook her head. With the seasoned Russian drinker's gulps, Mikhail imbibed the vodka. Then he spread out his arms and Sarah was expecting a shower of endearments, but instead he pulled her to her feet and his deep voice declaimed passionately, 'Last month they said we had lost. We were hunted animals, *moya Sarochka*, in hiding. But we did not yield. Our unconquerable will kept us steadfast. We shall smash General Kornilov. We, the Bolsheviks, the voice of the people, stood up and shouted, no Kornilovs, no Junkers, no Cossacks, no counter-revolutionaries, shall take Petrograd.'

'Misha,' Sarah said loudly, 'I know what's happening is earth-shattering but I want to talk to you. I have to talk to you. Privately. I have a seat booked on a train leaving for Archangel tomorrow.'

'Why?' Mikhail looked astonished.

'Because I'm thinking of going home. Because I'm . . .'

From downstairs there were loud shouts for Mikhail Mikhailovitch. Comrade Irina ran into the room, the tension sparking from her body like electricity, and said he was wanted immediately. With a wave of his hand, indicating Sarah should wait, Mikhail was gone.

For several hours, Sarah waited, during which there was general pandemonium inside and the sporadic rattle of machine-gun fire outside, the light faded and somebody came in and lit a lamp. At one point, when there appeared to be a lull in the crisis, she wandered down the stairs. Nobody took any notice of her, and of Misha there was no sign. In one room she saw a temporarily unmanned telephone so she went in and lifted up the receiver. After a long pause a voice asked her what number she wanted. She said the British Embassy and there was an even longer pause and a great deal of crackling, but eventually she was connected. She left a message saying Miss Whitworth had met friends in Petrograd but nobody was to worry, she would be escorted back. In another room Sarah saw a samovar and went in and poured herself a glass of tea. With the tea in her hand, she walked slowly upstairs and sat down in Misha's office.

Every time somebody charged into the room, the draught made the paraffin in the lamp flare, and strangely shaped shadows quivered over the walls. The noise both inside and outside lessened and the rat-a-tat of guns died away completely. It was quite dark now; fewer people pushed open the door and started searching for papers. In the corner there was rather a nicely shaped sofa so Sarah walked over, collected the documents strewn across it into a neat pile, and having placed them on the floor stretched herself out. By heck, she'd like to bring order into this chaos, get a filing cabinet and get to work. She smiled to herself. Then none of the comrades would be able to find anything, would they? Resting her head on the curved arm of the sofa, she gazed at the shadows flickering across the walls.

What was happening in Petrograd as she lay here assuredly was of earth-shattering importance. Events were taking place that could shape Russia's future. When Misha strode back, no doubt unsurprised that she was still here but full of joy to see her, she had to make a personal decision that would affect *her* future . . . She must have dozed off because the sound of the voices made her start. Where was she? Why were those ominous shadows crowding in on her? As she sat up, easing the crick in her neck, she heard Misha's voice. He was in a boisterous mood, his laughter ringing out, but he was not alone. They swept into the office, a couple of dozen of them, and somebody turned up the lamp. The room glowed with light, bottles of vodka and an assortment of glasses and tumblers appeared and were filled. Then Mikhail leapt on to the desk and made an impromptu speech. General Kornilov's army had been scattered in ignominious rout; the tide of the revolution had turned and it would sweep through Russia, cleansing, purifying, leaving the debris of the past stranded on the beach to wither and fossilise. He held his glass up to the ceiling and the long hair swung over his shoulders as he proposed a toast.

'*Za Revolyutsiyu! Za nashe budushschee! Za nashu novuyu Respubliku!*'

Euphorically, the comrades laughed, cheered, and quaffed their vodka. Or at least the majority of them did.

There were one or two of the men whose grim, watchful faces were untouched by the excitement, though they hailed the revolution, the future, the new republic as loudly as any. Sarah had seen several such faces during the long journey from Odessa to Petrograd, and they worried her.

Jumping from the desk, Mikhail strode towards the sofa and sat down with his arm round Sarah's shoulder and the touch of his hand sent a quiver down her spine and the muscles of her groin contracted. Surprisingly – maybe it was the vodka, though he was a heavy drinker who held his liquor well – he told the comrades that she was his dear friend, his Sarochka, who came from England but was a true friend of the revolution. Again the majority took this information in their stride, smiling at her, one or two cheered, but those other faces stayed watchful, as if mentally chalking up a black mark to Mikhail Muranov.

'You want to talk to me, I know,' he whispered to her in English. 'We shall go upstairs e're long, *moya lyubimaya, moya dikaya angliiskaya roza.*'

The endearments sounded a hundred times sweeter in Russian.

Eventually the noisy, exhilarated, ever-argumentative comrades dispersed, to snatch a few hours' sleep, or to return to revolutionary duty. With Mikhail's arm around her they squeezed their way up the narrow winding staircase that led to the topmost floor and into a small room in which the sloping eaves formed the ceiling. Slowly they kissed and Sarah could taste the vodka in his mouth, but its taste was sweet. Rapidly they undressed and lay together on the narrow bed.

For a while after they had finished making love they clung to each other, Misha's lips brushing her damp skin, her fingers stroking the silkiness of his hair, silvered by the moonlight shining through the small uncurtained window. Then, one arm still around her, the other gesticulating towards the slats of the wooden ceiling, Misha started to talk excitedly about the revolution and what their next moves should be. First they must gain control of the Petrograd *soviet*, by a democratic vote, of course, then

. . . With half her mind she listened to his deep, melodic voice, infused with a different sort of passion.

That he loved her had ceased to astonish Sarah. Whatever mundane chemical reaction, or emotional and intellectual attraction, or primeval life-force, drew one particular man to one particular woman, and *vice versa*, operated for her and Misha. But, and it was a large but, she was only one of his loves. She had to take her place alongside his love for Mother Russia and his passionate involvement in the Bolshevik revolution. Which was fair enough because she had her dreams and plans for the future, too, and moreover Russia was not her country. She did not instinctively, historically, from hard-won personal experience, understand its problems. It was not her revolution, and throughout these last few hours she had felt an outsider, a deeply interested one, but personally uninvolved. And the sloping eaves above her head reminded her of the attic room at The Grove, which Anne and Con moved into with glee when Aunty Sarah came to stay. How she longed to see Kessie and Tom and the children, to walk through the streets of Manchester and Mellordale, to climb over the moors to Netherstone Edge, to feel the fresh North Country wind on her face.

'Misha, I have my seat booked on the train for Archangel tomorrow, if tomorrow hasn't already turned into today. What time is it?'

'I have not the least idea.' Then with a puzzled frown Mikhail said, 'Why should you be thinking of leaving tomorrow?'

Sarah explained about England being her home and her feeling of detachment from the revolution. With a roar Misha sat up. The revolution was not a parochial Russian affair, it was the last step on the road to international Socialism, the true brotherhood of man. Capitalism had been a necessary step – Sarochka had read her Karl Marx, so she knew that – but its days were numbered which meant England's hours as a world power, a dominant shaping force were, too. The future lay with Russia and the revolution, with what *their* chief of men, Vladimir

Ilyich Ulyanov, called Lenin, had recently described as Communism.

At that Sarah sat up and they had quite a fierce argument. She found herself sharply telling Mikhail he knew nothing about twentieth-century England, which had changed since Oliver Cromwell and John Milton's days, defending her native land with an ardour she would not have dreamed of using at home. As sharply she said Marxianism had a distinctly authoritarian ring for which she for one did not care, and it conveniently overlooked the problems of nationalism, as she herself had once done. He caught her in his arms, smothering her against his broad chest.

'*Obozhayu tebya, Sarochka moya.* Go home, if you must, for the time being. Then you shall come back, *moya lyubimaya*, or I shall come to fetch you. We shall build the new world together, in peace. We shall have two children,' he roared again, this time with laughter, 'a boy like you and a girl like me! We are destined for each other. A few months, a year, cannot separate us.' Releasing the bear-like grip, he sank back on to the pillow and drew her down on to his body. Softly he quoted, '"Sole partner, and sole part of all these joys, Dearer thyself than all".'

'Misha, *moi lyubimyi.*'

He was her dearest, dearest love, but she was going home. For the time being, any road.

PART THREE

16

'It is good to have you back,' Kessie said for the umpteenth time. 'I have missed you.'

Sarah reiterated how good it was to be back, which was not the whole truth. Maybe it was having left Russian soil, for Reni was as far from Petrograd as London, but she was missing Misha dreadfully. She was also suffering from an acute sense of dislocation, made worse by the confusion of the old Julian calendar to which the Russians still adhered, and which meant she had lost a fortnight of her life on the voyage from Archangel to Dundee. Sarah trusted that once the Bolsheviks assumed power they would bring Russia into line with the rest of Europe by adopting the Gregorian calendar.

Kessie had lost weight, her slimness now verging on thinness, and there was an edge to her voice which emphasised how tightly her nerves and reserves were stretched. This was not surprising, for one of the first things Sarah learned was that Tom had returned to active service. Kessie informed her that the great British summer offensive, aimed at breaking out of the Ypres Salient and capturing the Belgian ports, was bogged down on a ridge called Passchendaele which was only a few miles outside Ypres. *Bogged* was the correct word because the Flanders' weather had been appalling throughout August and was notoriously dreadful in the autumn, so that the battle had developed into an even more horrific shambles than the Somme. The savagery in Kessie's voice made Sarah decide she would not enquire why her brother had seen fit to return to the front.

As if Kessie hadn't enough worries on her fragile shoulders, once more living in the dread of receiving the buff envelope which would regret to inform her that Captain E. T. F. Whitworth had been killed or hideously wounded, Alice Conway had come to live at The Grove.

'So she's expecting a baby and it's not her husband's,' Sarah said crossly. 'That's her look-out. She's a big girl. She owns that barn of a place in St John's Wood. So why on earth is she living with you?'

'Well,' Kessie explained, 'she went down to see her sister and naturally enough, I think, she told Verena the baby isn't Johnny's, it's Guy's. Apparently they had a terrible scene. Verena virtually threw her out and almost uttered the words "never darken our doorstep again". Alice came straight here from Sussex and she was in tears when she arrived, Sarah, and I don't remember ever seeing her cry. She said how miserable she felt with Guy in that ghastly Passchendaele battle and how lonely it was in that great big house with nobody to talk to . . .'

'Except a cart-load of servants. And you said, "Why don't you come and stay with us until the baby is born?"' Sarah mimicked the husky middle-class tones. 'Oh Kessie!'

There had been many a time in Reni when Sarah had longed to talk to her sister-in-law about Harry and Misha and her tangled emotions, but now she was back home and had the opportunity she didn't mention either of them. Well, other than as folk she'd met along the way when she was responding to Kessie's demands to know all about her experiences and what it was really like in Russia, or when she was showing her the photographs Jenny had taken. Kessie was fascinated to hear about a Bolshevik with long blond hair who quoted Milton by the ream and when she commented, 'He looks a flamboyant character. He almost leaps out of the picture, doesn't he?' Sarah almost told her the truth. The moment passed, and she didn't. Maybe it was because she didn't want to burden Kessie with her emotional problems, or maybe it was because she was no longer sure about how she felt. Were she and Misha really destined for each other? Or had it been one of those

184

wartime passions? A memory that she would for ever keep to herself?

Within twenty-four hours of her return Sarah realised that the England she had left in August 1916 was a very different country from the one she had come back to in September 1917. The euphoric excitement of waving the boys off to the war and cheering the gallant wounded as they returned had disappeared as if it had never been; the majority of Londoners were grey-faced and war-weary, grimly hanging on until that elusive victory was theirs. They also did a lot of moaning although, despite the air-raid damage, in comparison to Petrograd or anywhere Sarah had seen in Russia London remained a stable, well-run, well-organised city. Comparatively speaking, Londoners had little to moan about. Nobody was being shot down in the streets, nobody was actually starving, though the U-boat attacks on British shipping had taken their toll and there were food shortages. Sarah did comment on the long lines outside the shops.

Kessie corrected her, 'Queues.'

'What?'

'Standing in line, moving along in turn, that's what it's called. A queue. Hence queueing.'

'Since when? Why?'

'I don't know. New phenomenon. New word. Anyway, it's become popular. Queueing's a way of life for lots of women now. We have a splendid lady called Mrs Higginbottom who comes in twice a week to help Maggie with the heavy jobs and according to her . . .' Kessie adopted a strong Cockney accent, '. . . you gets the wire the Maypole or the Home 'n' Colonial 'as extra sugar or marge and off you shoots to queue up.'

'I see,' said Sarah.

Anne and Con had willingly gone up to the attic bedroom and Sarah was ensconced in the first floor bedroom which no longer overlooked the velvety lawn and flower borders, but a small piece of grass and a large patch of dug-over earth in which Peg Leg Pete, the ageing gardener, grew vegetables. (Why he was called 'Peg Leg Pete' Sarah had never enquired because though now rheumaticky, he possessed both limbs.) The only flowers Kessie had not sacrificed to the dig for victory campaign were those in her conservatory, though even there tomato plants were interspersed with geraniums.

A couple of days after her return Sarah was sorting through the junk she had accumulated during her year in Roumania and Russia when Maggie knocked on the door with the mid-afternoon post. Among the letters was one in Jenny's handwriting, with a Scottish postmark. The letter informed Sarah that Jenny's brother Hamish had been blinded during the battle for Vimy Ridge.

When I consider how my light is spent
Ere half my days, in this dark world and wide . . .

Milton and Misha went hand-in-hand, the longing for him quivered through Sarah's body and she had to concentrate hard to read the rest of the sombre letter. Jenny said Hamish was bearing up well and was at a convalescent hospital in Scotland, near where the Newfoundland Regiment with its strong Scottish connections had its headquarters. He was learning to deal with his disability before being shipped back home, and Jenny thought she'd try to travel with him, as a nurse on the hospital ship to Newfoundland, because she was dying to see her parents, her brother Callum, her sister Fiona and her homeland. If she did go, she would certainly come to London before she departed.

Then Harry telephoned, shouting down the receiver as folk did who were unaccustomed to this method of communication. To their astonishment, when Sarah and Jenny had reached Archangel the first thing they had seen on the quayside was one of the snub-nosed, high-wheeled Lanchester lorries being swung on board the waiting ship. They had then learned that Commander Locker-Lampson had decided the situation in Russia had become so dangerous the time had come to evacuate his armoured car squadrons. So they had voyaged back to Scotland in Harry and the other lad's company, and during the days at sea he had made it clear that he was prepared to forget that Mikhail had ever existed. When they had parted amicably on the dockside in Dundee, Harry asked if he might contact Sarah in London.

His voice was now bellowing down the line, asking if he might take her to the theatre. Sarah hesitated before replying but she did like him and had made it clear, she hoped, that she still loved Misha. She said she would meet him in central London because it was a long way from Bethnal Green to Highgate, but Harry insisted on collecting her from The Grove. Perhaps it was being engulfed by women – Maggie opened the door, Kessie came to greet him, pregnant Alice sashayed down the stairs, the girls bounded out of their playroom – or maybe it was the middle-class affluence of the house and its occupants, but Harry stood shuffling his feet, twisting his cap in his hands, answering questions without his usual chirpiness.

Sarah was irritated by his unease and the evening was not a success. The irritation with Harry added to the general restlessness from which she was suffering. She told Kessie she was going up north for ten days or so, both to see old friends and old stamping grounds and to fulfil a short lecturing tour that pacifist and Socialist friends had begged her to undertake, speaking about her first-hand experiences and knowledge of the glorious Russian revolution.

'You will come back, won't you?' Kessie asked rather anxiously.

'I expect so,' Sarah said, though actually she wasn't too sure that she would, not to live permanently at The Grove.

To be back in Manchester and Mellordale, to walk through the grimy, soot-blackened streets, even to smell the pervading stench of the gasworks, were grand experiences. Now a heroine in her own right, one of Doctor Inglis' brave nurses who had shown the world what British women could do, she was greeted with enthusiasm.

Her lectures were well attended. Sarah had however warned the organisers that though she would praise the revolution and its emphasis on women's equality, though she would talk about the terrible sufferings of the Russian people and *their* desire for peace, though she would hammer her renewed conviction that Thou Shalt Not Kill was the supreme commandment, she would not pretend the Bolsheviks were good English Socialists, nor would she say they themselves were pacifists as such – they were more than willing to fight for their revolution. When she was true to her word Sarah was noisily heckled by outraged Socialists and/or pacifists as much as by anti-Bolshevik jingoists, and at times the meetings were as rowdy as in the old suffragette days. The only welcome difference was that nobody shouted what was she, a woman, doing up there on the platform in the first place?

At a particularly rowdy meeting in Blackburn a middle-aged man stood up on a bench near the front of the hall, shaking his fist at Sarah. The muscles in his neck bulged as he shouted, ''Ow canst tha talk like that, Sarah Whitworth, about crawling on ower bellies to the Hun, begging for peace, when ower lads are within inches of victory at this vurry minute. And yer brother, ower Captain Tom, theer wi' 'em and all. Shame on yer cowardly soul.'

With difficulty Sarah remembered Mrs Pankhurst's advice to would-be suffragette orators. Never answer a personal attack. She was only too agonisingly conscious that her brother Tom was there, fighting in the Passchendaele mud.

Crouched in the dug-out, scribbling the message for his runner, out of the corner of his eye Tom watched the rat. It was as large as Kessie's cat Jasper, so gorged with blood, so bloated with dead flesh, it was waddling. It reached the end of the subsiding duckboard and belly-flopped into the mud. Tom's eye went on watching as slowly the thick brown slime engulfed the rat's vainly struggling weight until the last tip of its long grey tail had been sucked under.

Handing the message to his runner, he said, 'Get this to Battalion as fast as you can, Sharples.'

'Yes, sir.'

When Tom had last seen Battalion HQ it had been functioning in a slightly larger hole in the ground than this one, the Company HQ, of which he was in command. Between the two dug-outs lay a crazed, blasted, shell-shocked landscape of jagged tree stumps rising from the morass of mud, a bogged maze of old communication trenches, huge craters filled with slime and bodies, and smaller cavities reeking with foetid water, all wreathed in the poisonous yellow fog of slowly sinking gas.

Both Tom and Sharples knew the more appropriate words were 'get the message to Battalion if you can' but Sharples saluted and lifted the waterproof flap that hung over the gap leading into the dug-out. As the flap moved, Livesey's screams surged in with the rain. Sharples took no notice of the sound but bent his body low and squelched out into the mud of the sap. In one corner of the dug-out, similarly oblivious to Private Livesey's screams, Lance-Corporal Henderson continued his obsessive attempts to get the field telephone working, while in another corner Private Duty peered into the tea which was warming with infinitesimal slowness in the canteen on the cooker. Only Guy Kendle momentarily lifted his head as the screams echoed and receded with the movement of the flap before writing a few more lines on the envelope of one of Alice's letters, crossing out several words and sucking his pencil. It astounded Tom that in such circumstances, during the briefest of respites, Guy who looked as cold, haggard and exhausted as he himself felt, could switch his mind to concentrate on writing poetry.

Since their abortive attack on the Boche positions early that morning Livesey had been trapped on the concertina wire that lay in the quagmire in front of them, screaming for his mother, for help, for anything to relieve his agony. Guy had led one attempt to rescue the lad, Tom another, but they had lost three men in the process and Tom refused to try again until darkness fell – should Livesey live so long.

'Tea up, sir.' Private Duty handed Tom a tin mug.

'Well done.'

Tom had no idea what his servant's real name was. He had enlisted as A. Duty which Kessie thought showed a mordant sense of humour. She was eager to find out more about the man but Tom had pointed out that if he'd wanted people to know who he was, where he came from, and why he'd enlisted, he wouldn't have exhibited what Kessie called his mordant sense of humour. Private Duty was a servant in a million, well-spoken, well-read, to be seen in quiet moments scanning Virgil in Latin, consequently never 'one of the boys', but respected by the other lads for his abilities as scrounger and wangler and for his steadfastly unflappable temperament.

Rising to his feet, though it was not possible for a six-footer like either of them to stand upright in the dug-out, Guy accepted his mug of tea, sipped it and murmured, 'The nectar of the Gods.'

From the pocket of his fleecily bedraggled 'teddy-bear' jacket he took a squashed packet of Oros cigarettes, more usually known as 'Horrors', and proffered them to Tom. 'Is that all you have?' Tom said angrily.

'What have you to offer?' Guy snapped back.

Tom had no cigarettes left, so he took an Oros and lit it from a piece of burning paper provided by the ubiquitous Duty. Coughing violently – God his chest hurt but he might as well die in comparative happiness from bronchial pneumonia as from anything – he inhaled on the revolting tobacco. While they drank their tea and smoked their cigarettes, above the thunder of somebody else's barrage the Boche reminded them of their more immediate presence. Handing his mug to Duty, Tom jammed on his tin helmet and waded out into the mud of the sap. The rain made a slapping sound as it hit his 'battle bowler', ran across the rim and fell on to his mackintosh. He shouted to his observer who shouted back that it was nothing to get excited about, sir, but Tom put his head cautiously over the edge of the trench and peered through his smeared binoculars to make sure. There was no sign of a German attack, only a few whizz-bangs sending up spumes of mud and the machine-guns to their right cackling away like maniacal hens, their phosphorescent tracer bullets briefly glowing through the gloom.

Back in the dug-out Duty handed him the refilled mug and Tom gulped another mouthful of the hot, sweet, stewed tea. Guy drawled, 'What did you say to Battalion?'

'We're facing uncut concertina wire to a depth of a hundred feet. We're enfiladed by Boche machine-guns positioned in pill-boxes on a slight incline. We've lost most of A B and C Companies and God knows where the rest of the Battalion is. Or maybe HQ does? Half our casualties suffocated in the mud, which isn't surprising because even the rats are drowning in it now. I thought I'd seen it all on the Somme, but this is beyond Gehenna. Unless and until they can get reinforcements up, with artillery, I have no intention of obeying orders for a further attack. For reasons that escape me, because I'm too tired to think, we shall do our best to hold on. Signed Captain (acting Major) Whitworth, Member of Parliament. PS We need cigarettes urgently. Hot baths, hot food, dry clothes and warm beds wouldn't come amiss.'

At this recital of what front-line troops would like to say to Battalion, or better still to Division, Guy smiled slightly. Tom managed a wry smile back.

'If we're holding on,' Guy's drawl was at its most languorous, 'I'll plod my weary way o'er the lea and see what's happening in Bilge Alley and other salubrious points west. En route I shall convey words of cheer to our long-suffering lads, though what they will be my imagination has not yet decided.'

Wearily, he started to pull his cape on but immediately Duty was by his side, helping to haul it over the teddy-bear jacket. Placing his 'battle bowler' on his dirty matted brown hair – if golden Alice could see you now, Tom thought – Guy tapped the tin helmet three times for luck and made for the waterproof flap. Outside, Livesey's screams echoed loudly and a hysterical young voice shouted, 'For Christ's sake, why doesn't he put a sock in it?'

Why didn't he? Tom thought savagely. Why didn't Livesey peg out? Why did he go on, hour after hour, lying impaled on the iron thorns of the wire? Because he was, or he had been, a lusty lad and the will to live was fiercer than the agony of living?

A few seconds later the single rifle shot twanged through the murky air and the screams stopped. Guy's head slewed round towards Tom and they both guessed who had ended Livesey's crucifixion. There were few left from those who had joined the Pals Battalion at the beginning of 1916, and of the few none was a better shot than the late Private Livesey's particular mucking-in pal, Private Fielden. Neither Tom nor Guy spoke. They had seen and heard too much for the action to surprise them. Then the flap swung open and a young Lieutenant entered the dug-out. Tom's exhausted eyes noticed the two pips on his shoulder and the crown set in the sunburst that was the insignia of the Australian Imperial Forces. Where the hell had be sprung from? Was he a straggler from their last, mutual, bloody encounter with the Boche in Polygon Wood?

'Is there a Captain Whitworth round here?' The young man made no effort to salute his superior officers and his voice had a touch of that Aussie-Cockney whine.

'Yes,' Tom said.

'Hello, sir. Farrell's the name. Was sent out on a recce. See if any members of the British Army are still functioning.' That remark would have you on a charge with some buggers I could name, Tom thought, but he had the highest respect for the Aussies as fighters and their lack of deference appealed to him. 'Came across a pill-box full of Manchesters and rats. About five of the men alive. The rest dead. Couldn't get any of them to answer to begin with. They've had it, sir. You know?' In answer to the laconic query, Tom nodded. He'd almost had it himself. 'Finally persuaded one of them to talk, though he wouldn't budge. Said his name's Hinson and if I could find a Captain Whitworth, they might come out for him.'

'You'd better see to it, Piper old lad,' Guy said, 'I'll take over until you get back.'

Out in the sap the klaxon sounded and all hands in the dug-out stretched to pull their respirators from their canvas holders. Before he donned his, Tom said he must check all his lads had theirs on. In yesterday's gas attack a blank-faced, glazed-eyed Duckworth had sat slumped like Hinson and his mates in the pill-box, making no attempt to don his respirator. It had been impossible to get him even to an advanced dressing station and he'd died vomiting the putrid poisonous slime from his guts.

With the rubber of his respirator clinging to his face, breathing deeply through the counter-reactionary chemicals in the box attached to the mouthpiece, Tom peered through the goggles. He raised his hand to Guy, transformed by the apparatus into a monster from outer space, and in return Guy raised his.

Followed by the equally monstrous vision of young Farrell, Tom squelched his way into the sap.

On the last day of her speaking tour Sarah climbed up to Netherstone Edge. The sun was shining, the sky was blue, the clouds high and white, and she sang as she left the hard pavements of Mellordale behind and walked up the lane past the late Ada Thorpe's little house which Kessie and Tom now used as their base in The Dales. Sarah bounced across the tussocky moorland grass and clambered over the stone-piled walls until she was perched on the black rocks of the Edge, with the clear north country wind blowing in her face. Down in the valley that ran from Upperdale through Mellordale to Lowtondale, the pall of smoke from the belching chimney stacks hung over its entire length. The mills were working round the clock again, as in the early days of the Industrial Revolution, though now they were weaving the cloth for soldiers' uniforms.

And she was, Sarah thought, pregnant.

Until she was certain of her condition, until her next period had failed to arrive, she decided to return to The Grove. She would then review the situation.

17

Back in London, September turned into October and the
dank autumn days drifted by. In Flanders it rained and
rained, the mud-bath battle for Passchendaele continued,
the columns of 'Today's Casualties' were as long as the
Somme's, the only difference being that quite a lot of folk
were openly saying the slaughter was futile and should
cease forthwith. While they waited for news of Tom and
Guy, life at The Grove went on.

Maggie kept the house running smoothly, Anne and
Con went to school, Anne worried where to move the flags
on her map of the Western Front, Kate and Mark played
and quarrelled, and Alice's presence was less tiresome
than Sarah expected. There were moments when she could
have hit Madam – 'The fire's going out, Sarah', 'Well, put
some more coal on it' – but Alice had never before lived
without a horde of servants or a personal maid. She was
immensely cheerful and she did her best to help Kessie.
The telephone rang a good deal, and soldiers of various
ranks and nationalities who had met Tom in the trenches
called. They all spoke of Major Whitworth – he had been
officially gazetted Major – as a legendary figure, with the
greatest concern for his men, the coolest of nerves and the
cheek of the devil, the last quality not unassisted by
the fact that he was a Member of Parliament and a friend
of the Prime Minister's.

The study had been turned into an office, full of filing
cabinets and bulging folders whose neat labels showed the
span of Kessie's activities: 'Widows', 'Pensions', 'Separ-
ation Allowances', 'Missing', 'Conscientious Objectors',
'Wounded', 'Special Hardship Cases'. In the mornings her
part-time secretary came in and in the afternoons, when

194

Kessie had her rest, Sarah buckled down to answering the queries and cries for help. Just occasionally the cabinet marked 'Women's Suffrage' which stood somewhat forlornly in the corner by the window, was opened. The Representation of the People Bill, including Clause IV which was the one which might give women over the age of thirty the vote, was trundling its slow way through the House of Commons, but with attention focused on Passchendaele there was little they could do but wait on events.

On the evenings when the rattles sounded the air-raid alarm – October appeared to be a favourite month for raids – they all went down to the basement where Maggie made a pot of tea for the adults and cocoa for the kids and they told stories or sang jolly songs while the Zeppelins throbbed overhead and the explosions shook the house.

And Sarah's next period duly failed to arrive.

Immediately she wrote a long letter to Misha, telling him how delighted she was, hoping he would feel the same way, but saying it might be wiser for her to remain in England until the baby was born. Then, if that was what he would wish too, she was more than prepared to return to Russia. Having posted off the letter c/o the house off the Suvorovsky Prospekt, Sarah prepared for a long wait for his response. Whatever he replied, she was deliriously happy. Fate had been kind to her, it had given her a second chance after her abortion, and she wanted this child as much as she had *not* wanted Edward Dawson's. From the start she intended to take every possible precaution to ensure its safe delivery. She would *not* rush around the place, and she would *not* undertake any further speaking tours. Alice's baby was due in December, she would then be returning to her house in St John's Wood, and Sarah decided if Kessie would have her, if she could face the prospect of another pregnant woman on her hands, she would stay at The Grove. Otherwise she would go back north and find herself a room. Half her wages with the Unit in Russia had been paid monthly into a bank account in London so for the moment she was not badly off.

In the afternoon, after she had posted off the letter to Misha, Sarah was crossing the hall when the door knocker banged. Standing on the doorstep was a telegraph boy who handed her the buff envelope and she felt the fear crawling over her skin. The envelope was addressed to Mrs E. T. F. Whitworth and it could, just possibly, be from Tom to say he was coming home on leave. On the other hand . . . Sarah stared at the envelope. What should she do? Waken Kessie who was having her afternoon rest? Leave her in peace a while longer? Go down to the kitchen and steam open the envelope, or simply open it, so that she could prepare Kessie for . . .

'Is it for me?'

Clutching her dressing gown round her, Kessie was standing at the top of the stairs, her eyes fixed on the buff envelope in Sarah's hand. Slowly she came down the stairs. When she reached the newel post, she stopped and in a trembling voice said, 'Open it for me, please.'

Fiercely, Sarah tore at the envelope. Taking a deep breath, she unfolded the telegram and perused its contents, but when she looked up at Kessie's anguished face momentarily she could not speak.

'What does it say? Tell me, Sarah, please tell me.'

As flatly as she could Sarah read out the message. 'Guy officially reported missing Stop That means dead Stop Break news to Alice who will not be informed Stop Not next-of-kin Stop I love you Tom.'

When Sarah looked up again she saw the same guilty relief on Kessie's face that she herself had felt on reading that it was not Tom who was dead, before she started to weep.

Whether it was Kessie's fault in trying to break the news as gently as possible, or whether Alice would in any case have clung like a limpet to Guy's being reported missing rather than killed outright or dead of wounds, Sarah could not know, but she remained preternaturally calm and confident.

'Men have turned up as prisoners of war, weeks, months, after they've been reported missing. What's the address of the bureau that helps to trace them?'

'It's in Carlton House Terrace.'

'I'll go this afternoon. Personally. I shan't telephone.'

In high spirits Alice returned to say they had been most helpful and Guy's details were being sent to the Bureau Pour La Recherche des Disparus in Switzerland. Even when, two days later, the announcement appeared in *The Times*' officers' casualty lists her attitude did not change.

'Captain Anthony Guy Christopher Kendle, Manchester Regiment, has been posted missing, believed killed, in the battle for Poelcapelle. Aged thirty-five, the eldest son of Mr and Mrs J. P. P. Kendle of Ryby Hall, Ryby-in-Furness, Lancashire, Captain Kendle was educated at Downside College and King's College, Cambridge. In 1903 he married Miss Arabella Florence Babington, a union blessed by one son. Having fought and been twice wounded on the Somme, Captain Kendle rejoined his Battalion for the commencement of the third battle of Ypres.'

In the evening Kessie and Sarah sat in front of the fire in the sitting room, a habit they had dropped into before retiring for the night, one respected by Alice and much appreciated by the surviving cat, long-haired ginger Jasper who curled up on Kessie's lap.

'At least Alice's belief in Guy's survival means she won't go into premature labour from the shock of his death. I suppose there is a thousand to one chance he might be alive.'

'I can't believe Tom would have sent that telegram if he had any doubts.'

Sighing deeply, Kessie said, 'I suppose I should write to Arabella Kendle. Arabella. The name suits her. I bet she sent that semi-obituary notice to *The Times*. "A union blessed by one son", and "the commencement of the third battle of Ypres" has a distinct ring of Mrs Kendle.'

Kessie did write and by return of post she received a few formally polite lines, penned in a tiny hand on thick notepaper edged with black. In them Arabella Kendle thanked Mrs Whitworth for her sympathy, but it was God's will. She trusted, God willing, that Major Whitworth would come through safely.

'She obviously thinks Guy's dead,' Kessie said bleakly. 'I

wonder if she cared for him at all? God's will! I've always been a good Lancashire Unitarian – though I doubt Mrs Arabella Kendle would pass us as Christians – but I think I could finish this war as an atheist.'

'You and me, too,' said Sarah.

Then a letter from Tom arrived, but after Kessie had read it she merely said, 'He sends everybody his love, but he doesn't say anything much about Guy.'

'There you are,' said Alice, 'if anybody should know what's happened to Guy, it's Tom, and obviously he's not sure.'

Later in the morning, when they were by themselves, Sarah said, 'What did Tom *actually* say?'

'He sounds at the end of his tether. You mean about Guy? Apparently, Tom went to rescue some Manchesters who were in a catatonic state. When he got back to their dug-out, A. Duty, that's his batman's *nom-de-guerre* . . .' Kessie laughed slightly, 'told him Captain Kendle had gone up the sap to inspect something or other and the German artillery had opened up. And well . . . Guy never returned. Nobody actually saw him blown to buggery. His body hasn't been found. So officially he's missing. I don't see any point in telling Alice. Let her hang on to her hope. At least until the baby's born.'

Looking at Kessie's sad, strained face, Sarah didn't see any point in informing her sister-in-law that she had two pregnant women in her house, both bearing children conceived out of wedlock. One crisis at a time was enough.

A few mornings later, towards the end of breakfast, Kessie started to sort through her usual pile of correspondence when, with slight surprise, she noted there was a letter with a Ryby-in-Furness postmark from Arabella Kendle. After she had slit open the envelope and read through the contents, in those suddenly clear tones that cut through the natural huskiness of her voice when she was angry, Kessie cried, 'The bitch!'

Sarah was draining her second cup of tea, Alice her usual coffee, but at Kessie's words they both dropped their cups into their saucers. The chinking of the china served to underline an epithet Sarah had rarely, if ever, heard on Kessie's lips. While they both stared at her, for several seconds she sat frowning before speaking slowly.

'I think you'd better read this.'

Kessie handed the piece of paper to Sarah who held it in front of her so that Alice could read it too. The page was half-covered in Mrs Kendle's minuscule handwriting and the untitled lines read:

> Scarlet in the sodden gloom,
> From Gehenna poppies bloom,
> Guns stutter from German lair,
> And stench of death hangs in the air,
>   In Flanders fields, my love, my love.
>
> Poppies in your golden hair,
> Garlanded hedgerows scented fair,
> Meadows drowsing, cathedral shimmering,
> Images Of the Pilgrims' Way,
> On long, sun-hazed, summer's day,
>   In Kentish fields, my love, my love.
>
> Here each crimson petal shed,
> Falls for multitudinous dead.
> At home, in spring, they'll grow anew,
> In hope, in peace, I'll walk with you,
>   In England's fields, my love, my love.

Alice snatched the letter from Sarah's fingers. 'Where's the original? This isn't Guy's writing. It's hers. Why hasn't she sent me the original?'

With a sense of foreboding, Kessie's epithet buzzing in her head, Sarah thought: she didn't send it to you at all, luv, though presumably Guy wrote it for you, not her. Kessie's head was bent down and when she looked up her hazel eyes were wide with concern. Even more slowly she replied.

'Alice, I want you to listen quietly and not to get upset. The poem was among Guy's effects, so of course it was sent to his wife, as next-of-kin. She . . . appears to be . . .' Kessie paused, searching for the right word, '. . . appropriating it. She says she has already sent it to a magazine, though she doesn't say which one, and they have agreed to publish. So it will be appearing any day now as . . .' Kessie paused again, '. . . as the last poem Captain Kendle wrote for his wife before he was posted missing. And it's an absolutely awful thing for her to have done but . . .'

'It's my poem. She can't have it published. It's not hers. It's mine.'

Alice's voice was definite but reasonable. She turned towards Sarah and with a smile, calmly but uncharacteristically, she explained. 'You see, before Guy went back this time, we snatched a few days in Canterbury and on a simply heavenly afternoon we walked along the Pilgrims' Way, just lapping up the beauty of everywhere and everything. And I had this ancient hat on, a big cartwheel creation, with poppies round the crown. Guy said I looked ravishing in it and he said he'd write a poem about me in "that hat" . . .' The implications of Mrs Kendle's actions penetrated Alice's mind and slowly her voice rose until she was screaming, 'It's not her poem. It's mine. How dare she steal it? She never went along the Pilgrims' Way with Guy. She never did anything with him. She refused him everything. She wasn't in love with him. She's incapable of love. She's wedded to an implacable God. She knows Guy wrote those lines for me. They're mine, they're mine . . .'

Pushing her chair back Alice stood up and started to pad round the room like a wounded tigress, screaming against Mrs Kendle, shouting that she was Guy's love and he was hers. She was going to tell the world, to claim her inalienable right to the poem, and the only good thing was that when Guy came back there would be no question of not getting a divorce. As Alice's hysteria mounted Kessie tried to soothe her, begging her to sit down, but to no avail, and in the end Sarah briskly slapped her face and forcibly sat her in a chair.

Standing over the shaking, sobbing Alice she said, 'Now listen to ex-Nursing Orderly Whitworth. If you go on like this you'll harm your baby. What's Guy going to say about that when he does get back? Take a deep breath, take several deep breaths, and then up you come with me. I'm going to give you a sedative and you're going to have a rest.'

Sarah could see Alice debating whether to vent her feelings further, or whether to obey ex-Nursing Orderly Whitworth's instructions. Somewhat to Sarah's surprise, she obeyed. After she had settled Alice in bed, staying by her side until she was at least calm, if not asleep, she came back downstairs and joined Kessie in front of the fire in the sitting room. They both agreed that unless Guy had left specific instructions to the contrary, which in the Gehenna of Flanders' fields it was doubtful he would have done, the poem was the property of his wife who, according to Kessie, was fair-haired, if not as golden as Alice, so the description fitted.

'Do you know, I think she's taking her revenge on me, too.' Graphically Kessie described her disastrous visit to Ryby Hall. 'Why else would she bother to send me a copy of the poem and the information that it's being published?'

'Like you said, she sounds a right vindictive bitch.'

Charitable as ever, Kessie slightly backtracked on her use of the word. 'She's been badly hurt. Not that that excuses her behaviour.'

'Alice has plenty of friends in Fleet Street.' In their suffragette days she had been the WSPU's highly regarded press liaison officer. 'She can get them to trumpet the truth about who "my love, my love" really is.'

Almost pityingly Kessie looked at her. 'Sometimes Sarah, you are a sweet innocent. No journalist is going to trumpet the news that the gallant captain's last declaration of love, and hope for the future, was penned for his mistress, not his wife. Not at this grim moment and certainly not if the poem catches on, which, you never know, it might.'

The very next day the poem was printed under the title 'Poppies'. It was accompanied by a full-length studio portrait of Guy in his captain's uniform and a smaller photograph of 'my love, my love', in which Mrs Kendle looked well-bred and attractive, by her side the son who resembled his dead father. Two days later the citation announced that Captain A. G. C. Kendle had been awarded the Military Cross for his bravery during the battle for Polygon Wood. Within the week single sheet copies of 'Poppies' by Captain Guy Kendle MC had been printed, with his charming be-capped head at the top of the page, wreathed in scarlet poppies, the poem itself set in a larger ring of entwined poppies. The first print-run sold out within the day and Kessie's casual comment that the poem might catch on was vindicated with a vengeance, as thousands more copies were printed.

'It's a nauseating title and setting.' Alice tore one of the sheets into fragments and dropped them into the wastepaper basket. 'Guy will throw up when he sees it.'

Alice then became frenetically active, smoking at a rate that alarmed Sarah. The magazine that had first printed the poem, finding itself with a percentage of a gold-mine, was uninterested in her complaints. While some of her journalist friends professed to be sympathetic to Alice's predicament, as Kessie had predicted not one word appeared about the true identity of 'my love, my love'.

'All she's done is to set tongues wagging,' Kessie sighed. 'The gossips are having a lovely time. The connection be-tween her pregnancy and Guy Kendle isn't difficult to make.'

The newspaper gush about 'Poppies' continued alongside its phenomenal sales and the personal titbits, presumably fed by Mrs Kendle, about the man who before the war had explored the world in between being the loving husband and father who enjoyed the beauty of his family's north Lancashire estate. Kessie said she thought revenge had slightly unhinged Arabella Kendle, because the publicity was completely out of character for the pious, reserved, upper-class woman she had met on her visit to Ryby Hall.

Suddenly Alice changed tack, announcing that though she still regarded Mrs Kendle as a liar, a cheat and a thief, all those people she personally cared for knew Guy had written the poem for her. What she wanted to discover, on the missing Guy's behalf, was what his wife had done with his other poems, the ones Tom had said were really good and that he was intending to publish.

'What's happened to them?' Alice demanded. 'I'm going to Ryby Hall to find out.'

'You're doing nothing of the sort,' Kessie said sharply. When Alice started to protest, even more sharply she said, 'If you do, you're not coming back here. A visit to Ryby will achieve nothing except more trouble. Perhaps Mrs Kendle is arranging publication of Guy's other poems. I'll write and ask her.'

Alice's protests subsided. Sarah had forgotten how formidable her sister-in-law could be when her spirit was roused. Kessie duly wrote but this time no reply arrived.

While all this was happening Sarah was suffering badly from morning sickness. Fortunately there was the separate bathroom and toilet at The Grove, plus an outside toilet in the basement area, so if one was occupied she rushed into the other, dousing whichever toilet she used with eau-de-cologne to disperse the stench of her retching. Damn Alice for hogging centre stage but that was the way she was made, and Sarah wasn't. She certainly could not give Kessie her news until the 'Poppies' uproar had subsided.

When Harry telephoned yet again Sarah decided a night out, a few hours away from the emotionally charged atmosphere of The Grove, would be a good idea. As a condition of accepting his invitation, however, she insisted they met in central London, selecting the well-known rendezvous in front of Swan and Edgar's department store in Piccadilly Circus. She saw him pacing anxiously up and down as she descended from the tram at the bottom of Regent Street and the minute he saw her he dodged through the traffic to be by her side. After he had eyed her appreciatively, and said how nice she looked, he asked if it would be all right if they had a meal first at Lyons Corner House in Coventry Street? Irritated by his deference, Sarah said of course it would. He insisted on buying a posy of violets from one of the flower sellers sitting at the base of Eros's statue in the middle of Piccadilly Circus and when they reached the Corner House he insisted on tucking his arm under Sarah's to escort her to the second floor restaurant. When they had found a table in the crowded room, he insisted she order exactly what she wanted – within the confines of the Public Meals Order, of course.

Sarah chose sausage and mash, which she liked; but seeing Harry's disappointment at her plebian selection, she ordered a pudding too. He was obviously determined to do her proud. Had she been selfish in agreeing to meet him? Was she needlessly raising his hopes?

While they waited for the elderly, harassed waitress to bring their orders, they chatted about this and that and how strange it seemed to be back in England. When their food finally arrived they managed to discuss the news from Russia without once mentioning Mikhail Muranov's name, though 'our special correspondents' all agreed he was the most colourful character the Bolsheviks had thrown up.

In the corner of the restaurant, on a small dais, a three-piece orchestra was trying to compete with the conversation of the diners. Having finished a selection from 'Merrie England', the orchestra went into 'It's a Long Way to Tipperary' which produced a round of patriotic applause, though Tom said it was viewed with ironic contempt by the troops who never, ever, sang it on the Western Front. Sarah had to admit she found the strains haunting and maybe because she did she suddenly decided she owed it to Harry to tell him the truth.

'Harry, after I've told you what I'm going to tell you, if you want to empty the teapot over my head or walk out on me, I'll understand.' Sarah took a deep breath and said, 'I'm expecting. It's Mikhail Muranov's.'

Very slowly, Harry placed his serviette on the slightly stained white tablecloth. The buzz of conversation, the clinking of cutlery on plates, the upraised voices calling 'Waitress', the dying notes of 'Tipperary', thumped in Sarah's head. Of all the things she had imagined Harry might say, he said the totally unexpected.

'The swine. Giving you a baby and leaving you in the lurch.'

'Oh no, Harry, no, no. It's not like that.'

Neither she nor Tom had ever been great ones for explaining their motives and actions – it was Kessie who liked to go into the detailed reasons why – and the orchestra's launching into a jolly selection from Gilbert and Sullivan did not help what Sarah reckoned was a less than lucid résumé of the situation.

'You have written to him?' Harry said when she finished. 'If a woman was having my child, I'd like to know.'

Hadn't she made even that clear? Sarah said of course she had written to Mikhail but she didn't expect a reply for some time, with the chaos in Russia.

'Will you go back there?'

'I expect so,' Sarah laughed slightly. 'Until I hear from Mikhail, how can I be sure?'

'What are you going to do in the meantime? Stay with your sister-in-law? Isn't it time you told *her*? Are you all right for money?'

Sarah assured him she was for the moment fine financially. She explained about her wages in Russia being paid into a bank in London, so she now had a banking account and a cheque book, just imagine! Smiling at her attempt to lighten the conversation, Harry glanced at his wrist-watch.

'If we're going to the theatre, we'd better get our skating boots on.'

'Do you still want to take me then?'

The grey eyes looked straight into hers.

'Of course, I do. I told you, Sarah, and I meant it . . .' Harry paused for a second before continuing. 'I love you. If you ever want my help, you've only to ask.'

From her comfortable position on the rug in front of the fire, with Jasper stretched by her side, Kessie looked up as Sarah entered the sitting room. She smiled as her sister-in-law crossed the carpet and dropped on to the rug. Holding her hands up to the flames Sarah said, 'It's parky outside.'

'Did you have a nice evening?'

'Lovely, thanks. We had a meal and then we went to see *Dear Brutus*. It's not one of Barrie's best plays, bit sloppy, but enjoyable.'

While Sarah continued to warm her hands, from underneath Jasper Kessie pulled a copy of *Britannia*, the patriotic women's paper edited by Christabel Pankhurst. Showing it to Sarah she said, 'I've been catching up with their latest news. You might like to know the Women's Social and Political Union has finally ceased to exist. No fanfares. No fuss. A fairly bald announcement. Christabel and Mrs P. are forming a new party. The WSPU is dead! Long live the Women's Party!'

An involuntary sigh came from Sarah.

Kessie was well aware that her sister-in-law had lost patience with the Pankhursts long before she had, but the unsung demise of the WSPU had obviously struck a half-forgotten nerve. So many memories, so much energy, determination, hope, suffering and comradeship were entangled in those four initials, WSPU, and for several minutes they both sat silently. When Sarah continued to stare into the leaping flames a slight frown furrowing the bridge of her nose, Kessie had the distinct impression her thoughts had switched to other matters.

Has she finally told Harry she's expecting a child? Kessie wondered. Is she about to give me the startling news?

Relaxing her back against the armchair, stroking Jasper's thick fur, Kessie gazed at her sister-in-law. The aura Sarah radiated was of an eminently practical, sensible, no-nonsense lass from Lancashire, and with her small neat figure and remarkably unlined skin, despite her thirty-four years she still seemed very much a 'lass'. Yet in actuality, once you scratched beneath the surface, examined Sarah's record in detail, and came to know her as well as Kessie did, her actions had always been out-of-the-ordinary. They tended to be unpredictable and she possessed the same wild Whitworth strain as Tom, which Kessie felt sure came from their gipsy ancestors. How many other sensible Lancashire lasses who had some knowledge of sexual matters would return from heroic nursing in Russia, pregnant, unmarried, and this time, it would seem, cheerfully determined to bear and bring up an illegitimate child?

'I think you ought to know, Kessie. I'm expecting.' The

anticipated announcement was, in typical Sarah fashion, dropped like a brick. 'But don't worry. I'm thinking of going back to Manchester and finding myself a room. You've quite enough on your plate with Alice and your own kids and Tom away and . . .'

Kessie interrupted the flow. 'Do stop being stupid, Sarah. You've been stupid quite long enough. Did you seriously imagine I didn't know? I have had four children myself and I had terrible morning sickness with the twins. Did you think I was taken in by all that nonsense with the eau-de-cologne? I just decided to keep quiet until you wanted to tell me. Unless you actually *want* to go back to Manchester – and having your first baby is an experience to be shared, isn't it? – you're more than welcome to stay here. We can rechristen The Grove Number One Field Maternity Hospital!'

As Kessie giggled, Sarah buried her face in her hands and her shoulders were shaking, but not with responding laughter. Hastily pushing Jasper out of the way, Kessie moved the few feet across the rug and put her arms round the heaving shoulders.

'Sorry. Didn't mean to be flippant, but you have been a goose, keeping it to yourself. I am glad for you. I know how much you love children.' Kessie paused and looked down at the shiny black hair which was all she could see of Sarah's head. There was no question of her dearest sister-in-law not remaining at The Grove, but she could foresee all sorts of future difficulties. How should she phrase her enquiry? Slowly she said, 'Are you considering matrimony? I do actually think it's a good idea for all concerned.'

Sniffing back the tears, Sarah looked up. 'Harry Sewell isn't the father, if that's what you're thinking. It's . . .'

'The Bolshevik with the long blond hair who quotes Milton by the ream.' Kessie smiled down at her sister-in-law, as she interrupted again. 'Did you imagine I hadn't guessed *that*?'

18

At twenty-two minutes past ten the next morning it arrived, the cable from Misha! Untangled from its garbled English, which was one of the problems of communicating with Russia at any time, particularly when the communication was filled with Miltonic references, it read:

Sabrina fair, I feel I am happier than I know. Stay where thou art. Pandemonium, the high capital of Satan and his peers, the reign of chaos and old night, gorgons and hydras and chimeras dire, yet hold sway here. I shall come for you. Ensure it is a girl for me, though a boy for you will do. I adore you. Misha.

Experiencing only a flicker of disappointment that Misha had accepted her sensible suggestion of staying in England until the baby was born rather than urging her to join him in Russia whatever the difficulties, Sarah showed the telegram to Kessie who laughed and said Mikhail sounded a wonderful character. She also said the cable settled the matter of Sarah's staying at The Grove, an observation with which she agreed. They similarly agreed, with Alice due to give birth in the middle of December and in her emotional state, to keep the news of Sarah's 'interesting condition' quiet for the time being.

For forty-eight hours Sarah was euphoric. Her exhilaration increased with the news that on 6 November Canadian troops had actually captured the village of Passchendaele – though from the piles of flattened rubble linking the shell-holes it was difficult to imagine anything had once stood there – followed by the news that on 7 November, according to the Gregorian calendar, Mr

Kerensky's Provisional Government had fled Petrograd and the Bolsheviks had taken control of the Russian capital.

Then, early in the morning of 9 November Violet Mudge, the younger of Kessie's two prewar living-in maids, turned up with her great news. Sarah had wakened Kessie and they were sitting round the table in the dining room, sipping tea and watching Vi tuck into the eggs and bacon Maggie had produced when, bursting with excitement and importance, she told them how she had come by the news.

Turning towards Sarah, she explained, 'I work at a munitions factory in the Grays Inn Road, you see. We make the fuses for shells. I'm an examiner now and I have to check all the fuses wif me gauge. It has to be dead level. If it's not, they ain't no good.' She returned her attention to Kessie. 'On the night-shifts we have our dinner hour 'tween midnight and one o'clock. Well, it gets ever so stuffy in that cowshed we work in, all that hot brass flying from the lathes, so unless it's pourin' cats and dogs, or there's a real pea-souper, we usually goes outside for a breath of air. Most of the ambulances come up from the stations at night now, you know, so people won't get upset by seein' how many casualties there are. Well, whole convoys of 'em drive up the Grays Inn Road every night.' Vi turned to Sarah again. 'They're goin' to the Royal Free 'Orspital, you see, which ain't far from our factory.' Back her head went to Kessie. 'The ambulances chug along ever so slow and their backs are open, you know, so we walks alongside, cheerin' the boys up, givin' 'em fags and sweets. We have a whip-round every Friday – that's our pay day – to buy fings. You often see somebody what you know and guess who I saw this mornin'?'

Vi paused, but her expression said neither Mrs nor Miss Whitworth was actually to start guessing.

'I saw Ernie Read! You remember Ernie, Mrs Whitworff, he used to work at the ironmongers in the High Street. Well, he was at a casualty clearin' station outside Eeps when Major Whitworff was brought in. Ernie said he wasn't hurt bad, but bad enough Ernie finks to be home soon. And I said to myself, Violet Mudge, I says, Mrs Whitworff may not have heard the news, so the minute you finishes your shift, you're goin' straight up to the The Grove.'

Kessie did have that effect on people as dissimilar as Dorothy Devonald and Violet Mudge, Sarah thought. Vi proceeded to tell Kessie that her sister Ruby had gone to pieces somefink chronic since her husband Alf, which in Cockney fashion she pronounced 'Elf', had been killed at the Bullecourt place, which as most folk did she pronounced 'Bullycourt'. On his very last leave Elf had said Bullycourt was a place to be avoided, almost as if he'd known, and Ruby just had to pull herself together. Elf wasn't coming back and all the wishing and all the tears in the world wouldn't bring him back.

Listening to the voluble young woman, sitting with considerable self-possession at Kessie's breakfast table (a notion which would have appalled her before the war), Sarah had difficulty in recalling the moon-faced maid who had spoken only to echo her older, perter sister Ruby. By taking her out of service to assemble fuses for shells, the war had undoubtedly been the making of Vi. All over the country there were thousands of Violet Mudges and though they were still being denied the vote, to the eternal shame of British politicians, surely they were not going to lose their self-confidence?

Vi's good news lifted Kessie's spirits – though what a lunatic world it was when you were delighted to learn that your nearest and dearest had been wounded. After they had received the official telegram, another one arrived from Tom, informing them he was coming straight to The Grove, not to another hospital in England, which was even better news.

Tom had again been hit in the shoulder but, within the shortest while of his long-awaited homecoming, Sarah realised her brother's physical wound was comparatively unimportant and that there was another reason why he had been sent to his home environment to recuperate. For those cool nerves of which his fellow soldiers had spoken with admiration were shattered.

The following dank November days were, to say the least, difficult ones. Tom had a racking cough but was virtually chain-smoking. He had finally given up rolling his own and was continually sending Effie, the young lass who helped Maggie during the day, to buy another packet. He was feverishly restless but could not be persuaded to rest and any sudden noise made him jump like the veritable startled rabbit. His temper flared with or without pretext, which bewildered the children who had been waiting to see him for months. He vented his rages on Kessie, yet he was constantly touching her, slipping his hand into hers, his arm round her shoulder, kissing her hair. With Sarah he was reasonably controlled, asking about her experiences in Russia, how she assessed the implications of the Bolshevik seizure of power in Petrograd, yet his attention was distracted when she answered.

At night, sleeping in the bedroom next to Tom and Kessie's, Sarah often awoke with a start, for the moment thinking it was the rattle of the air-raid alarm that had awakened her before realising it was her brother shouting. Recalling her own memories of waking up sweating and panting in the nights after the Cossack massacre, she knew Tom was re-living the horrors of Passchendaele.

Alice's presence he resented inordinately. At the best of times when he was infuriated by somebody Tom could be abominably rude, and these were the worst of times. Even though the door was shut, as Sarah passed the sitting room in the middle of a dismal, fog-wreathed morning, she heard her brother shouting.

'Doesn't she realise Guy's dead? Haven't you told her?' As Sarah retreated up the stairs, he was yelling, 'It's macabre. He's dead, you hear, dead, dead, dead.'

Fortunately, Alice appeared impervious to Tom's behaviour, wrapped in her own concerns about how much her back ached, how fed up she was with being enceinte and how she couldn't wait for the baby to be born. Kessie told Tom she could not, and would not, throw Alice out, so on the occasions when she mentioned Guy and his poems Tom either glowered or stalked from the room. An anguished Kessie said to Sarah she didn't know what to do to help him. She had suggested a holiday in the peace of the Isle of Wight but he wasn't interested, and in short spells he did appear to find comfort in the children's company. They both agreed they would not mention Sarah's pregnancy at the moment, and she said she reckoned all Kessie could do was to exercise the utmost patience, because heaven knew Tom needed her. Briskly, she told her brother that keeping the home fires burning wasn't a barrowful of laughs, Kessie had her burdens too, and he should give some consideration to her health and well-being. All Tom said was, 'Yes.'

Towards the end of November, a month that had started so well but was now as gloomy as the fogs it produced, Sarah returned from doing some shopping to find Maggie in the hall, talking on the telephone.

'Hang on, please, will you? She's just come in. Miss Whitworth, that is, not Mrs.'

Dumping her shopping basket on the floor, Sarah took the drumstick-shaped receiver and said, 'Hello' into the upright mouthpiece.

'Hello, is that you Sarah?'

The tones were unmistakable. Sarah cried, 'Dorothy! Where are you?'

'In Hampstead. Staying with Stephen. We landed in Newcastle yesterday after an *awful* journey from Archangel. But I won't start explaining everyhing over the telephone. May Stephen and I come round? We're simply dying to see you and Kessie and everybody.'

'I'm not sure.'

'What do you mean?' Dorothy was unaccustomed to being refused entry to The Grove. 'Why ever not? Is something wrong?'

'Tom's back from Passchendaele. He's not well.'

'Oh, I see. Ask Kessie, will you, and give me a ring back? She knows Stephen's number. I shall be here for a few days, before I go to see the parents in Cheltenham.'

When she returned Sarah mentioned the telephone call to Kessie who said she'd love to see Didi and Stephen but she'd have to consult Tom. He said he was dining with Lloyd George on Monday night so Kessie could invite Fred Karno's troupe round that evening if she wanted. Then Jenny telephoned to say she was in London prior to sailing for Newfoundland with her brother Hamish. After consultations with Maggie about the food situation, Kessie decided to have a small dinner party on the Monday evening.

In the middle of the Monday afternoon, while Kessie and Alice were both having their rests, Sarah was in the kitchen helping Maggie with the preparations when Tom put his head round the door. He said, 'A young Australian lad I met over in Flanders has just been on the telephone. He doesn't know a soul in London, so I've invited him to dinner too.'

After Tom had gone, Maggie sniffed loudly. Sarah said, 'Thoughtless creatures men, aren't they?'

Maggie gave another sniff. 'I'll manage. Somehow.'

In the evening the young Australian was the first to arrive, just before Tom departed for his dinner with Lloyd George, about which the Aussie lieutenant had apparently been informed. Casually, Tom performed the introductions.

'Rupert Farrell, this is my wife . . .'

'How do you do, Mrs Whitworth. You're every bit as attractive as the photographs your husband sticks up in his dug-outs.'

'Thank you.'

Kessie had gone to considerable pains this evening. She was wearing a turquoise and white spotted silk ensemble, the bodice trimmed with turquoise velvet, the skirt layered, with a full-sleeved white tulle blouse. Her chestnut hair was swept back and entwined with matching velvet ribbons, and marquisite drop ear-rings, a present from Tom, completed the picture. Sarah reckoned Kessie had made the effort to cheer herself up as much as to impress anybody else.

'This is my sister Sarah who'll tell you all about Russia.'

'How do you do.' Lieutenant Farrell's grip was hearty. 'Be interested to hear about Russia.'

'And this is Mrs Alice Conway who's staying with us *temporarily*.'

Alice was resplendent in a stiff taffeta, mandarin style housecoat and Sarah noted that Rupert Farrell did not bat an eyelid, nor look embarrassed by Alice's condition, as some of their soldier visitors did. Had she absorbed Tom's emphasis on *temporarily*? After Tom had excused himself young Farrell gazed round the sitting room, commenting that it was a well-proportioned room, asking if he could see the rest of the house? Slightly surprised, Kessie enquired if he was interested in architecture.

'I was training to be an architect when the Mother Country called. I believe I answered the call because I wanted to travel. That part I don't entirely regret. I've seen Egypt, Gallipoli, France and Flanders. Now London. It's an architectural mess, but interesting. I like what I've seen of it.'

'Good,' said Kessie. 'Sarah, will you show Lieutenant Farrell round? Or shall we call you Rupert?'

'Call me Rupert. Old Piper said you weren't stuffy.'

Neither are you, Sarah thought, as she showed Rupert round the house. He was sturdily built, fresh faced, with eyes that looked accustomed to vast distances. When Sarah asked, he confirmed that he came from the outback where his parents ran a sheep station. When you'd seen one sheep, he added, you'd seen 'em all. His manner was laconic, but his tour of the house was thorough. He was good with kids which sent him up in Sarah's estimation, making the twins and Anne and Con, all of whom were in their pyjamas ready for bed, roar with laughter as he inspected their bedrooms.

As they came back down the stairs, Jenny had just arrived. Sarah had rarely seen her other than in grey orderly's uniform, or in a sensible skirt and jacket, but she too looked swish this evening. The coat and hat Maggie had in her hands were glossy beaver, Jenny's short red hair had been well set and she was wearing a gold and

214

green dress with a tabard-type tunic and buckle shoes which gave her the appearance of a jolly medieval minstrel. Sarah introduced her to Rupert Farrell.

'Pleased to meet you, Miss Macdonald.'

'And me you,' Jenny grinned.

'You're not English?'

'No. I'm a Newfoundlander. You're not English either.'

'No, Australian. Nobody has anything but praise for your lads. Not after Beaumont Hamel.'

'My elder brother was there.'

'Was he? We were with the Newfoundlanders at Broodseinde. They're jake.'

Jenny laughed and withdrew her hand, which Rupert was still holding. Their conversation had had little connection with the way they'd been smiling. They'd obviously taken to each other.

'Jenny'll tell you all about Russia,' Sarah said as she led them into the sitting room.

Immediately she introduced them Jenny and Kessie established the rapport she had anticipated. Jenny said she was sorry Major Whitworth couldn't be here as she'd been dying to meet him because he looked so *gorgeous*, a comment which made Kessie giggle in her old manner. And would Kessie – they were on christian name terms from the start – please congratulate him on his DSO? Tom had been awarded the Distinguished Service Order, to accompany his Military Cross and bar, for his bravery and qualities of leadership in the battle for Poelcapelle. Although the newspapers had had a field day writing about the gallant hero, it was a subject not mentioned in Tom's presence.

With the same enthusiasm as she took to Kessie and Rupert, Jenny took against Alice. To Sarah's dismay Alice started to talk in her obsessive way about 'Poppies' and Mrs Kendle and what she'd done with Guy's other poems. To begin with neither Jenny nor Rupert had the faintest notion what she was talking about, but gradually, despite her hostility, Jenny's attention was caught.

'Gosh, she sounds awful,' she burst out. 'How could any

woman do that, if the poem was written for you?' Then Jenny frowned. 'Is Captain Kendle alive then? I thought he was dead.'

Simultaneously Rupert said laconically, 'He is', and Kessie loudly, 'He's missing.'

Sarah looked at Alice's beautiful face. Did she really, truly, still believe Guy was alive somewhere? Or at the back of her mind did she know the truth? Had she created the fantasy of his survival in order to survive herself? How long would she, could she, hold on to this delusion which, as Tom had shouted, had a macabre quality?

It was with considerable relief that Sarah heard the front door knocker bang. A few seconds later Dorothy bounced into the sitting room, apologising for being late. She'd been waiting for Stephen. Didi hadn't changed in manner or attire, casually dressed in a navy blue skirt and a thick high-necked jumper. She hurled herself into Kessie's arms, embraced Sarah and Jenny enthusiastically, shook Rupert's hand briskly, and looked astonished to see Alice.

'Oh hello. Are you expecting? Nobody told us. Stephen will be surprised. I'm sure she'll be along shortly. Had to dash down to the Unit's headquarters.' Dorothy turned to Rupert, 'That's the Scottish Women's Hospital Unit. We're just back from Russia.'

'So I've gathered.'

'Well go on,' Jenny said when they were all sitting down, sipping drinks. 'Tell us. What happened after we left? How's Doctor Inglis.'

'Not terribly well.' Dorothy leaned forward in her chair, 'Shall I tell you? Would you like to hear?'

She would obviously have died of disappointment if Kessie or anybody had said no, but they were all genuinely interested – well, Sarah couldn't vouch for Rupert Farrell. After saying she didn't know where to start, crisply Dorothy embarked on her recital.

'We went to Hadji Abdul which wasn't a bad place, up in the Carpathians, wooded hillsides, lots of walnut trees, and the hospital was in an apricot orchard. They're delicious, fresh apricots and walnuts, as long as you don't eat too many. We were attached to the First Serbian Division and we weren't frantically busy. It was quite hot when we first arrived but then the weather turned fearfully cold, not as bad as Reni, but bad enough, and Doctor Inglis collapsed. Stephen had to take charge and frankly, I thought "our Elsie" should have been sent home. Stephen said there was no hope of that and she was worried sick about the Serbians. Elsie, I mean, not Stephen. You know how she was always going on about "her" Serbians? Well, she said the Russians were using them as "cannon-fodder" and if we didn't get them out of Russia, there wouldn't be an able-bodied male Serbian between the ages of eighteen and forty left. Stephen told me all this. That's really why we stayed as long as we did. Elsie wouldn't move until she was certain the British Government had agreed with the Russians to get the Serbians out. Anyway, finally, we packed up at the end of October. It was the most beautiful early evening as we left, I shall always remember it, but the journey to Archangel was simply fearful. We were in second-class compartments, and some of the Serbians had dysentery which some of us caught. That was jolly.'

At this comment, Rupert stirred in his chair. If he had been at Gallipoli, Sarah reckoned he knew something about dysentery.

'Elsie looked simply dreadful. Honestly, at one point I thought she was dying, but she rallied. She is a tremendously plucky old buzzard. The worst part of the journey was we knew we were racing against time. The ice closes in on Archangel harbour in November and then it's totally blocked until the spring. Can you imagine being stuck in Archangel for six months? When we reached the ghastly dump the Bolsheviks had already seized power in Petrograd, there was a general strike in progress, and then the Bolsheviks took control of Archangel. And this order was issued that no British citizens were to leave Russia. I must say Elsie and Stephen were tremendous. Elsie tottered around telling us to Stick to Our Equipment!'

Sarah and Jenny both laughed. Dorothy joined them before she continued.

'Sorry about that, chaps. Unit joke. Somehow Elsie and Stephen persuaded those hard-faced Bolsheviks in Archangel we were an exception to the order. Us and our Serbians. There were four ships in the harbour waiting for us. We got our ambulances and X-ray cars and ordinary cars and all the equipment and thousands of Serbians loaded on to them. It was quite a job, I can tell you, and it was perishing cold. We steamed out of Archangel in a convoy and HMS *Vindictive* arrived to escort us. I can't tell you how we cheered!

'The ice was already closing in. You could see great chunks of it banging against the boat. We were on board the *Porto*. Well, we ran into a simply fearful storm and the *Porto* got separated from the rest of the convoy. Then our engines broke down. There we were, adrift in the White Sea. We were a ghost ship. There were icicles everywhere, and fog wreathing the bows. It was just like *The Ancient Mariner*. I expected the albatross to appear any minute. We were a lovely target for a passing submarine. You'll never guess what Elsie did while we floundered about in that eerie isolation. One by one, she called us to her cabin – she was just lying there, poor old thing – and asked us to sign on for another tour of duty in Macedonia!

'Anyway, the chief engineer was Scotch and he said he'd get Doctor Inglis and the rest of us back to Scotland if it was the last thing he did. He and his boys worked like navvies and I lent a hand – it's quite fun down in the bowels of a ship – and he did it. He got the engines working, and off we steamed again. Then, somewhere off the Orkneys, we ran into another fearful storm. Honestly, this time I wanted to die, and Elsie was looking absolutely grisly. When the storm died down we saw a smudge of land and we sang "The Road to the Isles", especially for Elsie. I could have swum for the shore, honestly I could, but we didn't dock in Scotland, we steamed down towards Newcastle. We were escorted into the Tyne, we were limping a bit by then, and we dropped anchor to allow the Serbians to be taken off first. You won't believe it, but that night there was an absolute blizzard. The *Porto* broke her moorings and there we were being bashed and battered in the Tyne! We all thought we were drifting out to sea, back to Archangel!

'In the morning we disembarked in Newcastle. Was I glad to be home! Elsie walked off with all her medals pinned to her uniform. I must say it brought a lump to my throat because she looked . . . well . . . almost on her last legs. It was bitterly cold on the quayside, the sleet was driving up the river, but she thanked each of us personally. She invited us all to visit her in Edinburgh, though she said she'll be coming to London soon, before she sets off for Macedonia. Personally, I think she needs a jolly good rest before she sets off anywhere.'

As Dorothy finished her story, Maggie came in to say dinner was ready. Dorothy was saying she couldn't think what had happened to Stephen when there was a bang on the front door.

'Saved by the knocker. That must be her.'

Maggie went to answer and a few seconds later Stephen came into the room. She was in her uniform, the calf-length skirt and long belted jacket, the upturned hat with its tartan ribbon. Her square face had a set, stony look. At a woman's entrance Rupert Farrell automatically rose to his feet but as Stephen stayed silently by the door, her expression frozen, Kessie, Dorothy, Sarah and Jenny also stood up. Only Alice remained seated.

'What is it? What's happened?' said Kessie, moving towards her.

Staring past Kessie towards Dorothy, Stephen said, 'Do you remember, Didi, when we were adrift in the Tyne Elsie said, "Who cut the moorings?" I said, "Nobody cut them. They broke". She's cut her moorings. She died a few hours ago.'

19

It was a foul day, bitterly cold, not actually snowing though the Pentland Hills were white-topped from a recent powdering, but with an icy wind tearing up the Firth of Forth. From early morning the light had been murky and it was growing steadily murkier. In their Scottish Women's Hospital Unit uniforms Dorothy, Jenny, Stephen and Sarah sat in Miss Macdonald's ancient carriage which rocked from side to side as the horses clattered down Princes Street. At the far end, the spectacular drop of Arthur's Seat was a brooding silhouette. The carriage turned right and the two horses pulled hard up towards the Royal Mile, where at one end the turreted towers of Holyrood Palace were sooty smudges, at the other the ramparts of Edinburgh Castle looked sombrely down. When they reached the square in front of St Giles' Cathedral, 'queueing' in the line of vehicles waiting to disgorge their mourners, Sarah saw Harry standing in the crowd, obviously searching for them. Dorothy and Jenny grabbed her arm.

'Gosh look, it's Harry, bless him,' Jenny said, 'Wasn't it nice of him to come?'

He was in his Petty Officer's uniform and when they stepped from the carriage he greeted them with a salute. 'Your sister-in-law told me you'd travelled up, Sarah. I wanted to pay my last respects.'

'Follow us,' said Stephen.

As privileged mourners they were conducted down to the chancel and Harry sat by Sarah's side. Although she had ceased to believe in God, she found the service in the packed cathedral extremely moving, the emotion starting when the congregation sang one of Doctor Inglis' favourite hymns,

220

'Sunset and evening star, and one clear call for me'. At the end of the service, buglers from the Royal Scots Regiment sounded the Last Post, though it was the following jolly strains of Reveille, played fast in the shortened version, that choked Sarah's throat. While four huge, bearded Serbians lifted the coffin on to their shoulders, to bear it slowly down the nave, the organ thundered into the 'Hallelujah Chorus'. Sarah put her head back and stared up at the cathedral roof but she could hardly see it for her tears, and by her side Jenny was sobbing.

Outside, the Serbians laid the coffin reverently on to the waiting gun carriage, draped in the flag of the Scottish Women's Hospital Unit, the Union Jack below the red, white and green colours of the National Union of Women's Suffrage Societies of which Doctor Inglis had long been a member. Slowly the procession set off, the gun carriage drawn by six grey horses, followed by two open carriages bearing the floral tributes, then those in which Doctor Inglis' relations and the Serbian ambassador representing King Peter and Crown Prince Alexander were seated. The long line of carriages followed the gun carriage as it rattled towards the Dean Cemetery. The sky was darker and it had started to rain, everywhere and everything dripping dankly, as if weeping for Edinburgh's honoured daughter. Despite the filthy weather the crowds were thick on the pavements, men doffing their hats, kilted soldiers saluting, women wrapped in shawls and bonnets bowing their heads. Some of them were weeping too, for before the war Doctor Inglis had toiled long and hard in Edinburgh's hospitals and wynds.

When Doctor Inglis had been laid to her last resting place in her native land, they drove back to Miss Macdonald's house in the swaying carriage. Harry was invited to accompany them and the cook had hot toddies waiting and hot water for baths. Sarah availed herself of this luxury, changing out of her damp uniform into a more comfortable, voluminous jacket and skirt. Not that anybody appeared to have noticed her thickening waistline, but then nobody was expecting her to have a child.

221

They said goodbye to Jenny who was staying in Edinburgh. She was travelling to collect her brother to sail for Newfoundland within the next few days. She said, 'You will write, Sarah, won't you?'

Sarah promised she would and wondered if Lieutenant Rupert Farrell would be among Jenny's correspondents.

When they caught the London-bound train from Waverley Station, Dorothy and Stephen were studiously tactful in talking to each other to allow Harry and Sarah to have a private conversation. Solicitously he said, 'Are you keeping all right?'

'In the pink, thank you.'

'Make sure you don't catch a chill from this afternoon.'

'Any news of what's likely to happen to your squadrons?'

'No. Still drawing our pay and twiddling our thumbs. Not that I'm complaining. We get extra special pay, you know. Commander Locker-Lampson saw to that when he formed the armoured car squadrons.'

'Yes, you told me.'

Poor Harry, he was obviously dying to spend his money on her. Belatedly, Sarah decided she had better give him the news from Russia, to dampen his ardour. 'I've heard from Mikhail. He's delighted we're having a baby. He says I'm to stay here for the moment and he'll come and collect me as soon as he can.'

Doing his best not to look shaken by the news, Harry said he was glad for her sake. After a long pause he said, 'I was that shocked when I read about Doctor Inglis's death in the paper. How old was she?'

'Fifty-three, I think.'

'Did you know she was that ill?'

'No. Though looking back I should have done. Mind you, it wouldn't have made any difference if I had realised. Stephen says she knew she was dying. She'd known for several months.'

Disbelievingly Harry stared at Sarah before asking, 'What was it?'

Briskly she mentioned the usually unmentionable. 'Cancer. Stephen says she was convinced she'd live long enough to see the war won. And for women to get the vote.'

The train plunged into a tunnel. When it emerged into the grey November light – it was 30 November, St Andrew's Day, Scotland's patron saint – Sarah said, 'She walked off the ship in Newcastle unaided, you know. She had all her medals pinned to her chest and she stayed on her feet just long enough to say goodbye to each of her "gels" personally. She was a proud, patriotic, maddening, authoritarian, compassionate old tartar. And I'm proud to have known her.'

'Me too,' Harry said softly.

It was only when Tom started to talk about Doctor Inglis that he regained any of his old confidence. He had decided to speak in the debate on Clause IV of the Representation of the People Bill, to make votes for women the subject of his first speech since his return from Passchendaele, but to begin with he had stammered and almost lost the thread of his argument. Kessie could see his fellow MPs were listening politely only because he was the Honourable and *Gallant* Member for The Dales, the extra word being accorded him as a serving soldier. She leaned over the edge of the Ladies' Gallery, willing him to be the eloquent, scathing orator, the skilled parliamentarian she had known.

Tom tied in Doctor Inglis' sudden tragic death with the fact that the young women who had served with her, who had been with their field hospitals in the heat of the battle, who had driven their ambulances through all hellfire, who had endured two of the most terrible retreats of the war, in Serbia and the Dobrudja, these same young women were, by this honourable House, considered unfit to vote. Welcome as the Representation of the People Bill was as a whole, he considered it disgraceful, a continuing black mark against his sex, that women were being denied the vote on the same terms as men. With some of his old passion, he finished by saying, 'It has been left to a Rou-manian to appreciate what apparently the men of this

223

country cannot. May I remind you what the Prefect of Constanza said of the late lamented Doctor Inglis and her Hospital Unit? "No wonder England is a great country, if her women are like that."'

As Tom sat down to cheers and cries of 'Hear, hear?' Kessie sighed with relief. He had surmounted another barrier on the tortuous road to recovery.

Living with Tom was, at the moment, a bit like walking a tightrope stretched across a field of broken bottles. One false move, one slip of the foot, and they were both cut and bleeding. But Tom had decided he wanted to go to The Dales and asked her to accompany him. Maggie and Sarah were willing to look after the children so at the end of the week they caught the train north.

Being back among his 'ain folk', involving himself in his constituents' problems, seeing the love they had for him, the touching faith in 'ower Major Tom', did him a power of good, though when they were alone in the little end-of-terrace house that dear old Aunt Ada had bequeathed to Kessie, Tom still slipped into sombre silences, his hands still trembled as he lit yet another cigarette. At the end of their first week in Mellordale he had a bad nightmare.

Hastily, Kessie lit the paraffin lamp by the side of the bed. Fortunately she always woke up quickly, her mind clear. As the glow of the lamp spread round the room Tom stopped shouting and sat up in the bed, his head in his hands, his shoulders heaving, his breath rasping. Kessie knelt upright and put her arms around him, his head dropped on to her breasts, and she stroked the thick black hair. Slowly he sank back on to the pillow, pulling her down with him, holding her so tightly she could hardly breathe.

'You're so warm and you smell so sweetly, Kess. The touch and the scent of the living, not the dead.'

Silently they lay together, the heat of their bodies stoked their desire and slowly, sweetly, they made love. It was the first time they had succeeded since Tom's return from Passchendaele, for even the art of love-making, which he had previously taken for granted, had deserted him.

Perhaps it was because of this and also because they were in the double bed that had been their honeymoon bed, in a house that held happy memories, that for the first time Tom described his worst recurrent nightmare.

He was crouched in a shell-hole, the sound of the five-nines thundering in the background, when Guy came towards him. In the brilliance of the magnesium flares, he could see that Guy was wearing his respirator. Guy lifted his hand, the same way he had that last time they were together. Then he pulled off his respirator. Each time he made the movement Tom breathed a sigh of relief – no gas attack after all. Each time he expected to see the carefree smile break across Guy's face, the brown eyes shining, but each time there was a grinning skull beneath the respirator and baby rats were nesting in the eyeless sockets, as Tom had seen them nest in so many skulls.

Kissing his face, Kessie said, 'Oh Tom, my love, you're here, you're alive, and if there is an after-life it isn't like that for Guy or for any of them. It's only like that for the living with their memories. You mustn't forget them, my darling, you won't forget them, but the memories will fade, that's the saving grace of the living.'

'I know I've been a sod to you, Kess,' Tom held her tightly, 'but I love you, I love you.'

The next morning, looking quite cheerful, he announced that he was going up to Ryby Hall. The one concern Tom shared with Alice was wishing to know what had happened to Guy's other poems. 'Poppies' he regarded as a sentimental trifle that Guy had dashed off to please the current love of his life. According to Tom, some of his other poems possessed real passion, density of imagery, complexity of metre, and should most definitely be published. He had therefore written personally to Mrs Kendle who had replied promptly, thanking Tom for his sympathy and his beautiful description of her husband's last hours on this earth. Yes, she had admitted, several poems other than 'Poppies' had been included among her husband's effects, but in her opinion they did not reflect her husband's true character and view of life. She very much doubted that he himself would, on further consideration, have wished them to be published and she did not therefore intend to seek publication.

Tom had been furious. 'Poppies', he presumed, reflected her view of a man she had never understood, otherwise she could not have penned such rubbish, and she knew damned well the poem hadn't been written for her in any case. There the matter had been left. Until now. Kessie decided there was no point trying to dissuade Tom from visiting Ryby Hall. He had a great belief in his charm and powers of persuasion, when he chose to exercise them. She merely commented, 'Use all your charm on her. You'll need it. Your Lancashire accent isn't half as strong as it used to be, but it'll still amaze our Arabella, I assure you. Don't push her too hard. I think both she and Alice have gone slightly off their heads, if for different reasons, and if Arabella is pushed into a corner she could do anything with Guy's poems.'

After Tom had left the telegram from Sarah arrived, announcing that Alice had given birth to a bouncing baby girl weighing in at 7lb 4oz. Kessie trusted nobody would convey this information to Mrs Kendle, otherwise Tom's mission was surely doomed. The next day one of Sarah's brisk letters came.

> The Grove,
> Highgate,
> London N.
> December 16th,
> 1917.

Dear Kessie,

You did well to be up north! What a time we had with Alice! She screamed the place down, though in fact she had a remarkably easy labour for a first baby, which yours truly was able to deliver without difficulty. She yelled she wasn't going through this again, not even for Guy. She's still talking about him as if he's alive, so we're going to have to do something about it pronto, Kessie me luv.

The baby's a sweet little thing, fair-haired like Alice but with a look of Guy, and Alice has called her Margaret Jane. Madam is recovering fast, holding court in bed, telling all and sundry about the awfulness of her labour. She says God has obviously had the boot in for women from the dawn of creation, regarding Eve as responsible for the Fall, not that weedy little Adam who cravenly blamed everything on to her!

I'm fine. The children are fine. I trust all is well in The Dales and Tom is in better spirits.

See you soon,
Luv Sarah.

Kessie was delighted to hear the news and Sarah's letter made her smile, but she wondered how she was going to tell Tom that the child-bearing season was not yet over. In his present state he was unlikely to notice Sarah's condition until she became huge; if she ever did – she was carrying snugly. Despite his own past record with women, Tom could at times be very stuffy about the sexual behaviour of those close to him and he would not be pleased to learn that his favourite sister was with child, an illegitimate child. Oh well, it would sort itself out, Kessie supposed.

It was Friday evening before Tom returned from Ryby-in-Furness. He'd been delayed by a heavy fall of snow over the north Lancashire fells which had blocked the railway line. The wind was howling down from the moors and Kessie was propped up in bed reading when she heard Tom thumping up the stairs. From the glowering expression on his face as he came in, Kessie did not think the visit had been a success. He crossed to the bed and kissed her.

'You're freezing,' she cried.

'How's your heart?'

'Fine, thank you, it's been having lots of rest.'

'Good. I'm going to have a shave and then I'm going to make love to you.'

'Don't bother about shaving.'

227

After they had again enjoyed a sweetly passionate climax and were lying in each other's arms, Kessie said, 'Alice has had a daughter. She's calling her Margaret Jane. You will be nice to them when we get back, won't you? And what did Mrs Kendle have to say?'

Tom stretched his bare arms in the air, the fine silky black hairs that grew from his wrists to his elbows were a dark brown colour in the light of the paraffin lamp. Kessie remembered the first time she had seen him partly naked, washing himself in Sarah's room, and how the hairs on his arms and chest had fascinated and excited her. They still did.

'You know *her* problem, don't you?'

Kessie looked at him. 'You think that's every woman's problem.'

'Not true. It's not Stephen's for one. Nor Dorothy's I suspect. I reckon they'd both die of shock if a man touched them. A healthy love life is good for everyone. It will be obligatory in my new world.'

Kessie smiled and repeated, 'What did Mrs Kendle have to say?'

'She told me she'd destroyed Guy's poems because they were written under stress – true – and were the unpatriotic product of a temporarily diseased mind.'

'Oh Tom! She can't have.'

'I don't believe she has. I produced a mixture of charm and religious mumbo-jumbo. I said Guy's soul would find no rest, he'd wander in Purgatory, if his poems weren't published.' Kessie started to giggle but stopped abruptly as Tom said savagely, 'I could have killed the bitch. But I think I put the fear of God into her. She won't publish at the moment. You were right about backing her into a corner. But she'll keep the poems, locked away somewhere in that joyless place. God, what a household! I was so browned off and angry, I nearly started to walk home through the snow.'

Slowly his rage subsided and Kessie decided she had better mention Christmas. Tom said, 'What about Christmas?'

'Well,' Kessie chose her words carefully. 'Philip Marchal has invited us to spend it at Chenneys. I'd like to accept the invitation. It'll give me a complete rest. And Maggie could do with one, too. The children will have a lovely time there.'

'How often have you been seeing him?' Tom demanded.

Suppressing a sigh, keeping her voice as light as possible, Kessie replied, 'I've seen him once since he came back from the United States. He took me for a meal at the Savoy Grill – which I thoroughly enjoyed. He wrote to invite us to Chenneys.' She paused but there was no response from Tom, so she went on. 'Can we make a bargain? If we go to Chenneys, Alice will obviously come with us. She can have a lovely time too, being waited on hand and foot, just like her old society days. Then in the New Year I shall make sure she goes back home and brings Margaret Jane up in St John's Wood, where she can also decide what to do about Johnny. You know, that old thing, her husband.'

With her mouth clamped shut Kessie waited while Tom lit a cigarette, had a cough, and blew out several smoke rings. Finally he said, 'All right, it's a bargain. As long as bloody Alice disappears from under my feet.' Giving Kessie an injured look, he added, 'Of course I'll be nice to the baby. I like kids.'

You liked bloody Alice once upon a time, Kessie just stopped herself saying out loud.

20

Sarah had no particular desire to spend Christmas at Chenneys, though she took Kessie's point that it would give them all a complete break. On the morning of Christmas Eve they travelled down to Kent by train. There were two limousines to meet them at the local station which was just as well, because Alice and her baby's impedimenta and the nursemaid she had hired to look after Margaret Jane virtually filled one of them.

Philip Marchal was waiting to greet them in the entrance

hall at Chenneys, his expression as haughtily sardonic as of yore, his manner as coolly detached, though by his undemonstrative standards Sarah reckoned he was pleased to see them. Nearly a year away from England's shores had obviously not lessened his affection for Kessie, who was treated to his warmest smile and a softening of those cold grey eyes.

In the evening, after an early meal in the lovely panelled dining room, they trooped into the entrance hall, where a piano had been placed underneath a standard lamp, close by the huge open fireplace in which a mound of logs was burning. The families of those who lived and worked on the estate were already seated, all wearing their Sunday best and looking somewhat self-conscious, and near the fire was a group of convalescent officers and their nurses from the hospital wing. Among the patients, the three pips on his shoulder denoting his captain's rank, a man with a long neck and fine brown hair had his head bent low over the carol sheet in his hand. Swiftly Alice moved towards him, placing her hands on his shoulders.

'Guy darling, you managed to get here after all. How heavenly!' Startled, the man jerked his head upwards, a tic in his cheek twitching compulsively. Looking down into the face that bore no resemblance to Guy's, disappointed but not noticeably discomforted, Alice said, 'I am sorry. I thought you were somebody else.'

It had been all very well, Sarah thought, for Kessie to say they would discuss Guy's death with Alice once the baby was born, but in practice, with her talking about him vivaciously and on the whole *rationally*, as if he were in the trenches or sitting behind the lines in the officers' club in Poperinghe, unable to wangle Christmas leave at home, nobody had yet done so. Sarah didn't reckon it was her business, but they were definitely going to have to do something about Alice, and fast.

Fortunately, Tom was with the children and had missed the exchange, but Sarah saw Kessie frown and Philip's supercilious eyebrows rose an inch. Still, there was nothing to be done at the moment, so Sarah joined her brother who in unconventional fashion was sitting on the stairs with the children grouped round him. When everybody was organised, Kessie took her place at the piano. Then one of the servants handed out candles, another came round with a taper, and when they were all lit the main lights were switched off.

'Oh . . . h . . . h.' The gasps of pleasure and the children's squeals of delight sounded round the hall.

Philip was not a playwright for nothing and his dramatic instinct had effected the prettiest sight, the flames leaping in the fireplace, the candles on the Christmas tree and in folks' hands wavering and flaring, casting shadows on the carved ceiling and walls, illuminating the faces. Kessie rippled several chords on the piano and Sarah joined the assembled throng, men and women whom the war had brought here from all over the British Isles and Empire, employees who had probably never strayed beyond the boundaries of Kent, in lustily singing the favourite carols. The children's voices piped above the adults' contraltos and sopranos, tenors and baritones, and they finished with a rousing rendition of 'Hark the Herald Angels Sing'.

Sarah only wished that Misha could have been here sitting beside her, for atheist that he was he would still have relished the spectacle and the harmony of the carol service. She had received a Christmas greeting from him, assuring her in good Miltonic manner that time would soon run back for them, to fetch the age of gold. How soon, he had not intimated.

Philip had gone to immense pains to make the festivities enjoyable – or seen that his servants did, any road – and Sarah had to admit Christmas Day and Boxing Day were as pleasurable as Christmas Eve. Luxurious good taste had its attractions – log fires burning in every room, exquisitely set tables groaning with food, servants waiting to blow your nose for you – so long as you forgot about the men in the trenches and the women surviving as best they could in the back streets. The weather was seasonably kind too, hoar frost glittering in the rising sun, the days cold but bright.

For most of the time, in the highest of spirits Alice joined in the fun, but on a couple of occasions, wrapped in her mink coat and matching Cossack-style hat, she suddenly went outside, to pace up and down the terrace.

'I could kick myself,' a worried Kessie said to Sarah. 'I completely forgot she met Guy here at Chenneys. I don't know what's going on in Alice's head but the memories are obviously crowding back. And she has only recently had a baby, which can do peculiar things to some women. Philip says she ought to see a doctor. He knows one of those psycho-analysts whom he thinks could help her. How are we going to persuade Alice to see him?'

'I dunno,' Sarah replied, 'but I'm darned sure Philip's right.'

'I'm going to be a coward,' Kessie said, 'and leave it until after Christmas.'

The 27th December dawned with a heavy clinging mist. Once or twice the sun looked as if it might break through but it gave up the struggle. Maybe it was being cooped up indoors but the children started to quarrel, nothing serious, merely the usual 'You can't have it, it's mine', and the outraged cries of 'Mummy, what do you think Mark has done?', or Kate, or Anne, or even as the day wore on, dear little Con. Margaret Jane was in a bad temper too, crying a good deal, and Alice fussed around giving what Philip described as her 'Earth Mother, dressed by Moly-neux, performance'. In the middle of the afternoon, before tea, Tom said to Sarah, 'What about a breath of air, Sal, before we gorge ourselves yet again?'

Outside it was dank and chill, the bare branches of the trees skeleton-like against the leaden grey sky, moisture sploshing from the laurel bushes, scarves of mist sitting on the yew hedges, floating through the rose garden. From the terrace they followed the path that led towards the summer house and despite his still-edgy temper and his intense irritation with Alice, Tom seemed to be more in control of himself. As they walked briskly along, he voiced Sarah's ambivalent emotions, wondering what the hell the two of them were doing spending Christmas in a place like this, though he reckoned as far as the landed gentry went Philip Marchal was among the less poisonous.

'I remember saying something like that to Kessie when we first met. As far as mill-owners went, her father had a good record.'

Tom laughed. 'Don't worry, Sal. We'll shake everything up, even things out, *après la guerre fini*.' Savagely he added, 'By God, we will!'

They had reached the summer house. He pushed the door and it opened, so they went inside. It was chill in here too, with a slightly musty smell, but Tom sat down on the wickerwork sofa, took out his cigarettes and lit one. Realising he wanted to stay for a while, Sarah sat herself on the cushions by his side. Following on from his comments about what they would do in England after the war was over he started to talk about Russia and the Bolshevik Revolution.

'I'm impressed by the calibre of their leaders, Lenin, Trotsky, and that Mikhail Muranov has real fire and passion. Good intelligence too, I imagine. You met him, didn't you?'

'Yes,' said Sarah.

Half Sarah's mind listened to Tom saying he was not a Marxian, never had been, never would be, but maybe the Bolshevik variety was what Russia needed. The other half debated whether this was the moment to give her brother the news that would, sooner rather than later, because she was already four months gone, literally stare him in the face. She decided his state of mind had improved considerably and therefore it was. Having come to her decision Sarah proceeded with her customary no-nonsense, let's-not-beat-about-the-bush style.

'I didn't just meet Mikhail Muranov, Tom. I got to know him intimately. In fact, I'm expecting his baby.'

'And do I gather you're having this one?'

The question shot out in Tom's sharpest tones, though from the slight twitch of his lips Sarah thought he regretted having asked it. In a way she deserved it, and she knew that on principle Tom had never forgiven her for getting rid of Edward Dawson's child, much as he'd disliked Edward personally. She felt she should also make allowances for the shock of her announcement. In answer to the question she merely nodded. Silently Tom stared at her while he took his cigarette packet from his jacket pocket and lit another one from the dog-end of the first, which he ground into the floor of the summer house with his heel. Then the questions flowed from him in a gentler manner. Was she by any chance married to Mikhail Muranov? Did he know about the child? With the current chaos in Russia when was he likely to come to collect her? Or when did she intend to travel there? Was that her intention?

'Yes,' Sarah said. 'As soon as possible after the baby's born I shall go back to Russia, to fight with Misha for the brave new world.'

'I see. I presume Kessie knows all about it?'

Sarah nodded again. Tom glanced at her loose jacket and the flicker in his eyes admitted that he been neither observant nor in a condition to be given the news. Then he put his arm round her shoulder and made a typically Tom comment. 'Bloody hell, Sal, you aren't half a liability.'

She rested her head on his shoulder. After a few seconds of the comforting physical contact they rarely indulged in, Tom pulled her to her feet. 'It's cold. Come on, let's walk back to a nice warm fire and muffins and tea.'

When they were walking towards the house Sarah said, 'You've taken the news very well.'

'What did you expect me to do? Behave like a mid-Victorian father? You're thirty-four years old, Sal, and I'm your brother not your keeper, as you have on occasions told me in no uncertain terms. I shan't object if you sort your life out. If I were you, I'd start by marrying Mikhail Muranov. Makes everything simpler and there's a good deal to be said for marriage. I should know.'

'Yes,' said Sarah, 'Kessie's one in a million.'

In the early evening, after the children had gone to bed, they went upstairs to change for dinner. After they had reassembled downstairs they waited for Alice to appear, and waited, until eventually Philip instructed one of the servants to tell Mrs Conway dinner was ready to be served. The maid returned to say Mrs Conway was not in the room and the nursemaid Miss Jardine said she had not been in to kiss her daughter goodnight as usual. Kessie was deeply concerned at this news, so Philip immediately instructed his staff to search the house in case Mrs Conway had met with an accident. At Kessie's request the aged footman was sent to the hospital wing, where she thought Alice might possibly have gone in search of the captain whom she had imagined was Guy. He returned to say nobody had seen Mrs Conway in the hospital, but one of the nurses had noticed a light in the summer house.

'That's it!' Kessie exclaimed. 'That's where she's gone.'

Tom swore under his breath and lit another cigarette. To an extent Sarah shared her brother's reaction, though it wasn't really Alice's fault if she'd gone slightly off her head. Life had been kind to golden Alice until the moment Guy was killed and she was ill-equipped to deal with tragedy. Sarah also reckoned they were partly to blame for allowing her to live the lie of Guy's survival.

Despite both Tom and Philip's protestations, Kessie insisted on going with the search party to the summer house. Sarah stayed with Tom, who was restlessly tense and chain-smoking. It was a good half hour before they heard voices in the hall and Philip immediately limped out of the room. Tom moved to the open fireplace, where he kicked one of the logs which fell with a splutter of yellow flame into the glowing redness.

The door opened and Alice swept towards the fireplace, her hands outstretched to warm them in front of the flames Tom's kick had stirred. Almost unbelievably, she was wearing a silver lamé evening gown with roses forming the straps across her bare shoulders. Diamond ear-rings glinted in her lobes and her golden hair was piled high. The hem of her gown was however wet and bedraggled and strands of hair were straggling down her cheeks and shoulders.

Behind her were Philip, his face impassive, and Kessie, her forehead furrowed with anxiety.

As she moved across the room Alice talked nineteen to the dozen, about how cold it was and she shouldn't have worn her high-heeled court shoes because they were impractical for walking and the heel had come loose on one of them which was a nuisance and was there a good cobbler in the village? Then in a conversational tone, addressing nobody in particular, she said, 'He didn't come. I waited and waited. I can't think what's happened to him.'

Much as Sarah had never cared for Alice, it was pathetic to think of her in that freezing summer house, with the wind lashing the sleet around it, dressed in one of her Paris evening gowns, waiting for the dead Guy.

'Who didn't come, Alice?' Tom's voice was low. Kessie moved towards him, shaking her head, but he repeated, 'Who didn't come, Alice?'

Sarah doubted anybody was going to stop her brother now. His friendship with Guy Kendle had possessed an intensity forged by the circumstances in which they had met, slept, eaten, fought, and one of them had died. Tom could no more continue to live with the lie of Guy's existence than Alice could apparently live without it. Yet she could not live with it and stay sane, and Sarah reckoned somebody had to tell her the truth. Kessie apparently reached the same conclusion because she stood limply, her arms by her side, as for the third time Tom repeated, 'Who didn't come, Alice?'

'Why Guy, of course.'

His voice trembling with emotion Tom said, 'He's dead, Alice. He was blown to buggery in the mud Field-Marshal Haig and his merry men believed we could, and should, with stiff upper lips, fight our way through. For your own sake, for the sake of that baby asleep upstairs, face the truth, Alice. Guy's dead.'

Her cornflower blue eyes opening wide, Alice turned her head towards Tom.

'You never really liked me, did you? It took me a long time to realise that.' A deep shiver ran through her body and she said, 'I think I shall have a nice hot bath. I adore the peacock in your bathroom, Philip.'

Seizing her by the bare shoulders, shaking her, Tom said, 'Did you hear what I said? Guy's dead.'

As Sarah, Kessie and Philip all moved towards Tom, fearful that he might lost control of himself, Alice said, 'Yes, I heard. Will you come and talk to me while I have a bath, Kessie?'

When Kessie returned downstairs, having seen Alice to bed, Tom had disappeared into the wildness of the night. She wanted to go in search of him but Sarah and Philip dissuaded her, arguing that it was best to let him walk his anguish out of his system. While they ate a belated dinner, Sarah enquired after Alice and if she now accepted the truth about Guy, fiercely as it had been delivered.

'She went to sleep like a baby, but I honestly don't know what's going on in her mind. She does need help. Professional medical help.'

Kessie put her face into her hands and Sarah saw the intense concern for *her* in Philip's face as he said, 'May I suggest Alice and the baby and Miss Jardine stay here for the time being when you return to London tomorrow? I will make enquiries about finding the right sort of help.'

Gratefully Kessie looked up at him, acknowledging that she had sufficient problems of her own without the burden of Alice's.

A fortnight later, back at The Grove, Kessie decided to give a celebration-cum-belated birthday party. After nearly sixty years of struggle, on 10 January 1918, the House of Lords passed Clause IV of the Representation of the People Bill which meant that women over the age of thirty would have the right to vote in the next and subsequent General Elections in democratic Britain.

Kessie was in two minds about inviting Alice who remained down at Chenneys. According to Philip, her moods were still volatile and he was uncertain whether she had accepted the fact of Guy's death. In principle she had agreed to see his psycho-analyst friend, but in practice she kept finding reasons for postponing the consultation. However, Philip thought attending the party would do her no harm and he offered to escort her to London. Sarah had to admit that though an aloof, apparently cold fish, towards those within the charmed circle he was a considerate man.

When Philip and Alice arrived at The Grove on the evening of the party, she was wearing one of her Paris model evening gowns. This little number had a white skirt embroidered with tiny green stars, and a matching shawl worn over a sleeveless, slinky green taffeta top, with the real touch of *haute couture* being provided by the armlets which were of the same green taffeta material, only stiffened, and which stretched from her knuckles to her elbows. Alice looked absolutely stunning and apart from a tendency to skip from subject to subject like a butterfly among the summer flowers, though with less apparent purpose, she sounded almost as normal as she looked.

'I do wish I'd been in the House of Lords. It must have been exciting.'

'No, it wasn't actually, was it?' Kessie looked at Sarah who shook her head. 'You know how little space there is for *women* in their Lordship's Chamber, so we were crowded into one of the committee rooms, waiting for the news of the debates to be relayed. When we heard Lord Curzon was due to speak we wondered if he was going to make one of his speeches about "The Gauls are at the gate, hold them back, lest the walls of manly imperial power come tumbling down", and thwart us at the eleventh hour. We learned he wasn't in the sweetest fashion. One of the parliamentary policemen put his head round the door and bellowed, "Lord Curzon is h'up, ladies, but 'e won't do you no 'arm"!'

'How delicious!' Alice's bell-like laughter pealed out. Then, with the most innocent expression she said, 'I gather getting himself "h'up" is not one of one Lord Curzon's problems.'

'Naughty, naughty,' Kessie giggled before saying, 'I

suppose I'd better give my speech. Tom insists I do, and some people have to leave early.'

'Kessie wants everybody in the sitting room,' Sarah shouted. 'Bring your glasses with you.' Sarah saw Harry, whom she had invited, gawping at the mounds of food Maggie had somehow managed to provide and she tucked her arm into his. 'That includes you, me lad. You can guzzle away to your heart's content later.'

When everybody had crowded into the sitting-room, Tom held up his hand and in a toast-masterish voice said, 'Pray silence for your hostess, the distinguished suffragette, the campaigner for women's rights, who's married to some MP or other whose name escapes me. Ladies and gentlemen, I give you – Kessie!'

Amid the laughter and cheers Tom spanned his hands round her waist and lifted her on to a chair. After telling him she could have climbed up herself, which brought more cheers, in her husky voice, Kessie started to speak.

'Many of you will remember those conversations we used to have at Clement's Inn . . .' the cheers rang out again, 'and in prisons up and down the country, with the wardresses bellowing "Keep quiet, you women".'

Amid the groans, Dorothy who had spent more time in His Majesty's prisons than anybody in the room, jumped on to a chair and waved her clasped hands above her head, a gesture which produced more cheers. Whatever her feelings about being denied the vote, she had accepted this invitation.

Kessie continued: 'Remember those eager conversations we had about the rallies and processions we should organise in London and Manchester, in every city and town in the land, once we had the basic right to vote. Well, life rarely goes according to the best-laid plans. Our victory has come in time of war, a terrible terrible war, in which victory has not yet been won. The dreadful days in which our limited triumph has been achieved have given it an anti-climactic quality. There are those who have already started to say that given our sterling war efforts we should have won the vote anyway, therefore all our prewar efforts were a waste of time. I'm sure that will become a popular theme when we who fought are dead and gone.'

'Perish the thought!' Stephen boomed. 'Which birthday did you say we're celebrating? Your thirty-third, old thing, or your one hundred and thirty-third?'

Amid the laughter Kessie called out, 'Will you kindly stop heckling me! In my opinion, the talk about our war work is standing the matter on its head. In the first place, when we embarked on our militant campaign in 1905, who imagined there would be a Great War in 1914? In the second place, well, just think back to 1905, think what things were like for women. Had we not fought, had we not started to change the whole attitude towards women, had we not set the tone for others to follow, then I do not believe, I really do not, that so many women would have been capable of stepping into their roles in this war.'

'Hear, hear!' Sarah smiled as Philip Marchal's voice joined the shouts of approval.

'When I speak of us suffragettes rousing the masses of women by our example, who roused us? They're not with us tonight, as they were not with us in the Houses of Parliament the other day. That does not alter what they did. I know Mrs Pankhurst and Christabel were the tinder that lit my confidence and courage and determination. And I'd like to pay my tribute to them.'

'Well said, old thing,' Stephen boomed again, and Alice shouted, 'Hear, hear!' Sarah agreed with Kessie's generous tribute, but there were fewer cheers than for some of her earlier remarks.

'With the achievement of votes for some women, we have breached the barriers of male superiority. It's a historic breach. Of that I have no doubt. But let nobody doubt that we've only made a gap in the barriers. An enormous amount remains to be done before they're all broken down. Though I hope to live long enough to see them smashed in my children's lifetime, Stephen.' Waving to Stephen, with a lovely smile Kessie then turned towards Tom. 'In our children's lifetime. And on this reasonably joyful occasion, I'd like to pay my tribute to, and to thank, the men who battled with us through the years. Not least to my not entirely unknown husband.'

Tom took her hand in his, raised it to his lips and kissed it gallantly, to further cheers and cries of 'ah . . . h'. The glasses were charged and Kessie proposed the toast: 'To votes for all women within a very short while! And to the equality of the sexes in a world at peace!'

Dorothy shouted herself nearly hoarse over the first part of the toast and Sarah drank to the second part with greater fervour, before she led the singing of 'Happy belated birthday, dear Kessie.'

After the guests had dispersed, some to stuff their faces at the buffet, some to talk, some to depart, Sarah joined Harry who had obviously enjoyed stuffing *his* face with Maggie's delicious food.

'There must be a lot of memories wrapped up in this evening for you,' he said.

'There are,' Sarah agreed, 'though as Kessie said, it's not exactly how any of us imagined we'd celebrate the achievement of votes for women.'

Harry was not at his ease, blast him. Why couldn't he just relax and be his cheerful self? Why couldn't he realise that most of Kessie and Tom's friends were pleasant folk who had their own doubts and worries, and the surface differences of accents, manner and dress were merely matters of money and confidence? She had invited him because she was fond of him and because they both knew they might never meet again. For Harry had finally been discharged from the Royal Naval Air Service, and having been transferred to the army he was due to report for further service on Monday morning.

'Hello, Harry.' Dorothy bounded over to them. 'Has Sarah told you? Stephen and I are off to Macedonia soon. Stephen felt we should go. It was what Doctor Inglis wanted. Won't it be fun if you're sent to Salonika and we meet up there?'

Sarah caught Harry's eye and they both smiled, their idea of 'fun' and Didi's being dissimilar. Somebody in the dining room called out her name and with an 'Excuse me', off she bounded. Harry looked slightly hurt that she should arrive and depart so swiftly but Dorothy was like that with everybody, not just him. To cheer him up, Sarah said, 'You haven't had a proper chance to talk to Tom yet, have you? Come on.'

Despite his own edginess, Tom remained good at putting uncertain folk at their ease, concentrating his attention as if they were the one person in the room he wanted to talk to. Harry soon relaxed into his chirpy, amusing, sensible self, until the clock on the mantelpiece chimed midnight prettily, the golden pendulums swinging backwards and forwards. Pulling a wry face Harry said, 'I suppose Cinderella had better be on her way. Thanks ever so much for inviting me. I have enjoyed myself.'

'Look after yourself, Harry. Come back soon.'

Sarah held out her hand, which he clasped for a longer time than polite manners permitted, before he wished her and Tom the very best of luck. After Harry had gone her brother said, 'Where does he fit into the picture? He seems a decent enough bloke and he obviously dotes on you.'

'He's a good friend,' Sarah said briskly.

'I see.' Tom gave her his devilish grin.

21

The next afternoon Philip escorted Alice, and Margaret Jane, to The Grove for tea. They all agreed it was imperative that Alice receive medical help and while she was here Kessie might be able to persuade her to consult the psycho-analyst. They had only just arrived when the front door knocker banged and from the hall the instantly identifiable, mellifluously carrying tones of Alice's husband, Johnny Conway, were audible.

Oh heck! Sarah thought. What had brought him round, unannounced, at such an inappropriate moment? Kessie had deliberately not invited him to the party last night, though she knew he was currently in London on leave. Alice's reactions to her husband's voice were alarming to say the least. For a few seconds she listened in wide-eyed silence, then, clutching Margaret Jane in her arms, she jumped up and rushed into the corner behind the piano where she cowered, clasping the baby tightly to her bosom. The minute Alice was on her feet, Kessie moved quickly but not fast enough, because Maggie gave her usual tap on the door and as usual entered almost immediately. Behind her was Johnny, arms already outstretched, ready to make his usual dramatic entrance.

'What's he doing here? Get him out. He's not coming near my baby. Get him out. I'm divorcing you, do you hear? I'm marrying Guy. Go away. I don't want you. Don't you dare come near my baby. I know what you want. You want to take her away from me. You can't have her.'

It was Philip who shut the door in the startled Johnny's face, but Alice went on screaming for several more seconds. Then she started to sob, terrible sobs that were dredged up from the depths of her being, and a frightened Margaret Jane howled in concert with her mother. Trying to comfort her, Kessie said to Sarah, 'See to Johnny, please. Make him go away. Tell him I'll see him later.'

Cautiously Sarah opened the door in case he was still behind it, but he was in the hall where Maggie was standing by his side like a guard-dog. Sarah gave her a brief smile and she disappeared down the basement stairs. In his uniform which, unlike Tom's, looked as if it had never seen a speck of dirt, let alone mud, Johnny was extremely handsome, fitting the role of junior staff officer to perfection. From behind the shut sitting room door, the sound of the sobbing was fearful and he clutched at his officer's stick and started to bang it against his leg. Sarah recalled seeing him perform a similar action as the hero in Philip's play, *Love me for Ever*.

'I'm sorry, Johnny, but I think you'd best go.'

He stopped banging the stick and pivoted round to face Sarah.

'But she's my wife. I'd no idea she was . . . was . . . in such a state. I think somebody might have told me. I mean, I am her husband. I do care about her, you know. What's being done? I mean, she shouldn't be up and about in her state. She should be in a . . . a . . . secure place, being properly looked after.'

A virtuous, blustering note had crept into his voice and Sarah felt herself bridling. But she took a deep breath because it wasn't exactly his fault if his wife had fallen passionately in love with another man, had that man's child, and gone off her head when he was killed.

'Look Johnny, we all know Alice needs help, but honestly you aren't the person to give it. Not at the moment. So why don't you toddle off somewhere and come back in . . . Well, give us a ring first. Then you and Kessie can have a good talk.'

'It doesn't strike me that Kessie's help has done Alice much good to date.'

Sarah could have slapped his face. Furiously she said, 'If it wasn't for Kessie, your wife, who doesn't want to know about you and whom you haven't seen in months, would be in an even worse state.'

'Now look here, Sarah, I'm not being spoken to like that. I'm Alice's husband and . . .'

'To blazes with your proprietorial rights. They don't mean a thing.'

'They do legally. Legally I have the right to . . .'

The sitting room door opened and Philip limped into the hall. His face impassive, he nodded towards Johnny whose whole demeanour changed to one of hearty bonhomie.

'Good to see you, Sir Philip.'

Sir Philip. Sarah's eyes opened wide but then she realised that because of Kessie and his feelings for her she met a Philip Marchal few people knew. When he spoke his voice was chillingly clipped and incisive, and with his cold appraising eyes and cold detached manner he was a daunting figure.

'I am about to telephone a clinic run by a friend of mine who is a *psycho-analyst*.' Philip enunciated the word with glacial clarity. 'He studied in Vienna before the war. I shall ask him if your wife can be admitted immediately. Do you have any objections, *as Alice's husband*?'

The emphasis on 'as Alice's husband' was ironic, indicating that Philip had overheard their slanging match. Johnny had no objections. On the contrary, he couldn't thank Sir Philip enough for his help. While they waited for the operator to ring back on the long-distance call, part of Sarah felt sorry for Johnny, desperately filling the empty air with irrelevant chatter, flailing in a situation beyond his grasp, but part of her liked him less than she once had. The way he was kow-towing to *Sir* Philip while trying to maintain a man-to-man relationship was pretty nauseating and she couldn't see any future for him with Alice.

The telephone trilled, Philip was connected to the clinic and organised Alice's admission for tomorrow. After he had hung up the receiver he turned to Johnny. 'In my opinion it will be wiser if you do not contact your wife at the moment. Therefore, I shall not give you the address. Write to me, Jonathon, and I will keep you informed of her progress. The child may remain at Chenneys where she's been staying with her nursemaid, an admirable woman.'

Vainly trying to hide his surprise at Philip's casual announcement that 'the child' had been at Chenneys, without argument, without seeing Kessie or Alice, expressing his heartfelt thanks, Johnny left. Sarah reckoned he was only too relieved to dump the problem of his wife in *Sir* Philip's hands. Thoughtfully she gazed at Philip.

'I wouldn't like you for my enemy.'

Heavily sedated, Alice stayed overnight at The Grove. Kessie contacted her sister Verena who apparently held forth about the dangers of women kicking over the emancipated traces, as Alice had done, but in this extremity she agreed to overlook her sister's appalling behaviour and to visit her at the clinic which was in Sussex, not far from her country house. She did not, however, offer any help with Margaret Jane.

In the morning Philip arrived with the nurse he had organised. Sarah had to admit he was a quietly efficient bugger. In her quiescent, semi-drugged state, Maggie and Tom assisted Alice down the stairs. The glossy fur coat in which she had arrived yesterday hugged her tall, slim figure but Kessie had not dressed her hair and underneath her fur hat, tied in a loose bow like a girl's, its golden length flowed down Alice's back. The pity was evident in Tom's expression, the particular blankness of Maggie's showed even she was touched by Mrs Conway's condition, and Sarah's own heart ached.

In the hall Philip and the nurse took over, leading Alice towards the front door. Suddenly she stopped, shaking off their arms, and turned towards Kessie who, Sarah could see, was fighting back the tears. With a flash of her incisive, imperious clarity Alice said, 'Where am I going? Where's my baby? Where's Guy?'

'You're very tired, Alice. You're going to have a rest,' Kessie said huskily. 'They'll be waiting when you come back.'

Trusting, childlike, Alice nodded, but something was still troubling her. Moving her head fretfully, she said, 'I never meant to hurt you, Kessie. You're my very best friend. We women shouldn't hurt each other, should we?'

As Kessie shook her head, hugging Alice tightly, Sarah wondered when in particular she had hurt her truly best friend so deeply that it bothered her at this moment? Then, in a stronger New York accent than Sarah had heard her use in years, as if she were a young society belle, Alice said to Philip, 'Do I know you? Have we been introduced? I'm Alice Hartley. Shall we dance?'

Kessie put her head round Sarah's door. 'That was Philip on the telephone. He says Alice has settled in at the clinic, but her doctor thinks she should have peace and quiet for the time being. No visitors.' She advanced into the room, frowning slightly. 'I asked Philip to register Margaret Jane's birth but it's already been done. By Jonathon Fitzgerald Conway, father, occupation actor. What do you think about that? Giving him the benefit of the doubt, I suppose he did it for the best. But Alice will go ma . . .' Kessie bit off the end of the word 'mad' because Alice was already on the brink of madness. 'She'll hit the roof when she finds out.'

'Let's worry about it when she's recovered,' Sarah said briskly. 'And it really isn't your problem, Kessie.'

With Alice's departure a comparatively peaceful, relaxed atmosphere had returned to The Grove. Tom's nerves were still easily jangled, but that had become a more appropriate word than shattered. He had melancholic moods and Kessie said she sometimes woke in the night to find him standing by the window, or that he'd gone out for a lonely walk, but the nightmares were infrequent, he'd stopped venting his rages on Kessie and had again become solicitous for her welfare. He spent a lot of time with the kids and the sight of Tom sitting on the sofa, with Kate on his knee, Mark tucked by one arm, Con by the other, Anne hunched at his feet, reading *The Forsaken Merman,* the children's faces responding to their father's expressive voice, warmed the cockles of Sarah's heart.

The girls adored him, dramatic Kate and highly intelligent Anne competing for his attention with dear little Con sweetly accepting that she had his love. Consciously or unconsciously, Anne was his favourite child, and the bond between father and eldest daughter was of the strongest. His relationship with his only son was more difficult and Sarah reckoned this was partly because, as one boy among three girls, far too many folk pampered and petted Mark, treatment his father did not accord him. Then Tom brought his son a set of toy soldiers, beautifully painted lead figures of dragoons, fusiliers and grenadiers, which delighted Mark. Sprawled on the floor the two of them arranged their troops in battle order, with Anne deeply interested in the proceedings. When Tom started teaching Mark how to bowl, using the corridor as a run-up, Kessie said cricket could wait for the summer months and it wasn't doing his shoulder any good.

Lloyd George renewed his offer of a post in his Government, dangling the possibility of a full ministerial job before Tom. When he turned the prospect down Kessie was invited to take tea at the House of Commons with the Prime Minister, but she refused that offer.

'It's up to Tom,' she said to Sarah. 'I just want him really well again, and he's definitely not in a mood to be pushed. If he thinks he can do more good staying in the army, on home-leave, acting as an independent goad, let him.'

Sarah was enjoying her pregnancy no end, though it would have been even more enjoyable if she could have shared it with Misha. As that was not to be, she wrote to him regularly, telling him what was happening in England, describing the heart-stopping moment when the baby quickened and how she could now feel it pushing and burrowing in her womb. She tried not to be too disappointed when no replies came, but the newspapers informed her that Mr Muranov was with Mr Trotsky in the thick of the Bolshevik negotiations with the Germans for a separate peace treaty, negotiations which the English newspapers considered shameful and disgraceful. Sarah didn't imagine Misha would be enjoying them greatly, but a peace treaty was essential for the survival of the infant Bolshevik Republic. It also provided good reason for him not having the time to write to her. She contented herself with the letters that arrived from her friends.

Jenny's letter was curiously uninformative and Sarah could only presume that her return to her island home was failing to live up to expectations. Harry's letter was chirpy and uncensored. Without betraying state secrets, he felt he could inform Sarah he was reattached to the dear old armoured cars, army version, and as they sailed across the ocean blue and neared their unknown destination, the air was distinctly hot and humid, there was a lot of sand about and camels and blokes in long white nightdresses. The unsubtle clues made Sarah laugh. Harry was clearly head-ing for, and had probably by now arrived in, the Middle Eastern theatre of operations. It was a safer zone than the Western Front and she sent up a prayer: may he come back soon in the same condition he went out.

Dorothy and Stephen's letter, jointly addressed to Kessie and Sarah, was in fact penned by Didi, with 'Bless all your cotton socks' added by Stephen. Didi wrote as she spoke, matter-of-factly but vividly. They'd sailed across the Mediterranean, up the Aegean Sea, and into the Gulf of Salonika where the water was incredibly blue and the air amazingly clear. At the moment it was jolly cold and they could see the soaring Macedonian peaks thick with snow. There hadn't been an actual offensive for some time but conditions up in those barren hills and soaring mountains were pretty grisly, they gathered, freezing cold in winter like now, boiling hot, fly-infested and dysentery-ridden in summer. Some of the boys in the wards had already been in hospital five times. There were lots of NYD cases to keep Stephen on her toes, they were certainly needed and jolly glad they'd come out. NYD officially stood for 'Not Yet Diagnosed', she informed them, but was translated by the troops as 'Not Yet Dead'. There was a PS. Would they tell Alice there was a Scottish Women's Hospital Unit already in Salonika, raised and funded by American women.

'I *shall* write and tell her that. Maybe it'll help cheer her up.' Kessie had been given permission to write to Alice and she regularly penned her chatty letters.

Then one afternoon, Maggie came into Sarah's room with a cable that had just arrived. It was from Misha, proving that some at least of her letters had reached him. It read:

Forgive me, Sabrina fair. I leave the written word to Milton. With him who can compete? Here we battle against the evils that would throttle our lustily mewing republic. I think of you every day my wildest of English roses. We shall be together soon. Your adoring Misha.'

Blast him for being an even worse correspondent than she herself normally was, but bless him for cabling, and just what – or who – had prompted Maggie's comments as she handed over the envelope?

Having long since ceased to regard Sarah as an upstart, instead treating her as an ally in the battle to protect Kessie's well-being, with a sympathetic sniff Maggie had said: 'Such a shame your husband's such a long way away, and you can't get to him, and he can't get to you, Miss Whitworth, with all this revolution business going on. I don't know why they can't let us alone to get on with our own lives. And I shouldn't be calling you "Miss Whitworth", should I? What do I call you now?'

What indeed? Sarah marched down the corridor and into the study where Kessie was working.

'What's all this about *my husband*?'

'Ah.' Kessie swivelled round in her chair. 'Well, I haven't been bruiting it abroad, I assure you, but if anybody's asked, I've lied, I admit I have, and said you married in Russia but the revolution and everything has separated you from your husband.'

'You had no right to, Kessie!' Sarah exploded.

'No,' she agreed calmly, though there was a flush on her cheeks. 'It makes everything simpler, particularly for Tom. I think you should consider his career, Sarah.'

'And what do I do when the baby's born and the registrar wants to see my marriage lines?'

'Say they were lost in the revolution. He won't go to Reni to check.'

'There's quite a few folk know I'm *not* married to Mikhail. Harry, Stephen, Dorothy, Jenny and the others who were with the Unit in Russia.'

'No, they don't. Well, apart from Harry and he won't say anything. The others can't know whether or not you were *secretly* married. Actually, I've already written to Stephen and Dorothy, and Jenny, sort of suggesting you and Mikhail married secretly in Reni.'

Sarah felt her anger and astonishment at Kessie's unilateral actions rising, but she tried to control them, saying, 'If I married Mikhail, why didn't I stay in Russia? Why did I come back here?'

'You didn't know you were expecting when you left. Which you didn't, did you? Otherwise you might not have come home. With the chaos in Russia, it seemed wiser to leave temporarily.'

'I see. I deserted my husband in time of trouble.'

'No, you didn't. *He* was worried about your safety. If you prefer it, because he knew you were expecting.'

'You've worked it all out, haven't you?'

'Yes,' Kessie admitted.

'How dare you?! I know exactly how Alice is going to feel when she's faced with the *fait accompli* of Johnny having registered himself as Margaret Jane's father.' Sarah stamped her foot and swore, 'Bloody furious!'

It was a *fait accompli* unless she went around shouting, Kessie's a liar, I'm not married, and I don't know whether I ever shall be. Sarah had to admit she knew *why* her sister-in-law had resorted to such underhand tactics. Despite the war and the loosening of moral codes, a heavy stigma still attached to illegitimacy and her being married indubitably made everything simpler for the Whitworths. She was living at The Grove, as her money dwindled partially off Kessie, for whose loving support she was enormously grateful. Though she continued to feel angry for several days – it was a matter of principle and she would marry, or not marry, Misha in her own good time – there really was nothing to be done.

She was debating whether to write to tell Misha that Kessie had married them off when the news came through that the embattled Bolsheviks had moved to Moscow, re-declaring it the capital city. Politically Sarah understood the reasons why – Petrograd was associated with the old regime and closer to the West, while Moscow was the ancient centre of Russian nationalism and further from hostile forces – but personally the news threw her into a panic. She had lost contact with Misha. By the time the cable arrived, giving her a new address in Moscow, she was so relieved she couldn't be bothered informing him of their 'marriage', which in any case was known only to a small circle of friends.

Early in March Kessie was finally given permission to visit Alice. She returned to say the clinic stood in beautiful surroundings which must be soothing for broken minds, the staff seemed sympathetically understanding, and Alice had accepted the fact that Guy was dead, though she was unlike her old self, quiet, almost withdrawn, liable to start crying.

Then out of the blue Jenny telephoned.

'I'm back, Sarah, back in dear old England!' After Sarah had expressed her delight and astonishment Jenny continued volubly. 'I can't tell you what it was like at home. Oh everybody was nice to me – in fact I was treated as a heroine. But I found the continuing patriotic enthusiasm pretty amazing, considering the casualties per Newfoundland's population must be among the highest of any Allied country. Nobody asked whether the sacrifices were worthwhile. And they're not enthusiastic about the Russian Revolution either. But it's what's happening in our family that really upset me. Hamish is fine. He's come to terms wonderfully well with his blindness. His fiancée is a great girl and they're determined to marry soon. No, it's Callum that's the problem. And my mother. She's devoting her entire life to him. She ignores my sister Fiona and poor old Popsky. She didn't show much interest in me either. I guess in one way her fierce devotion to Callum is touching but in other ways it's awful. He's turned into a gas-cough racked, evil-tempered child. The whole household revolves around him. Anyway, one day I was walking along the cliffs, watching the Atlantic breakers dash against the rocks, and I didn't feel three thousand miles from England. I felt three million, totally cut off! Part of me will always love Newfoundland but I don't really belong there any more. So I decided Fiona and Popsky will just have to work out their own salvation. And I got the first passage I could back to England.'

Jenny paused for breath. Then, as she continued, the

euphoria that had been in her voice while she raced through her explanations took command.

'Actually Sarah, I've been back a week. Guess what? Rupert Farrell met me in Liverpool. You remember him? The Aussie lieutenant. Well, we kept in touch and he managed to get leave and it fitted in beautifully with my return and . . . well . . . it just sort of happened. We're lovers, Sarah! Gosh, I can't tell you how happy I am! Are you there, Sarah?'

'Yes.'

'You haven't said anything.'

'You haven't given me the opportunity, luv!'

With a laugh Jenny went on, 'Gosh really Sarah, you might have told me you and Mikhail were married. There was I thinking you were going to marry Harry. Well, didn't we all?'

For a few seconds she paused, allowing the slightly accusatory tone to waft down the telephone line, before asking if Doctor Inglis had known? Or had they rushed off and made their vows in front of some Bolshevik official in a civil ceremony? Sarah cursed Kessie but found herself papering the tissue of lies by replying that nobody in the Unit had known and it had been a civil ceremony in Reni.

'When's the baby due?' So Kessie had passed on this information, too.

'Towards the end of May.'

Jenny put forward her sister-in-law's alternative line of explanation for Sarah's returning home. 'I expect Mikhail was worried about your safety, with the baby and everything. You must miss him dreadfully. Was it him you met that last night in Petrograd when there was all that hoo-ha at the Embassy, and you wouldn't tell even me where you'd been?'

Sarah admitted it had been Misha she'd met. Jenny then invited her to dinner before Rupert returned to France, Sarah said she would consider the invitation, and with further rhapsodies about how happy she was, Jenny rang off.

The next morning Philip telephoned and Sarah took the

call because Kessie and Tom were out. His voice at its most clipped, he said he was down at Chenneys and he thought he'd let them have the news before it broke officially; the long-awaited Boche offensive had started and the distant thunder of the guns was the most terrible they had heard, worse than the Somme, worse than Passchendaele. In the evening a less ebullient Jenny telephoned again. Rupert's last few days' leave had been cancelled, he'd been ordered to report back immediately. It looked serious, didn't it?

The situation grew more serious as the Germans broke right through the British lines on the Somme front, retaking all those Picardy towns, villages, hamlets and woods so bloodily captured in 1916, advancing further than any army had on the Western Front since 1914.

Climbing up to the attic on Easter Sunday morning to give the girls their Easter eggs, Sarah heard Anne crying. When she opened the door the child was hunched on her bed, staring at the map of the Western Front and the large green baize board that adorned the bedroom walls. The items pinned to the board – a selection of the postcards from Tom and Sarah and Uncle Pip, a copy of 'Poppies' and a photograph of Uncle Guy, Daddy's medals and Aunty Sarah's Russian Cross of St George and the Roumanian decoration from Queen Marie – these were unmolested. But the Union Jack marker flags were scattered over the floor and little Con was crawling around, her own eyes brimming with tears, gathering them up.

'I'm not doing it any more,' Anne sobbed loudly. 'I hate the Germans. They won't win, will they, Aunty Sarah?'

'I shouldn't think so.' Sarah seated herself on Anne's bed. 'Come on, see what I've got you. I painted them myself, like your Daddy and I used to do when we were little, though he wasn't a dab hand with a paint brush.' Con stood up and trotted to her side. Anne gave long shuddering sobs and sniffed repeatedly but she too moved towards Sarah to examine the painted eggs. Despite her anguish at the large dent the German advance had made on her map, anything about her Daddy, including what he'd done when he was her age, engaged her interest. Sarah said, 'It's Easter Sunday. The Resurrection. Do you know what that means?'

'It's when Jesus woke up from being dead,' Con said.

That was one way of putting it. Sarah ruffled the soft auburn hair and little Con gave her the sweetest smile. 'It also means you must never give up hope. Not even when things appear to be at their blackest.'

Within ten days Sarah herself was clinging to the hope that it was always darkest before the dawn and all the rest of those optimistic clichés. For though the German advance on the Somme front had been halted, they launched a further onslaught against the British lines in Flanders and in two days they recaptured more blood-stained places, Neuve Chapelle, Loos, Messines. Then Field Marshal Haig's Order of the Day to his troops was published: 'With our backs to the wall, and believing in the justice of our cause, each one of us must fight on to the end.'

Over the weekend Tom was tense and moody, but with the continuing grim news from Flanders weren't they all? The Germans had retaken Passchendaele, the ultimate symbol of senseless British sacrifice and suffering. On the Monday evening, during their evening meal, it was Kessie who was notably quiet but she had a bad cold developing. When they were in the sitting room, drinking their tea by the fire and she said she was going straight to bed Sarah assumed it was to nurse her cold, but at the door she paused and said,'Tom's going back. Don't nag him, Sarah. 'Night. See you in the morning.'

Before Sarah could collect her thoughts, Kessie had shut the door. In the silence Tom lit a cigarette. Sarah had to say something, she couldn't let a shattering announcement like that pass without comment.

'Why, Tom, why? Is it this backs to the wall gup?'

Inhaling on his cigarette he looked at the glowing red tip before gazing at her. 'Partly. For Haig to have issued that "gup", we're in real trouble, Sal. And we are. They're routing them out from everywhere, anybody who can breathe, stand up and hold a rifle, and some who can't.'

'You're among those who can't. Or shouldn't. Your hand's shaking now.' Tom threw the cigarette into the fire and dropped both his hands into his lap. 'God knows you've done your bit. Think about Kessie and the kids. And don't tell me you're a born survivor, please don't.'

Leaning his head against the back of the chair, staring up at the ceiling, slowly, quietly, her brother said, 'You should understand why, Sal. You've been closer to the reality of battle than most women. You should understand about loyalty and comradeship and that yawning gap between us and the uncomprehending civilians. And don't worry, I've learned to live with fear. I'm rested, I shan't go under. I need to see it through, not just for my lads, for myself.' Tom lifted his head and looked straight at her. 'We're damned well not going to be defeated, Sal.'

She let out a long sigh. In a crisis she would go to aid Jenny or Dorothy or Stephen, or Vera and Agnes, or any of the Unit. In the last few days, pacifist or no pacifist, she had found herself praying we would hold on. We couldn't be defeated, we damned well could not.

22

Down in Steephill Cove the nets were drying across the lobster pots, the sail of a just-beached fishing smack fluttered in the slight breeze, and the waves frothed up the shingly incline. Outside the cottage with its thatched roof dropping almost to the shingle, a large woman stood with arms akimbo, gazing out to sea, and an old man sat on an upturned boat, smoking his pipe. The sun was dancing on the water, brightening the fresh green of the trees on the arms of the cove, deepening the orange colour of the cliffs.

It had been Kessie's idea that Sarah come to the Isle of

Wight to await the birth of her baby in the peace of Willow Bank. Initially she had been miffed, to say the least, at the way her sister-in-law was organising her life, and she'd said so. But Kessie had become upset, and accepting that she'd acted with good intent, Sarah had shut up and travelled with Jenny for company. Now she reckoned Kessie had been right. The beauty and serenity of the island had to be good for her and the babe. Here you'd hardly know there was a war on, that across the sea a halted German army was facing an undefeated British one, that Tom was there, Rupert was there, among the millions of men poised for what? The final offensives? Or the continuing war of attrition?

Yet even here you couldn't escape the war completely, Sarah thought as she watched the ship with the Red Cross markings sail slowly out of sight past Ventnor, carrying another contingent of wounded from Le Havre to Southampton.

At an unaccustomed leisurely pace, she walked across the grassy headland and up through the woods towards Willow Bank. By the time she reached the wooden gate at the bottom of the long sloping garden, Sarah was out of breath and she decided she'd best curtail her perambulations because the babe was due any day now. As she opened the gate, in the corduroy trousers and open-necked shirt she'd taken to wearing, Jenny came flying down the path, waving a newspaper. Her expression was grave. Had the Germans launched another offensive? Had they broken through again?

'Sarah, you know I've been down into Ventnor? Well, I bought an early edition of the evening paper. I want you to sit down.'

Solicitously, Jenny shepherded her towards the wrought-iron garden table that stood on the lawn beneath the shade of the willows. It was the table they'd been sitting round in the beautiful summer of 1914, when Tom had arrived with the news that Austria had declared war on Serbia. With Jenny fussing around her, Sarah lowered her body into the wrought-iron chair.

'Now promise me you won't get too upset?' Clutching the newspaper in her hand, Jenny sat down in the chair opposite.

'Jenny, if you want me to go into labour, you'll keep saying things like that. If you don't, you'll tell me what's happened.'

'It's your friend Alice Conway.'

Alice? What had she done now? According to Kessie, she was well on the road to recovery and her doctor had allowed her to return to her house in St John's Wood, with Margaret Jane and her nursemaid.

'You know there was an air-raid on London last night?' Sarah nodded. They had seen the news briefly in the morning paper. The words tumbled from Jenny's lips. 'Well, your friend's house received a direct hit and she was . . . she was killed.'

For a moment Sarah sat absolutely stunned, unable to grasp the news. Alice killed? She could not have been, not Alice. In the tall trees at the bottom of the garden the nesting rooks' cawing rose to a furious crescendo and the sunlight glancing through the willows made fretwork patterns on the table. Silently, Jenny pushed the newspaper towards Sarah and there on the front page Alice's beautiful face smiled grainily up at her, with an inset picture of men digging through the piles of bricks beneath the gaping walls of Alice's house. Barely absorbing the words, Sarah read that the American-born Mrs Conway, prewar socialite and suffragette, the wife of the well-known actor Jonathon Conway who was currently serving his country on the Western Front, had been a victim of last night's Zeppelin raid on the capital. Miraculously, her baby daughter had been rescued alive, and at the moment of her untimely death Mrs Conway had been thirty-two years old.

Despite the fact that she had not cared greatly for Alice, Sarah found herself peculiarly affected by her death. Maybe it was the shocking unexpectedness. No, it was the waste, the sheer waste, the apparently never-ending toll of death this fearful war had created.

At six o'clock the next morning Sarah went into labour. It was the archetypal cycle of impervious nature, she thought: Alice being killed, her giving birth.

It was a glorious day and she could see the sun pouring through the large windows as the sweat poured off her body. Calm, comforting, cheerful, Jenny stayed by her side, and Mrs Dobell the housekeeper came in with cups of tea, reiterating what she'd been predicting for the last fortnight, from the way Mrs Murrynoff was carrying it was definitely a boy. Some time in the late afternoon the doctor appeared, not a bad chap, but Sarah wished it had been Stephen. He said she was doing nicely, no problems, but first babies were notoriously slow and it would be several hours before anything happened. He'd call back after his evening surgery.

Soon after the doctor had left the baby decided to get a move on. The contractions came faster and harder and Sarah's body was racked with pain. 'Unto the woman He said, I will greatly multiply thy sorrow and thy conception; in sorrow thou shalt bring forth children.' Why should she think of a God in whom she did not believe, of scriptures learned long ago in the dingy Methodist chapel in Mellordale?

'Scream, Sarah, if you want. I don't mind. I'm sure Mrs D doesn't, do you?'

'I bellowed like a bull when all o' mine were born,' Mrs Dobell said.

Sarah had no intention of screaming. Despite the pain, alternatively raking, stabbing, leaden, she was bearing this child in joy.

'Gosh Sarah, it's coming, I can see the head. It's blond. Like Mikhail. Don't worry. I'm with you all the way. Just push, Sarah, push. That's my girl. Push.'

With the evening sun filling the room with golden light, Sarah felt the baby leave her body and she heard Jenny cry 'Eureka!' as she lay drenched in sweat, gasping happily, mind and body relieved from pain. Downstairs in the hall the grandfather clock chimed the half-hour. She hadn't heard the baby cry. Oh God, or gods, or fate, you can't be so cruel, it can't be stillborn, not another death, not death before life has been given. The sound of the chimes died away. In a panic Sarah struggled to sit up and as she did so the baby wailed faintly. Putting her face into her hands she sank back on to the bed. Above the baby's cries she started to sob and the tears trickling through her fingers were scalding hot.

Cheerfully Jenny's voice said, 'Don't you want to know what it is?' Not really. She was just grateful, unutterably grateful, that her and Misha's child was alive and well. 'You were wrong, Mrs D. It's a girl. What are you going to call her, Sarah?'

'Tamara,' Sarah sobbed. 'Misha's favourite sister is called Tamara. And I think it's a *luvly* name.'

Jenny sent off the telegram to Kessie and the cable to Mikhail, dictated by Sarah: 'It's a girl for you, Misha. She's beautiful. I've called her Tamara. We want to be with you. Please write. All love Sarochka.'

His return cable came within the week, expressing his rapturous delight. There were however no quotations from Milton, no suggestions that he would come to her, or that she should go to him, but Sarah was well aware that a full-scale civil war had broken out in Russia. Her joy was therefore marred, but she had Tamara who *was* a beautiful baby, with Misha's fair hair, her own dark skin and eyes, and who filled her with jubilant bliss.

After Kessie had telegraphed her delight at the news, she wrote describing Alice's funeral:

It was a beautiful day. I think that was fitting for Alice, blue skies and sunshine. We buried her in Highgate cemetery and all sorts of people I hadn't seen in years turned up, which was a tribute to Alice I appreciated. Funerals are as much for the living as the dead, aren't they? Christabel came and we had a civil conversation afterwards. Mrs Pankhurst's on another tour of America, as you may have read, shouting about the Irish and the Bolsheviks. I really do feel somebody should keep her quiet, don't you? Or not allow her to travel.

Johnny was given compassionate leave to attend the funeral. He looked handsome and grief-stricken. Half the mourners didn't know about Guy and the fact that Alice and her husband had ceased to live together. Those of us who did, pretended we didn't. I gave a small funeral tea and when the others had gone, Johnny and Philip and I discussed the future. Well, actually, we didn't. Johnny was vague. In his grief, until the war is over, etcetera, he couldn't think straight, but he leapt at the suggestion that Margaret Jane and Etty Jardine remain at Chenneys for the time being, with Philip acting as the baby's guardian. Philip has been so helpful and people who say he hasn't got a heart, let alone of stone, don't know what they're talking about.

Oh, there's one other thing. In the last months of her life, Alice was sufficiently *compos mentis* to make a new will. She left everything in trust for Margaret Jane, which means she's a very rich baby, or will be a very rich young woman. She named Philip and me as executors and trustees. Not Johnny. Nor her sister Verena. I don't think Johnny was over-pleased by this.

I bet he wasn't, Sarah thought, and she wished Alice had *not* named Kessie as the trustee of a large fortune. And when it's anything to do with you, Kessie me luv, Philip Marchal's heart overflows with helpfulness.

Before she left the Isle of Wight, with the utmost reluctance but deciding that as she had acquiesced in Kessie's plot she might as well do the deed in the island's remoteness, Sarah registered Tamara's birth in Ventnor; father Mikhail Muranov, politician; mother Sarah Amelia Muranov, née Whitworth. The registrar professed to know Major and Mrs Whitworth intimately, which Sarah doubted, and was only too eager to believe that her marriage had been solemnised in the town of Reni in southern Russia in July, 1917, and the certificate lost during her journey to Archangel.

When they returned to London Kessie expressed her gratitude that Sarah had registered Tamara's birth as a married woman. Sarah grunted. 'Look, we must have a talk, Kessie. I've come back here because frankly, I've nowhere else to go. I've no money left. But I can't stay here for ever, living off you. I assure you I don't intend to. I shall find a job and get a room and put Tamara in a nursery until . . .'

'Do shut up. I don't expect you to stay here for ever. I have plenty of money. I'll pay you to be my secretarial help, if you want. There's mounds of work to be done. You stay here until you hear from Mikhail. Agreed?'

Hunching her shoulders, pulling a face, Sarah agreed. She recalled old Mr Thorpe, Kessie's Dad, with whom she'd always got on well, once saying to her, 'People under estimate Kessie's strength of character because she's such a nice, charming lass. But when my daughter sets her heart on something, she usually gets her own way.'

So Sarah continued to live at The Grove, feeding, bathing, changing Tamara herself, pushing her in the perambulator in the summer sun; no nursemaids for her. Kate and Mark showed intermittent interest in their new cousin, Anne gave her opinion that babies didn't do much, apart from sleep and cry, but little Con loved helping Aunty Sarah and playing with Tamara. When she wasn't lavishing attention on her baby, Sarah helped Kessie with the continuing piles of letters, cries for help, visiting soldiers, and with plans for further breaches of male superiority. She also packed the weekly parcels for Tom. Life in the trenches appeared not to have changed because he continued to write asking for candles, decent English matches – French ones were known as 'Asquiths' or 'Wait and Sees' – Oxo, soap, toothpaste, bars of chocolate, lime juice tablets, and cigarettes.

Sarah also became involved in the photographic exhibition Jenny was organising. Prompted by Kessie, Philip had helped set it up, and he said that whether Jenny was aware of it or not, she was interested in violence and she'd make an excellent war photographer, except nobody would allow a woman, including those who had witnessed its horrors, to undertake such a role. Intrigued by this comment Sarah re-examined the photographs of the scenes she too had witnessed.

What Philip had observed was true. All Jenny's most vivid, arresting pictures had an element of violence; peasant women in the market square at Reni, wringing the necks of scrawny chickens; a menacing line of the Rolls-Royce armoured cars humped beneath mantles of snow, beside the frozen Danube; a mongrel dog licking the face of its dead master; a child's body sprawled among the sunflowers along the railway track; and those terrible photographs she had taken during and after the Cossack massacre.

The official opening of Jenny's exhibition was arranged for four o'clock in the afternoon. Philip sent one of his limousines to collect them – the petrol allowance by courtesy of the War Propaganda Bureau, Sarah presumed – and with Tamara in her arms, wrapped in a beautiful shawl dear old Ada Thorpe had crocheted for Anne, she climbed into the back of the vehicle. Sarah intended to enjoy her baby's company on all possible occasions, and what other folks thought about that could go hang.

When they arrived at the gallery a posse of reporters and photographers was gathered on the pavement, watched by an interested crowd. Sarah assumed it was the clout of Sir Philip Marchal and Mrs Tom Whitworth's backing for the exhibition that had drawn the press, though when she saw Jenny emerge from the gallery and wave frantically at them, she thought maybe it was her attire. For Jenny was wearing cyclamen-coloured pantaloons with a darker purple silk blouse which, apart from being *outré*, in Sarah's opinion clashed with her red hair. The chauffeur opened the rear door of the limousine, Kessie and the children stepped on to the pavement, but the minute Sarah and Tamara climbed down it was they who were surrounded.

'Where exactly were you and Mikhail Muranov married?' 'Why've you kept it a secret?' 'Get a photograph of the baby.' 'What do you think of your husband's Bolshevism?' 'Why are you in England?' 'Are you returning to Russia?' 'Does your brother support the Bolsheviks?'

'Come on, Mrs Muranov, be a sport. You're an emancipated woman.'

The questions descended on Sarah like a sudden hailstorm, flash-bulbs flared and popped, Tamara started to howl, photographers jostled each other to get better snaps. Jenny and Kessie were both shouting and together with the chauffeur were trying to force a way through the mêlée, but for several minutes it was pandemonium, until Philip appeared with a policeman. For once Sarah was delighted to see him.

When they were safely inside the gallery, with little Con amusing a calmed Tamara and Sarah sitting with a welcome cup of tea in her hands, she said, 'Sorry about that, chaps, as Stephen would boom.'

'Don't worry about us.' Smoking a cigarette through a long holder, Jenny strode up and down in her cyclamen pantaloons. 'It's good publicity for me. It's poor old you I'm sorry for. I tried to telephone but you'd already left.'

'How did they find out?' said Kessie.

Sarah looked at her accusingly. 'Either your registrar friend on the Isle of Wight just happened to let slip the information that Mrs Muranov, formerly Sarah Whitworth, had given birth to a daughter not long since, or journalists followed their journalistic noses.'

'Bit of both,' Jenny said cheerfully.

Anne, Kate and Mark all had *their* noses pressed over the rail of the red velvet curtain behind the display window, having climbed on to chairs to obtain a better view of what was happening outside. Anne said, 'They're all still there, Mummy, prowling about.'

'Will you get down,' Kessie said. Reluctantly the twins did. 'That includes you, miss.'

With a last look outside, Anne jumped to her mother's side. Philip said, 'It might be wiser if you make a statement.'

'I'm not saying anything,' Sarah snapped.

Eventually she succumbed to Kessie and Jenny's pressure, rather than to Philip's, though it was he who issued the statement on her behalf. It said that Mrs Muranov had returned to England to await the birth of her child. She would be returning to Russia to be with her husband once the situation had calmed itself. In the meantime she wished to be left in peace with her daughter and she would make no further statements, lest they be misinterpreted and exacerbate an already difficult situation.

The newspaper coverage Sarah's story received the next morning was vast. The captions read: 'The Suffragrette and the Bolshevik', 'Love spans the political chasm', 'Love blooms in the revolution', and Tamara's howling face, peering from the crocheted shawl, was captioned, 'Daughter of East and West'.

After they had perused the coverage over breakfast, slightly defensively Kessie said, 'You'd have registered Mikhail as Tamara's father, anyway, wouldn't you? Some reporter would have found out sooner or later. Just think of the uproar if they'd discovered you weren't married.'

'I just hope Misha's sense of humour is in good working order,' Sarah said.

23

Sarah's letter to Mikhail was one of the longest she had ever written. She explained about their 'marriage' which she could not now deny, at least not without hurting her sister-in-law and her brother, both of whom she loved dearly. She reiterated her wish to be by his side, and in the final paragraph she said how much she loved him and missed him. Sarah found this the most difficult to write, for even with Misha, expressing deep personal emotion did not come easily.

It was the intrusion into her private life that she hated

most about the reporters who continued to accost her as she wheeled Tamara in the perambulator, begging for the 'human interest' story. When Sarah resolutely refused to say anything, or to lose her temper, they wrote largely inaccurate pieces. Slowly, however, the interest died away.

The news of her 'marriage' also produced a stream of letters, some abusive, calling Sarah every foul name under the sun, with the rest from Bolshevik sympathisers in Britain. Of those, about half seemed to Sarah cranky in the extreme, but to the other half she replied seriously, emphasising her own belief that the role of women in the new state was particularly exciting. There was one bonus from the sensationally untrue news that she was married to Mikhail Muranov. Sarah was asked to translate articles and pamphlets which kept her abreast of Bolshevik activity, kept up her Russian and earned her some much-needed money. For though Kessie was only too happy to lavish her 'filthy lucre' on Sarah, she hated being dependent even on her dearest sister-in-law.

It was the end of July and from Misha there was still no response to her long letter.

Tom's weekly letter arrived and Kessie gave Sarah the customary résumé. 'Tom says the Americans who are training with the Manchesters are indecently well-paid, fed, and clothed, compared to the Tommies, that is. Apparently they're all issued with safety razors too, so he's got his eye on one of those. He appears to be growing quite fond of his Yanks, though he says they're arrogant and full of the uncomprehending eagerness and enthusiasm the Pals Battalions had in 1916.' Kessie paused, 'We can only pray they don't go the same way as most of the Pals. And it's Tom's opinion the influenza epidemic has been caused by all those rats that have multiplied in their millions in the trenches. They've transmitted a modern-day plague. The reason why the troops haven't gone down with the 'flu to anything like the same extent as civilians is because they've become immune to rats.'

'I see.' Sarah considered it as good an explanation as

any for the epidemic that had swept across the war-torn world, gleaning another harvest of deaths, but which, thank heaven, had missed The Grove.

'And the best of news is the last bit. He's been promised leave, glorious leave!'

When Tom arrived home, Sarah had still not heard a word from Misha.

Her brother was looking tired but in control of himself, and he assured them the tide finally had turned in the Allies' favour. It wasn't propaganda gup, he'd been there on the Somme on 8 August when they had counter-attacked. The Boche were fighting as they'd always fought, he said, stubbornly and bravely, but they were on the run.

'Oh Tom!' Kessie threw her arms round his neck, right there in the middle of the sitting room and Sarah envied her sister-in-law's uninhibited emotion. 'How long? How long before it's all over?'

Tom said obviously nobody could know for certain, but he reckoned two to three months. Kessie looked up at him. 'Why don't you accept one of those offers of home-duty, and exert your influence as a hero who also happens to be a politician?'

'I'll give the suggestion due consideration.'

It was the first time he had hinted that he might have done his bit and need not return to active service. Kessie dropped her head on to his chest, he held her tightly, kissing her chestnut hair, and Sarah crept out of the room.

Her brother made no comment about her 'marriage' to Mikhail Muranov, though he was ever so good with Tamara. He asked if she was still intent on going back to Russia and if he should make enquiries about the possibility of her travelling at the moment. Sarah shook her head. Kessie had already made a similar suggestion, offering to use her friendship with Lloyd George. Misha's silence had left Sarah sick at heart, but she reckoned her commonsense was reasserting itself. Maybe he had been angered by the British press coverage of their 'marriage'; she felt sure he still read the English papers. She did not doubt that his days were filled and fearsome, but if he really adored his Sabrina fair, his wildest of English roses, then he could darned well find the time to get some message through and to respond to her expressed desire to be with him. Until he did, she was not contacting him again; she was making no effort to travel to Russia.

When Tom had been home a week Kessie said they were going to The Dales. He was making a major speech at the Free Trade Hall while he was up north, and she wondered if Sarah wanted to come with them. Sarah said yes.

The main hall of the Free Trade Hall was packed to capacity and half an hour before the meeting was due to start they'd had to close the doors, leaving hundreds milling around in Peter Street. Taking her seat on the platform next to Kessie – Tom had asked them both to be on the platform with him – Sarah looked at the mass of faces and watched her brother bow his head in acknowledgment of the storm of cheering and clapping. In his uniform he was every inch the dashing hero, but Sarah was remembering the times she had climbed up to Netherstone Edge with him, his eager audience of one. She was recalling his young voice battling with the wind, practising his oratory, vowing that one day he would fill the main hall of the Free Trade Hall in the great big city of Manchester.

Tom intended this speech to be the speech of his political life and from the moment he started to speak, quietly but with his resonant voice and his excellent diction carrying across the tingling silence, Sarah knew it would be. For one and a half hours he spoke, weaving a verbal tapestry of rhetoric, humour, and serious political analysis. He devoted a long section to the irrevocable social and economic changes that had already occurred in England as a result of this cataclysmic war and that would continue in the Socialist future, stressing the long overdue and welcome emergence of women into the front ranks of society.

The last part of his speech was the bravest and boldest,

for Tom dared to say that as a man who had fought in the front-line trenches on the Somme and at Passchendaele, he had to tell them the front-line troops did not regard the Germans as monsters but more often as poor buggers like themselves, stuck there for reasons they didn't always understand. This did not mean either he or his lads were 'soft' on the Germans, but it did mean – and he believed he was speaking for millions of British soldiers, dead and alive – there must be a peace treaty which, while it acknowledged victory over the Kaiser's militarism, did not grind the whole German nation into the dust. For if we, the victors, did not show magnanimity, then our victory would be as dust.

Having antagonised a sector of his audience, Tom drew them back into his spell as he swept towards his peroration. It was the same spell Misha cast, the rich reverberations of the voice firing the blood, mesmerising the senses, exalting the spirit, igniting the belief that anything was possible on this earth that mankind desired to make possible. Tom flung out his left arm, the audience seemed to catch its breath as one being and the only thing missing from the old days was the thick black hair, too close cut now for Tom to run his hand through it, or for it to flop on to his forehead with the intensity of his conviction.

'Not a hundred yards from this building, on a black day close on one hundred years ago, peacefully assembled men, women and children, were murdered for demanding their rights as citizens. Of the Peterloo Massacre, Shelley wrote: "Rise like lions after slumber, In unvanquishable number!" We, their grandchildren, are the lions who have emerged from the jaws of hell. Rise in your unvanquishable numbers . . .' Both Tom's arms swept upwards. 'Let your voices clamour to the heavens. Rise and fight for your rights, for an England that is a land of hope and glory, for equity and justice throughout the world, for peace not in our time, but peace for all time.'

The congratulatory telegrams and letters poured into the house in Milnrow. In the streets of Mellordale Tom virtually had his right-hand shaken off (which didn't do his injured shoulder any good) and his back thumped into coughing fits by folk expressing their appreciation of his speech. There were only a few telegrams or epistles which said he should be court martialled and shot at dawn for his treacherous, traitorous, 'conshie' talk.

Among the telegrams were ones from Jenny – 'Gosh I wish I'd been there!' – and from Philip Marchal expressing his approbation.

'I didn't know he was a Socialist,' Sarah said, 'nor an optimist.'

'Well, no, he isn't,' Kessie admitted. 'But his plays aren't right-wing, now are they? They hold a very cracked mirror up to the society he knows. I do see his point about the difficulty of preaching equality when you own a place like Chenneys. But Philip always says, come the revolution, he'll disappear gracefully. And in the meantime, he's giving a goodly number of people a decent living on the estate. Occasionally, I think he'd like to be an optimist.'

The newspapers mostly agreed it had been a brave, if several considered, misguided speech, and that Major Whitworth had emerged from the war not only as a hero but as a formidable political figure who might, one day, develop into a statesman.

When Kessie and Tom returned to London Sarah stayed on at Milnrow with Tamara. She needed a breathing space, she needed to sort out her emotions, and she reckoned she could do that best here, where her roots were. Within a few days of settling herself in, the letter from Kessie arrived.

The Grove,
Highgate,
London N.
September 13th
1918.

Dearest Sarah,

You had better hear the news from me. Tom has decided to return to active service. His anger with armchair patriots, war profiteers, and generally uncomprehending civilians – all of whom he's had a basinful of in the last weeks – and his desire to see it through to the end, which can't be long now, have overwhelmed him. He leaves for France more or less immediately.

Do stay at Milnrow as long as you want, but come back here as soon as you can. You know how much I value your support when Tom's away. Give Tamara a kiss for me.

Fondest love, as always,
Kessie.

The news shocked Sarah. She had not expected Tom to go back again. But he was a born survivor; more than ever after that speech in the Free Trade Hall he must be a survivor. She wrote a brief letter in response to Kessie's – there wasn't much she could say if Tom was already on his way back to France – explaining that her services were needed in The Dales so she expected to stay up north for a while.

At The Grove they were sheltered from the harsher realities of wartime life on the home-front by Kessie's money and by being the family of a nationwide hero. Back here at ground level the hardships hit Sarah like a tornado. The introduction of rationing for a few foodstuffs had made the situation a little more equitable for those without money, but long queues for other foods in short supply still wound round the shops. Those outside the coal depots started in the early hours of the morning. Women huddled in shawls waited for ages and if they were lucky they pushed the old perambulators, barrows and home-made boxes on wheels back home, half-filled with dusty coal.

Here in The Dales the plans for women's future equality tended to fade in the face of the immediate problems. How to ensure that bereft old women who couldn't stand in queues didn't starve for lack of food or warmth. What to do about a woman with five kids under the age of seven, six months gone with another, whose husband had been killed weeks ago and not one penny of whose pension, beggarly as it was, had yet come through. Where to park the kids of a sick woman whose husband as far as anybody knew was still alive in Flanders, who were living in a rat-infested house down by the River Mellor. (Rats were not unique to the trenches.) How to obtain compensation for three lasses badly injured in an explosion at a munitions factory, which had palpably been caused by managerial negligence and greed for profit.

The woman who had run the Mother and Baby clinic had, alas, been a victim of the influenza epidemic and the organisation was in a mess, so Sarah took over there, pushing Tamara down the cobbled streets into the centre of Mellordale, letting her enjoy the company of other babies. From her variegated jobs and her translations she earned just enough to keep the two of them.

Occasionally, in rare quiet moments, she daydreamed of Misha, and when she scooped the post from the mat and shuffled through the envelopes Sarah could not stop herself hoping there might be one with a Russian stamp, though what she would do in the unlikely event of Misha's actually writing and asking her to go to Moscow, she did not now know. Sometimes at night, lying in her solitary bed, usually when she was overtired, her body ached for the warmth of his, for their passionate conjoining. She had scaled the heights of love with him, he had made the blood race through her veins, he had extended the range of her emotions. Nobody could take the memories from her. Above all, he had given her a child.

24

'It's Daddy!' Without knocking Anne came bursting into the study. 'It's Daddy.'

'What is?' Wearily, Kessie looked up from her desk. 'Shut the door, there's a draught.'

Anne almost stamped her foot in her excitement and frustration at Mummy's unusual obtuseness. Waving her hand through the open door she babbled, 'He's in the hall, Daddy, he's here, he's come, in a taxi, it's Daddy.'

Slowly, Kessie stood up. Was Anne playing a game? No, she was too sensitive a child for that sort of practical joke but it couldn't be Tom. She'd had no word, no telegram, and he hadn't long gone back. Then she heard Kate and Mark and Con's voices high with delight and the deep rumble of Tom's responses, and she ran down the passage and into the hall. There he was, Kate in his arms with his cap on her head, Mark and Con gazing up at him, all three of them chattering away. He saw her, gently he swung Kate to the floor where she marched up and down, the cap swivelling lopsidedly on her head, and took Kessie into his arms. For several seconds they just stayed there, holding each other tightly. Kessie had always sworn she would not cry when Tom came home or returned to the war, but his arrival this time was too sudden, too unexpected and she was not prepared. Quietly she sobbed. She felt Tom kissing her hair and she heard him murmuring, 'Kess, Kess, Kess.'

'Daddy, Mark's taken your hat,' Kate wailed dramatically, her little legs chasing after her brother who was running up the stairs with the cap on his head. 'Give it back, you horrid boy.' That was one of Anne's terms for Mark which his twin sister had adopted. 'Make him give it back, Daddy.'

After they had sorted out that little rumpus, Kessie wanted to know how Tom had managed to wangle leave so quickly and how long he was home for. He said he wasn't actually on leave. He'd been hauled out of the front lines, a situation to which he had no objections, and ordered to report forthwith to Doullens to meet 'a Cook's Tour' of visiting MPs and journalists. When he reached Doullens after the usual chaotic journey they'd already left and the Colonel to whom he'd reported, a sympathetic chap he'd met in Ypres last year, had suggested that as he wasn't due to report back to his battalion for a week he amused himself for the next few days. So he'd hitched a lift to Boulogne, crossed on the butterfly boat to Folkestone (*au fait* with Western Front slang, Kessie knew that meant a leave boat), and he had three clear days of home comforts.

As the children started to pull him into the sitting room, Tom stumbled, and when he sat down on the sofa, with them crowding around him, Kessie realised he could barely keep his eyes open.

'When did you last sleep properly?' Tom leant his head against the back of the sofa and said he couldn't exactly recall. In her firmest voice Kessie said to the children, 'Right. Off you get. Daddy's going to have a sleep. Would you like a bath first?'

'Love one.'

It was agreed he would also like a cup of tea and a bite to eat after his bath and the children scurried down to the kitchen to 'help' Maggie prepare a tray. Kessie went upstairs to run the water and bare-footed, wrapped only in his dressing gown, Tom disappeared into the bathroom. While she put his dirty underwear, shirt, and socks into the laundry basket on the landing and hung up his khaki jacket and slacks, Kessie thought of the personal adjustments they would have to make once this bloody war was over. For the best part of three years she had run their lives, taking virtually all the decisions major and minor, and it was to her authority the children responded. 'Daddy' was a figure who appeared from time to time, to be greeted with euphoria, and to spoil the children abominably – even in the worst days after Passchendaele he had usually given in to them. There had been moments during his periods at home, dearly as she'd loved his presence, when Kessie had resented his 'interference' in problems he knew nothing about. Oh well, she thought as she touched the purple and white ribbon of Tom's MC and bar and the red and blue of his DSO on his jacket, they wouldn't be the only family in England with those sorts of problems to resolve '*après la guerre*'.

From the bottom of the stairs Anne shouted up, asking

if Daddy was ready for his tea. Kessie said no, he hadn't yet emerged from the bath. Looking at her wristlet watch, she decided it was time he did. Outside the bathroom door she called 'Tom' but there was no reply, so she put her head round. His right arm was hanging over the rim of the bath, the silky black hairs stuck in damp clusters, the dirty water was lapping round the black hairs at his throat, his right foot was wedged between the taps, his head was on one side, and he was fast asleep.

It took Kessie several minutes to waken him, kneeling by the side of the bath, shaking him. When she did, he shot upright and the water sloshed over her blouse and on to the floor, soaking her skirt, and his left hand stretched out for . . . what? His revolver, his respirator? The sodden blouse and skirt clinging to her limbs, Kessie stood up and crossed to the towel rail, holding out the large, fleecy bath-towel for Tom to wrap himself in. Slowly, exhaustedly, smiling faintly at her, he climbed out of the bath. Looking at his body she thought he couldn't weigh an ounce more than the twenty-three year old she'd first met. He lurched towards her but as she tried to put the towel round him, he let it fall to the floor, slipping his wet arms around her, bending his head, kissing her with a deep instinctive passion.

Kessie had no memory of shedding her clothes. She was on her feet, close to the ivy-patterned wallpaper, their damp bodies and mouths were entwined, he was thrusting himself inside her and she was tight because it had been weeks since . . . She sighed, 'Oh Tom', as she always did when he entered her body. Her senses entered a realm of gold that in their years of passionate loving they had not before touched and Tom had to be living through the same intoxicated, exultant, breathless, straining, swaying rapture. Then her mind was transported beyond adjectives, beyond erotic images and they were one single two-headed being locked in love, in all that was beautiful, pure, holy in the world. From the moment she sighed 'Oh Tom', until the moment her moaning pleasure gasped 'Yes, yes, yes', neither of them spoke.

Then Tom panted, 'Oh Christ, Kess, I love you.'

Languorously he kissed her face, her hair, her shoulder, she felt his weight heavily upon her, she pushed against him, and slowly he slid to the floor. He made two further movements, pulling his long legs upwards into a v-shape, putting his left arm round his chest, and he was asleep. Naked against the wall, with Tom lying naked at her feet, Kessie shivered as the perspiring heat drained from her skin. Stepping over his body, she knelt down for the bath-towel which she wrapped round herself.

'Tom.' She shook his shoulder. 'Tom darling, wake up.' She went on shaking him, harder and harder. 'Tom, please wake up.'

It was no use, no use whatever. He was spent, from the battle-fatigue, travelling and love-making of fabulous sensation. What on earth was she going to do? Well, wash herself first, and then . . . ? She couldn't possibly move his weight. She'd have to get Maggie to help; but Tom was stark naked. Stretching out her hand for his dressing gown which was lying across the bathroom chair, she draped it over his recumbent form. Could she get him into the garment? She managed to put his left arm into the sleeve and started trying to slide the gown underneath his body but she couldn't lift him.

'Mummy.' It was Anne's voice and she was tapping on the door. 'Isn't Daddy ready for his tea *yet*?'

Crouching on the floor, with the bath-towel clutched round her, her hands attempting to lever Tom's back, Kessie felt an attack of giggles about to overcome her. Anne knocked again. 'Mummy, are you there? Daddy, your tea's ready. There's crumpets and a piece of snow-cake.'

With the greatest difficulty Kessie controlled the incipient giggles and came to a decision. Maggie was an unmarried woman – she could hear Tom saying 'Give her a treat' – but there was nothing else to be done. Clearing her throat, she called out to her daughter, 'Daddy's fallen asleep. I can't move him. Will you ask Maggie to come up, please?'

Tom slept until nine o'clock on the Sunday morning. The children brought him breakfast in bed to make up for being unable to give him crumpets and snow-cake last night. When they'd reluctantly left the bedroom, Kessie told her husband what had happened after he'd withdrawn from her and the proceedings.

'Maggie kept her eyes fixed on the wallpaper as she hoisted you into a sitting position. I wrapped the dressing gown round you, and while she hauled you upright I tied the belt, to cover your well-endowed indecency. With the children pushing and pulling, between us we carried you into the bedroom and rolled you under the bed clothes. Not by a twitch did Maggie wonder what I was doing in my underclothes, which was as much as I'd put back on before she arrived.'

'To think I missed all that!'

The next two days flew past in inverse speed to the way in which the previous weeks had limped by. He took the children to the cinema to see a Charlie Chaplin film and Kate spent hours draped in a shawl, imitating the little flower girl Charlie had rescued.

'I think you're right,' Tom said. 'She's a born actress.'

When the two of them were in bed, reading as they often had in the old days, Kessie put her book on the counterpane and said, 'Can you get me permission to come with you to Folkestone tomorrow? I'd like just a few hours to ourselves. And when the war *is* over, we're having a holiday. By ourselves. It's all right for you, but I've had the children all day and every day for the last three years. My idea of bliss is to be without them for a while.'

Tom laughed and said he took the point. In the morning he arranged a pass for Kessie to accompany him to a 'restricted' coastal zone. In the afternoon he collected the children from school, wearing his uniform which delighted his offspring. They had an early tea together, the taxi arrived, he kissed his daughters and patted his son on the head, and Kessie and he drove to Charing Cross station. How she hated its frenetic wartime atmosphere, soldiers everywhere, entraining, detraining, changing their French and Belgian money at the bureau on the platform, saying emotional, or suspiciously casual, or ignorantly cheerful farewells to their wives, parents, girl friends and children. The ladies of the town were unobtrusively trying to accost lonely, lost-looking lambs, scattering like startled birds when a policeman appeared. According to Tom, the members of women's allegedly oldest profession had done yeoman service in France and Flanders, infecting thousands of soldiers with venereal diseases, causing them to be sent to the VD hospitals in Rouen and Le Havre, saving them from death at Passchendaele or wherever. Kessie considered that a sick comment but probably only too true.

It had been a lovely day and as the train rattled through the rows of back streets south of the River Thames, through the ever sprawling London suburbs and out into the countryside, they watched a glorious sunset, the sun a red disc in the sky, slowly sinking to the horizon. Tom's name had obtained them a first-floor suite in the grandest hotel on the Leas in Folkestone and after they'd had a meal Kessie said she'd like to go for a walk.

The lovely day had turned into a beautiful night, the sky a deep blue-black, the stars crystal bright, the full moon shedding a platinum light. Arm-in-arm, at a leisurely pace, they walked down the wide steps of the hotel, through its gardens, across the road and the grassy expanse of the Leas, to the edge of the cliffs. The moon was cutting a shimmering path through the darkness of the sea, shining on the trees that grew thickly from the cliff tops down to the beach, illuminating the roofs of the blacked-out houses, the troopships crammed into the harbour, the shadowy figures moving around the docks.

Tom put his arm round her shoulder, she rested her head on his, and after a while he said, 'It is all over, Kess. The agony's being prolonged because the buggers can't agree on armistice terms. Some of the Boche regiments are giving up without a fight. Not all, though. We encountered the 23rd Prussian Division the other week, the Invincibles, and they fought as if they were still invincible.'

Kessie let out a long shuddering sigh. What was there

to say? Except, don't go back, don't re-encounter the Invincibles. Slowly they walked along the Leas, elegantly beautiful in the moonlight, and then Tom said, 'It was a splendid day when I crossed the Channel this last time. I stood on the deck watching the white cliffs appear on the horizon. They were dazzlingly bright in the sunshine, and I wanted to cry. This is my country, this little island is what I know and understand, it's what I've fought for, and we *are* going to make it a land of hope and glory. And I'll tell you something else, when I come back next time, it'll be the last time I see the white cliffs of Dover from the sea. I'm not setting foot out of England again.'

'Oh Tom!' Kessie protested.

He said he wasn't joking, he'd had foreign parts, and if anybody ever mentioned rain-sodden England to him again, he'd refer them to Picardy and Flanders. They walked back to the hotel, laughing and joking, with Kessie saying other parts of France were beautiful, and sunny, and was he going to refuse to attend international Socialist conferences and personally she'd love to go to America and India.

Gently, sweetly, they made love, falling asleep in each other's arms. When Kessie awoke in the morning she was still tightly clasped in Tom's embrace. They had breakfast in the suite, then all too soon it was time for him to leave. She brushed his uniform and adjusted his tie, and they went down into the lobby. Kessie was glad they had breakfasted privately because innumerable officers, young and old, came up to slap 'old Piper' on the back or to say how good it was to see Major Whitworth again. She realised how greatly he had earned the admiration of his peers, and in some of the fresh young faces there was near-idolatry. Not altogether idly, she wondered how many of them would carry the respectful admiration into the peace-time years when Tom was again an impassioned Socialist MP.

The taxi he had ordered to take him down to the harbour arrived. Normally he'd have walked the short distance, he said, but with so many troops tramping down the path at the end of the Leas to embark for France, he'd spend the entire time saluting. The elderly porter held open the hotel door and the driver carried Tom's bag down the steps. They followed him, stopping by the cab.

The terrible moment of farewell had come again, the gnawing of the stomach, the tearing of the nerves. This had to be the last time, Tom would soon be home for good, he was a survivor. Kessie had finally come to believe that.

On 8 November Sarah travelled to London with Tamara. The reason for her visit was twofold. Maggie had written to say Mrs Whitworth was not at all well. Sarah was aware that Tom had appeared for a few days in October and that Kessie had gone to see him off in Folkestone. Soon after her return she had apparently developed a cold which she couldn't shake off, and in Maggie's painstakingly written opinion it would do Mrs Whitworth no end of good to see Mrs Muranov who might also, with her medical knowledge, know what was wrong with Mrs Whitworth.

Exhaustion, strain, four years and three months of war, Sarah reckoned.

The other reason for her journey south was to raise funds. Not a word had come from Misha who was still hale and hearty because his picture and various intemperate remarks appeared in the newspapers from time to time, causing reporters to contact Sarah to discover what she thought of her husband's views. Although she didn't tell the reporters, she had shut the door on that episode of her life which *had* proved to be one of those wartime romances, but it had given her Tamara and briefly shown her what passion was, so she had no regrets and only the very occasional private weep. Her life now lay in The Dales serving her own folk, and for a start she had her eye on a building in Mellordale where she hoped to open another 'People's Centre'. She needed money for the enterprise and several of her old moneybags contacts lived in London.

Kessie was looking *very* tired and her skin had its waxen pallor.

'I don't know what you're doing out of bed. Come

on. Upstairs. Ex-Nursing Orderly Whitworth will brook absolutely no argument.'

'I'm waiting for the war to end,' Kessie said. 'I want to be on my feet.'

'You can wait in bed and get up when it does.'

There was an atmosphere of quivering expectancy. On the train coming down from Manchester nobody had been able to talk of anything else. Would the armistice be signed today? Tomorrow? Or would the war drag into next week?

Just after 11 o'clock on the morning of 11th day of the 11th month of 1918, Sarah was working in the study at The Grove. Tamara was at her feet, sitting up beautifully straight now, poised ready to crawl, her dark eyes darting round the new surroundings. Suddenly, the maroons were fired and for the first time in years the church bells started to peal.

Sarah knew it was all over.

With her face in her hands, almost unable to think or to feel, she sat immobile until Tamara pulled insistently on her skirt, showing her mother a pencil that had dropped from the desk. Within minutes the factory hooters were blasting away for victory, vehicles were tooting their horns, bicycle bells trilling, rattles whirring, voices shouting, singing, cheering. Picking Tamara up, gulping down the lump in her throat, Sarah carried her into the hall. She met Kessie at the foot of the stairs, they closed in a silent embrace, and a squashed Tamara started to struggle and yell as her mother and her aunt's tears sploshed on to her face.

'It's ended, Sarah, it's finally ended,' Kessie sobbed. 'Oh thank God.'

The children came home from school, given a half-holiday of rejoicing, waving the Union Jacks they'd been issued with. Kessie opened a bottle of champagne and everybody had a sip. Anne said she liked the taste, so did Mark, but Con and Kate said it was horrid and complained that the bubbles tickled their noses. Licking from Sarah's finger Tamara shared the positive reaction, trying to lick her mother's other fingers, pulling a cross face when they did not taste so nice. In the bright autumn sunshine the children went out to join the celebrations and in London at least the weather was in tune with the wonderful news. Jenny telephoned to say the scenes in the West End were unbelievable. She was out taking photographs and it was going to continue for hours. Why didn't the Whitworths come on down? Kessie said she didn't feel she should go but Maggie and Sarah could take the children. They arranged to meet Jenny at her studio apartment at four o'clock.

It was three o'clock, Kessie's pretty mantel-clock with its golden pendulums whirling round had just chimed, the exuberant cacophany in the streets outside continued, enthusiastic bellringers were still pealing out the victory carillons, and they were drinking a cup of tea before Sarah departed for the greater excitement in the West End. In more sombre mood, they were remembering the millions who had not lived to see this day. Sarah thought of Alice and Guy, of little Tania and Mr Lohvitzky and Doctor Inglis, and wondered what Misha was doing at this very minute.

Anne came bounding into the room, excitedly telling Mummy they'd all had a ride in a wheelbarrow Sergeant Tomkins had decorated with flags and was pushing round and round the green, and up and down South Hill. In her hand she had a telegram which she gave to her mother.

'I didn't hear the knock,' Kessie said. Anne explained she'd met the telegraph boy at the gate, before she ran to the window where she hopped up and down excitedly.

After she'd read the telegram Kessie frowned, then the frown cleared and her expression became as blankly frozen as a marble statue's. At her mother's sudden, terrible silence Anne stopped hopping up and down.

'What is it? What's happened?' Sarah said.

The telegram fluttered from Kessie's fingers. She was sitting as if turned to stone. Her heart thumping, a nameless dread quivering through her body, Sarah picked up the telegram. It read:

T 339. Regret to inform you that Major E. T. F. Whitworth 18th Manchesters killed in action 7th November. Field-Marshal Haig sends his sympathy.

PART FOUR

25

The haunting strains of the 'Londonderry Air', which had been one of Tom's favourite pieces of music, greeted them. The packed congregation rose to its feet as David Lloyd George escorted Kessie and the children down the nave of St Margaret's Westminster, the parish church of the House of Commons. Sarah followed behind.

The children were dressed in black coats, the girls in long black stockings, ankle-strapped shoes and velveteen berets, Mark in black knee socks and laced shoes, the thick black hair he had inherited from Tom forming its own mourning cap. Kessie was wearing a black velvet two-piece with a straight calf-length skirt and a matching picture hat that shaded her face. In high-heeled court shoes she was slightly taller than Lloyd George but his stockily robust figure, looking crumpled as ever in its frock-coat and mourning waistcoat, made her appear the more slender and fragile.

It had taken three months of their Prime Minister at his most persuasive to convince Kessie that his friends, admirers and colleagues wished to pay tribute to her late husband. At any memorial service for Tom she had insisted that a woman's voice be upraised and Sarah had agreed to read the first piece they had chosen.

When she mounted the elaborately decorated pulpit, the reds and golds heightened by the ribbons of February sunlight filtering through the stained glass of the windows, Sarah felt herself trembling. Momentarily, she stared down at the mass of upturned faces. Sitting with the members of the Government was a resplendent figure representing

King George and Queen Mary. Tom's batman was here, Private Duty, and Dorothy and Stephen back from Macedonia, and Philip Marchal who had been quietly, ubiquitously helpful, and Jenny was here with Rupert who was among the survivors. Dear old Harry had survived too, though he was not yet back in England . . .

People were coughing and clearing their throats. Sarah gripped the ornate rim of the pulpit and from somewhere Tom's voice whispered, 'Come on, Sal. This is our big moment. The buggers are waiting for you to utter. Come on, lass, you can do it!'

Clearly, steadily, she read from the Gospel according to St John, Chapter 15, verse 12. '"This is my commandment, That ye love one another, as I have loved you. Greater love hath no man than this, that a man lay down his life for his friends . . ."'

When she had finished Sarah knew she had done it well and as she returned to her seat, with the organ playing the sweetly lapping sounds of 'Sheep may safely graze', Kessie pressed her hand and smiled slightly.

Learning that Tom had been killed as the victory bells pealed out and they rejoiced in his survival had made the impact of his death a thousand times more shattering. How could they have been so stupid, so unutterably stupid, she and Kessie had asked themselves over and over again, as to have forgotten the time factor in the notification of death, and not to have realised that Tom could already be cold in his grave? Kessie's grief had been, and still was, an almost tangible thing, as if she were wrapped in a barbed wire of pain, but she had not collapsed. Somehow for part of each day she had kept on her feet to provide a façade of normal life for the children, and Sarah had never admired her more. Not yet five years old the twins were blessedly too young really to understand what had happened and were as much affected by the general emotion as anything. Con realised she would never see her beloved Daddy again and as for Anne . . .

While the choir and congregation sang 'There is a green hill far away without a city wall', Sarah glanced at Anne's tense face, the mouth clamped shut. Conscious of the attention, the dark eyes that were so like Tom's flickered up towards her aunt. There was no hint of shared grief in her face, little trace of the distraught child who had sobbed and screamed in Kessie's arms that her Daddy hadn't been killed, it was a mistake, they'd muddled him with somebody else, he wasn't dead, he wasn't, he wasn't.

Up in the pulpit Tom's colonel was saying his piece about what a gallant, caring officer Major Whitworth had been and quoting from that poem the Canadian doctor, John McCrae, had written during the second battle of Ypres: 'In Flanders fields the poppies blow Between the crosses row on row . . . If ye break faith with us who die We shall not sleep, though poppies grow In Flanders fields'. Like Tom and Guy he had died, and Sarah wished the colonel could have quoted from one of Guy's 'real' poems, but Mrs Kendle had not produced them and his 'Poppies', popular as it remained, was not appropriate for this occasion.

Immediately after the armistice, while they were numb with shock, Lloyd George had announced the General Election and Sarah had been invited to contest Tom's old seat in The Dales. Though she knew she was being offered on a plate the dream she'd had for years, the dream of standing for Parliament, she had turned the offer down. Maybe she should have had the strength to seize the opportunity, but she had not. It had been with an effort that she and Kessie had gone to the polling station, to be among the first women to drop their voting papers into the ballot box. It was the moment for which they had fought for over thirteen years, but to say it was a hollow one failed to express Sarah's leaden emotions and even less, she suspected, those of her sister-in-law.

The bright sunshine was lightening the dense images and dark colours of the Milton window. Atheist that he was, how Misha would love to sit with her in this beautiful church in which John Milton had worshipped and married. Out of the dark skies she and Tamara had received a Christmas greeting from Misha, with a quotation from

Milton naturally: 'And joy shall overtake us as a flood, When everything that is sincerely good And perfectly divine, With truth, and peace, and love, shall ever shine'. Misha had given no indication when, or how, joy would overtake them, and though Sarah had written back because she loved him, damn him, she wanted to be with him and she wanted Tamara to know her father, she had only a slender hope that he would respond positively. To take a baby into the continuing bloodiness of the civil war in Russia, without knowing what they were going into or even whether they were wanted, was unthinkable.

Dashingly handsome in his uniform, Johnny Conway stepped into the pulpit, managing to hold his head so that his noble profile was shown to best effect to most members of the congregation. The beauty of his delivery, however, made the oft-heard words of the 23rd Psalm sound as if he had just composed them, while he lay down in green pastures.

The two parcels, one very large and hard, the other slightly smaller and softer had arrived not long before Christmas, but they had received so many packages – some folk had sent toys for the children, as if they were orphans and Kessie weren't comfortably off – that Sarah didn't take much notice of them. In the early afternoon, while Tamara was having her nap, Kessie said she supposed they'd better see what was inside.

'Oh God!'

Having opened the softer package, Kessie was holding up the jacket of Tom's uniform which was crumpled and caked in mud. Crusted flakes of French soil fell to the carpet as she unfolded the sleeves. Round the left breast pocket there was a large stain, the ribbons of his Military Cross and Distinguished Service Order were a dark rusted red, and as Sarah stared at them she knew it was her brother's blood. They had forgotten the ritual of officers' effects being returned to their families, that they would include the dead man's uniform, with the clammy, musty stench of the charnel-house clinging to it . . . Sarah put her hands to her mouth to gulp down the horror.

'Oh God!' Kessie repeated, as she dropped the jacket to the floor and threw Tom's socks and shirts, his 'British warm' and his teddy-bear jacket across the carpet, before frantically scrabbling at the wrappings of the larger, harder parcel.

'Don't Kessie, don't,' Sarah cried out, 'leave them.'

She was like a wild creature as she pulled off the last piece of brown paper to reveal the gramophone, now battered and scratched, that she had given Tom when he first went off to war. Underneath was his haversack which frantically Kessie tipped upside down. Everything he had carried with him from the Somme to Passchendaele to those last hours on the Sambre canal cascaded on to the carpet.

A half-used bar of soap and his shaving tackle, including the safety razor latterly acquired from his Yanks; the crayon drawing Kate and Mark had scrawled as their first farewell gift, now tattered to strips; the papier mâché figure Con had made, no longer even faintly recognisable as a cat; the cigarette lighter Kessie had given him, its gold dulled and dented; the copy of Shakespeare Sarah herself had bought him, dog-eared and mildewed; the sampler with 'Daddy' in the centre that Anne had embroidered, its colours faded; photographs of Kessie and the children, and a group picture from that day at Chenneys, a smiling Alice and Guy side by side, Tom with his right arm in a sling, the other round Kessie, Anne grinning up at her Daddy, Sarah with the twins and little Con. On top of the pile lay a bundle of letters, the ones from Kessie tied with uncharacteristic neatness by a ribbon, emphasising how precious they had been, together with the five-year diary Maggie had given him.

Kessie's fingers fluttered through the pages of the diary and Sarah, her own body shaking, feeling as if every nerve and sinew had been put through an infernal mincing machine, caught a glimpse of her brother's handwriting and the date of the last entry, 6 November 1918. Kessie clasped the diary to her bosom and gave a terrible, soul-shivering howl whose sound still haunted Sarah today.

When she had recovered some composure, they took the blood-stained uniform down to the bottom of the garden, doused it in paraffin and set it alight. Watching the cloth burn blue and green in the flames, the scent of death in their nostrils, in long trembling gasps Kessie said, 'I don't . . . think . . . I can live . . . without him.'

'Yes you can. You have to, Kessie. For the children, for me, for a whole heap of folk who love you and need you. The pain will fade.'

'That's what . . . I told Tom . . . when he was . . . so distressed by Guy's death . . . and the nightmares of Passchendaele . . . what I didn't know . . . then . . . was the intensity . . . of the initial . . . agony.'

For the first time Sarah appreciated how Alice could have deluded herself about Guy, for at times she could not believe that Tom was dead, not her best beloved brother who had been part of her life since her first conscious memories, not Tom who had so much to live for and so very much to offer his fellow men and women.

The choir was singing 'Abide with me'. She'd heard her brother sing that some and often, his baritone voice always deepening on 'fast falls the eventide'. As the plangent notes echoed and the trebles of the choirboys shivered upwards, Sarah took a deep breath to control the welling tears.

Kessie had been obsessive about wanting to know exactly how Tom had died, reading the letter from his colonel over and over again. Sarah was filled with apprehension and slight impatience when only last week Kessie informed her that Private Duty was about to be discharged from the army and was coming to see them.

What an emotional afternoon that had been.

There he sat in the armchair Tom himself had so often lounged in, the rough, ill-fitting cloth of other ranks' uniform sagging around his thin body, but at his ease, a mystery man who'd obviously had the highest regard for his 'officer bloke' as with a wry smile he described Tom. Prompted by Kessie, in his quiet cultured voice Private Duty told them the battalion had met stiff, last-ditch resistance as they approached the Sambre canal. In the crisis he'd gone up with Major Whitworth to try to effect the crossing of the canal. When they reached the pinned-down men, with their experienced NCOs wounded, inexperienced subalterns jittery, and raw recruits demoralised, one of the lads was lying wounded by the pontoon bridge the company had been attempting to erect. Cautiously, he and Major Whitworth started to crawl towards the man. Before they proceeded a few yards, the sniper's bullet hit Major Whitworth.

'He died instantly?' Kessie had already been told this. The bullet had lodged in Tom's heart. 'He didn't suffer?'

Private Duty replied yes, and no, to these questions. Insistently, Kessie asked if there had been any pain on his face?

'None at all, Mrs Whitworth.' After a few seconds' reflection, he added, 'There was a slightly surprised expression.'

'Yes, there would be. He didn't expect to be killed.'

Then Kessie wanted to know about the burial service. In an even quieter voice Private Duty painted the scene, filling in the details she was so desperate to hear. It had been a cold morning but the sky was rain-washed, the sun bright, with scudding white clouds, and the padre had known Major Whitworth and put some genuine emotion into the words he had recited thousands of times in the previous four years. There had been a large crowd of officers and men, many of whom should not have been there, but nobody had said a word because it was Major Whitworth's funeral. When the Last Post was played, some of the lads had broken down and wept. The coffin had been draped in the Union Jack and her husband had been given one of the more elaborate, distinctive Celtic wooden crosses as his headstone. The soldier who had affixed the details had known Major Whitworth too and instead of the standard stamped-out strip of metal, he had painted the words which read:

Major "Tom" Whitworth DSO, MC and bar, MP. 18th (Pals) Battalion Manchester Regiment. Killed in action on the Sambre Canal. November 7th 1918. R.I.P.

Halfway through the recital Kessie started to cry softly, though begging Private Duty to continue, and Sarah felt the lump in her own throat thickening. The sympathetic account from the man who had been at Tom's side as he died and was buried, appeared to have satisfied a part at least of her sister-in-law's obsessive need. When Private Duty was leaving Kessie asked if she might know his real name?

'I prefer not, if you don't mind, Mrs Whitworth. The cloak of anonymity suits me. It absolves me from responsibility.' He paused before he said softly, 'I would have died in place of Major Whitworth, if I could.'

How extraordinary, Sarah thought, that the child who had been born in the dark, damp, terraced house down by the River Mellor, in the smoky cotton town of Mellordale in the county of Lancashire, thirty-six years ago, should have died Major Whitworth, killed by a German sniper's bullet in the last days of the Great War; and that she should be sitting here, fiercely brushing the tears from her cheeks, as the organ soared into the last, heart-rending section of 'Nimrod'. The reverberation of the organ trembled into silence, David Lloyd George rose to his feet and mounted the steps to the pulpit to deliver the final memorial oration.

The Prime Minister was at his very best, the mane of white hair rainbow tinted by the sun-reflected colours of the stained glass, the liquid voice flowing with grief and affection, for he had genuinely liked and admired Tom. At the end, arm outstretched in familiar gesture, he quoted, 'He was a man taken all in all, We shall not look upon his like again.' Then in a softly dying, but magically audible voice, he recited the last stanza of the poem Laurence Binyon had written at the start of the war, which had acquired such poignancy in the last four years:

They shall grow not old, as we that are left grow old;
Age shall not weary them, nor the years condemn.
At the going down of the sun and in the morning
We will remember them.

In the tingling silence Lloyd George resumed his seat.
Kessie's head was bowed and her shoulders were shaking
and Sarah was glad the service was nearly over because
she didn't think she could take much more of the emotion,
never mind Kessie.

Escorted by the Prime Minister, with people inclining
their heads as they passed the packed pews, to the resounding,
triumphant strains of the 'Trumpet Voluntary' played
by a bandsman from the Manchester Regiment, Kessie,
Sarah and the children walked down the nave and out into
the fading late afternoon sunlight of Parliament Square.

With a slight sigh of relief, Sarah shut the front door behind
Stephen and Dorothy, the last to leave of those who had
been invited back to The Grove after the service. It had
however been a surprisingly relaxed, pleasant affair, or
maybe they had all exhausted their emotions in St Margaret's Westminster.

As she made to turn towards her sister-in-law, Sarah
was thinking about the proposals Kessie had made the
other day. Namely, that she sell The Grove which was
haunted by Tom's ghost, probably Willow Bank too because
they had spent so many happy family holidays on
the Isle of Wight it would be impossible to visit for years
to come, and that she buy a larger house which they could
share, with Sarah and Tamara having their own private
flat. Kessie said she wanted to return north as there was
nothing to keep her in London now. Sarah could resume
her Socialist, feminist, pacifist activities in Manchester,
Maggie would come with them, they could afford to employ
help with Tamara and she didn't want to hear any
nonsense about money because of that commodity Kessie
had plenty and as a good Socialist it was her duty to spread
it around.

Sarah was smiling at the memory of her sister-in-law's definite tones, glad that she felt able to plan for the future, and was about to tell her she accepted the proposals, gracefully and gratefully, when Kessie let out a sharp cry of pain. Clasping her right hand across her left arm, she started to breathe heavily. In the few seconds it took Sarah to reach her, she was already gasping for breath and she half-fell into Sarah's arms. Looking into the upturned face, drained to an ashen colour, Sarah saw the dilating pupils of Kessie's eyes. Frantically she called for Maggie before gently lowering Kessie's body to the floor and catapulting herself towards the front door. Throwing it open she ran into The Grove, shouting at the top of her voice.

'Stephen, Stephen, come back, come back. Kessie's had a heart attack.'

26

Ten days after Kessie's exhausted heart had almost stopped beating, Sarah stood by the window in her bedroom at The Grove. Since Tom's death they had entered a long, dark tunnel and she wondered when they would finally emerge. The plan to return north with Kessie, the plans she herself had begun to make, to put herself up for selection as the Labour candidate at the first feasible by-election, to start campaigning with the Peace Movements to ensure no similar holocaust ever again gripped the world, were once more distant dreams. It did not occur to Sarah's sense of family loyalty that she had any option other than to give her dead brother's children the love and stability they needed, with their father killed and their mother so desperately sick, both within the space of four months.

At the bottom of the garden by the apple tree, close

to the spot where they had burned Tom's uniform, she suddenly noticed all four children. It was a blustery Saturday afternoon of fast moving March clouds, bright sunshine and heavy showers, and the black clouds were building up again. Sarah put out her hand to unlock the window catch, to push up the frame and to call the children in. What the heck were they doing? Anne had a spade in her hand, there was a mound of earth by the tree and she was digging the spade into the ground and throwing up another scattering of soil. Taking a quick look at Tamara to make sure she was asleep, Sarah sped across the room, flew down the stairs and out through the conservatory. As she raced down the garden the cold sploshes of rain hit her face. When she reached the apple tree the children were staring at a mouldy, disintegrating box that Anne's spade had just unearthed. Grabbing the twins by the shoulders, Sarah commanded, 'Inside, all of you, this instant.'

Gusted by the wind, the rain was now falling in slanting sheets and Con and the twins ran as fast as their legs would carry them, but Anne slumped on to her heels, staring fixedly at the box. In the last ten days Sarah had needed to exert the utmost patience and self-control with her niece, repeatedly telling herself the child loved Kessie as much as she had loved Tom and was possessed of an above-average intensity of emotion which was making her behave so wildly. She hauled her niece to her feet and Anne lifted her face upwards, the copper-coloured hair hanging in wet strands beneath her tam o'shanter, her eyes burning like Tom's. The continuing defiance in the dark eyes said Anne was not going to move of her own volition, so Sarah picked up the spade and prodded at the box which collapsed at the second jab to reveal the decomposing remains of Amber, the dead cat which had been buried beneath the apple tree.

'That's what you wanted to see, isn't it? Well, you've seen it. That's what a dead body looks like after it's been in the earth for a while. Are you satisfied?'

With an impassive expression Anne eyed Amber's remains. 'Is that what Daddy looks like? Is that what Mummy will look like if she dies?'

'Mummy is *not* going to die.' The consultant had said he believed Mrs Whitworth's indomitable spirit was pulling her through. The child's terror lest her Mummy die too, was the reason, Sarah presumed, why she'd performed her disinterring act now rather than after Tom's death. Briskly she said, 'It's what we'll all look like one day.'

'I shan't. I'm going to be cremated and have my ashes scattered from the top of Netherstone Edge.'

A simple memorial service for Tom had been held on the crags of the Edge which Sarah had attended with Anne and Con, though Kessie had been unable to make the ascent and had vetoed the twins' participation. On a bright, cold winter's day hundreds of folk from The Dales and survivors from the Manchester Regiment had climbed to Tom's favourite haunt on the Lancashire moors.

The rain was beating on them, splashing from the bare branches of the apple tree, but Sarah reckoned it was important to let Anne talk, if she wanted. Whilst she started to shovel the earth back into the cat's grave, Anne said, 'Miss Vernon says Daddy's soul is in heaven. Is it? She says he's watching everything I do. Is he?' Miss Vernon was Anne's headmistress from whom Sarah had received a letter about her niece's increasingly disruptive behaviour at school. 'Can he hear in heaven, too?'

'I don't know, luv. But if he is listening and watching at the moment, I don't reckon he'll be pleased with you. This was your idea, wasn't it?' Nodding, Anne took the shovel from Sarah's hand and furiously attacked the diminishing mound of earth, slinging it back to fill up the grave. The rain dripping from her, Sarah waited until the child had completed the task and stamped the earth muddily flat with her Wellington boots. 'Shall we go in now and get out of our wet clothes? If you promise not to do anything like this again, we can all have a game. You can choose. Lotto, pelmanism, Newmarket, whatever you want.'

'Oh Aunty Sarah,' Anne flung the spade to the ground and herself into Sarah's arms, her slight, soaking wet frame shaking. 'I don't want Mummy to die. I don't want her to go to heaven with Daddy. Heaven sounds a stupid place, if you have to watch and listen all the time.'

There was no instant, overnight improvement in Anne's behaviour. She continued to roam around like one of her father's gipsy ancestors, snapping at her sisters and brother, complaining bitterly that 'Tammy' kept her awake by howling all night. 'Tammy' was the children's pet name for Tamara, though there was nothing affectionate in the way Anne was currently using it. She continued to shut herself into her bedroom and to worship at Tom's shrine, sitting cross-legged in front of the large photograph of him in his uniform which she had decorated with a laurel wreath and black ribbons, surrounded by his medals, including one for Distinguished Services to the United States army; his gazettings from second-lieutenant to major; the sampler she had embroidered which Kessie had let her have back; dozens of smaller photographs of Tom through the ages, starting with the tousled haired lad in the darned jumper, reach-me-down trousers and clogs, standing outside their house in Inkerman Street, Mellordale; and the always fresh vase of flowers, some of which came from the bouquets that made her mother's hospital room look like a florist's shop. And she continued to fill scrapbooks with every newspaper photograph and article about Tom that she could find.

Sarah considered the obsession downright morbid, though fortunately the other children did not follow their older sister's example. Then Kessie showed her the poem Anne had written entitled 'My Daddy'.

> The bells rang out
> We were victorious.
> The telegram came
> Regretting to inform us . . .
>
> Why was it Daddy?
> Why was he there?

Only four more days . . .
It was cruelly unfair.

I loved my Daddy
With all my heart.
Now he is dead
And my life has tumbled apart.

Kessie said she thought it best to let Anne have her shrine, which might help her to put her young life back together again. Reluctantly Sarah agreed, mainly because Kessie herself looked so frail and fragile, as if any puff of wind would blow her away, the chestnut hair emphasising the pallor of her skin, the hazel eyes huge in the thin-ness of her face, her breathing shallow, her voice huskier than ever. Still, Sarah did not receive any more letters from Miss Vernon, so she presumed Anne was being less disruptive at school.

When the consultant was reasonably satisfied that Mrs Whitworth would pull through, she was transferred from the nearby Whittington Hospital into which she had been rushed on that awful night, to a private nursing home in the countryside round Muswell Hill, run by two ex-suffragettes. Unlike many war widows the one thing Kessie did not have to worry about was money and Sarah really appreciated how an ample supply of 'that commodity' relieved the pressures.

Not long after Kessie had settled into the nursing home, towards the end of April, Philip Marchal called to see Sarah at The Grove.

When they were decorously seated either side of the fire in the sitting room, he said, 'I don't want to bother Kessie with any of this, because it would only upset her, but I feel you should know, Sarah. Johnny Conway has been offered a contract in Hollywood which he has accepted. From his attitude, I infer it is a lucrative contract. He is exercising his self-appointed rights as Margaret Jane's father and taking her with him to the United States.'

'What! But he knows she's not his child and he knows

Alice's intention and dearest wish was to have her brought up in England, to be an English lady.' Recalling the afternoon when Alice had screamed at her husband that he wasn't having Margaret Jane, Sarah felt her dander rising on the dead woman's behalf. 'Can't we stop him?'

'No.'

The definite negative made Sarah blink. Philip gave her a slight smile before he said, 'Jonathon hinted that if we tried to stop him, both he and Alice's sister might raise difficulties about her will which, as he so picturesquely pointed out, was made when his poor dear wife was in a nursing home for nut-cases. Had she been in her right mind, Hollywood's newest hero observed, his poor dear wife would have made her husband and her sister the executors of her will, and the trustees of her daughter's fortune.'

'He knows darned well she'd have done nothing of the sort, in or out of a nursing home.' Sarah had reckoned there'd be problems about the damned will and she could see why Philip didn't want Kessie troubled by any of this. 'I imagine Alice's sister does, too. Aren't people buggers?'

'Only too often, Sarah, only too often.' Philip's laughter was both amused and sardonic. 'There is the question of Alice's mother in America. She has been deluging me with inordinately long letters, blessing me for acting *in loco parentis*, but understandably yearning to see her dead daughter's child. Mrs Hartley, of course, knows nothing about Guy. To her, Margaret Jane is Johnny's daughter. I suspect he has been playing on the devastated, lonely old woman's feelings.'

'Why's Johnny so keen on taking Margaret Jane with him?' Sarah looked at Philip. 'Is it to revenge himself on Alice?'

'I would suspect so. Don't worry. I shall remain a trustee and executor of her mother's will.'

Philip's tone was chilly and Sarah remembered saying she wouldn't like him as her enemy. She didn't reckon Johnny Conway would find it the most pleasant of experiences.

In the middle of May, Anne showed Aunty Sarah the pictures in the newspapers of the well-known actor, Jonathon Conway, waving farewell to England's shores as he sailed to seek further fame and fortune in Hollywood. Mr Conway was accompanied by his eighteen month old daughter whose American-born mother had, alas, been a victim of the last Zeppelin raid on London, and by her nursemaid. Etty Jardine had consulted Philip when Johnny had offered her the job in America and he had said she should accept, for she was Margaret Jane's surrogate mother. Sarah suspected that Etty was also going in the role of Philip's spy.

'Ladies and gentlemen.' Adjusting the conical witch's hat, pulling her black cloak around her, Anne emerged from behind the bushes in the garden at The Grove. 'We are presenting this play in honour of the birthday girl Tamara, who is one year old today.'

'Hurrah!' Harry clapped his hands, Dorothy and Stephen, Jenny and Rupert, and the other guests joined in, while the birthday girl wriggled on Sarah's knee, pulling at the necklace round her mother's neck.

'I'm sorry we've run out of programmes but we didn't expect so many people.' Anne gazed at the audience sitting in deckchairs, garden chairs and every spare chair from the house. 'The play is entitled *The Witch's Lesson*. It is written by Anne Whitworth.' She tried not to smile as Harry clapped and cheered again, 'And it is performed by the Whitworth Players.'

Bowing, almost losing her witch's hat, Anne scurried back into the bushes. After a few seconds her friend Wilfrid marched to the centre of the lawn which had recently been returfed after its wartime use as a vegetable garden. Clad in his Boys Brigade uniform he blew a fanfare on his bugle, whereupon the twins appeared from the bushes. On their heads were gold cardboard crowns, their older sisters' velvet party cloaks trailing behind them. Sarah consulted her programme. Master Mark Whitworth and Miss Kate Whitworth were playing King Florizel and Queen Halcyon;

indeed all the leading parts were being played by members of the Whitworth family. With one of Sarah's white nightdresses hitched round her waist, tinsel wound in her auburn hair, waving a silver wand, Miss Constance Whitworth was the Good Fairy, while Miss Anne Whitworth was the Wicked Witch.

The plot was about the king and queen wanting a baby, an heir to the throne of Dreamland, and the play was very well written for a not yet ten year old, observantly and amusingly based on the traits and foibles of the Whitworth family. King Florizel and Queen Halcyon quarrelled violently but presented a united front when under outside attack, the Good Fairy was endearingly sweet and reasonable but backed off initially when it came to a fight with the Wicked Witch, which Anne herself played to the hilt. Just when the birthday girl was growing restless, standing up on Sarah's knee, pointing to the grass and imperiously crying 'Da, da da', Con came towards them, waving her silver wand.

Handing the wand to Harry who sat grinning with it stuck in the air, she picked Tamara up and trotted towards King Florizel and Queen Halcyon. 'Your Majesties, here is your baby daughter. I bought her for you at a shop on the Isle of Wight, so she will be a very good baby.'

The lines made Jenny hoot with laughter. Con turned towards the Wicked Witch, 'Will you be her other guardian? Will you be good and kind?'

'I will,' said Anne, 'now I see you have been sensible and bought a little girl, after all.'

'Bravo!' Dorothy shouted.

In Con's arms Tamara started to struggle and to yell, so she lowered her cousin to the ground and while Kate dramatically recited the lines which happily wound up the play, Tamara tottered across the grass, beaming at the audience.

The performance had not really been for the birthday girl, who was far too young to appreciate it. Sarah had dropped the suggestion of putting on a play, letting it lie until Anne picked it up, to give the children, Anne in particular, something to take their minds away from their mother who remained in the nursing home. Her idea seemed to have worked, and with an excellent birthday tea laid on by Maggie, despite the continuing food shortages, and the sun shining as brightly and the air as warm as on Tamara's natal day, a good time was had by all.

The close friends stayed after the mothers of Tamara's fellow babies and those who'd had 'bit' parts in *The Witch's Lesson* had departed and the children had gone to bed. In the slowly gathering June twilight they sat out in the garden, sipping glasses of Maggie's elderberry wine. Jenny's was a farewell appearance, temporarily anyway, for she was off with her camera to Germany.

To the point as usual, Dorothy said, 'Have you actually got a commission? Or are you going on spec?'

'Sort of both.'

'What does that mean?' Dorothy demanded.

'Our Miss Macdonald is dying to see what's happening in Germany, whether the Fatherland will follow the Russians into a full-scale civil war and go Bolshie in defeat. A magazine is interested enough to have helped her obtain travel documents,' Rupert said laconically. 'Our Miss Macdonald is also convinced her photographs will be so brilliant the whole of Fleet Street will be panting for them, aren't you, sweetheart?'

'If I'm not convinced,' Jenny said tartly, 'nobody else will be. You want to try being a woman.'

'Do I?' Rupert eyed her curves in their blue and green pantaloon and blouse outfit, and she stuck out her tongue at him.

Sarah found their relationship baffling, but then other folk probably considered hers and Mikhail Muranov's downright peculiar. After all, they were supposed to be married. The week after Tom's memorial service at St Margaret's Westminster, Rupert had sailed for Australia. Having said hello to his family and taken a look at the sheep, he'd decided to sail back to England, and Jenny. Their affection was mutual and on the new free-and-easy level that was operating in certain, though by no means all, sections of postwar society, they seemed happy enough.

'They're trying to push us back where they think we belong, you know.' Dorothy looked accusingly at Rupert, but it was Harry who said, 'I presume by "they" you mean men?'

'I certainly do.' Dorothy turned to Sarah, 'I remember you saying our war work could turn out to be a sort of boomerang, hurled by men in their hour of need, which they'd expect to return to hand once the war was over.'

'Did I? Wasn't that clever of me?'

As the Johnnies came marching home again, the Jills were being thrown out of work without so much as a thanks-a-lot. The popular press had already taken to calling women, who only six months ago they had been lauding as indispensable heroines, selfish, clinging blacklegs if they wanted to keep their jobs.

'We're not just trotting back home like good little girls,' said Dorothy, who had never been a good girl.

With Tom dead and Kessie *hors de combat* Sarah had received scores of letters from women in The Dales. She told her friends about them, saying, 'It does seem that far too many women are accepting the back-to-the-kitchen sink orders. Some of them are angry at their treatment but they still have that inbred deference that comes from centuries of being second-class citizens.'

'They may be deferential at the bottom of the heap,' Dorothy said, 'but the more educated types are thronging the Women's Services offices, demanding to be found new jobs.'

'Good for them,' said Jenny. 'We've all got to stand up and fight on our own two legs.'

Infuriated by Dorothy's contemptuous reference to those at the bottom of the heap Sarah snapped, 'It really isn't as simple as you two seem to think. You want to try standing up and fighting without a penny to your name and kids to support.'

'If you're not going back to Russia, why don't you do something about changing the situation?' Dorothy demanded. 'I thought you wanted to stand for Parliament.

Goodness knows we need a woman, lots of women, in the House of Commons.'

Sarah made no reply. She had no intention of answering Didi's implied question – are you going back to Russia? And she still found it difficult to talk about Tom so there was no way she was explaining why she had not stood at the General Election, nor why she could not stand at the moment. It didn't matter because Harry galloped to her defence. Huffily he said the situation in Russia was impossible and until it calmed down obviously Sarah could not return with a small child. Her current concern was caring for her brother's family. Dorothy apologised and the temperature subsided.

'If you want a humble man's opinion . . .' Rupert began.

'Don't overdo it, lover,' Jenny said.

He ignored the interruption. 'You're facing the same sort of problems women did in Australia, once they'd won the vote.'

'All women haven't won the vote,' Dorothy said fiercely. 'I haven't for one.'

'You have in principle,' Rupert said patiently. 'My sister was a suffragist, so I've lived with the pre-vote euphoria, and the post-vote depression. What Sarah said about boomerangs was true in Australia. Once my fellow-countrymen had recovered from the shock of women fighting for the vote, they did their best to return to being their old, beery, superior selves.'

Dorothy looked at him coldly. 'Well, they're not doing it here. And I'm not suffering from depression. I'm lobbying hard for the Sex Disqualification Removal Bill. That'll open the legal profession to us. And we'll finally have both sexes sitting on juries and dishing out justice, and not before time.'

' 'Tis true,' Stephen twitched her nostrils, 'we've so many areas of discrimination to attack now, it's difficult to know which to storm next.'

'If you want another humble man's summary,' Harry said, 'I think you took twelve giant steps forward during the war. You've been pushed six steps backwards since the armistice and *they* will go on trying to push you right back. But you'll resist, at all levels of society. Too many women left their homes, tasted freedom, or took over the responsibilities of keeping the home fires burning, for any of you ever again to be willing to be treated like doormats.'

'Well said, Harry old thing!' Stephen boomed.

In the twelve months he had spent in the Middle East driving the armoured cars through incredible conditions in the Persian mountains, Harry had matured and acquired greater confidence. Since his return to England he had been a comfort to Sarah, a man she could talk to as she had to Tom or Misha. She had in fact told him what the situation was in regard to Mikhail Muranov and that she now doubted she and Tamara would go to Russia. Harry's increased confidence did not apparently extend to emotional matters and he had made no comment about that.

Jenny hiccoughed into her glass of elderberry wine. 'Gosh, this stuff's potent. Are you strong enough to carry me home, lover?'

'If I could hump full marching order as a ranker in Gallipoli and France,' Rupert replied, 'I can manage you through London.'

'Thank you,' Jenny hiccoughed again before asking, 'is Kessie going to accept Philip Marchal's invitation and spend the summer recuperating at Chenneys?'

'I think so,' Sarah said.

27

The summer holidays were nearly over, the children due to return to school, and all manner of people from Mr Seagrave the heart specialist, to Vera Johnson who had been engaged as Kessie's nurse, were saying it would be wise for her to remain at Chenneys. The roses were creeping back into her cheeks, but the children did tire her, bless their spirited hearts. In London they had their Aunty Sarah to look after them and they could continue to visit Chenneys until such time as their mother's health was truly on the mend. Nobody forecast when that would be.

'You think I should stay here then? And you're sure you don't mind looking after the children?'

'Yes I do,' said Sarah, 'and no, I don't. For the time being.'

Philip said little, wisely in Kessie's opinion, but then he'd said his piece, softly, tenderly, not long after she had first arrived, to be installed in her own suite on the ground floor of the west wing: bedroom, sitting room and newly converted bathroom, with an adjoining bed-sitting room for Vera and the children's rooms nearby but not too close to disturb her.

'I hope you will find some peace of mind and body here, Kessie,' Philip had said. 'Stay as long, or as short, a time as you wish. You know my dearest wish. That you will one day feel you can become the mistress of Chenneys, as you already are of my heart.'

It had been a pretty speech and Philip's devotion, tact, and sensitivity to her needs, continued to astonish Kessie. He had a surprisingly practical streak, or maybe that was how his family, without leaving the slightest imprint on English history, had over the centuries acquired hundreds of acres of prime Kent land, not to mention substantial acreage of central London. Practically, Philip's devotion extended to commissioning a bright young inventor to design and build a battery operated bath-chair, in which Kessie was able to buzz around the ground floors and out into the garden. The contraption, which the children christened 'Norman' after its young inventor, gave Kessie a mobility which cheered her a little.

She was still at Chenneys when the misty, melancholy month of November came in and with it the first anniversary of Tom's death and the armistice. People said it must be a comfort to have the children which was true, though on her bad days Kessie could hardly bear to look at Mark who physically was so like his father. Had she been given the terrible choice – the children or Tom – she would have chosen Tom.

By her bedside Kessie had the photograph Philip had taken of him in his uniform and she spent hours gazing at the quizzical expression in his eyes and the slight smile hovering over his lips, telling herself she should not. And she spent hours reading through his diary, running her fingers over the unstylish elementary school handwriting which Tom had given individuality by loops and twirls, telling herself she should not. Some of the entries had a savage passion that made her weep however many times she read them, so many of the names contained within its pages belonged to the dead, and there was the added poignancy of Tom's idiosyncratic spelling. A few of the entries made her laugh.

June 18th 1916 Henshall reported this a.m. 'There's a big gun outside, sir. What shall I do with it, sir?'; and *January 30th 1917* Sergeant Protheroe brought last night's patroll safeley back in filthy conditions. He informed me they lost their way in No Mans Land. Suddernly in the dawn light, they saw this sentry 'with a frill round his middle and one of them funny hats on'. Protheroe thought it was a Jock so he yelled, 'Don't shoot. 18th Manchesters.' The sentry yelled back, 'Ach, mein Gott!'

Each time Kessie read the last, hastily written entry of November 6th, 1918, the tears rolled down her cheeks.

Foul day. Everyone in foul tempers. The men quartered in misserable leaky barns and the rations didn't arrive. Battersby's company detailed to efect the crossing of the canal tomorrow a.m. Not my doing! Battersby's suberltans are inexperienced 'agonies' and he's a born dugout king, leading from anywhere except the front, bound to survive and bluster about his heroic war. [Captain Battersby had not survived; he'd been killed a few hours before Tom.] He's got Sergeant Buckley with him but if Buckley's hit there'll be trouble. [Buckley had been hit.] The end can't be long now, we all know it can't and the knowledge is keeping us going, just about. Then it's Kessie, the children, England, home and beauty! What will it sound like when the guns stop firing?

Christmas was a bad time too, faith lost, memories haunting. So was New Year's Day, 1920; Kessie's natal day, her thirty-fifth birthday. Sometimes she felt one hundred and thirty five and sometimes she felt she looked it, her face sharp and thin, her breasts top-heavy in the angularity of her body. But she was only half the biblical lifespan and her comparative youth was another problem. Since Tom's death the only men to have touched her had been doctors, or servants lifting her, or a friend lightly embracing her, but the sexual desire had not died. Sometimes it was quiescent for weeks and Kessie thought, that's it, gone, spent, only the passionate memories left, but then it crept into her blood again until her whole body ached for the caress of Tom's fingers, for his lips, for the hardness of his loins against hers.

Spring came, faint stirrings of hope anew. Even more slowly, starting in the bathroom as she had last time her heart had been affected, Kessie began to take a few hesitant steps. It was a difficult process, both because she was scared of what she might do to her heart and because she was seldom left alone. Vera was an excellent nurse, a tactful companion, happy to stay silent, stitching away on her *petit-point* embroidery, but she obviously saw her task as never being far from Kessie's side and she was unhappy when Kessie buzzed away in her bath-chair.

It was in one of the corridors, when she had climbed out of 'Norman' and was holding on to the panelled wall, taking a few breathless steps, that she met Philip whom she'd imagined was in his study writing. He did not say, what the hell do you think you're doing here? as Tom would have, but discarding his walking stick he lifted her back into the contraption.

'I think that's enough for one day. A few gentle steps at a time, eh?'

That was her main complaint against Philip. He never argued with her, he never upbraided her, he never raised his voice, however bloody-minded she might be. Oh, to have a lovely, rip-roaring row like the ones she'd had with Tom!

By the Easter holidays she could, slowly, walk several yards by herself without gasping for breath. Mr Seagrave who visited her regularly shook his head and said she was an amazing lady and he wouldn't have believed it unless he had seen it with his own eyes.

Now it was nearly the end of May and soon she would have been here a year, months without pressures in which her health had improved immeasurably. She was ambulant, if not exactly hale and hearty, and the children had accepted life's new routine, weekdays in term-time in London with Aunty Sarah and Maggie, weekends and holidays at Chenneys with Mummy and Uncle Pip. It was not a situation, however, that Kessie felt could continue indefinitely.

Tamara's second birthday dawned with clear skies and bright sunshine; maybe she was a lucky child, Sarah thought, who would be blessed with fine weather throughout her life. Sturdily built like the father she did not, and now seemed unlikely ever to know, the wide Ukrainian features and fair hair contrasted beautifully with the dark Whitworth eyes and skin. That was not subjective mother love speaking. Most folk said what a lovely little girl she was.

These days Sarah rarely visited Chenneys, but she'd come down this weekend so that Tamara's birthday could be celebrated with her cousins and her Aunty Kessie. In the afternoon they all trooped out to the lawn that spread its immaculate green between the rose garden and the ornamental lake, Kessie buzzing along in her contraption. Apparently, every May troupes of local morris dancers gave a display for charity in the grounds of Chenneys and

311

Kessie had asked that this year the event might coincide with Tamara's birthday.

The audience, composed of the county society, folk from the village and the estate, was already seated. To a patter of applause the first troupe pranced to the centre of the grass, and a hefty lot of lads they were. Clad in white shirts and breeches, with bright sashes across their shoulders and wound round their middles, the little bells jingling from the frippery round their knees, the ribbons on their upturned pork-pie hats flowing in the gentle breeze, they waved their sticks and handkerchiefs. Solemnly, they bowed first to Tamara, who was sitting on a high chair of honour next to Sarah before turning to Philip and the rest of the audience.

Two of the heftiest looking lads jangled their hand-bells and the dancers were off, picking up their feet, banging their sticks one against the other, the little bells tinkling below the clang of the hand-sets, the sun shining on the whiteness of the costumes and the green of the grass. It was a pretty, pagan, English spectacle and Sarah reckoned faintly ridiculous in this postwar era.

'Does it remind you of the Pethick Lawrences in the old days?' she whispered to Kessie. 'They were great ones for preserving the time-honoured pastimes of true working folk.'

Her shoulders shaking with laughter, Kessie hissed, 'Shut up.'

Sarah glanced at Philip who was looking po-faced. Last year, he'd told them, one of the more enthusiastic novices had wildly swung his stick and knocked a fellow-dancer out cold. No such excitement this year.

'Kessie,' Sarah whispered again, 'after the birthday nosh, do you think we can slip away for a while? I want to talk to you, serious-like.'

Kessie whispered back that they could meet in the summer house.

When the display had finished Philip made a stiffly polite speech of thanks – he could do with lessons in public speaking from Kessie – and they repaired to the marquee in which the birthday 'nosh' was laid. It was a spread and a half, thought Sarah, covering the trestle tables draped in white cloths and adorned with floral decorations: wafer-thin sandwiches, potted meats, raised pies, trifles, jellies, sponge cakes, iced cakes, fruit cakes, cheesecakes, with the *pièce de résistance* a four-tiered birthday cake, on top of which sat an iced model of a teddy bear, a dolly, and a golliwog, and two slender golden candles.

Sarah asked Harry if he would lift Tamara up to blow out the candles, a gesture which he appreciated because he liked coming here even less than she did and perhaps in protest, tended to lapse into his I'm-only-a-Cockney-lad manner. Tamara was fond of him, and she did look sweet in the ruched silk dress Kessie had bought for her birthday present, blowing kisses with self-confident *élan* as the guests sang 'Happy birthday, dear Tamara'.

Leaving her daughter in Harry's safe hands, Sarah made her way to the summer house. 'Norman' was already parked outside, the downstairs windows were open to the warm air, and the door was ajar. Inside, Kessie was sitting with her feet up on the wickerwork sofa, where Sarah herself had sat with Tom on that chill December day. There was no point living with the memories, it was the future she wanted to discuss with her brother's comparatively young widow who, bless her guts and courage, was looking almost like the old Kessie, with one startling difference.

Last weekend, to Sarah's astonishment, the girls had returned from their visit to Chenneys with their hair cut short into their necks, straight fringes and straight sides providing a hirsute proscenium arch for their faces. They all obviously fancied themselves and Kate went around holding her neck at a Johnny Conway angle, allowing her 'Buster Brown' style to be seen to best effect. They told Aunty Sarah that Mummy had had her hair cut too, but it wasn't until she saw Kessie last night that the symbolism of the gesture struck Sarah. For the glorious waist-length hair that Tom had adored had not merely been cut, it had been bobbed, parted on the left, so that it fell across

Kessie's forehead, flicked on to her cheeks, and tapered into her neck. The effect was startling, though the style suited Kessie, giving her an up-to-date elegance, and the shearing of her and her daughter's long hair had to be a statement that she was preparing to face the future without her beloved husband.

'Right. Fire away,' Kessie said as Sarah sat herself down in one of the wickerwork chairs. 'If you want to say you can't go on looking after the children, and you're fed up coming to Chenneys, I know, Sarah, I know.'

'No, that's not it.' Sarah still regarded it as her duty to care for the kids, until such time as Kessie had sorted out her future.

'Oh,' her sister-in-law looked surprised.

'No, it's . . .' Sarah had done a rough rehearsal of what she wanted to say. She expected Kessie to agree with her, probably be grateful that she had voiced both their feelings, but it was a tricky, delicate subject. 'Look Kessie, you know how much I loved Tom, as much as you did in a different way. I know how much he loved you, but Tom was always a realist and he'd want you and the children to be as happy as possible, now he's gone. I'm not daft about Philip Marchal, as you probably realise, but he's daft about you and I reckon the best thing you can do now is to marry him.'

With a smile Sarah looked at Kessie who did not smile back but sat with an unfathomable expression on her face. Slightly surprised by the lack of reaction, having got the crunch point over, Sarah reckoned she'd better elaborate.

'I thought I ought to let you know, as Tom's sister, that I've no objection to the marriage. On the contrary, like I've said, I think it's what you should do. Chenneys is a beautiful place. I know you find peace here, as Philip does. He's in a position to give you everything, Kessie, and he not only can, he's dying to take all the burdens from your shoulders. He loves the kids because they're yours. And they like him. They're used to Uncle Pip. Anne may kick up a bit when you tell her you're going to marry him, but she'll get over it.'

314

Kessie's expression had not changed, her silence was almost as daunting as Philip's. Sarah felt herself floundering, filling the empty space.

'Frankly, Kessie, people are starting to talk. Let 'em you may say, if you know about the gossip, but I reckon you've always cared more than I have, for example, about your good reputation, and the gossip may affect the children. You know what folks are like. In fact, there's been a bit of tittle-tattle at school already. I haven't said anything because I didn't want to bother you, but Anne came home in a state the other week, and Con was crying, and I gather it was to do with their Mummy living down at Chenneys.'

'Really?' Kessie's husky voice had the clear tones Sarah hadn't heard in ages. 'What are "folks" saying? That I'm leaping into bed with Sir Philip Marchal? He should be so fortunate. Do they imagine my heart attack was a blind, a cover, so I could rush down here a few months after my husband was killed, to carry on with my secret lover?'

'Don't be silly, luv. I'm sorry I mentioned it. But a lot of people who admired Tom, not just the malicious gossips, find it difficult to grasp what you're doing here, month after month, a young widow living in the same house as a highly eligible bachelor.'

'If I marry Philip, that'll make it all right, will it?'

'Well, yes,' Sarah said lamely, 'though that's not why I think you should marry him.'

'How kind of you.'

Swinging her legs to the floor, far too swiftly Kessie rose to her feet and started to pace across the floor. Sarah realised she had made the most appalling blunder, not just putting her foot into Kessie's sensibilities, but clomping in with her indiarubber boots.

'I'm leaving Chenneys all right. Not because of what mean-minded "folk" who've nothing better to do are saying, but because I feel I can't impose on you any longer. Or delude Philip. I like him very much and in a way I wish I could love him. I wish I could marry him. It would tie everything up so neatly, wouldn't it? And I have your blessing, too, as Tom's sister.'

Heck, that had been a supreme misjudgement. Kessie swung round towards her, catching her breath hard as she moved. 'But you see, Sarah . . .'

'Don't Kessie, don't get excited. I'm sorry. I . . .'

'No, you just listen to me for a minute.'

She took a long trembling breath and Sarah did not know whether to shut her up, or to let her talk. Which would do less harm?

'You see, Sarah, I can't marry anybody for the fore-seeable future. If ever. For me marriage is very much a physical as well as a mental thing. That's the way it was with Tom. Something else you'd better understand, Sarah, is that part of me died with Tom. Even if I were capable of making love, the part of me that belongs to him couldn't do it. Maybe one day . . . if I live so long . . . but not yet . . . Sarah . . . not yet . . .'

Her breath was emerging in long, sobbing gasps, she was shaking, and Sarah ran towards her, telling her to stop talking, trying to make her sit down, but Kessie shook off her arms and her voice rose as she reiterated all the things she was not going to do, she was incapable of doing. Then she half-collapsed. Sarah was dragging her towards the sofa when the door was flung open. Philip moved across the floor at a pace that belied the lameness of his leg, rudely thrusting Sarah aside, gently lowering Kessie on to the sofa.

'My darling, whatever it is, whatever she's done to you, it doesn't matter. Breathe slowly, slowly, my darling, there, there, that's it, slowly, slowly.'

For several minutes he concentrated his attention on Kessie, and Sarah might not have existed. A shaft of sunlight was streaming through the window, playing over the pale clamminess of Kessie's skin, highlighting the tints in her bobbed chestnut hair, emphasising the elegance of Philip's hand as he stroked her face and throat. He calmed her and slowly her breathing became regular, though it remained shallow. As Sarah stood watching, appalled by the passion she had unwittingly unleashed in Kessie and the damage she had done her beloved sister-in-law, none-theless she could not but believe she had been right in her presumption. Kessie should marry this man who loved her with a passion that equalled her own, with a devotion not given to many men to hold, nor women to receive.

Fortunately the train was half-empty, so Sarah, Harry and Tamara had a compartment to themselves. Even more fortunately the child had by now exhausted her tears and tantrums at being dragged away from Chenneys and she fell asleep stretched across the seat, her head in her mother's lap. Sarah looked at the tear-blotched face, and the ruches of the silk party dress stained with icing and marzipan – they'd had a ludicrous scene about the teddy bear, the dolly and the golly decorations from the top of the birthday cake which at that particular moment Sarah had been determined her daughter was *not* bringing home with her – and she felt like bursting into tears herself.

Avoiding Harry's concerned gaze, she leant her head against the back of the seat and stared out of the window. The twilight was gathering, in the orchards of the Garden of England the last of the blossom glimmered in ghostly fashion on the trees, the unfurling leaves of the hops were stretched high on their poles, patterned against the darkening sky, and the conical roofs of the fat round oast-houses were acquiring sharp silhouettes. Sarah recalled Harry talking about his family's hop-picking holidays during those days in Galatz.

'Do you want to talk?' he said. 'Will it help?'

Would it? Sarah reckoned she owed him some explanation because all she'd said, tight-lipped, fighting back the tears, as she'd marched up to him after the scene with Philip, had been, 'I'm leaving. With Tamara. There's a train at seven-fifty. If you'll come with me, I'll be grateful.'

Then she'd packed and gone down to Kessie's room where Vera had been embarrassed, almost as if she'd had instructions not to let Sarah in. Not that it had mattered because the doctor had already been. Kessie was sedated and drifting into sleep, so she'd just bent down and kissed her. After that she had found Tamara, happily playing with Con and the twins in the deserted marquee, and they'd had the full Russian firework display, with a dose of Lancashire truculence thrown in. The children had been bewildered and upset. Anne had asked, 'What's the matter, Aunty Sarah? Why are you going? It's Tammy's birthday.'

At least they hadn't been worried about Kessie. Sir had kept that quiet, ordering Sarah from the summer house to fetch one of the younger manservants who had carried Kessie round the back of the house to the west wing. Sir had told the children Mummy was tired and had gone to bed early, which was nothing new in their young lives.

Immediately Philip emerged from Kessie's suite they'd had their scene, standing in his study, his *sanctum sanctorum*, which was lined with books from rug scattered, polished wooden floor to oak-beamed ceiling. On the walnut desk Sarah noticed the neatly arranged piles of paper under the coloured glass paperweight, the sharpened pencils, the quill pen and the silver inkwell. While Philip spat venom at her in a voice that never rose above conversational level, through the open lattices windows the scent of the summer flowers wafted.

'I have no wish to know why you upset Kessie. You will never again upset her like that in my house. I believe you care for her, Sarah. Your actions since your brother's death proclaim that you do. I had believed you to be possessed of a fund of good, north country commonsense, apart from the fact that you're a war-trained nurse. So what possessed you to upset Kessie's delicate equilibrium, I cannot imagine. Nor can I, at the moment, forgive you. I suggest when you leave tomorrow you . . .'

'Don't worry, I'm leaving tonight.'

'That would seem stupid, and unfair to your daughter, who is greatly enjoying herself.'

'Just leave my daughter out of it. If you consider Kessie's welfare your business – which she doesn't – Tamara's is mine. I'll tell you how I upset Kessie, whether you want to hear or not. Because I said I thought it would be a good idea if she married you.'

'How dared you! You impertinent, interfering . . .'

'Bitch?'

318

Philip's expression showed his distaste for her intemperate language. His voice at its iciest, its pitch remaining low, he said, 'We are scheduled to be in Mellordale for the opening of your brother's memorial hall on midsummer day. That is obviously an occasion Kessie will struggle to attend at all cost. Doctor Fortescue, happily, does not believe you have seriously harmed her heart, so she should be well enough to make the journey to Lancashire. Until then, I suggest you keep out of the way.'

'Do I have your permission to go on looking after Kessie's children, my brother's children? It's still term-time, you know. Or are you keeping them here too, out of my way?'

He did not bother to reply but the answer was obviously no, the children would return to The Grove tomorrow night as usual.

'I'll do what I want and what Kessie wants. Not what you see fit.'

With that Sarah had, as they said, swept from the study but she did not reckon she had come particularly well out of the confrontation. But she had been off-balance, sick at heart herself, and he'd given no quarter, made not one whit of allowance for her distressed state.

Looking across the compartment at Harry's kindly, troubled face, briefly she outlined what had happened to make her leave Chenneys. When she had finished he said, 'I think he's a sod, if you'll pardon my French, after all you've done for Kessie and the kids in the last eighteen months.'

'I think he's a sod too, at times.' Sarah laughed slightly and Tamara stirred in her lap. 'But your family haven't been lords of the manor for nine hundred years without leaving some trace. And he's like a tiger when it comes to protecting Kessie. I don't know what she'll do now, seeing she was planning to leave Chenneys. I've put the kibosh on that for the time being, haven't I?'

The train clanked into a station and Sarah watched a porter lighting the gas lamps on the platform. Suddenly Harry said, 'Can I speak my mind?'

'Why not? Everybody else has today.'

Slowly he said, 'I think you probably were misguided to speak to Kessie about marrying Sir, though I know you did it out of concern for her future. But I think you should leave her to sort her own life out now. She is in better health, she has plenty of friends and him to fall back on, and she's not short of money, her own, or his. And I think it's about time you started living your own life again, Sarah. I think you ought to start thinking about standing for Parliament. I mean, it's ridiculous that that Lady Astor should be the first woman Member of Parliament. She wasn't even a suffragette!'

The indignation in Harry's voice as he made this last statement caused Sarah to smile. The train clacked into motion, and with it the pace of Harry's speech accelerated.

'Are you staying in England, Sarah? I mean, definitely. And if you are, what are you going to do about being married to Mikhail? Because you're not, are you? I mean, I know you're not, though I'll never breathe a word to anybody, of course, you know that. But I've been wondering if maybe you could get a divorce, or have the marriage annulled, or declared invalid, or illegal, or something. Officially, I mean, seeing it never happened. I mean, Kessie knows lots of important people, and so do you. And well, if you could get a divorce or something, I'd consider it a great honour if you'd consider marrying me. And I'm making a pig's ear of it, as usual. But I love you, Sarah, and I always will. I know you don't love me but I think we could make a go of it and Tammy likes me, doesn't she? And I believe you have a real task to fulfil, helping ordinary people who aren't too good at helping themselves, doing something about all the injustices there still are. And I'd be honoured to help you.'

Silently, Sarah stretched out her hand which he took in his. She couldn't speak, because the tears she'd held back for hours were crowding into her eyes and constricting her throat.

28

Miscalculating so badly and upsetting Kessie had disturbed Sarah more than she had bargained for, as had Harry's touching declaration of love and faith in her. She had been drifting on the tide of being pregnant, having a baby, waiting to hear from Misha, Tom's death, Kessie's collapse, and giving the children the stability and love they desperately needed, for so long now that she had almost lost the habit of taking clear-cut decisions. Harry was right. She had to make up her mind about her own, and Tamara's future.

On Sunday night the children returned from Chenneys. Just before she went to bed Anne said, 'You and Mummy haven't quarrelled, have you, Aunty Sarah?'

'Good heavens, no. What gave you that idea?' Anne's dark, sensitive eyes indicated that if the atmosphere at Chenneys hadn't worried her she wouldn't have asked the question, so Sarah added, 'I had a bit of a dust-up with your Uncle Pip, that's all.'

The answer satisfied Anne, the slight twitch of her lips announcing that in any 'dust-up' between Aunty Sarah and Uncle Pip she was on the feminine side of the barricades. From the children Sarah learned obliquely that Kessie was all right. Mummy had stayed in bed all day because she was tired after the morris dancing and the birthday party, but they had been in to see her before they left.

On Monday Sarah dashed off a brief note to Kessie, expressing her contrition at her well-meant but clumsy interference, begging her sister-in-law's forgiveness, telling her to forget everything Sarah had said, and hoping to see her before too long. In the evening Jenny and Rupert came for supper, both briefly in the same place at the same time and for once both discussing the same subject, namely the shortly to be opened Tom Whitworth memorial hall in Mellordale.

A memorial fund for Tom had been set up immediately after his death, and Sarah had been invited to be on the committee which had Kessie as its chairman. Thousands of pounds had poured in and Kessie's suggestions had been adopted; namely that the money be used to endow a scholarship to Ruskin College, Oxford, to enable a working class lad like Tom to enjoy a higher education, and to build a memorial hall for the use of the people of The Dales. Kessie had offered a large piece of ground she still owned not far from the Thorpe cotton mill in Mellordale as the site of the hall, and she had nominated Rupert Farrell who had been training as an architect before the war as its designer. From the start there had been rumblings about Rupert's youth, the fact that he had no 'letters' after his name and his status as a colonial, but Kessie's collapse had stilled them, nobody wanting to thwart, or argue with, Tom's widow in her parlous state of health.

'What do you think about the building?' demanded Jenny, who had just returned from a visit to The Dales. When Sarah said she hadn't been in Mellordale for a while and had not therefore seen it in its completed state, Jenny whipped dozens of photographs from her folder. 'Go on, give us your honest opinion, as Tom's sister.'

Since the scene with Kessie, Sarah had gone off her role as Tom's sister, but after she had examined the excellent photographs she gave her honest opinion that the completed memorial hall lived up to its design, of which she had always approved. The exterior had the strength and solidity of the best of the old moorland cottages and coaching inns; the clean uncluttered lines and open spaces of the interior appealed to her no end; the surrounding lawn, flower beds and trees, and particularly the children's play area, were lovely.

'Thank you, ma'am,' Rupert said in his normal laconic fashion, but he was obviously pleased.

Jenny said there was an incredible hoo-hah going on in The Dales, with people shouting that the memorial hall was an eyesore, not what they'd expected, and an insult to Tom's memory. 'Gosh, what do they want in a Lancashire cotton town? St Basil's Cathedral? Dozens of onion-shaped domes? Or another of those over-decorated, gloomy Victorian buildings, with huge staircases and long dark corridors eating up the space?'

'They're conservative folk in The Dales. Most folk are, you know, most of the time. They have to be jollied along.'

'That's a depressive, élitist remark, coming from you.'

Sarah smiled and said she liked the building, Kessie loved it, and a spot of controversy never hurt. Jenny who herself had become a decidedly controversial figure, dashing into places and situations still deemed unsuitable for a woman, wearing her corduroy trousers and her sheep-skin jacket, with her camera slung over her shoulder, said she supposed not.

After she and Rupert had gone, looking forward to seeing Sarah in Mellordale on midsummer day for the grand open-ing ceremony, she recalled Kessie in one of her now-rare giggly moods saying she had a vision of Jenny and Rupert climbing into bed and greeting each other: 'Hello, nice to see you. Gosh, hang on a minute, lover, while I check the film in my camera.' 'Not to worry, sweetheart, I want to check the elevations of the second floor.'

Could they continue indefinitely to lead their own lives, meeting occasionally? Sooner or later wasn't one of them going to say: I want to put roots down, I want a home, a family? Wasn't that what human relationships were all about? Still, without doubt, Miss Macdonald had emerged from the war years a confident, dedicated, emancipated woman. The pity was there weren't more like her.

On Tuesday and Wednesday Sarah went down to the voluntary centre which was being run on a shoestring in the Kings Cross area. Late in the afternoon she put her head round the door of the dingy room in which Stephen held her Wednesday clinics. In an unusually tetchy voice she was saying to a pinched-face woman who could be any age up to sixty, but was probably in her twenties, and had four snivelling kids hanging on to her skirts, 'If you don't

323

take any notice of what I tell you, there's not much point your coming to see me, now is there? Rub the ointment in every night and see they take the pills every day. Off you go. See you next week.'

After she had handed a sweet from her tin to each of the children and they and their mother had trailed out, Stephen leant back in her chair. Clasping her hands behind her cropped hair, she let out a long exasperated sigh.

'One of those afternoons?' Sarah asked.

'One of those afternoons,' she agreed.

They brewed a pot of tea on the Primus stove and while they were drinking it, Stephen said, 'You wouldn't like to have a good old argy-bargy with Dorothy, would you?'

'Not particularly. Why?'

'Being a bit tiresome at the moment. The latest theme is I'm wasting my time here, sapping the energy I should be devoting to achievable ends. The only hope for the future, according to madam, is to organise from the top, getting the women with brains and gumption and the rest of it into the key jobs, and then their – our – influence will percolate down to the hoi-polloi. An afternoon of Mrs Macnamaras – she's expecting another, of course – and I have a mote of sympathy with Didi, but as a philosophy,' Stephen smote the scrubbed deal table, 'no!'

It sounded like the old, rather than the latest Dorothy to Sarah, who said she didn't think she could be of help.

'I dunno. Didi respects you. Come and have supper with us one night soon.'

On Thursday there was a letter from Kessie which made Sarah feel happier. It read:

Dearest Sarah,

There's nothing to forgive. I know you meant well. Don't we all at times, with somewhat disastrous results? I expect Philip behaved like a *bugger* to you. He honestly does not realise how ferocious he can be. Accept my apologies on his behalf. I'm feeling much better. Perhaps you helped me to spit some of the accumulated spleen from my system. The episode also taught me that I

324

cannot afford to become emotional, quite apart from it not being the done thing in England to scream and yell. I shall be staying here for the time being. When we meet in Mellordale for what will undoubtedly be another emotional occasion – though I am looking forward to it, and the photographs of the Memorial Hall are splendid, aren't they? – we must have a long, civilised discussion.

I do appreciate how much you've done for me, Sarah, since Tom died and believe me, I shall be eternally grateful.

My fondest love, as always,
Kessie.

P.S. In answer to your query why we had our hair cut short, which I didn't understand, the answer is because I was fed up with mine. Took simply hours to wash and dry! The girls plagued me to let them have theirs cut. It's fashionable, you know.

Ah well, Sarah thought, so much for symbolism which she'd always viewed with suspicion.

On Thursday evening she came to her decision. She would return north. There was as much grinding poverty and unemployment, and as appalling housing conditions in parts of London as in The Dales, with as little sign of the 'homes fit for heroes' and the jobs promised by Lloyd George, but Lancashire was her native county, she could get out on to the moors, the lungs of the cotton towns, and personally she now needed gulps of strong fresh air to keep her going. In The Dales she could take Tamara around with her, or get her into a nursery, so she could work full-time. The more Harry became involved in her political activities, the more he put his job in the garage in Knightsbridge at risk, and the time had come for her to sever her frankly non-existent links with Misha and to join her life with Harry's. She knew he would be willing to come north with her, Tamara did like him and needed a father, and once back on her native heath she could think about standing for Parliament.

Friday Sarah devoted to her daughter and to personally collecting the children from school and seeing them off on the train for Chenneys. When she returned to The Grove Maggie met her in the hall, informing her that a *person* had called, he'd been insistent that he must see Mrs Muranov, so she had put him in the sitting room.

The person was Bob Prendegast who had been among those who'd written to Sarah when the news of her 'marriage' to Mikhail Muranov had broken. He'd kept on writing, eventually they'd met, and he reminded her a bit of poor old Edward Dawson in his ardent Marxian days before he'd marched off to fight and die for King and Country. Like the young Edward, he was intense, spotty, liable to sweat and to be dogmatic, but a well-meaning lad who genuinely yearned to be of help to his fellow men.

When she entered the sitting room Bob greeted her with an air of suppressed excitement, and his voice was low and confidential. 'I have an urgent message for you, Mrs Muranov. An emissary has come from Russia. He's in the country . . .' Bob's voice dropped to a whisper and he glanced round the room, presumably to ensure no spying lackey of the imperialist British Government was hidden behind the piano. '. . . illegally. The emissary has a personal message from Russia for you, Mrs Muranov. He's only here for a couple more days and I have to ask if you will be willing to meet him, and to swear on your oath as a true Socialist to reveal nothing of where you are taken, or what passes, to anybody.'

Sarah's heart was thumping. It was the long awaited emissary from Misha who had come too late, but never mind. She had a Kessie-like urge to giggle. All this whispering in the middle of the sitting room, the secrecy, the mention of oaths, was ludicrous but it was Bob's big moment, real cloak-and-dagger stuff, and obviously he expected her to swear silence before he imparted further information. With as straight a face and as steady a voice as she could muster, Sarah did so. From his inside jacket pocket Bob proceeded to extract a sealed envelope containing her 'instructions', which solemnly he handed to her.

'Mrs Muranov?'

'Yes.'

Apart from the fact that she was clutching her copy of Milton – that instruction had obviously come straight from Misha and convinced Sarah the rendezvous was genuine – she was now the only person left standing on the platform of Manningtree station, so the identification was not difficult.

Sarah followed the man, who was wearing the leggings and jacket of a farm labourer, out into the forecourt where he assisted her into a trap. With a pull on the reins and a flick of the whip the horse set off at a steady trot. The weather had been dreary most of the week and today was another of those grey English summer days, a heavy sky merging into the horizon, not raining but with the threat of drizzle in the air. Rural Essex which was unknown to Sarah looked flat, bleak and uninviting. The driver said not a word as they trotted over a bridge, past fields thick with vegetables, and along a road running parallel with a river. Within a short distance they came to a muddy path which led to an isolated stone cottage standing above the reeds on the river bank.

'That's it,' the driver nodded. 'Your visitor's waiting there.'

Helping Sarah down from the trap, he nodded again, pulled on the reins, the horse turned and off they trotted back towards Manningtree. Sarah looked at the cottage where a wisp of smoke curled from the chimney. Gingerly, she made her way down the muddy path. There was no door knocker, so she thumped with her hand. Nothing happened, so she turned the door knob and it opened. Putting her head into the small dark hall she called out, 'Anybody at home?'

'*Da. Kak ya tebya zhdal! Sarochka moya, Sabrina moya, moya samaya dikaya izo vsekh angliiskikh roz!*'

It was Misha's voice. Sarah stood transfixed. Not for one second had she believed, suspected, or understood that it was Mikhail Muranov himself who had travelled clandestinely to England. She realised now why Bob

Prendegast had been urged to secrecy and had impressed its need upon her.

'If this is summer in England, *bozhe moi!*, what is winter like?' Misha's voice roared. 'I am frozen, *Sarochka moya*, come to warm me.'

Slowly, in a stunned, dazed state, Sarah walked into the room that led off the cubby-hole of a hall. There he was, a greatcoat round his shoulders, huddling over the wretched fire in the dank dark room. As she came through the doorway he stood up, the coat slipped to the stone floor, and he held his arms out wide.

'*Moya lyubimaya, kak ya skuchal po Tebya!*'

Disbelievingly, Sarah stared at him. Like Kessie he'd had his hair cut. In place of the pageboy length there was a close-cropped blond stubble, of which she did not think she approved, though it emphasised the breadth of his features and the noble line of his head. With the velocity and noise of a shell Misha hurtled towards her, enveloping her in a great bear hug, holding her up in the air, carrying her towards the miserable fire.

'Will you kindly put me down?'

'"Nay, lady, sit",' Misha pulled a wooden chair to one side of the fireplace. Gesticulating with his hand, he continued to quote, '"If I but wave this wand, Your nerves are all chained up in alabaster, And you are a statue".'

'There's nothing wrong with my nerves, thank you. What are you doing here, Misha?'

With a grin he peered into her face. '"Why are you vex'd, lady? Why do you frown? Here dwell no frowns, nor anger; from these gates Sorrow flies far; see here be all the . . ."'

'For heaven's sake, stop quoting at me. I'm not vexed. I'm just astonished to see you after two years and ten months and a few days, the odd cable and Christmas greeting. As a good atheist I can't think why you bothered to send *those*.' Sarah shivered.

''Tis cold in here. Can't you do something about this fire?'

Partly because her brain was reeling, her emotions like

328

tangled hemp, Sarah set to work to resuscitate the fire.
Briskly, she riddled out the choking ash, while Misha said,
'Have you brought photographs of our beautiful daughter?
How I yearn to see her!'

'No I haven't brought any photographs.' Sarah removed
the large unignited lumps of coal. 'You've managed to
contain your yearning well enough. She's just had her
second birthday.'

'Sarochka!' he roared. 'What do you think I have been
doing in these terrible years? What do you imagine has
been happening in Russia?'

'What do you think I've been doing? Pass me some of
the kindling.'

'What?'

'The bits of wood in the basket.' Sarah waved her hand
impatiently and Misha handed her a bundle of firewood.
'My brother was killed in France, four days before *our* war
ended, my brother Tom.'

The softness of his tones as he expressed his sorrow made
Sarah shiver, not from the chillness of the room. The desultory flame ignited the kindling and she placed cobs of coal
on top of the wood, while Misha went on, 'You knew I would
come for you the first moment I could. You know you are
my sole partner, dearer thyself than all.'

'How long have you been in England?' Sarah stretched
out her hand for a newspaper lying on the floor, opened
out the pages and held them across the grate to encourage
the flames.

'A few days,' Misha murmured. 'I have political reason
to be here. When it was decided we required to make
personal contact with our comrades of influence in England, it was for you, *moya* Sabrina, for your sake, I
personally made the journey.'

The flames were leaping yellow and orange behind the
newspaper, the heat was turning the pages brown, and
Sarah pulled them quickly away before they caught fire.
Screwing them into a ball she dropped the paper into the
hearth, stood up and looked at her dirty hands.

'Where do I wash?' Misha waved his hand towards

the far corner of the room. 'When do you go back?'

'On Monday morning, on the tide.'

'Are you expecting Tamara and me to return to Russia with you?' With a surprised expression – why else had he come? – he nodded. 'Oh Misha, you're wonderful.' Good as his English was, he failed to catch the ironic English usage and with a wide smile he held out his arms. 'Do you really think I've been sitting like Penelope, weaving my tapestry, waiting for Odysseus to come and fetch me?' Ducking under his outstretched arm she walked to the scullery door, where she turned and said, 'For all you know, I might be married.'

'You cannot be married,' he roared. 'You are married to me. You are my wife.'

Hoist with my own petard, or Kessie's petard, Sarah thought, as she worked the hand-pump over the sink and washed the coal-dust from her hands. When she returned, the fire was blazing merrily, Misha was standing in front of it, a bottle of vodka was sitting on the mantelpiece behind him, and he was holding two filled glasses, one of which he handed to her.

'*Za nashe budushchee*!' he threw back his head, quaffing a mouthful. '*Za nashe blestyashchee budushchee*!'

'Oh Misha, don't,' Sarah sipped at her vodka. 'It's too late. You left it too long. I've made up my mind. My future is here.'

'Mamma, feed duckies. I want bwead. Please. Feed duckies.'

Sarah gave Tamara the hunks of dry bread from the paper bag and with her arms outstretched she trotted to the edge of the pond, into which she threw a large piece.

'Break them up, luv, into little bits.'

It was a beautiful Sunday afternoon and half Highgate was out strolling on Parliament Hill Fields, but then it had been a beautiful morning, had it not? Enfolded in Misha's arms in the narrow bed, Sarah had watched the dawn break through the small uncurtained bedroom window of the cottage, a pearly luminous light which had taken on a pink tinge before a band of gold had struck the wood of the frame, all four small panes of glass had glittered, and slowly the room had been bathed in sunlight.

Without difficulty Misha had persuaded her to telephone The Grove – it had been quite a hike to the nearest public telephone box. Last night, in his arms, her passion had returned, bursting like the April buds in primrose season, to remind her that all the pleasures of the world were locked in their two entwined bodies. Within the space of the next few hours – the agreed train for Manningtree left Liverpool Street station at six forty-five this evening – she had to take the most monumentally clear-cut decision of her life.

'Mamma, more bwead. Duckies hung'y. Bwead, please, Mamma.'

And as vitally, or more vitally, the decision which would affect her daughter's whole life. Holding out her chubby hands for the bread, Tamara beamed up at her and the sun shone on her blond hair. She was Misha's daughter too, as he had repeatedly said. But it was preposterous of him to arrive without warning in England and to send her a message *after* he had been here for several days and attended to his political business. And then blithely expect her to pack up, turn her back on her native land, and to sail with him to Russia.

By the edge of the pond Tamara was chatting to two little girls who were with their nursemaid, pointing to the ducks and giving them pieces of bread to throw. This was the life her daughter knew, middle-class English affluence. But she had already decided to take Tamara back north to a harsher, harder life, had she not? Lancashire was not civil-war torn Russia, however, and Misha had neither denied nor played down the horrors of the last years and the crimes the Bolsheviks themselves had committed, though he had argued passionately that they had been a necessary, transitory evil. And when he had spoken of the future, of their future, of Russia's future, of the world's future, in the dawn of the Communist age of justice and equality which would be as roseate and golden as the sunlight that had spread across the bedroom, the blood had raced through Sarah's veins, her

331

spirits had been uplifted, her conviction fired, as they had not been in months.

There was an heroic quality about Misha. He had a breadth, an expansiveness of feature, intellect and personality that perhaps came from the vastness of his country, from the wind howling across those desolate northern wastelands, rippling through the acres of golden wheatlands in the Ukraine. Maybe Misha was right and this small offshore European island had exhausted its buccaneering, inventive energy; too many of its brightest and best had fallen on the battlefields of France and Flanders. Sarah was a long way from being convinced about that, but maybe she and her daughter should fight for the brave new world in Russia. Bugger politics, it was her daughter's father she wanted to be with, whose life she wanted to share.

Tamara was trotting back with her friend Barbara and her mother who were also out taking the air. Mrs Larwood asked if Tamara could come to Barbara's birthday party next week? Sarah said, yes, she thought so, and Tamara tucked her hand into Barbara's and said confidentially, 'What you want for birfday pwesent?'

'Dolly's pram. A big one wiv silver wheels.'

Scandalised, her mother said nice little girls didn't ask for things, they waited to see what they were given, and with justification Barbara protested that she had been asked. Mrs Larwood tut-tutted at Sarah – weren't children awful at times? – and mentioned the growing controversy surrounding the Tom Whitworth memorial hall which, from the pictures she had seen looked very sparse, spartan and modern, she felt, and what did Mrs Muranov think?

Everybody was expecting her to be in Mellordale on midsummer day and Sarah very much wanted to be there, as Tamara expected and wanted to be at Barbara's birthday party next week. She could not just uproot the child, but children were adaptable and Misha was her father. Nor could she just leave without saying goodbye to anybody, to Kessie, to the children, to dear Harry who would be shattered by her departure, though she had not committed herself to him. There was no time to discuss the situation

332

with anybody and she couldn't even telephone Kessie because in the current circumstances neither the butler nor Philip himself would connect her.

Either she caught the train to Manningtree with Tamara this evening, or she did not. It was an immensely simple, inordinately complicated, matter. If they did not appear at the cottage Misha would be amazed, maybe desolate, but he would return to Russia on the tide tomorrow morning. It would serve him right for being so spectacularly confident that nearly three years of semi-silence were of no account when two people were destined for each other. She must not come to her decision for reasons of pettiness or false pride, but from the sensible, considered logic of the situation.

The children had left for the station and the journey back to London a couple of hours ago but Kessie had stayed on the terrace at Chenneys, relaxing in the early evening sun, watching the butterflies fluttering through the herbaceous borders, listening to the bumble of the bees and the peal of the church bells drifting on the still air. She could just about bear the sound of their chimes which had none of the clamour of those terrible victory bells. It was going to be a beautiful sunset, the sky was an exquisite eau-de-nil colour, and the ribs of pink cloud tinged by the carmine disc of the sun were arching across the heavens like the imprints of the receding tide on a sandy beach. Despite herself, the shiver ran down Kessie's spine.

'Are you cold?' Philip said immediately. 'Shall we go in?'

As she shook her head he smiled, a sad tender smile, and she suspected he knew why she had shivered. They were two of the three survivors from the six who had sat here on the terrace, watching the sunset on that heavenly August day in 1916. Alice, Guy and Tom were dead, an average casualty tally from the Great War for Civilisation.

Kessie broke the silence. 'I had a chat to Anne this afternoon. She says people are saying nasty things about me. I don't think I can go to The Dales to open Tom's memorial hall, and come back here, without further nasty things being said, do you? It would seem the moment to make the break.'

Taking out his cigarette case, Philip opened it, extracted a cigarette, shut the case, tapped the cigarette on its flat surface, put the case back in his pocket, drew out his lighter, cupped his hands, flicked the wheel of the lighter, and lit the cigarette. All the movements had an elegant precision which belied the emotion Kessie's senses could feel. When he spoke his voice had a particularly back-of-the-throat drawl.

'People will stop saying nasty things if you marry me, Kessie, as I believe Sarah pointed out.'

With a long sigh, Kessie said, 'Oh Philip, you know how fond I am of you, but I can't marry you, you know I can't.' She glanced towards the Tudor pile of the house. 'You need an heir and there's no way, however much my health improves, that I can give you a child.'

'I have already told you, I have no urgent desire to reproduce myself. Chenneys will survive without a product of my loins. I would have four ready-made step-children, of whom I am extremely fond. We met at the first night of *Love me for Ever*, did we not, Kessie? I shall love you for ever.'

Having quietly made his statement Philip lay back in his chair, staring at the darkening pink of the ribbed clouds. Kessie asked herself why she didn't marry him, the ideal, devoted husband for a semi-invalid war widow? And wasn't she a lucky lady to be given a second bite of the marital cherry, with the postwar preponderence of women over men? Tom would want her to be as happy as possible, as Sarah had said, and as she had also said the children liked and were accustomed to 'Uncle Pip'. Frankly, though Kate occasionally still cried for her Daddy, her and Mark's memories of their father were fading fast and they would both take to life at Chenneys like ducks to water. Con was too sweet-natured to buck at anything. But what about Anne, who had adored her Daddy and worshipped his memory? Would Tom have wanted his children to be brought up as the step-children of *Sir* Philip Marchal? Did she want to be

Lady Marchal? No. But not to marry him because he had a title and was rich would be ridiculous. Wouldn't it?

What were the options?

To return to The Grove, where Tom's ghost haunted every room. Not feasible. To resuscitate the idea of going back north and sharing a house in Manchester with Sarah? Possible. With her precarious health it would put a burden on Sarah's shoulders and anyway, Kessie had the feeling she was considering marrying *her* faithful swain, seeing that Mikhail Muranov had let her down so wretchedly. Maybe the three of them could share a house, with the children, because neither Sarah nor Harry had any money, and that was one thing she could provide. Kessie decided she would discuss the subject with Sarah in Mellordale after the opening of Tom's memorial hall. Perhaps after she had been back to her Lancashire roots, to where it had all started for her and Tom as young suffragette and Socialist, her mind would be clearer.

'I will give you an answer soon, Philip. I promise.'

'I can wait, Kessie. For as long as it takes for the answer to be affirmative.'

Rowing out to sea in the small boat in the early morning mist was an eerie experience and Sarah sat holding Tamara tightly in her arms. Fortunately, she was sleepy after her unexpected train journey last night and the lateness of her bedtime, and Sarah herself was feeling pretty exhausted, in a state in which she was prepared to let things happen. She gave a cry, however, as the dark shape loomed through the mist, but Misha put his arm round her shoulder, assuring her it was their waiting trawler.

As he clambered on to the ship, carrying Tamara in his arms, she woke up and started to cry. When she saw her mother in the small boat bobbing on the waves below, she screamed, 'Mamma, Mamma', struggling furiously to escape from her father's grasp.

'*Dorogaya moya, nenaglyadnaya moya.*' Misha tried to pacify his daughter but she screamed and struggled even more frantically as Sarah was hauled on board and she did not stop until she was once more in her mother's arms.

'Go away.' Tamara pushed at Misha who had pulled a doll from his pocket and was dandling it in front of her. For Sarah his delight in his daughter was a pleasure to behold, if not at the moment for Tamara who howled whenever he came near her, frightened by his over-excited, over-boisterous, over-affectionate attention.

The palaver with which they were being received on board, the captain saluting Misha, bowing to her and Tamara, made Sarah realise that Mikhail Muranov was a very important Bolshevik person and hierarchical deference had not been banished with the revolution, not yet anyway. Sarah's Russian ear had grown slightly rusty but she understood the captain saying he wished to sail immediately, to which Mikhail agreed. One of the sailors was ordered to conduct Commissar Muranov and his family to their cabin, when suddenly the sun pierced the mist and it truly was as if the curtain were rising on a stage, to reveal the distant spectacle of the low-lying Essex coast, the mouth of the river, the huddle of houses on the water's edge, all bathed in a soft pink light.

Holding Tamara in front of her, Sarah stood against the side of the trawler as it throbbed into motion, and with Misha's arm round her shoulder she watched as slowly the boat moved and slowly the distant land receded. The fresh wind fanned Sarah's cheeks and Tamara was fascinated by the wash of the bows, the undulations of the waves, and particularly by the cries of the wheeling, swooping seagulls. When Misha imitated their raucous, demanding shrieks rather well and not too loudly, Tamara was faintly amused.

They stayed watching until the coastline became a blur, a smudge, and was then no more, the last sight of Sarah's native England. For better or for worse, fate had called to her and she had answered.

'*Za nashe budushchee!*' Misha said softly.

Sarah turned to him, gently he kissed her and Tamara, and his daughter gave him the hint of a smile.

'To our future!' Gently Sarah kissed him back.